COWARD AT THE BRIDGE

James Delingpole

POCKET
BOOKS

LONDON • SYDNEY • NEW YORK • TORONTO

First published in Great Britain by Simon & Schuster UK Ltd, 2009
This edition published by Pocket Books, 2010
An imprint of Simon & Schuster UK Ltd
A CBS COMPANY

1 3 5 7 9 10 8 6 4 2

Simon & Schuster UK Ltd
1st Floor
222 Gray's Inn Road
London
WC1X 8HB

www.simonandschuster.co.uk

Simon & Schuster Australia
Sydney

A CIP catalogue for this book is available from the
British Library.

ISBN: 978-1-84739-386-9

Typeset by M Rules
Printed by CPI Cox & Wyman, Reading, Berkshire RG1 8EX

James Delingpole is a journalist, broadcaster and author of six books including *How To Be Right*, *Thinly Disguised Autobiography* and the Dick Coward series. He writes for the *Daily* and *Sunday Telegraph*, the *Daily Mail*, the *Mail On Sunday*, the *Sunday Times*, *The Times* and the *Independent On Sunday* on everything from rock to culture to politics and gardening. He is married with children and lives in south London.

Further praise for *Coward at the Bridge*

'Tempered by the carnage of war, Dick's antics have more meat and less sauce than those of his antecedent Flashman, whose racy adventures Delingpole creditably updates' James Urquhart, *Financial Times Magazine*

'Vigorous, witty and elegant . . . A welcome corrective to the Spielberg-Hanks version and promises a lot more excitement to come. Jolly good show, Delingpole' *The Spectator*

'Impressive and enjoyable. A very entertaining journey . . . A rattling story, full of action and laughs and gut-wrenching fear. Roll on Vol.2' Marcus Berkmann, *Daily Mail*

'A literary equivalent of *Saving Private Ryan* . . . Delingpole has a fine ear for dialogue' Andrew Roberts, *Mail on Sunday*

'Very funny and always delightfully non-PC' *GQ*

'A gripping yarn for men who don't want to go to sleep' *Daily Echo*

'With echoes of George MacDonald Fraser's fictional *Flashman*, *Coward on the Beach* was an action-packed story full of wry humour and vivid detail. *Coward at the Bridge* is another joyful addition to what promises to be a 10-book series . . . Not since Anthony Burgess's *Earthly Powers* has a novel had such a seductive opening line: "Did I ever tell you about the time I found myself locked in a cupboard with a stunning 17-year-old nymphomaniac who couldn't keep her hands off me?" How can anyone fail to read on?' *Tatler*

'A cracking story from the off, with our hero locked in a cupboard with a nymphomaniac Dutch blonde . . . It is a shamelessly frivolous take on history, but the author's zest and inventiveness carry the day' *Mail on Sunday*

'War is an awfully big adventure, best appreciated vicariously, at a great distance in space and time. James Delingpole's splendidly entertaining second no[vel] . . . [Flashman]-sque ubiquity in the Secon[d World] . . . [*Coward at t*]*he Bridge* is 'war-buff heave[n] . . . Del[ingpole] . . . [Harr]y VC' *The Spectator*

Also by James Delingpole

COWARD ON THE BEACH

To my father, who must be quite sick by now of never once having had one of his son's books dedicated to him.

Contents

ARNHEM AND THE LANDING GROUNDS
17/18th September 1944

N

1 mile

4th Para

1st Para

1st Air Landing Brigade

Asylum

Wolfheze

Kraft's SS Battalion

Oosterbeek

Heelsum

Hartenstein Hotel

Lower Rhine

Driel

Rail Bridge (Destroyed)

II SS Panzer Corps

Arnhem

Arnhem Bridge

Pontoon Bridge

SS Panzergrenadiers

Elden

To Nijmegen

Leopard
Tiger
Lion

© Richard Delingpole

OPERATION MARKET GARDEN
17th September 1944

ENGLAND

Felixstowe

Margate

Calais

Dunkirk

FRANCE

Bruges

BELGIUM

Brussels

Antwerp

German front line

Start point

Eindhoven

101st Airborne

Grave

82nd Airborne

Maas

Waal

Nijmegen

Lower Rhine

1st Airborne

Arnhem

HOLLAND

Rotterdam

Amsterdam

GERMANY

Siegfried Line

THE RUHR

Essen

20 miles

© Richard Delingpole

Cupboard Love

Did I ever tell you about the time I found myself locked in a cupboard with a stunning seventeen-year-old blonde nymphomaniac who couldn't keep her hands off me? Worst moment of my life.

Well, top ten anyway.

Yes, I know what you're thinking. You're thinking, Dear old Grandpa doth protest too much. But you don't yet know the circumstances and you don't know the occasion.

The occasion was one of the more unfortunate operations in the annals of British military history, a show in the Netherlands in September 1944 known as Market Garden. The circumstances will require a little more explanation.

First, the cupboard. It is set into the wall of the large, airy drawing room of one of the numerous well-proportioned villas which abound in this lovely, leafy enclave of *haut bourgeois* Holland. If you didn't know what to look for – the hinges aren't obvious and the keyhole is discreetly hidden within the eye of the toucan on the exotic, rainforest-print wallpaper – you probably wouldn't even notice it was there. Hence its appeal as an emergency hiding place.

At a push, it can accommodate two people – but only so long as they press themselves close together and don't wriggle around too much. Extensive movement, certainly, is quite impossible in this cramped, narrow space, which was designed to house books, not humans. Were you, for example, to find a female hand straying inexorably towards your crotch at the most unsuitable of moments and you wished to pull sharply away, you would have great difficulty doing so. Rather, you'd have to remain stiffly as you were and take it like a man.

This is what I do for the first minutes of the girl's attentions. To be perfectly honest, it takes me most of that time to convince myself that she really is doing to me what I think she's doing. It all seems so jolly unlikely.

I mean, put yourself in our shoes: during the last week this tranquil resort town to the west of Arnhem has been bombed, shelled, machine-gunned and mortared almost to rubble, with barely a brick or tree left undamaged; the air is rank with clogging dust and the throat-catching stench of rotting flesh merged with cordite; there are Germans everywhere, many of them, happily, dead, but many more of them alive and on the hunt for people just like us: surviving soldiers from the 1st Airborne Division; Dutch men and women brave enough to risk their lives by concealing them.

No one in their right mind would think about hanky-panky at a time like this, I'm saying to myself, as this innocent young Dutch girl's hand slips beneath the dangling flaps of my Denison smock and begins negotiating its way inside my trousers. It's some sort of nervous tic, that's all. Trembling hands brought on by the constant shelling: that'll be it.

From outside there's another of those guttural shouts which drove us to hide in the first place. It's followed by the crunch of glass and splintering wood, as the remnants of one of the window frames are rifle-butted or jack-booted open. They never were ones to knock politely first, the Germans.

I tense, waiting for the almost inevitable grenade blast, thinking how little protection these thin wooden walls will offer when it comes.

But providence is on our side. There's no grenade. Perhaps they're Wehrmacht, not SS.

'Is there anybody here?' a voice calls out in German. 'Is there anybody here?'

Whoever it is then picks his way through the window – lands on the floor of the room we're hiding in with a loud thump – pauses awhile and then scrunches through the debris of glass and fallen plasterwork towards the front door.

'Ground floor clear,' he calls to his comrades, who surge in moments later.

You can hear two or three of them galumphing up the staircase and down into the cellar to inspect the other floors. Several more pairs of boots stomp around the room in which we are hiding.

I scarcely dare breathe. It's this Dutch girl's shell shock I'm particularly concerned about, for she seems quite unable to stop her hand brushing against my John Thomas in what, if I didn't know better, I'd almost believe were caressing motions. Mind you, what was it Price said when this girl first showed an interest in me a week ago? Something like: 'I'd keep off, if I were you. She's only just escaped from that loony bin up the road.' That was just his sense of humour, though. Surely?

More thundering feet, this time on the way down from upstairs.

'Upper floors clear, Herr Hauptmann.'

'Cellar also,' reports another.

Good. Now piss off somewhere else, why don't you? I mentally urge them.

A born telepath, clearly, for almost immediately their captain replies, 'Excellent. Feldwebel: get this room cleaned up and bring me a table and more chairs. It will serve very well as our interrogation centre.'

Interrogation centre?

I'd like to think that I'd misheard. Or that this was my German playing tricks on me. Unfortunately, it never does, for as you know, Jack, I speak the lingo fluently. If I didn't I'd have died a dozen grisly deaths by now.

'*Jawohl, Herr Hauptmann*,' says his sergeant, and in less than an instant – God, there've been times when I wished it could have been German soldiers under my command, not British ones – furniture is being shifted, debris swept and further chairs retrieved. One of them, by the sounds of it, has been placed directly in front of our hiding place.

Christ! We're in for it now, I think. If they're going to use this room for interrogation purposes, we could be stuck here for hours. Days, even.

We've got no food. Nothing to drink. My back and neck are already killing me from being in this cramped position – and we can't have been here more than five minutes. The tiny cracks in the door won't allow nearly enough air in. And then there's this girl's shell shock. If it is shell shock. It seems to be getting worse.

Crickey, what if Price is right. What if she really is one of the nutters who escaped through the walls after we bombed the Wolfheze asylum? Whether she is or she isn't, what she's doing to me now isn't arousing, it's just ruddy dangerous. That rustling noise she's making against my battledress: I don't know how loud it is on the other side of the cupboard, but from where I am it sounds like Krakatoa erupting.

I clasp my hand firmly over hers and the nervous shaking, erotic massage or whatever it is stops. I hold it there to make damned bloody sure. Don't want to miss a word they say outside. The captain has given the order for the prisoners to be brought over. His clerk is setting up a writing desk; a lieutenant is being summoned to assist with the interrogation. Whether we like it or not, we're about to get a ringside seat.

More scuffling, stomping and furniture-shifting. Then, the

muffled sound of tramping boots from outside the house – British Army-issue boots – marching in perfect unison.

'HALT,' yells a German-accented voice. The boots keep marching. 'HALT!' screeches the voice.

'PLATOON. PLATOON,' bellows a voice which could only be the property of an English regimental sergeant major. 'HALT!'

As one, the boots crunch to a halt.

Now there is a burst of angry shouting, followed by derisive laughter, and still more shouting. I can't hear every word but I can work out the gist: the German officer is trying to impress on his captives that he is in charge now; the prisoners are telling him where to get off; the German is making threats.

There! A volley of shots. Warning shots, one hopes.

No cries of pain: that's promising. No laughter either.

The angry fellow seems to have made his way inside the building now, for next thing I know he's yelling almost in front of my cupboard.

'These prisoners. Do they belong to you, Herr Hauptmann?'

'They do, Herr Hauptsturmführer.'

Hauptsturmführer. That's an SS rank.

'Then I would suggest that you teach them to show their victors more respect,' says the Hauptsturmführer.

'In the Wehrmacht we are taught that respect must be earned, not given automatically.'

Utter bollocks, of course, as I know from my own experiences on the Eastern Front. Still, got to hand it to the cheeky Hauptmann. Not only has he got balls of steel but he's a damned useful wind-up merchant.

As you'd expect, there are sharp intakes of breath all around, and from the SS officer a testy pause.

Then, the Hauptsturmführer says icily, 'In that case, Herr Hauptmann, may I request that when you have finished questioning your prisoners in the Wehrmacht way, you allow my men to investigate them using SS methods. Then afterwards we can compare notes and see which style works best.'

'These *Engländer* are my prisoners and they shall remain my prisoners.'

'Then—' begins the Hauptsturmführer, in a voice full of menace.

'However,' interrupts the Hauptmann in a more conciliatory tone. 'If you would care to assist at this interrogation, I would more than value your presence.'

The SS officer appears temporarily mollified. More chairs – and another table for the SS unit's own clerk – are brought in, then, without further ado, the first prisoner is marched in and the interrogation begins.

'Good morning, Sergeant,' says the Hauptmann. 'You must be very tired. Are you sure you vould not like to sit down?'

'Thanks, but I'd rather stand.'

'As you vish. Now, Sergeant, could you kindly tell me your name.'

'McTavish. Jock.'

'You are from Scotland, zen?'

No answer.

'Answer the Hauptmann!' snaps the Hauptsturmführer.

'You are from Scotland?' asks the Hauptmann.

'Can't really say,' says the Sergeant and I'm hardly surprised. With a name as unlikely as that, odds are that he's one of the Division's numerous German-Jewish volunteers, fighting incognito.

'Ven did you volunteer for ze glider pilot regiment, Sergeant McTavish?'

'I can tell you my serial number, if that helps.'

'Sergeant McTavish, please do not play these games. You are vearing a glider pilot's uniform vith a glider pilot's vings.'

'My mother always used to say it can be a mistake to judge by appearances,' says McTavish.

6

The SS officer chips in nastily, 'She was a Jew perhaps, your mother. With a hooked nose. A hooked nose like yours, Sergeant McTavish – *wenn das wirklich Ihr Name ist.*'

Crikey! I don't know what those last comments have done to poor McTavish but if he has turned anywhere near as sick and pale as I have then he's done for.

But these German Jews, if he is a German Jew, are made of sterner stuff.

'79341201,' says McTavish in a calm, even voice. 'Now don't let me detain you, please. I know you've got quite a few more of us to get through.'

'Give him to me,' says the Hauptsturmführer in German. 'I will make him talk.'

On the other side of the wall, I can imagine McTavish being careful not to adjust his expression.

'Take him away,' the Hauptmann commands one of his guards, ignoring the SS man's request. Then: 'Next prisoner.'

Now, I'll say one thing for those two or so hours I spent hiding in the cupboard with a nubile, gorgeous, panting Dutch girl that day in Oosterbeek: it didn't half show the British soldier in a splendid light. He can be a tricky customer, your Tommy – bolshie, sarcastic, truculent, stubborn, far too often ready to disobey an order if he thinks there's half a chance he can get away with it – but by golly when the chips are down, his natural bloody-mindedness is the making of him. It makes him ferocious in attack, tenacious in defence and – should you be unlucky enough to capture him – the biggest pain-in-the-bum POW this side of Airey Neave.

Just listen to the way these chaps are handling their interrogation. All right, so one or two of them are gulled by the Hauptmann's easy manner into giving away rather more information than an intelligence-trained chap like myself might prefer (just a unit's designation here, a pub or street name there – but it's enough, you know, it's enough). But the majority of them stick so rigidly to the principle of name, rank and number, you could almost be eavesdropping on a dramatised training manual.

What's more, they rarely miss a chance to rub Jerry's nose in it. It's like being at school again, listening to the boys at the back of the classroom testing how far they can cheek the master without being thrashed. And the Germans of course don't like it one bit. The Hauptsturmführer is itching to have them all shot. Even the unflappable Hauptmann is fast losing his patience. Someone, quite soon, I have a nasty feeling, is going to find himself being made an example of . . .

Speaking for myself, I find this note of tension in the proceedings rather a relief. As I'm sure you can imagine, no matter how charming the company, being cooped up, squashed and skew-whiff in an airless cupboard for two or three hours, is both maddeningly uncomfortable and mind-numbingly tedious. It's the tedium that worries me most for there's always the danger I'll fall asleep. And what if I snore or if my head lolls and thumps against the wall? What if this Dutch girl gets another attack of the shell-shocked tremblies?

Outside, there's some sort of commotion as a particularly troublesome prisoner is brought in. Another sergeant.

'This is the man I told you about, Herr Hauptmann. The man who cost Schweitzer his foot,' says one of the guards in German.

'Vot is it zat you find so funny, Sergeant?' the Hauptmann asks his captive. '*Vielleicht sprechen Sie Deutsch?*'

The Sergeant, whether he speaks German or no, quite sensibly doesn't reply.

'Sergeant, while resisting capture you cost me one of my best men. Do you think this is a laughing matter?'

The Sergeant mutters something I can't hear, partly because it's under his breath, partly because Blondie's hand has gone to work again. And this time I know it isn't shell shock. I can tell by the way, taking advantage of my momentary distraction, she's some-how managed to dart her hand inside my shredded battledress and grab a hold of the end of my you-know-what, which she is now pumping very determinedly between thumb and forefinger.

Madam. This is neither the time nor the place! I think, trying to drag her hand away. But from my awkward position this is harder than you'd imagine, and when finally I do get sufficient purchase to give her hand a salutory, crushing squeeze, she says in a whisper so loud it almost counts as talking, 'Let go or I scream.'

It's at this point, that I begin properly to appreciate what a pickle I'm in. Price – as ever, blast him – was right. This is not just some ordinary sweet Dutch girl who took a fancy to me a week ago because I am such a splendid, handsome and generally lovely fellow. She is, in fact, one of those women one used to imagine were a male fantasy, but who one now belatedly realises do actually exist: a totally insatiable, utterly fearless succubus who is never happier than when practising sex under the most dan-gerous of circumstances and most imminent risk of discovery.

All of which distraction has led me to miss some of the pro-ceedings next door. Annoying, since I now recognise the Sergeant's voice – war abounds with such coincidences – as that of Price himself. By the sounds of it he's in an even bigger mess than I am.

Instead of surrendering nicely, as far as I can gather, he not only booted one of his captors in the privates, and broke another's wrist, but also sent a third staggering backwards onto a *Schuhmine*, which cost him one of his feet. Why the Germans didn't shoot him immediately I can't imagine. But the way Price is carrying on, they'll surely soon remedy this oversight.

'Well, it wasn't me who put it there, was it? "Hoist by your own petard", that's what we say in Blighty.'

Shut up, man! Shut up! I'm mentally urging him. Well, one

part of my mind is. Another's wondering how on earth to stop this missy carrying on with her appalling tricks.

Or maybe, another part of me is thinking – possibly the one marked 'randy young bugger who never gets quite enough of what he thinks he deserves' – maybe, if I just let her get on with it and bring events to their natural conclusion, she'll be content enough with that.

Unfortunately, as if reading my thoughts, she decides to make new demands on me. With her spare hand she takes the nearest one of mine and guides it gently towards one of the breasts she has helpfully exposed by slipping off her dress.

Well, I know what she'll do if I refuse to obey orders: she'll scream, won't she?

A jolly nice breast it is too. Perky. And very excited.

Oh God, no, please. No, please don't do that. But she has, I'm afraid: the girl has started to breathe very, very deeply.

No, worse than that. She has started to moan.

Quickly, before anyone outside hears, I stop playing with her nipple.

'Don't stop or I scream,' she says.

This time, someone outside ought definitely to have heard. The only reason they haven't is because the Hauptsturmführer is screaming to his fellow captain in German, 'Give this impertinent pig to me. I will show him how we treat prisoners who try to escape!'

'If he goes on in this way, then I might well give you that pleasure,' says the Hauptmann, his patience now exhausted. 'Sergeant Price,' he says. 'You are no doubt familiar with the SS?'

Deep sighs from Blondie. What am I going to do? How can I shut her up before it's too late?

'Do not misunderstand me, I am a man of my word. This is your very last chance to cooperate –'

'I will scream,' warns Blondie, as yet again I try to stop the manual nipple-stimulation which is making her so damned noisy.

Buggeration! You're damned if you do and damned if you don't.

'Sergeant Price, do you understand me?'

Oh God, she's moaning again. Louder. And louder. And louder.

'Sergeant – what was that?' says the Hauptmann.

'What was what?' says the Hauptsturmführer.

'There. In the wall behind us.'

'A rat. Probably a rat.'

'It almost sounded human.'

A pistol cracks. Bang! And, damn it, wouldn't you know, a hole appears in the cupboard wall barely an inch above my head.

'Can you hear him now?' asks the Hauptsturmführer – rhetorically, since even Blondie now seems to recognise the gravity of the situation.

'Sergeant Price?'

'That's me.'

'I'm asking you one more time –'

I don't believe it. She's back at it again already. Breathing heavily.

There's nothing for it. I don't want to do this but I'm going to have to. With the hand that isn't compulsorily attached to Blondie's breast, I reach for the razor-sharp knife strapped to my leg. Steady now. Don't want to alert her. I've got hold of the grip. It's coming smoothly out of its sheath. There. Ready . . .

'Tell us all you know now and we will spare your life. Otherwise I shall have to pass you over to the Hauptsturmführer for further questioning –'

Not much longer now. I shall have to get this over with quickly. Is the blade sharp enough? Yes. Can I achieve all I need to do swiftly in so confined a space? We'll just have to see. It's my only hope.

'So, Sergeant Price. The choice is yours. Do you wish to live? Or do you prefer to die?'

Sighs. Loud sighs from my cupboard-mate.

'Hmm. The options are so tempting. Let me think that one over for a moment.'

'Enough. Enough of your games!'

I go to work with the knife, in long swift cuts. The girl screams!

'What was that? What was that?'

The moment has come. And I'll bet you thought I was exaggerating when I said it was among the worst of my life. Well, you don't now, Jack, do you?

But first, I want to take you back two or three months, so I can explain how I got into this mess in the first place.

2

Leave it to Daphne

It's getting on for 10.30 a.m. by the time Price and I trudge with our kitbags down the long gravel drive, over the moat bridge, through the great creaking oak door with its Civil War bullet holes, and into the lofty entrance hall of Great Meresby. We did try calling from the station, but no one answered.

Damn it, where is everyone?

We're hot; we're exhausted; we've not eaten since lunchtime yesterday and we're dying for a brew.

'Griffiths? Griffiths? Griffiths? GRIFFITHS?' I call to the four corners of the vast, dark-panelled hall.

'G-R-I-F-F-I-T-H-S?' joins in Price, in a parade voice to waken the dead. And at last there are stirrings down one of the corridors.

A doorway opens and a woman in riding kit appears. She's so pale and thin that I scarcely recognise her.

'Darling?' she says. 'Darling, is that really you?'

'Mother. Are you all right?'

But she isn't all right, clearly she isn't, for she dives for my neck with all the desperation of a torpedoed matelot seizing the very last life ring, and she buries her head there for a long while, sobbing. I've never seen her sob since the news came that my elder brother John was dead.

'Mummy,' I say softly, stroking her consolingly on the back. 'Mummy.'

'I'll go and find us a brew then,' says Price.

'He told me you weren't coming back,' says Mother eventually.

'Who did?'

'Your father,' she says.

'What? He told you I was dead?'

'He wouldn't say,' says Mother, looking fixedly at me with teary eyes, as if desperately trying to convince herself that I'm not a ghost. 'He just said . . . he just said you wouldn't be coming back.'

My father, the General, is – as you'll remember – a somewhat temperamental fellow given to violent mood swings and brisk judgements. But even by his erratic standards, giving a mother to understand that her best-beloved son is dead does sound a little extreme.

'Where is he?'

'Gone fishing. With Griffiths.'

'He's taken the butler fishing? Good Lord, Mother, he really has lost his marbles.'

'Darling, we're very short-staffed. All the men have been called up; most of the girls have been lured by the wages at that awful bomb factory.'

'So we'll be having to fix our own breakfast this morning, Mother, is that what you're saying?'

'I fear so, darling.'

'Damn this wretched war.'

In the kitchen – hardly much point going to the drawing room: it's not as though there's anyone left to eavesdrop – Mother joins Price and me for a brew while we fill her in on our adventures. Price has found, secreted in a cupboard, a pound of the very excellent India tea we brought back from the East and which

Griffiths had assured Mother was all finished. As we chat, Price widens his search, convinced that there may yet be further treasure troves to be unearthed.

Naturally, as warriors must do when talking to their mothers, I edit out all the unpleasant stuff. This has the happy bonus of keeping things nice and short. So, just the sketchiest of accounts of the landing on Gold Beach and the capture of Port-en-Bessin, then straight into the sort of jolly gen more likely to tickle her fancy.

'And who should we bump into at the casualty clearing station on the beach? Why, only Gina Herbert.'

'Oh darling, that's too extraordinary. And how was she?'

'Bearing up, you know, after, er . . .' I trail off, unsure how much Mother knows about the affair. Being a friend of Gina's father, my godfather Johnny, the Earl of Brecon, she ought I suppose by now to have heard everything: Gina's clandestine marriage to a Commando captain; the officer's tragic death in action; Lord Brecon's fury at his daughter's deception; Gina's decision to cut herself out of her own inheritance as a gesture of defiance . . .

'Yes. All *that*. Still, father and daughter appear to be on speakers again now,' says Mother, and inwardly I breathe a sigh of relief. Not, of course, that there's much likelihood of Gina ever reciprocating my feelings. But suppose one day she did, well, it's always a bit nicer being married to a girl whose estates cover half of Wales than one who has renounced land and title because of some silly family tiff.

'Though only just,' Mother adds. 'You'll have heard about her current beau, no doubt?'

'God, is she still with that greasy Frog?'

'That was rather her dear papa's reaction. "An English Commando officer, I can forgive," he said. "Even if he was a touch below the salt, poor chap. But a Frenchman? Does the girl have any idea how much time and energy her ancestors have spent trying to wipe fellows of his persuasion from the atlas?"'

'Handsome fellow, mind,' chips in Price, casting me a mischievous look. 'A lot better-looking than some of the desperadoes I've seen chasing her.'

'You don't surely think she's serious, Tom?' says Mother. She only calls him that when Father's not around.

Price doesn't answer, for he has been distracted by a splendid new discovery behind the bleach bottles underneath the butler's sink.

'View halloo!' he announces, whipping a linen towel from atop a wire basket to reveal more than a dozen eggs.

I glance upwards. I thought I heard a noise, like someone tapping on the ceiling. But no one else appears to have noticed.

Mother gasps. As you may remember from my last visit to Great Meresby, eggs have been in decidedly short supply. Or so our staff have been telling us.

'Poached, scrambled, boiled or fried, Lady Emily?'

'Goodness, Tom. It has been so long I scarcely remember enough to form a preference.'

Price laughs throatily in that way I all but never hear him laugh except in Mother's company. Mother has always been fond of Price – their shared love of horses, not to mention all he's done these last six years to keep her favourite son alive – and that affection is clearly reciprocated.

'Then why not let's have all four!' declares Price. And Mother giggles her approval.

Oh no, really, this is too much. It's like watching your grandfather trying to dance the jitterbug. Pull yourself together, man! I'm tempted to tell him. Cheerfulness just doesn't suit you!

Tap tap tap. There's the noise again. Louder this time.

Mother casts a quick, uneasy look upwards, turns slightly red and says, 'We'd better keep our voices down.'

'What?' I say, starting to panic. 'I thought you said he was fishing.'

'Not your father,' she hisses back. '*Daphne*. This is her writing time.'

'Daphne?' I protest, pulling a face of the direst agony. 'Oh God. WHY?'

She may be Mother's best friend but she is *such* a frost.

Mother signals frantically for me to mind what I say. The pipes in the kitchen probably carry every word.

'Darling, we needed each other,' she says, then adds under her breath, 'Well, I can't speak for Daphne, I'm not sure that Daphne needs anybody. But when your father led me to believe I'd lost a second son in four years, I certainly needed her.'

'But, Mummy,' I protest, like the petulant child I always seem to revert to after half an hour in Mother's company. 'It means you're going to spend the whole weekend whispering to one another, like you always do. And I'm only here for barely a day and a half. Price and I have to be off by tomorrow night, you realise that, don't you? Mummy, it really is too unfair!'

Price shoots me a look which I ignore. She's my mother and I can say what I like.

'Darling, if I'd known you were coming, of course I would have made time for you. But Daphne's come all the way up from Menabilly, and she only works in the morning, so whatever we do in the afternoon, we shall all have to do together. How about we all go for a jolly picnic: you, me, Daphne, Lucy – goodness, she'll be happy when she knows you're here. And, Tom, perhaps you'd care to join us too if you don't have other plans.'

'It would be my pleasure, Lady Emily,' purrs Price.

Oh Lord. I don't know who's going to ruin this weekend more: my father, Tom Price, or Daphne bloody Browning.

While Price, as promised, japishly prepares all those eggs for us in four different ways, I fill in Mother on the strange story of how it is Price and I came to be home.

You'll remember that our last adventure found us being called back from active service in France via a message passed on by no less a personage than Field Marshal Montgomery. Now this sort of thing is highly unusual and the natural impression I formed as a result is that we had been earmarked for a mission of the utmost secrecy and importance. Something to do with an airborne operation, I seem to remember thinking at the time, though this could just be hindsight.

Certainly, of the numerous possibilities Price and I speculated on during our Channel crossing home, none came remotely close to matching the scene that greeted us when we reported in, as per our orders, to an especially grim and barren-looking Army base in the suburbs of Birmingham.

'Are you sure this is the right place?' I say to Price, peering through the rickety wire fence. I've been expecting tight security, platoons of fit young men in red berets marching at the treble in tight formation, an air of vigour and purpose. The parade ground here – if you could flatter the meagre stretch of grass-tufted tarmac thus – appears not to have been used in months; the perimeter defences are so poor a child of three could negotiate them; and the place seems all but devoid of personnel, with even the gatehouse empty.

Price double-checks the address and nods grimly.

Then he cups his hands round his mouth and screeches, 'Guards to the gate! Officer reporting.'

Answer comes there none.

'I'll have someone on a charge for this,' I say.

'I'll have his bollocks on toast,' says Price.

'Awroit, gents, won't be a minute,' calls out a cheery voice from the window of a prefabricated building a few yards from the gate.

'"Awroit, gents"?' hisses Price.

Tragically, the very ill-turned-out and rank-smelling soldier who emerges from the prefab moments later has the same number of stripes on his arm as Price. So, after the man has saluted sloppily, glanced at our papers, and let us in through the gate, it's left to me to deliver the necessary rebuke.

'Sarnt, is it normally your practice to address visitors as gents? And stand to attention until I say otherwise. And do up your top button.'

'Sorry, sir, I don't mean to be rude,' says the Sergeant, fiddling with his top button. 'Only the OC likes to encourage an informal atmosphere round the base. "Seeing as we've such a shite job," he says, if you'll pardon my French, sir, I'm only repeating what the OC says. "Seeing as we've such a shite job, Sarnt," he says. "Let's not make things shiter on ourselves than they already are," he says. And I know it doesn't always give a very good impression to visiting officers, sir, but the truth is we don't get that many visiting officers, what with most operations having moved now to the other side of the Channel and the bulk of our unit transferred with them. And you'll forgive my impertinence, sir, for I'm only speaking as I find, but I've an idea that once you're both settled in here you'll find this informal atmosphere that the OC has created quite a breath of fresh air after all that spit-and-polish malarkey you find elsewhere in the military.'

'You'll let us be the judges of that, Sarnt. Now if you'll allow us to report in to the OC –'

'I would do, sir, only he's gone home for the weekend. Most of us do, if we aren't too busy – which we generally aren't right now – and if you don't mind me suggesting it, sir, I'd advise the both of you to do the same. So long as you're both back here by 09.00 hours – maybe 10.00 at the latest – Monday, the OC will look forward to meeting you then.'

'Are you, um, quite sure he's expecting us, Sarnt?' I ask, desperately.

'No doubt about it, sir. And, if I'm not speaking out of turn, may I be the first to congratulate you. You, Lieutenant Coward, sir, will be taking over as this unit's second i/c. And, Sarnt Price, you'll be taking over my job.'

'Would you mind filling us in briefly on what this unit actually does?'

'Briefly, sir? Well, our nickname is the Shitehawks, if that gives you any inkling.'

'Spell it out, man.'

'Sanitation, sir. Our task is to supply, coordinate, oversee, construct and dismantle the latrine facilities at every Army camp you care to name in Southern England. Well, I don't mind telling you what a hell of a job that was in the build-up to D-Day. Up to our necks in it, we were. At the American camps especially. Something to do with them having more generous rations, I suppose. The more that goes in, the more—'

'Thank you, Sarnt.'

'Pardon me, sir, if I've made you come over a bit squeamish. All our chaps do when they first arrive, but you'll get used to it, sir – everyone does in the end. "We may spend our weekdays knee-deep in shite, Sarnt," our OC likes to say. "But we'll spend our weekends smelling of violets." Now you have yourself a good weekend, sir. And you, Sarge. And we'll look forward to seeing you both on Monday. Ta-ra.'

Mother listens intently to the story, beaming throughout. I ought to tell you that, in the expurgated version we gave her, the word 'shite' was replaced by sundry gentle euphemisms. Things are different for your generation, I know, Jack. But in those days one didn't use potty language in front of one's mother.'

'But, darling, this is wonderful news,' she says when I've finished. 'You'll be able to come home, almost whenever you like.'

'Oh Mummy, really, you've got completely the wrong end of the stick. You don't honestly think that once we've squared things with their OC we're going to stay at that dump, do you?'

'Well, why ever not?'

'Mother! You heard what they do.'

'Well, I'm sorry, darling, but you're not going to convince me it's any more grim than sleeping in the mud and being shot at.'

'That's neither here nor there, the point is it's quite clear they've made some sort of clerical error.'

'The Sergeant you spoke to sounded pretty convinced they hadn't.'

'Mummy, you weren't there so you don't know. The man was quite clearly off his rocker. Besides, you don't think at a time like this the powers that be would drag experienced combat troops away from the front line to shovel up excrement, do you?'

'Maybe someone on high was trying to do you a favour.'

'A favour?' I yelp, quite aghast. Mothers, really. They've never understood the first thing about soldiering.

'It's a punishment, that's what I reckon,' says Price gloomily.

'Ever the optimist, Tom,' teases Mother.

'But from whom? Who would go to all that trouble to get us transferred like that, virtually in the midst of a battle? And who, for heaven's sake, would have the power? You'd need to be pretty high up.'

'Or have connections,' muses Price.

'Did you have anyone in mind, Price?'

'It's not as though you haven't made your enemies.'

He's thinking, perhaps, of the vindictive Air Vice Marshal who cost me my flying career. Or possibly, the half Colonel I couldn't help but cuckold one time. Or perhaps some kinsman of the one I shot in Burma. Or – yes, now I think of it, there are more than enough candidates.

'Maybe so, but is any of them really deranged enough to have gone to quite such elaborate lengths to see me undone? I think not, Price. In my experience, there's always less to these little problems than meets the eye. What we have here is a clerical error, pure and simple. We'll go back on Monday, have words with this ludicrous OC, and get ourselves removed from this, ahem, *mucky* situation before you can say Jack Robinson.'

Shortly after 1 p.m. – that's the official end of Mrs Browning's writing day – the picnic party sets off. Mrs Browning is how I always used to address her. Daffy D, sometimes, behind her back. To you, Jack, she'll be more familiar – if at all – under her maiden name Daphne du Maurier.

Ring any bells? Probably not, the speed with which literary reputations pass these days, but you might know some of her work. *Don't Look Now*, the film about a frightful red dwarf rampaging through Venice: that was one of her short stories. As was Alfred Hitchcock's shocker about the Nazi seagulls. *The Flock*, was it? But the thing she always remained best known for – and by golly did it use to irritate her if you brought it up, which is why I so often did – was a melodramatic murder mystery written largely for the enjoyment of hysterical women. Book by the name of *Rebecca*.

'Do remind me, Mrs Browning,' I used to badger her. 'Is it pronounced "Mander-lee" as in Camberley; or "Mander-lay" as in Kipling?'

And do you know what? I still can't for the life of me remember what her answer was. That was the difficulty I had when one of her biographers popped round for an afternoon to interrogate me about 'the real Daphne du Maurier I knew'. As I tried to explain to this incredulous young poppet – she clearly thought that to have spent time in Daffy D's presence was akin to being served private mass by the Pope – I was usually far too busy wishing her back home to Menabilly asap to pay attention to a single word she said.

Now this picnic. As is our family's wont, it takes place in our very favourite spot on the whole estate: the mill pond where Mrs Wilkins's dog got eaten by the giant pike and where I once disgraced myself with Gina. We loll in the sun, work our way merrily through Father's best Hock and gorge ourselves on the thick ham sandwiches Price has cleverly rustled up, courtesy of the huge haunch of gammon he found lurking in the cold room. Then afterwards, plunge into the icy water for a spot of traditional skinny-dipping.

Not Mrs Browning, obviously. Skinny-dipping isn't her style. Not Price either. So, in fact, it's just Lucy and I who take the plunge on this occasion.

'OPL,' orders Lucy, as she changes.

'What's that?' I say.

'Only Perverts Look – so don't,' she commands for the first time ever, when she slips out of her dress.

And when I do inadvertently look round before she's done I understand why. My, she's changed, the sweet, skinny, tomboyish little urchin I used to read stories to and share baths with. There's no mistaking her for a boy any more. Thank goodness all the men on the estate have gone off to war, because I know the sort of things I'd want to do to a girl shaped like that if I weren't her brother; and if I thought there was any danger of any of them doing it, why, I'd be after them with my shotgun.

'OK. Safe,' says Lucy, once she's in the water.

I strip off and join her. We swim to the deep bit and tread water for a while.

'It's topping to have you back,' she says.

'Topping to see you, Luce.'

'When Mummy thought you were dead I never did. I told her not to be so silly because you're going to make it through right to the end.'

'I'm glad to hear it, sis, but what makes you so sure?'

'Just a feeling in my bones. Same one that tells me I probably won't see this one out.'

'Luce! Don't ever say such things.'

'It's all right, I don't mind. Not now I'm used to the idea.'

'Well, I bloody well mind and it is not going to happen.'

'I expect that's what Patricia, Sarah and Victoria thought before the doodlebug got them.'

'If Hermann Göring sends so much as a gnat in your direction, I shall have his guts for garters.'

When we get out of the pond I'm told to avert my eyes again. Now I feel terrible for having wished all those young suitors away from that body. What if her premonition is right and she dies never having shared its charms with anyone?

We dry off in the sun by the willow – close enough to eavesdrop, if we want, on Mother's conversation with Mrs Browning, but generally more interested in catching up with one another's news.

'You're so much nicer than James,' she declares. 'Do you know what he said when I told him what I told you?'

'What?'

'He told me to stop being so morbid and said if I knew what real war was like I wouldn't joke about it.'

'Pompous oaf.'

'And when I told him I wasn't joking he said then I was a silly girl and shouldn't take premonitions seriously. He'd foreseen his death in action lots of times, he said, and nothing had come of it yet. And I said, "Still, James, we're all keeping our fingers crossed." Which, let me tell you, went down like a dose of cod liver oil.'

'I'll bet.'

'Sometimes I don't think he even realises how obnoxious he's being. These gongs he keeps getting don't exactly help. Nor does Father. You should have heard him when James cabled that he'd been put up for a DSO. It was all hail, the conquering hero. And make way, for Great Meresby's new young master.'

'Oh Lord, really?'

'Well, not in so many words, but I should be careful if I were you. We had his brigadier friend – Jumbo, is it? – round the other night. You know, the one who pulled strings to get you in the Commandos. The impression I got was that the rumour mill wasn't exactly working in your favour. Something you'd done to get in your OC's bad books? Whatever it was, I'm afraid Daddy hit the roof. "Can you get him out of there, Jumbo?" he said. "For the sake of our family name? I don't want him doing any more damage than he already has." I say, Dick, are you all right? I thought it better that you should know, that's all, and . . .'

'No, don't worry, sis. It's perfectly OK. I think you might just have helped me solve a mystery worthy of the great Daphne du Maurier herself.'

'Oh come now, Colonel Coward,' I remember that young biographer saying when she came for tea. 'You surely recall at least some of her bons mots?'

'Dick, please,' I said, patting the place next to me on the swing seat, in that distrait, I'm-a-sweet-old-boy-I-can-do-no-harm way which serves a chap so well past a certain age. Pretty little thing in her gamine way. Lesbian, no doubt, as so many Daffy D worshippers are.

'Dick then,' she said with a smile. But stayed where she was: QED.

'Bons mots, though? I'm not sure Mrs Browning was really a bons mots person.' (And at that point I had to try hard to suppress a snigger.) 'Saved them all for her books, I expect.'

'You must, though, have formed some impression of her character. Her personality?'

'Oh I did. I did, very much so.'

'And?'

'Absolutely bloody terrifying.'

The girl looked crestfallen.

'I can't be telling you anything you don't know, surely? Something to do with being an heiress, I imagine. That absolute assurance you get from having pots of money. It made her very certain of who she was and what she wanted and you crossed her at your peril.'

'Others speak of her emotional fragility.'

'Oh undoubtedly. Brittle as porcelain and mad as a fruit bat. Well, you'd need to be, wouldn't you, to dream up that frightful red dwarf. When she came up to Great Meresby, though, she tended to keep that side of things under wraps. Too busy being Mother's rock, I suppose.'

'You didn't think much of her, then?' said this girl lugubriously. I could see any second now she was going to pack up and go, for this wasn't what she wanted at all.

'Daphne du Maurier? Why, the woman was a marvel. For one thing, she was the only girl I ever knew capable of standing up to my father. Frightened the life out of him, in fact. And for another she saved my bacon. Perhaps when you've more time I could tell you all about it.'

'I'd love to hear it now, if you're not too exhausted.'

'Splendid. Then we shall make ourselves another pot of Darjeeling. You shall join me here on this most comfortable swing seat.' (It's never too late to convert 'em, say I.) 'And then I shall tell you everything you need to know. Not just about the small part she played in my own life. But also the rather more historically significant one she played in one of the greatest disasters in British military history.'

Dear me. Grandpa up to his old tricks again, you're no doubt thinking. But, Jack, this was no ruse. It is my view that the

Market Garden fiasco was as much Daphne du Maurier's fault as anybody's. Not because of anything she did, but because of who she was. And who she was, of course, was the wife of the man in charge of the tactical side of the operation, Lt. Gen. Frederick Browning.

In my family, taking our cue from Daffy D, we all knew him as Tommy. To the world at large, though, he was better known by his nickname Boy. Anyway, Boy, Tommy, Frederick, Lieutenant General, sir, whatever you want to call him, was a decent enough fellow. But I can't pretend I used to dread his visits to Great Meresby any less than Daffy D's.

First, he was such a stickler. I remember the first time he came to stay – not long after they'd got married; '31, '32 would that be? I would have been around fifteen at the time – I found myself sitting opposite him at dinner. And do you know the only words he exchanged with me the whole evening? 'I think, Master Richard, you'll find your evening shirt is missing a stud.'

It was later that same evening – or rather, in the small hours of the next morning – that I discovered another of his peculiarities. Unfortunately, the Brownings' guest bedroom lay next to mine, and I was woken in the night by the most appalling wailing noise. At first, I put this down to one of the numerous ghosts which supposedly stalk our ancestral seat, most likely the poor chap dispatched by his wicked stepbrother, Edward II-style, with a red-hot poker up the bum. Then, with dawning horror, I realised it was coming from next door and therefore, in all likelihood, comprised the orgasmic yelping of the rutting Brownings.

Except it sounded more like yelps of pain than of pleasure. Bondage secrets of our top lady novelist. I say, this will amuse Pricey, I thought, for in those days I'd forever be seeking new ways to curry favour with him. So I cupped my ear to the wall, in search of further evidence, and quickly found myself feeling rather shabby.

The yelps gave way to sobs; and sobs to soothing words from Mrs B. Poor Tommy had been having another nightmare.

It was all because of the First War, of course, as so many people's difficulties were in those days. One rarely talked about it because one simply didn't. But it's a wonder the country functioned at all in the twenties and thirties, populated as it was by a generation of sexually frustrated spinsters and widows on the distaff side, and on the male one by cripples and gibbering basket cases. My father, QED.

Anyway, old Tommy, I found out from Mother – who'd, of course, been sworn to secrecy by Daffy D – had had as bloody a time on the Western Front as anyone. Seems that, in 1917, his company was ordered to make a dawn attack on a wood riddled with snipers and machine-gun nests. It was supposed to be supported by tanks but as per usual they'd broken down. The attack went ahead all the same, and pretty soon, from an original compliment of seventeen officers, Tommy found himself the only one left alive. It was at this point, his dying comrades screaming and groaning all around him, that the Germans decided to launch their counter-attack . . .

Well, his sangfroid under fire that day won him a DSO, which many think should have been a VC, but underneath his nerves were shot, that's for sure. In their early years together, Daphne did for Tommy what she did for my mother, calming him down, soothing his troubled brow and all that. But by the time of the Second War – when Tommy, of course, was away most of the time running his 1st Airborne Division – the strain was beginning to tell.

I know this because of a conversation I overhear during the picnic by the mill pond. Something about a letter Tommy had written, asking if Mrs B could see her way to helping him buy a new boat.

'Ah, but has Tommy been a good enough Boy, do we think?' Mrs B says to Mother, with a scornful edge.

'Oh darling, you can't not. That would be too, too cruel,' says Mother.

'Three thousand pounds is an awful lot of money,' says Mrs B.

'And you're telling me you can't afford it?' says Mother.

'It's more the offhand way he asks for it. "A small amount of pence," he says, when it so patently isn't.'

'You'd rather he grovelled and pleaded?'

'Lord no. That really would be too ghastly,' says Mrs B with a sigh. 'No, I know that whichever way he asked I should be irked by it. Even his endearing little notes – "My dearest Mumpty", they begin – have begun to grate. What once sounded so sweet now just makes my toes curl. Isn't that just awful of me? Aren't I a frightful, frightful shrew?'

Mother goes, 'There, there, no of course not,' as best friends are supposed to do.

But at that moment my sympathy's all with Tommy. What a devil of a position to find yourself in: you're a senior officer, with a distinguished war record, good-looking, going places, soon to be given command of one of the most daring operations of the war. Yet you know that, whatever you achieve in your own right, you're always going to go down in history as the chap who was lucky enough to end up married to the woman who wrote *Rebecca*.

Unless, of course – and, it's that big Unless which to my mind explains Daffy D's pivotal role in the disaster that was Market Garden.

'A bridge too far.' That was what Lt. Gen. Browning supposedly warned Montgomery at the final planning meeting a week before the operation. Well, if that's really how he felt at the time, why didn't he call a halt to proceedings while he still could? He was Deputy Commander of the Allied Airborne Army, after all. It was perfectly within his power.

Well, there has been an awful lot of speculation on this one over the years. But for me it comes down to just three words, and two of them are a well-known brand of cigarette.

I'm not saying she was there actually whispering advice in his ear, *à la* Lady Macbeth. The operation was far too hush-hush for that. But I don't think it's too far-fetched to suggest that, when he had to make that difficult decision, what tipped the balance was the thought that here was the chance, the one and only chance, finally to do something in his life that would not only impress his unimpressible wife, but also might actually eclipse her fame for good.

All this I told to the young lady who came to see me, but none of it went into her book – I checked when she sent me my courtesy copy. The bit I thought would go in didn't go in either: my speculation as to the mildly suspicious closeness of Daffy D's relationship with my mother.

It was one of those ideas that occur to you on the spur of the moment. Not for the life of me do I really think that Daphne du Maurier and my mother might have been lovers. But I was feeling slightly mischievous that day, and thought it was the sort of fancy that might go down rather well with the lesbian lovely perched next to me on the swing seat.

She wasn't buying it, though – any more than she was ready to buy my other biographical titbit, God's own truth though it is. It has to do with that particular shade of maroon headscarf my mother favoured, and to which Daffy D took such a shine she began sporting it herself. She always wore one when she came to stay, furled round her neck in the manner of a cravat, which went rather well with her mannish, grey woollen trouser suits.

Anyway, the funny thing was, when a few years later Tommy was looking for a new beret colour to indicate membership of this new airborne division he was commanding – what shade should he have chosen but this very maroon. (Which the soldiers initially hated, I might tell you. Thought it was far too feminine a shade for a fighting man. Least they did until the Germans in Tunisia started calling them 'the Red Devils', after which they decided they rather liked it.)

So I told the pretty lesbian this and do you know what she said? She said, 'I'm afraid the story about Daphne du Maurier having chosen the shade of the 1st Airborne Division's berets is nothing but an urban myth.'

Whatever one of those is when it's at home.

We are all taking some of that excellent tea in the library when Father gets back. Price has stopped scowling; Mother's almost back to her usual self; Luce is snuggled up next to me on one of the window seats; and we're all listening to Daffy D, on unusually good form, as she spooks us with the tale of the skeleton found in the last century by some workmen, bricked up inside a secret room within the walls of Menabilly.

'I've been through the family papers, those the Rashleighs will let me have at any rate, but there's no mention of it anywhere,' she says.

'Well, it's not the sort of incident you'd want to advertise,' I say

'Yes,' says Luce. 'Perhaps the Rashleighs are holding the incriminating letter back: "Deare Mum, thanks for ye tucke. I am settling in well to ye new schoole. Please do not be crosse, but there's something I did in ye holidays, which clean slipped my minde. For my merrimente, while playing with ye impertinent servant boy Pippin, I bricked him up in ye walle and have since cleane forgotte in which parte of ye house it was . . ."'

Luce and I are the only ones who laugh at this.

'I don't imagine the poor victim found it a matter for joking,' says Daffy D coolly.

'No, no, I expect not,' I say, trying to keep a straight face.

Mummy does hate it so when we tease Daffy D. 'Do you have any theories on the subject?'

'Rather too many,' says Daffy D.

'The very best of which we shall see expounded in your next book, perhaps?'

'Perhaps,' says Daffy D, with a distant half-smile.

'WELL, AT LEAST WE KNOW WHAT WE'RE HAVING FOR DINNER!' bellows a triumphant voice from the hallway, and everyone in the room, Price included, freezes. 'EM? LUCE? WHERE ARE YOU? COME AND HAVE A LOOK AT THIS PAIR OF MONSTERS I BAGGED.'

'We're in here, darling,' says Mother.

'WHERE?'

'In the library.'

'AH.' There are stumpy footsteps as Father hobbles in, closely followed by our butler, Griffiths.

'Show 'em, Griffiths.'

Griffiths steps forward to show the two salmon he is holding, each by the tail. They're so long he has to keep his hands high to stop their noses touching the ground, and the strain of their combined weight is causing his arms to tremble. The fishing on our stretch of the Wye is, of course, pretty good. But rarely this good. No wonder the old man's so cheerful.

'I thought—' he begins. Then stops, suddenly, as for the first time he notices me. His expression changes from one of exultation, through shock to one which for a brief moment looks like pure, visceral loathing. But I don't think it can be, for having gaped at me for a while, apparently lost for words, he declares with renewed brightness, 'You? And Price too? You'll not have received my letter, then. Ah well, never mind. More than enough here to feed the five thousand. What, Griffiths?'

While Father disappears to clean up, I reflect with gratitude on the bounty of the Great Meresby estate. God knows, there have been moments in the past when I've had cause to rue its pleni-tude: the abundant salmon, trout and pheasant are, after all, the reason Father always manages to draw so many prize military bores to stay for the weekend. But on this occasion it has been my salvation.

Dinner that evening is more relaxed than any I can remember in years. For one thing, Daffy D apart, there are no crashingly dull guests to keep amused. For another, Father is exuding an almost reckless bonhomie and bounty. He invites Price to join us; he cracks open a magnum of Vintage '34 Bolly (though, as usual, he himself sticks to whisky); he seats me right opposite him at the head of the table; and he scarcely bats an eyelid when Griffiths enters solemnly to report that, the egg supply having been mys-teriously exhausted, we shall have to enjoy our poached salmon au naturel, not with Father's favourite hollandaise.

'I think I may have to reconsider my theory,' I murmur to Lucy after pudding, as Father calls for more champagne, so that he can propose a toast.

'Which theory?'

'The one identifying the miscreant behind our recent posting.'

'You think Daddy would have gone to all that trouble?'

'Don't you?'

'Now I think about it, yes. But if it was him, he's making quite a show of covering his tracks.'

'I'll say. I feel like the prodigal son.'

'Ladies; gentleman,' says Father, as Griffiths helps him to his feet. 'His Majesty the King!'

'His Majesty the King!' we all toast.

Then the next toast is proposed.

'To the new Master of Great Meresby!' says my father, with a pointed look at me I find hard to decipher.

Glances are exchanged. Lucy throws me a puzzled look. 'Search me,' says the one I give her in return.

'To the new Master of Great Meresby!' we all repeat uncertainly.

Does he mean me? My suspicion is no. Nothing he has ever said in the previous 99.9 per cent of our exchanges together has ever indicated such a delightful turn of events. This suspicion seems to be confirmed by the next toast, which is addressed to me personally.

'To Richard –' says my father, raising his glass.

'To Ri—' everyone begins.

'I'm not finished,' interrupts my father. 'To Richard. In the sincere hope that he enjoys greater success in his new home than he did in this one.'

Silence. In the first place, it's a bit of a mouthful, and in the second, well, what exactly is it supposed to mean? Something bad, probably. One of those really nasty surprises that Father does so enjoy springing on one in his sadistic way. But is this just a tasteless joke, a statement of intent, a threat or what?

'None of you going to join me? Ah well. If you'll all sit down – not you, Daphne: this is a family matter, so perhaps you'd care to make yourself at home in the drawing room till we're done. Then I shall explain.'

'Thank you, Ajax, but I prefer to stay where I am.'

'Darling, what is this about?'

'A surprise, Emily. Like the one Richard and Price chose to give me by turning up at Great Meresby, despite my express injunction to the contrary in the letter I left at their new posting and which they mysteriously claim not to have received. Now if Mrs Browning will kindly excuse herself . . .'

'Ajax,' says Daffy D, in that terrifying, icy way of hers and Lord, isn't it lovely not to be on the receiving end for once. 'When someone is on the verge of behaving very badly I find it often helps to have a disinterested party there to advise them that they are. For that reason, I intend to stay.'

'I'll tell you what bad behaviour is. Abandoning your comrades in their hour of need; cowardice in the face of the enemy. That's not just bad behaviour in my book. That's a capital offence, and if that boy had been under my command, blood relative or no, that's exactly the punishment I would have given him.'

'Ajax, I'm not sure any of us understands what you're talking about.'

'*He* knows, all right,' says the General, the angry finger he has jabbed in my direction quivering like an arrow that has just struck bullseye. 'He knows what he got up to in the landings on Gold Beach.'

'Sir, with respect, it was a mistake –' says Price.

'I'll say it was a mistake. Biggest one of that boy's miserable life. I've given him quite enough second chances, and now I'm quite done. He can have the house in Edgbaston, and that's all he'll inherit from me. The terms of the arrangement were perfectly clear: the estate ends up in the hands of the son who most deserves it and there's no longer any doubting which one that is.'

'Daddy, that is UNFAIR,' says Lucy. 'The war isn't over yet. Dick still has a chance to prove himself.'

'I'll thank you, Lucy, for keeping your nose out of matters you do not understand,' snaps the General. 'Even were the war to last another decade, Richard still wouldn't stand a cat in hell's chance of matching his brother's war record. Specially not once James's DSO has been confirmed.'

'*If* it's confirmed, Daddy. A lot of medal recommendations aren't, you know, or Dick would have had dozens by now.'

'Ha! Would he, by Jove?' the General snorts. 'And I suppose you were there to witness these numerous incidents of meritorious valour, were you?'

'No, Daddy,' sighs Lucy. 'No more than YOU were.'

'Proper little terrier in your brother's defence, ain't you, Luce?' muses my father. 'If only Richard had half your spunk –'

'Which he does, Daddy. He does!'

'Cowardice in the face of the enemy is a very serious charge,' says Daffy D.

'Do we not think it only fair that Dick should be given a chance to defend himself?'

'Deny, deny, deny! That's all he'll do,' says the General. 'That's all he ever does.'

'And your preferred response to a false accusation would be what exactly?' says Daffy D.

'False accusation? I'll have you know that this latest incident was witnessed by his OC himself.'

'Beg pardon, sir, but the OC was missing at that point, lost in the confusion of the landings,' says Price. 'It was his troop commander who thought he'd seen it. Then he realised later it had been a mistake but never got the chance to relay to the OC the correct version of events because he was killed shortly afterwards.'

'Handy,' says the General.

'With respect, sir, if he hadn't been killed he could have cleared Mr Richard's name.'

'We only have your word that he intended to do so.'

'There was a time, sir, when my word would have been assurance enough,' says Price, a touch unctuously, but you never know with Father. It's always worth exploring every avenue.

'Don't play the bluff honest retainer with me, Price. I'm damn near as furious with you as I am with young Master Yellowbelly there. If you'd had the presence of mind to do as the situation merited and put a tidy bullet through his head, we should all have been spared a great deal of unpleasantness.'

'And is young Master Yellowbelly to be given his chance to defend himself?' I say finally, my voice quavering in a way I wish it wouldn't for it plays right into my brute of a father's hands.

'I say, is that a gnat I heard whining?'

'Daddy, you are a pig and I HATE YOU!' screams Lucy, her face puce.

'Lucy!' says my father, his intonation somewhere between an admonition and a plea.

Lucy storms out.

Mother is in tears; Price is wearing that distant look I normally only see on his face after a particularly stiff engagement; Daffy D's face is set, her lips taut, her complexion the colour of a gravestone.

'Damn it, what is the matter with you all? I've given him Birmingham, haven't I?'

In later years, Mother, Price and I will chortle over this as one of the funniest things Father ever said. But at the time, none of us is exactly in the mood for laughter.

There is a long, gloomy silence, broken eventually by a clipped, upper-class voice pregnant with but barely contained fury.

'So you're not prepared to give Dick a fair hearing? And you're not prepared to give him a second chance?' says Daffy D.

The General says nothing. My guess is that he simply doesn't dare.

'Very well,' says Daffy D. 'If you cannot, then I shall have to ask someone who will.'

3

Christmas Comes Early

Do you know what happens when your parachute Roman candles and you hit the ground at 119 mph? I do.

It's not a pretty sight. You imagine strawberry jam but what you get is much more akin to a collapsing pink blancmange. The corpse – if he's lucky, for you'd definitely rather be dead than survive a jump like that – looks pink and quivery as you prod it curiously with your toecap, and realise what they say is true: no blood but every bone in your body is broken.

'Jumping to a conclusion,' is what my sergeant instructor at Ringway used to call it. Besides Roman candling – that's when your body twists as you leave the plane and your parachute fails to fill with air – there's the joyous possibility of getting your chute hooked on the tailplane, and trailing behind the aircraft screaming blue murder because you know no matter how long you delay the inevitable there's never going to be a happy ending.

And when your chute does inflate and you're floating gently down, that's the time when you're especially vulnerable to ack-ack or small-arms fire, which being as it's coming from below is going to hit you in the place where you least want to be hit. Unless, of course, it's an ME-109 come to strafe you, in which case you needn't worry, for when you've been hit by an explosive round from a 20 mm cannon, there'll be none of you left to worry with.

This is why paratroopers like to keep the gap between leaving the aircraft and hitting the ground as brief as possible. They manage this by dropping low, from between 800 and 500 feet, meaning that they spend no more than fifteen seconds in the air. But this presents problems of its own. First, it scarcely allows your pilot much margin for error. If he fails to hold a steady height, as happened quite a bit in Normandy, then it's jelly and blancmange all over the drop zone. Second, it leaves you very little time to sort out your other problem, which is the kitbag dangling from the rope tied to your leg.

Being a paratrooper, see, you're only as useful as the equipment you can carry with you into battle. Your weapons, your ammo, your food, your spare socks, your toothbrush, you name it – if it won't fit into your webbing, then it will have to go in the bag dangling from your ankle. Now you don't want to land on top of this bag because it's full of nasty hard things – mortar-base plates and suchlike – that can easily break your leg. And what you want even less is for the rope to wrap itself round you because then it can rip a limb clean off. Oh, and, if you are going to pack your bag with mortar bombs, for God's sake remember to make sure they're not primed. You'd think that one would be obvious, but it wasn't to the poor blighter I saw floating down once, about ten feet above the ground, when all of a sudden he starts rocketing up again, this time in a fountain of colourful bits.

Then, of course, there's your landing spot. If it's too rough, you're buggered because you're miles behind enemy lines alone with a broken ankle. If it's too wet, you drown. And if it's in a tree, well, it's probably the worst thing of all if the horrors I saw in Crete are anything to go by.

'*Nein! Nein! Bitte! Kamerad! Nein!*' I remember those young *Fallschirmjäger* crying out pitifully as they dangled from their trees like apples ripe for the plucking. But our infantrymen below weren't having any of it. Slowly, methodically, they picked off those shrieking German boys with the cool efficiency of a pest controller dispatching rats. There's no reason to think Jerry behaves differently when the positions are reversed.

And I haven't even told you yet what happened on the disastrous drop over Italy, but there'll be time enough one day for that, no doubt. Suffice to say that parachutes have never really been my number one favourite mode of travel. In my mind's eye, they always seem to be associated with things I'd generally rather avoid – like burning aircraft, jellied corpses and suicide missions into the deep unknown.

'Feeling windy?' says Price, as I stare blankly at the crumbling, lichen-covered headstones, lost in thoughts similar to the ones I've just rehearsed for you. God, I hate it when he's pretending to be solicitous. It's like Himmler trying to tell a knock-knock joke.

'What? About an interview for a job I don't even want? Hardly,' I say.

Price strains hard to bite back his instinctive rejoinder. It's about the only thing I'm almost enjoying about this wretched business, watching him suffer as he struggles to suck up to me and accommodate my sulky whims.

He'd never normally be sitting with me in a churchyard, for one thing. He dragged me here because he thought I'd like to see the twelfth-century church and I do. Nice village too: tranquil, a decent-looking pub called the Leg of Mutton, and a beck running down the main high street. But I'm not going to let on because that would be playing his game. He wants me to like this Lincolnshire village – Ruskington, it's called – because he wants me to get comfortable with the idea of staying here. 'Bet the hunting's not half bad round these parts,' he says at one point, a gambit so lame I'm not even going to dignify it with a reply. By the time the hunting season starts, the unit we've come to interview for will long since have been deployed overseas.

'Come now, Mr Richard. You know you don't mean it.'

'And what makes you think that?'

'Because I've explained it to you, haven't I?' he says, striving not to sound too cross. 'It's your last chance to put things right with the General.'

'And what if I made up my mind not to put things right with the General. What if I say, stuff him. Stuff the estate. Let James turn it into a golf course or a brothel or whatever he's got planned. Stuff everything.'

Price flicks his cigarette butt onto the pathway and grinds it with his boot.

'It's hard working for a living,' he says. 'Not that you'd know.'

'I'll manage. I've got ideas.'

'Ideas that will pay for your hunters, your champagne, your tailoring bills?'

'I've heard it said a fellow can survive without such essentials. Besides which, this thing I've been thinking of, I think I might enjoy it.'

'Are you going to tell me?'

'You'll laugh.'

'Try me.'

'I was thinking of writing a novel about our adventures. Several novels if it works out.'

Price laughs.

'Well, we have had some pretty good ones.'

'You think after six years of war anyone's going to want to buy a book reminding them what they've just been through?'

'Ah, but these books will concentrate on the lighter side, based more or less on our relationship.'

'What relationship?'

'Yes, that's just the thing my Price character will say. I'll make him a miserable bastard, even more miserable than you, but at the same time oddly indispensable – in the manner of Jeeves to Wooster. So, I suppose, I'll have to make my upper-class hero more chinless and feckless than he is in real life –'

'That'll be hard.'

We saunter back to the station, where someone from the base is supposed to be collecting us in half an hour. Price was so keen to get me here, we accidentally caught an earlier train, which is why we have time to kill.

'I've got a better plot idea which will make you a lot more money for a lot less trouble,' says Price, lighting up another fag.

'Do tell me.'

'There's a 4,000-acre estate with the best salmon fishing in the whole of the Wye Valley, in prime hunt country that stretches beyond Hay Bluff—'

'I think I've heard this one before.'

'Let me finish. Now, there's a fellow who could easily get to inherit all this. Only he won't because he's a stubborn berk, who'd rather spend the rest of his war shovelling shit in Birmingham, when he could be covering himself with glory in the finest unit in the British Army.'

'Oh, 1st Airborne Recce Squadron are the finest now, are they?'

'Are you disputing it?'

'Make up your mind is all I'm saying. You said exactly the same thing about 1st, 2nd and 3rd Parachute Battalions; and 10th and 11th Battalions; AND 156 Battalion. Until they turned us down, when you suddenly realised they were third-rate amateurs who made the Home Guard look like the SS Das Reich.'

You'll gather from this that Daffy D's attempts to parachute us into one of the several outfits comprising her husband's 1st Airborne Division have so far drawn a blank. 'I'll see what I can do, my own beloved Mumpty,' he apparently explained to her in his letter. 'But you must understand the final decision lies with my battalion commanders.'

And the battalion commanders, to a man, have decided no. They've all been very nice in their letters of rejection. 'Unit at full strength', 'No vacancies at this time', 'Pains me, truly it does, to turn down an application by two men with such extensive operational experience,' blah blah blah di blah ... But reading between the lines, I think I can fathom what the real problem is. With a war record including treachery, adultery, mutiny, desertion, drunkenness, reduction to the ranks, cowardice in the face of the enemy, and shooting a superior officer, our reputation has preceded us.

'Anyway, this 1st Airborne Recce lot can't be much cop at reconnaissance,' it occurs to me, as a distant whirring announces the approach of our pick-up vehicle. 'If they were they would have done their homework, and turned us down flat like all the others.'

'Well, if the OC has heard anything and starts asking you awkward questions just remember not to give him a straight answer,' says Price.

'Ah yes, because I'm such a brainlessly decent upper-class poltroon I find it almost impossible to lie unless my Jeeves-like companion reminds me?' I suggest, sarcastically.

Price grins.

'There may be life in this book of yours yet.'

Our driver introduces himself as Trooper Wood – Chopper Wood to his chums, you won't be surprised to hear. He has tiny hands and the cherubic features of one of those implausible, naughty yet adorable scamps you see on soap powder advertisements. He seems nifty enough behind the wheel, but then who wouldn't in this corner of England where the roads are so resolutely flat and straight.

Mounted in front of my seat is a weapon I recognise, the Vickers K machine gun. For old time's sake, while we're paused at a road junction, I rise from my seat, nestle the gun butt against my shoulder, take aim at a row of Junkers on an imaginary desert airfield and caress the trigger.

'Used one of them before, have you, sir?' asks Wood.

'Ages ago. Up the blue.'

'Quite popular with the SAS, I believe, sir, the Vickers K.'

'It was, it was. But we'd never have dreamt of going out with so few as this. It was three LMGs per jeep at the very least. Preferably five. Still, I suppose with Recce your primary purpose isn't to engage.'

'Oh it's not that, sir. It's a question of weight. We'd love more LMGs if we could have 'em, but the powers that be won't allow it. It's the main drawback of being airborne, sir. You can only take so much with you.'

'Still, I expect you get sufficient back-up from your Humbers.'

'Our what, sir?'

'Your armoured cars.'

Wood chuckles.

'Oh I like that, sir. I like that very much. We do like an officer with a sense of humour in Recce.'

Finally the horrible realisation dawns: these tinny jeeps, with no armour, only a rapid-firing pop gun on the front, and drivers just out of kindergarten, are what 1st Airborne Division, in its wisdom, has decided will spearhead the greatest Allied thrust on Germany since D-Day.

I try not to let Wood see how perturbed I am by this. It wouldn't look good coming from a prospective section commander. Or, formerly prospective section commander, as I think I've now become.

'So you're quite the man of action, sir,' continues Wood breezily.

'I wouldn't say that.'

'Oh that's what they all say, sir, men of action like you. But I'm not just saying this cos I can see your DFC ribbon or because you let slip back then, sir, that you were in the SAS. I could tell straight away, sir, soon as you opened your mouth. Gentleman killers, that's what I call your sort. Just like Mr Bland, my last section commander. Just like my old boss before the war. Gentleman killers all.'

From the back of the jeep comes laughter.

'Eh, Sergeant, am I right?' calls back Wood.

'Son, this gent has killed more Jerries than you've had sly ones off the wrist – and judging by the size of you, that's more than a few,' declares Price.

Wood looks momentarily uncomfortable at this, then cracks a smile.

'Nice one, Sarge,' he says.

At the guard house we learn that the OC is not back from his training run, but has left a message that Wood should show us round. The camp all seems much as you'd expect – barbed wire, Nissen huts, men being drilled, men cleaning weapons, men climbing up ropes – until we approach the firing range, where a black man is preparing to fire his Bren.

Now the fact that he's black is in itself unusual. Of course we have many negroes fighting alongside us for the Empire and damned fine soldiers a lot of them are too – but they tend generally to be found in askari units where they don't stick out so much. What strikes me much more forcibly than the man's skin colour, though, is the target he's aiming at.

Standing directly in his line of fire about 1,000 yards away is a tall, well-built man with his hands in the air. Either this dark fellow hasn't noticed or – worse still, it happens sometimes with men who've been exposed to too much combat – he's flipped his lid and doesn't care.

'*Nicht schießen!*' calls the man from the target area.

The black man ignores him and starts taking careful aim. His number two beside him appears to be complicit in this, for he makes no attempt to stop him.

'Cease fire!' I yell. 'Cease fire.'

His number two appears to whisper something in his ear. The black man half glances back and then resumes his aim.

Jabbing my index finger frantically forward I indicate that Wood should drive closer, yelling all the while for the bugger to cease fire. When he doesn't respond to the order in English, I repeat it in Swahili, just in case.

'*Nicht schießen*,' repeats the man one more time – a prisoner, brought here for interrogation, caught trying to escape? – before collapsing suddenly, hit dead centre in his chest by a single shot.

'My God, you blithering idiot, can you not obey an order when you hear one?' I say to the black man. I'm appalled to see he's got a huge grin on his face, which falters only slightly when he sees my pips.

'Sorry, sir, we thought you were Trooper Bleackley,' pleads his number two, a mole-like individual with very dark, silken, slicked-back hair. 'He's got two guineas riding on the outcome of this. We thought he was trying to chicken out.'

'Never mind Trooper blooming Bleackley. What about the fellow you've just gone and murdered?'

'Murdered?' says the black man. (Or rather 'Mairdered', for it would seem he hails from Liverpool.)

'Yes, mur—' I begin, only to cut myself short as, from the far end of the firing range, the apparent victim rises unsteadily to his feet, then waves both his arms and performs the delighted jig of a man whose recklessness has just earned him two guineas.

'Blanks?' I say.

'Body armour,' says the black man.

'How ruddy irresponsible!' I say.

'Good shooting, though,' murmurs Price.

When, finally, I come up before their OC, this incident is the first thing I mention. No doubt it's the last thing he wants to hear, some upstart lieutenant from an Army sanitation unit trying to lecture him on lax fire discipline. But I don't much care, for by this stage I've made up my mind: there's no way on God's earth that I'm going to throw in my lot with this fruitcake suicide squadron.

'Come out in one piece, did he, the tall fellow?' asks the OC, a white-haired, middle-aged, bluff country-squire type by the name of Maj. Gough. He arrived sweating and red-faced, an hour later than we'd arranged, pursued by a very strange little dog – like a cross between a poodle and a dachshund – which I later found out was a rare sort of terrier called a Dandie Dinmont.

'I think so, sir.'

'I'm most relieved to hear it. Losing Tiny would have played havoc with the men's morale. Being as he's so much bigger than the average trooper, the men all imagine that he'll cop the bullets that would otherwise have been aimed at them.'

The OC's jovial, straightforward manner rather disarms me. In civilian life he could be your favourite cuddly uncle.

'I'm sorry, sir, to have brought it up, it's just—'

'Freddie, please. We're all on first-name terms here. And, no, of course you did the right thing. The men will be duly reprimanded. But a fire-eater like you must know what it's like when you keep getting ops cancelled on you at the last minute. A chap's got to let off steam somehow.'

Fire-eater? What has that blabbermouth driver been telling him?

'Cancelled ops?'

'Twelve so far this summer. Allied headquarters can't decide what to do with us, that's the problem. They've got the cream of the British and American forces – thirty thousand airborne troops in all – kicking their heels, itching to make a difference, getting steadily more browned off as the days go by. Do you know what they're calling us now? First Stillborn Division. Our big worry is that the war will be over before we get a look-in. Largely thanks to chaps like your brother.'

'My *brother*?'

'I've got that right, haven't I? You've a dashing brother with lots of gongs in Guards Armoured Division? Well, the speed he and his chums are advancing across Europe is leaving us precious little to do. They keep overrunning our objectives before we can reach them, damned spoilsports.'

'I'll give you spoilsport but I'm not so sure about dashing,' I say.

'Sibling rivalry?'

'Heaven forfend. We're thick as Patton and Montgomery, my brother and I.'

'That bad, eh? Relieved to hear it. From what I gather, he's the most frightful shit.'

'Your intelligence is first-rate.'

'It is our job, rather. Now, do you have any questions before I give you your Christmas tree?'

'Bit early for that, I should have thought.'

The OC laughs and reaches into the top drawer of his desk. He removes something shiny and pushes it towards me. Of course, the cap badge of the Reconnaissance Squadron, with its two diagonal lightning flashes. The jagged-sided triangle they form does indeed look quite like a Christmas tree.

'You're still puzzled, I see,' he says. 'Those two flashes –'

'No, it's not that. I was wondering, don't you want to interview me first?'

By which, of course, I mean, Help! You haven't given me any room to wriggle out.

Obviously I can't say no to his offer directly. For one thing Price would never forgive me. For another I'm a moral coward. It's a bit like when you're trying to get rid of a girl you don't fancy, but can't quite pluck up the courage to tell her. So much easier to start behaving so unpleasantly that she thinks she's the one who wants to ditch you.

'Oh I don't think we've any need for that,' says the OC. 'I've seen your wings and your ribbons; I've half an idea what you and Sarnt Price have done and where you've been. Seems to me you'll fit in just perfectly as a section commander in 1st Recce. Say the word and the position's yours.'

Well, Jack, you don't survive as long as I have without a gift for thinking on your feet. My best hope, I realise, is to do exactly what Price asked me not to do in the cemetery.

'Freddie, I'm honoured,' I say. 'And in return, I feel it's only fair that I should be completely open with you. You ought to know the reason for my discharge in Burma.'

'Ah yes,' says Maj. Gough with a roguish smirk. 'That half colonel you shot. Had it coming to him, did he?'

'Er, yes,' I flounder, somewhat disarmed by his enthusiasm. 'Yes, he did.'

'Thank Christ for that. Thought you were going to tell me it was an accident. If there's one thing we don't need in 1st Recce it's poor shots.'

'Funny you should say that, sir, but I can't hit a barn door at twelve paces,' is what I should say at this point, but I can't for I'm just not that brazen. Instead, I glide swiftly on, towards another of my more spectacular misdemeanours.

'And the mix-up on the Eastern Front. That one's been pretty well hushed up. But it's as well you hear it from me than from anyone else.'

'Mix-up!' says the OC, his face glowing with delight. 'A marvellous turn of phrase to describe a business, I don't mind saying, I've been itching to ask you about all day. Now, are you going to show me or am I going to have to wait for some fortuitous occasion when we happen to be sharing a shower?'

I regard him with some astonishment.

'Your arse, Dick!' he roars, jovially. 'I want to see your arse! Not because I'm a pederast, though God knows, I saw enough of that going on in my days as a midshipman. I want to see that famous tattoo.'

For a moment I'm lost for words.

'Is it that famous?'

'Famous? How many other buttocks in His Majesty's Armed Forces are you aware of with a literary German obscenity tattooed on them by a Wehrmacht machine-gun troop at the battle of Stalingrad? Your arse is a legend!'

And so it is, blushing like a virgin bride, that I find myself leaning against the Major's desk, bottom sticking out, trousers round my ankles, in a way I never imagined I'd have to do again on leaving my prep school. There are no bodily secrets among fighting men, it's true, but I can't pretend it feels altogether comfortable having my buttocks pored over with such evident rapture by an ex-naval man. Especially not when there's a knock at the door and Maj. Gough says, 'It'll only be my adjutant. You don't mind if he has a look, too, do you?' Before I have time to say no, he calls out, 'Come.'

The door opens and, much to the enormous embarrassment of everyone save perhaps the OC, two men walk in and salute. One is clearly the adjutant. The other is a very tough-looking, heavy-set, older man with penetrating grey eyes, grizzled stubble and an expression so miserable it makes Price look like the Cheshire Cat. On his arm he wears a corporal's stripes.

'Frightfully sorry, sir,' says the reddening adjutant, about to wheel round and make a speedy exit. 'I thought you asked—'

'Never mind that, grab an eyeful, gentlemen, quickly, for I doubt you'll be offered another chance. Will they, Mr Coward?'

'I should say not, sir,' I say with feeling, for I was about to hoick up my trousers, and now feel I can't. What I still don't quite understand is how in God's name I allowed myself to be persuaded to do this in the first place.

But this, I'll come to realise, is one of Maj. Gough's extraordinary strengths as a commander. He could ask his men to pickle their bollocks and down them with a pint of urine and happily they'd do it for him because of the way he asks it: as if it's the most normal and natural and delightful thing in the world, something he'd happily be doing himself if only he could be half so lucky.

'*Leck mich am Arsch?*' says the adjutant, examining the Gothic script more closely. 'Would that be some sort of unit motto?'

'I'm sure Corporal Cholmondeley can translate,' says the OC.

'I don't speak German, sir,' says Cpl. Cholmondeley, very stiff and unamused.

'Course you don't, Corporal. Why is it I'm always forgetting?' says the OC in a teasing voice.

After Cpl. Cholmondeley has gone, and I'm finally decent again, the OC says, 'Splendid fellow, Cholmondeley. Not a natural for music hall I shouldn't say, but you should see him in action. What did you make of him?'

'He didn't seem very amused.'

'Ah well, he wouldn't, would he, being a Jerry.'

'Didn't—?'

'Yes, of course he did, but some of them won't admit it. Came to us from the Pioneer Corps. No sense of humour. Hunnish grey eyes. Square face. What more evidence do you need? Anyway, I wanted to give you an idea of the calibre of the chaps you'll be working with. We don't care where a fellow comes from or what his background is in this unit. So long as he's the best, that's good enough for us. Now, how soon before you can join us?'

'I'm not sure, sir,' I say, wondering how I can best let them down gently. I've served with chaps like this rather too many times before: decent, likable fellows with a can-do attitude and a devil-may-care-spirit. Problem is, I know too well where invariably they all end up.

'Freddie, please. You're among friends here. Isn't he, George?'

'Rather. Exactly the sort of chap the Recce needs.'

'I'm not sure that I am, actually.'

'Let us be the judge of that, Dick.'

'Look, I'm sorry for wasting your time, but I've decided I can't. I really can't join your unit.'

'But why ever not?'

'Well, I suppose I should have mentioned this earlier and I don't know why I didn't because it is quite a handicap for a chap in an airborne unit.'

'What? Spit it out.'

'Parachutes. I hate bloody parachutes. No, worse, I'm absolutely terrified of them. You see, whenever I've had anything to do with them, things always seem to go so terribly, terribly wrong . . .'

4

Mons Veneris

'Gently, you bugger, gently! No, not like that, you great merkin,' the Earl of Brecon bellows, laying his huge, rough beefy red hands on top of mine and seizing control of the rod.

'Like *this!*' he cries, blasting the back of my head with a flaming torrent of cherry brandy and whisky fumes. He lifts the rod very gently upwards, half crushing my knuckles in the intensity of his passion.

'There,' he says more softly, eyes following the darting, dappled shadow as it flicks with a brief flash across the pebble bed, then dives for the green-black cover of the deep water channel, heading fast and determinedly upstream. 'Let him run,' he whispers, giving me back control of the rod. 'Let him run! He's a beauty, that one. Take your time. Don't lose him. Don't you dare lose him, my boy, or I'll have your bollocks for raspberry jam!'

I do so enjoy my birthday treat with my Uncle Johnny. It's the same every year and I wouldn't have it any other way: a morning's fishing, just him and me, on the broad bend in the Wye directly below his family seat, Brecon Abbey.

You'll recognise it, no doubt, from the television. Whenever they need somewhere symbolising the magnificence in excelsis of the English upper classes, Brecon Abbey's the place they use. If it's an Austen adaptation it'll be where Mr Darcy lives; if it's that bugger Waugh, Brideshead. Not nearly as charming in my view as Great Meresby but the fishing and shooting are better, there's five times as much land, and the chap who owns it – my god-father, the 12th Earl of Brecon – is a hell of a sight more welcoming.

'Now, Dick, to business!' says Lord Brecon, once the salmon has been safely landed and he's popped the first bottle of Bolly.

'Oh God, must we?'

'Dear boy, it cannot be avoided. I have to think of my future neighbours. More to the point, my daughter's future neighbours. I do not want Great Meresby falling into the wrong hands.'

'You and James get on reasonably well.'

'And suppose he sells it on to a greengrocer. Or one of your Uncle Noël's unwholesome thespian chums. Or – ye gods! – some dreadful jazz musician. Come, Dick, you know what my daughter's like. You know how strangely drawn she is to anyone of whom I'm likely to disapprove.'

'Anyone who isn't a duke or a marquess, you mean.'

'Cheeky bugger! I'll have you know, I'm quite capable of moving with the times. Why, this evening I mean to put her next to a strapping young major general and, American though he may be, I certainly shan't reach for the shotgun if he shows an interest.'

'Gina's back?'

'Damn, what an ass I am. I had meant to keep it a surprise. Yes, she is. Expected this afternoon. Had some sort of falling-out with her web-footed inamorato – for which much thanks. Ever since we got the telegram, her mother and I have been working like blacks to find something more suitable.'

'Who is he, this American?' I say, trying to keep the hurt out of my voice, which, as you'll imagine, isn't easy. Hide of a hippo, and the subtlety of an area bomb raid: that's my Uncle Johnny. No wonder he and my father get on so well.

'Paratrooper, I think. Your cousin Richard is one of his company commanders. Bob Gavin? John Gavin? Something like that. Youngest US general since George Custer.'

'And look where it got Custer,' I mutter, pulling a face.

'Not good enough for her, do you reckon? Why, it doesn't half tickle me the way you watch over her,' he says, filling up my glass. 'You're like the brother she never had.'

Never, I think to myself, has incest seemed more compelling.

'But, you naughty chap, you've allowed me to ramble. We were supposed to be sorting out this business with your father.'

Well, I don't intend to bore you, Jack, by repeating what you know already. I explain to Uncle Johnny, as I have already explained to Price, that my mind is made up: I intend to see out the rest of the war in Birmingham, away from the action, for I've more than done my bit and I see no point in courting Father's favour with yet further acts of derring-do when it's quite clear he wanted to give the estate to James all along.

'Oh I think you're right, dear chap. You're absolutely right,' says Uncle Johnny, when I make the last point. 'I remember him saying almost as much at the memorial service for your poor dear elder bro. "And d'you know, almost the worst of it is, Johnny, I shall now have to pass on Great Meresby to that noisome runt."'

'My father actually said that?'

'Might have been "frightful brat", or "hideous worm", or "hellish spawn", I forget exactly, for he was in his cups and so I fear was I. But that was the general sentiment.'

'Oh,' I hear myself saying in a little-boy-lost voice. And I'm struck by a desperate urge to be with Mother, the only person I can think of in the world – her and my little sis, anyway – who could tell me that it isn't true and that my father certainly didn't mean it, he was just drunk and upset, that's all. Mother being ten miles away – somewhere on the estate to which I have been permanently denied access – I content myself with a long draught of fizz and lung-rasping Balkan Sobranie.

'Why so glum?' says Uncle Johnny, clapping me on the back, when eventually he notices how silent I've grown. 'It can hardly be news that Ajax has a softer spot for James, what with him being so tall, handsome, clean-limbed, sporty and chip-off-the-old-block, and you being – well – rather the opposite.'

I suck deeper on my cigarette and gaze glumly, unseeingly, towards my huge dead salmon. Some birthday this is turning out to be.

'Am I making things worse? Oh dear. Look, the point I've been trying to make, not altogether successfully, I grant you, is that I know your father, know him well, and whatever his faults he's a man of his word, do you see?'

I let out a weary sigh. If there's one thing worse than having a father as cantankerous as mine, it's the drip drip drip of people trying to persuade me what a splendid fellow he is.

'What I'm saying is that it's still not too late. Win more gongs than your brother and the estate's yours – and never mind which side of the sheets you were born.'

'Uncle Johnny, what are you on about?'

'The VC, obviously.'

'I meant – has Father got it into his head that James and I are illegitimate?'

'Not James, no.'

'But we're twins, for God's sake.'

'You'd never know it, though, would you?'

'So because we're not identical, Father's made up his mind that the child that came out first is a bastard, and that the one that looks most like him is the right and true heir to Great Meresby.'

'More or less.'

'But – but that's the most bonkers thing I've heard in my whole life!'

It's so completely bizarre and sudden and unexpected I can't make up my mind whether to laugh or cry. On the one hand, it explains an awful lot. And I suppose it does make me feel sort of better because it means my father's behaviour isn't about me but about the severe brain damage he must have suffered when that whizz bang took out his dug-out at Passchendaele.

On the other hand I can't also help feeling rather bitter and cheated. Imagine! The whole course of my life, my future happiness, the family name, everything, has been quite ruined, not because of anything I've been able to affect myself but because a tiny splinter of metal, twenty-seven years ago, decided to bury itself in the wrong bit of my father's head.

Maj. Gen. James Gavin – Slim Jim to his troops – is everything I dreaded: tall, intelligent, well turned-out, immaculate manners, matinee-idol looks. And hung like a horse, so the woman next to me volunteers halfway through dinner, causing me damn near to choke on my Petrus.

It's jolly scary, I must say, when women you've barely met start talking so frankly about sex. Jolly exciting, too. She must be a bit squiffy, which is fine by me. I too have spent most of the evening trying to drown my sorrows. Partly it's because of what Uncle Johnny told me this morning. Mainly, damn it, it's because he hasn't sat me anywhere near Gina.

Whenever I think no one's looking, I steal sour little glances across the silverware to where Gina is giggling her knickers off at everything the smoothy-chops, poster-boy Major General says to her.

Eventually the girl to my right, whom I've so steadily ignored I don't even know her name, drawls softly, 'And if you think he's big on top, you should see his undercarriage!'

'Hahaha, yes,' I go, as if she's said something seemly and innocuous about the weather.

'Never guess he had a wife, would you?' says my neighbour.

'Does he really?' I say, encouraged.

'And a daughter not much younger than that strumpet,' says the woman.

'Um, that's your host's daughter, actually,' I say.

'I know,' she says.

'Well, I think it's a bit much calling her a strumpet,' I say, keeping my voice down, not that I need to for as per usual at the Earl's dinners, most of the guests are exceedingly noisy and very well-lubricated. 'She's just being polite, that's all.'

Suddenly, I feel a pressure on my leg. It's my neighbour's hand and it appears to have been placed there very deliberately.

'Is *this* being polite?' asks the woman, whom I now wish I'd studied more carefully beforehand. Dark hair, dark sculpted lips, very attractive in a vampish kind of way, I seem to remember. I would try to confirm this except I'm far too embarrassed to risk eye contact.

'Um –'

'Or this.'

Now her hand has edged further towards my inner thigh. My chest is palpitating wildly. There's an unmistakable tightening in my crotch. Cripes!

'Because that's what he's doing to her, you know.'

'What? Feeling her, um, leg?'

'Maybe not literally. But still, she'll be wet enough by now.'

Her hand is now fully placed where it can feel my excitement. Oh God, oh God. What do I do?

I don't know how things look from the other side of the table – can they see where her arm's going? Have I turned as red as I think I have? – but something in our behaviour must have alerted Maj. Gen. Gavin, for he shoots my neighbour a brief, puzzled look, and then me, a much longer, harder one.

To cover my embarrassment I stammer, 'S-So, General. I gather you know my cousin, Richard Du Croix.'

'My finest Company Commander, sir. And you are?'

'Coward, sir. Lieutenant Dick Coward.'

'My godson, General,' chips in Lord Brecon. 'The one I was telling you about. Who thinks paratroops are a waste of time.'

What? I never said that. Did I?

Then through the fug of alcohol it comes to me. I suppose I did say something quite similar to Uncle Johnny while we were fishing. But only as a way of trying to justify my decision not to join 1st Airborne Recce. And only because I'd heard Price bang on in this vein after the debacle over Italy and I thought his argument quite clever.

The Major General looks at me intensely. My neighbour's hand retreats and so does my tumescence. There's no more effective a passion-killer, let me tell you, than a debate about tactics with a senior officer.

'Do you think paratroops are a waste of time?' he says.

Actually, I don't. But the wine has got the better of me and I can't resist putting the fellow in his place.

'Are you familiar, sir, with our General Slim?'

'I know the name.'

'Fine man. Commands our 14th Army in Burma, and he said to me something once on the subject of special-force units which I think may interest you: "Any well-trained infantry unit should be able to do what a commando can do. This cult of special forces is as sensible as to form a royal corps of tree climbers and say that no soldier who does not wear its green hat with a bunch of twig leaves in it should be expected to climb a tree."'

'You're saying there's no place in the military for elite units?' asks the Major General.

'I'm right with you there,' booms Lord Brecon. 'The only elite you need is the Brigade of Guards. Why, half the Johnny-come-latelies in these newfangled specialist regiments – the Commandos, the Paras and what have you – barely know how to hold a knife and fork, let alone which way to pass the port. And that's the officers, I'm talking about, not the other ranks . . .'

'Oh I do very much believe in elites and I've fought with most of them,' I say. 'My point is that it's madness creaming off the brightest and best of the line regiments if all you're going to do is squander them in hopelessly misconceived operations.'

'Like Pegasus Bridge?' says Maj. Gen. Gavin, as of course he would. It's the one airborne operation of the whole bloody war so far which has been a complete and unmitigated success.

On 6 June, a company of the Ox and Bucks Light Infantry in Horsa gliders landed virtually on top of the bridge, surprised the defenders, and then, with the help of some paras, held it through the night against repeated assaults from more powerful German forces. It was textbook stuff, exactly the sort of thing airborne troops are designed to do: strike quickly, hold briefly, then get the hell out.

'Pegasus Bridge was a fluke,' I say, to audible gasps from some of the more sensitive souls at the table. It's like saying that Dunkirk was an ignominious retreat, and El Alamein a graceless slogging match: people don't like having their glorious victories dragged through the mud.

'Tell it like it is, Lootenant,' says Maj. Gen. Gavin, smiling at my impertinence. 'You saying I should pack my bags and take my boys home with me, because, hell, you don't need any airborne-time wasters? You British are going to win this war on your own?'

'Oh, please don't do that, General,' purrs the radiant Lady Brecon, sitting to his left, in her soft New England accent. 'We do so enjoy having you here.'

'He doesn't mean it, Mummy. And he's twisting what Dick said,' says Gina, with a sharp, but not unamused glance at her neighbour.

With a grin, the Major General raises his palms in mock sur-render.

'All right, you found me out,' he's saying.

'You weren't calling General Gavin's men useless, Dick, were you?' prompts Gina.

'Certainly not. They're some of the best soldiers I've ever fought with,' I say.

Finally, I have the Major General's fullest attention.

'We had a few fall on top of us in Sicily last year,' I explain. 'Pilot error, as per usual. They'd been dropped fifty miles from where they were supposed to be, so they asked whether we'd mind if they joined us for a while. Jolly good company they were too, though they never did get the hang of our tea breaks.'

'Nor will we, Lootenant.'

'No sense of style or form, that's the problem with you colonials,' says the Earl. 'Eh, what, dear?' he adds for the benefit of his American wife.

'Too much style and form – that's the problem with you Limeys,' replies the Major General. 'There are times when I wonder whether we're fighting the same war. For you guys, it just seems to be a game, where what matters above all is to play by the rules. For us, the only thing that counts is winning.'

'Then pray God you never take up cricket,' says the Earl. 'You've already quite ruined Wimbledon with your poisonous professionalism.'

'If poison is what it takes to kill the enemy, then, Lord Brecon, I stand guilty as charged,' says the Major General.

'I hope you're not suggesting, sir, that our chaps don't know how to fight,' says the Earl.

'No, sir, I would never say that about our most trusted ally.'

'Spit it out. Say what you really think of us,' says the Earl.

'Now, darling, that's too unfair. You're putting our poor guest on the spot,' says the Countess.

'I don't doubt he's faced worse,' says the Earl.

'Ma'am, I'm happy to say what I think. I'd say your generals are too cautious in the advance, and your officers too reluctant to take the initiative. But when the chips are down, your infantry are a match for the best on earth; and when you lose, you die better than anyone.'

'On that cheery note,' says the Earl, 'might I propose that the ladies now retire?'

I'd like to regale you with some of Slim Jim Gavin's postprandial indiscretions, but I'm not sure there were any. Being American he hadn't got nearly drunk enough; and being a career senior officer destined for the greatest of heights, he was hardly going to shove in his tuppeny-ha'penny's worth with a junior officer like me present.

Besides, even if he had spilled the beans on his superiors – he clearly wasn't a fan of Field Marshal Montgomery, that much I gathered; nor of his own immediate superior Gen. Lewis Brereton – I doubt I should have paid much notice. The fact was, I was far too busy wishing the port-and-cigars stage of dinner over, so that I could get away and hook up with Gina.

It's not until midnight when finally I succeed.

'Dear God, am I glad to see you,' she says, when we bump into one another outside the Chinese room. 'Quick, before anyone sees us.' She grabs me by the sleeve and drags me in the direction of the conservatory. En route, she liberates a bottle of champagne, two glasses and a box of cigarettes.

As we brush slowly through the fecund, steaming torpor of the Earl's conservatory, Gina slips a hand into mine. I'm reminded of those walks we used to take at the Victorian fern garden in South Devon when I was recovering from my fever, and the grotto at the bottom where once, rather surprisingly, she used an Anglo-Saxon expletive – inevitably putting thoughts into my head of the sort of thing I wouldn't half mind doing to her. Crikey! The very thought of it, combined with all that wine, and this heat, and the fact that it really is her actual skin I can feel against mine, warm and not at all resistant, is almost enough to make me pass out.

'Do you want to stay in here? Or shall we go outside?' she says.

'Outside.'

'Me too.'

We walk to the edge of the terrace and pause for a moment by the stone balustrade, drinking in the view. It's a warm, clear night and you can see for miles: the bend in the Wye and silvery splashes of moonlight in the shallow rapids just beyond; parts of the drive sweeping through the oak-studded parkland, and what may be shadowy groups of deer; and in the further distance, the shooting woods and the inky foothills of the Black Mountains.

Gina takes my hand again, and we pass down the stone staircase and onto the lawn.

'Where are we going?'

'Somewhere. Close your eyes.'

Gina leads me carefully through the night.

I catch the scent of roses, some deep, rich and spicy, others more akin to peaches and lychees.

Then the roses give way to the cloying, heavy scent of jasmine – no, honeysuckle – and there's the crunching and skittering of gravel underfoot.

Then it's grass again, all springy, and there's a slight and very welcome breeze you can feel against your face and just hear – or imagine you can hear – ruffling the leaves.

I don't normally like being led like this. I hate the unknown, the gnawing anxiety that any second you're going to bump into something. Like going on night patrol. Tonight, though, is different. I'm half-cut, for one thing. But it's mostly to do with Gina: the trust I have in her; the joy I have in being with her at this moment, now, which I want to last for ever.

The final leg of our journey is steep and uneven. Gina has to pull me, hard, uphill and several times I nearly trip up. Then I do trip up and laughing, she collapses almost on top of me.

'All right, this'll do,' she says. 'Bet you've already guessed anyway.'

'The Mound?'

'The Mound,' she agrees.

The Mound is a mysterious knoll or tumulus whose purpose has never been ascertained. After the Sutton Hoo find five years back the Earl was sorely tempted to have it excavated. But the thought of all the sightseers it might attract quite put him off. And besides, he didn't want to kill the mystery.

I'd like to stay entangled as we are but Gina wriggles free.

'Now for God's sake give me some of that fizz,' she says. 'And a cigarette or I think I'll die.'

'But you don't smoke.'

'Didn't,' she corrects, tapping one end of the cigarette against the box with a practised ease I can only imagine she learned in France with that Free French colonel. 'Jesus!' she says, accepting my light and inhaling deeply. 'She didn't half put me through the mill.'

'Who?'

I fill both our champagne glasses.

'Your neighbour. The General's driver. The vampire.'

'His driver, was she? Seemed a bit too grand for that.'

'Not *just* his driver. He likes a nice, well-bred English girl, does Slim Jim Gavin.'

'So I noticed.'

'You can talk. What exactly was she doing to you under the table?'

'Whatever it was, I wasn't enjoying it.'

'Oh you poor, meek, innocent thing, you.'

'Unlike some I could mention.' I try to keep the tone light, but it comes across more petulant.

'Now, Dick, you're not jealous?'

'Of the most dashing thruster in the US military? Now what on earth would make you think that?'

'Dick,' she chides, with a flutter of her eyelashes. 'Dick,' she repeats, prodding me under the ribs. When that doesn't work she shuffles right next to me, drapes an arm round my neck and says in that light sing-song voice of hers, 'First, he's married. Second, he takes himself far, far too seriously. And third, I'm already spoken for.'

'What? When?'

'Well, since France, of course. You do remember our conversation in France, don't you?'

'Yes, of course I remember. I just . . . I didn't realise you were quite so serious.'

'However could you have doubted it?'

There's a look Gina gives you – I've mentioned it before where she fixes you with those marvellous grey-green eyes, turns you to liquid, and sucks you up like a straw. And when she does that you're finished. Whatever reservations you may have had, whatever things you had to say, whatever clever thoughts there were swirling round your head are gone, all gone. Your tongue lolls, your eyes spiral and if you're not careful you'll end up with a pool of drool on your dinner shirt. It isn't the first time that look has landed me in a frightful pickle and it won't be the last either.

Before I can stop to think – and it's just as well, for contemplation has ever been my enemy – our faces have drawn closer together, as if pulled by magnets. Then our lips meet and, rather than pull brightly away as I might have expected, they stay together resolutely stuck. Our mouths open, and with a thrill of anticipation I feel the softness of her outer lip give way to the moisture of her inner lip, just before the tip of our tongues meet, then wriggle past one another.

As our tongues plunge deep into one another's mouth, desperate, yearning and hungry, I'm thinking to myself, 'This can't go on. Nothing this good keeps going on.'

But it does go on. For how long I don't know, but long enough for me, emboldened, to reach round underneath her arm and place a hand on her right breast. She makes no attempt to move it away. Nor does she when I begin caressing her nipple, which is easy enough to find since her bra is already undone.

How did it get undone? Not me. Must have been her. And if it was her then she must want me to do this – as, certainly, her gasps seem very much to be confirming that she does – and that perhaps she'd like to go further still.

And fantastic though all this is, I'm not altogether sure I can cope with so much excitement in one go. I'm already fit to burst as it is. So I release her now very hard nipple from its grip between my thumb and forefinger, and I cool down, ever so slightly, the ardent grappling of our tongues. Very surreptitiously, though, for it would be awful if she noticed because I'd hate her to think anything was wrong.

She pulls herself free, cups my face in her hands and looks me in the eyes.

'Are you all right?' she asks.

'Better than all right,' I say, grinning weakly.

'Then –'

Gina is about to pull us back together again.

'Just want to take it slowly, that's all,' I say. 'Because I want it to last.'

'Oh, that's such a good idea. Me too!' she says. 'Drink and cigarette first. *Then* pudding.'

We snuggle together and sit in companionable silence for a while, blowing smoke towards the silvery Wye, our free hands entwined.

'Of course, we shall have to keep it a secret.'

Her unexpected tone of serious practicality rather throws me.

'Do you think?' I say, not altogether sure whether she means marriage, engagement or the mere fact that we're anything other than distant cousins.

'You know how Daddy reacted the last time. I'm not sure his poor heart could handle it twice.'

'I suppose not,' I say, morosely.

'Sweetheart –' she says, squeezing my hand.

Sweetheart!

'If it were up to me I'd be shouting it from the rooftops, you know I would. And Mummy wouldn't mind one bit, I'm sure. But Daddy, though we know he loves you like a son, doesn't think in that way. It's what comes with the title, I suppose. He thinks dynastically.'

'But surely the Coward bloodline –'

'My sweet, it has nothing to do with bloodlines, it's about social position. And you must realise it's not me saying this, it's Daddy – and I know how he thinks because it's exactly what he said last time with poor dear Guy. Daddy needs to know that Brecon Abbey is going to end up in the hands of the chap who can play the game. It's why he's so adamant I should marry someone with a title.'

'That rules me out, then.'

'Or failing that, an officer of high rank.'

'Met any nice generals recently?'

'Dick, I've told you I'm happy to wait as long as it takes. Daddy has a good many years in him yet, I hope, but—'

'Gina, we can't leave it till your father dies. That would be ridiculous.'

'I agree. I agree. The alternative would be to find some way of persuading him you're the right man to take on the estate. And –' a meaningful squeeze of my hand – 'to father an heir.'

'But how?'

'Darling, I just don't know. Great Meresby would have done, I'm sure. But Daddy's told me you've decided to bow out of that frightful competition with James and keep yourself safe in Birmingham instead, which I quite understand. We shall just have to think a bit harder, won't we?'

'You really think Great Meresby would be enough?'

'Oh, I know it would. If our estates were joined, they'd be the largest in all the Marches, and there's nothing that would tickle an Earl of Brecon quite like that.'

'Then that is what we must do.'

'No, Dick, I couldn't let you. If anything were to happen to you now, I should never forgive myself.'

'I'll just have to make sure nothing does happen then, shan't I?'

'Oh, Dick, kiss me, you're so brave.'

As I kiss her gently on her lips, she lets herself drop backwards onto the ground, pulling me on top of her.

'Again!' she whispers, as my body presses on hers, and I feel renewed stiffening down below. 'Properly this time,' she adds, dragging one of my hands back onto her breast, while sucking me deeper into her hot, wet mouth.

This is what I've always wanted. All I've ever wanted. Yet at the same time, I begin to think to myself, as her breathing grows heavier and she reaches behind hers so as to remove her bra completely, it's almost a case of too much too soon. If only I'd known beforehand I could have prepared myself better, both physically and mentally. As it is –

'I want you inside me, Dick!'

Oh my God, those words. It's too much. I think I'm going to—

'If you want to, Dick. Do you?'

And I have done. All messy and shrunken with no immediate hope of recovery. And definitely no means of disguising my shame, should she investigate my sticky underwear.

'I do Gina, I do so very much,' I say, kissing her gently. 'But don't you think that the longer we wait, the better it will be?'

After a beat, and not sounding quite as convinced as I'd prefer, she says, 'Oh, Dick, you are so, so adorable. And so completely unlike any other man I know.'

5

In the Flying Coffin

Down the runway, their roundels glowing a brilliant blue and red in the soft, early-morning September sun, the Halifax tugs are lined up in ranks, awaiting the signal to depart. Price and I are resting beneath the wing of our glider, wondering, just like everyone else, if that signal is ever going to come.

It's a pleasant enough place, the airfield at Tarrant Rushton: pretty WAAFs, cheery ground crew, delightfully authentic pubs heaving with besmocked, straw-chewing rustics straight out of Thomas Hardy. But after sixteen cancelled operations in a row there are many of our number who'd happily see the whole place flattened by a thousand-Heinkel air raid if it meant never having to hang about this cursed runway again.

Now here's one of the GPs come to inspect our Horsa. GPs is what we call the glider pilots, two to each glider. This one, a lieutenant, walks up to the stern of the aircraft, jumps up and catches hold of the tail. The nose lifts up, signalling that the balance is right, but then we knew that already. It's the third time he's done it in the last hour.

'What's his problem?' says Price.

'Being thorough, I expect.'

'Jittery, I call it,' says Price.

The GP takes our interest in his activities as an invitation to come and say hello. He's a pleasant-looking chap: young, guileless face with eyebrows arched as if in constant delighted surprise. In another life I imagine he would have made a very popular village parson.

'Hello,' he says, extending a hand. His shake is firm but his palms are baby-soft. Even less used to manual labour than my own. 'Pat Verney. Delighted to have you aboard.'

Price and I introduce ourselves.

'I say,' says Lt. Verney, catching sight of my pilot's wings and the diagonal stripes of my DFC. 'Oughtn't it to be you flying this kite?'

'Oh, any fool can manoeuvre a Spit,' I say airily. 'I expect it takes far more skill coaxing one of those things down.'

This isn't false modesty. I mean, have you ever seen a Horsa? Broad, ungainly wings; body like a long, fat, painful turd: the sort of thing an eleven-year-old might build before he'd gained a proper understanding of aerodynamics.

'You'd master in it moments,' says Lt. Verney. 'Two steering columns, handle at your feet controls the flaps; cast off about 3,500 feet – normal glide to about 2,000 feet, after which it's medium and full flap for the steeper dive you'll need to speed your way through any enemy unpleasantness. Didn't I tell you it was easy?'

'Sir, haven't you forgotten the bit at the end where you have to crash-land, under fire, in a crowded field, at the same time as three dozen other gliders laden with high explosive?'

'Now you mustn't worry about that, Sarnt. I can assure you that today's LZs are wonderfully spacious. Much more agreeable than the ones in Normandy.'

'At Pegasus Bridge, were you, sir?' says Price, hopefully.

'Goodness, no. I only got my wings last week.'

Price's face crumples.

'I'm most terribly sorry about the graffiti, by the way,' adds Lt. Verney, nodding towards the cockpit of his Horsa, beneath which someone has chalked, 'Up with the Fräulein's skirts.' (All the gliders have them: 'We are the Al Capone gang,' 'Up with the Reds,' and, in honour of our distinguished OC, 'Freddie's Flying Circus.') 'It really is most unfortunate. I'd been hoping to name her Penelope.'

'They're going to love him,' says Price when he's gone.

'Who?'

'The Germans. They'll be so busy being charmed by him, they'll forget how to fight.'

'Price, not everyone in this war has to behave like an insensate brute.'

'And when things go belly up –'

'*If* things go belly up, please, Price.'

Price rolls his eyes.

'If things go belly up and we're relying on the likes of that mummy's boy GP to hold the line, what's he going to do? "Oh I'm most frightfully sorry but I believe I am unacquainted with the PIAT. How about I take Jerry a nice cup of tea instead?"'

I should explain that this is one of the anomalies of the Glider Pilot Regiment. Unlike their American counterparts, who are whisked from the front line as soon as is conceivably possible, and are even allocated troops to protect them, British glider pilots are trained as infantrymen and are expected to stay and fight till the battle's over.

'Char's up,' says Chopper Wood, proffering a mug of tea. You may remember he was the baby-faced fellow who picked us up that day we went for the interview with 1st Airborne Recce Squadron at Ruskington. He's now my driver.

The first mug Wood gives to me, the other he's on the verge of drinking himself when he catches Price's look.

'Sorry, Sarge, I could only carry the two. But there's plenty—'

'It's all right. One's all I need,' says Price, snatching the mug from his hand. Wood looks momentarily shocked, smiles awkwardly, then heads back to the mobile canteen for another cup.

'Now, you're not going to be horrid all the way to Holland?' I say.

'Not unless he asks for it,' says Price.

'Price, I need the lad on side. You know how cut up he is, not being able to jump with his mates.'

'He's cut up? And how do you think I feel?'

Price has never quite forgiven me for my injudicious remarks to the OC regarding parachutes. A case of out of the frying pan, he believes, and into the bottomless pit of boiling acid.

'Wads anyone?' says Wood on his return, handing round a paper-wrapped bundle of cakes he's brought back with his tea.

'That's mighty generous of you, young fellow. I don't mind if I do,' says Price in a heavily sarcastic, pretend-friendly voice, as he helps himself to two. Unlike sentient beings, Price seems to get hungrier before an engagement.

He ignores the sharp look I give him and adds, 'But ain't you forgotten something?'

'What's that, Sarge?'

'Your parachute.'

'Eh?'

'You're right, lad. My mistake. In gliders, we don't get given effing parachutes,' says Price, turning to give me a hard, resentful look. 'Do we, Mr Coward?'

Sometimes people ask me what it was like to take off with that mighty air armada just after midday on 17 September 1944. 'Do you know what?' I reply. 'It made D-Day look like a Rotary Club outing to Bognor.' And if I'm feeling in lyrical mode, I'll treat them to the marvellous panoply we privileged fellows of the 1st Airborne Division witnessed as we flew over the sun-kissed southern reaches of our Sceptred Isle to our appointment with destiny across the Channel.

First, the slow, ungainly climb above the high-hedged fields of South Dorset, where nutbrown labourers have been transfixed into immobility as our gliders and their Halifax tugs cast their shadows on the ripened corn. The beach and pier of sunlit Bournemouth diminishing from view as we head northeast, over Hampshire trout streams and Berkshire woodland, past idyllic villages and sturdy market towns whose every citizen has poured from church and home to wish us all God speed.

Then, over Hatfield in Hertfordshire, the air traffic thickening as gliders and tugs from bases all over Southern England converge to form three parallel streams, each almost a hundred miles long. Below, two sights to stir the patriotic heart: the red-brick walls and knot gardens of Queen Bess's childhood home, Hatfield House; and also, heavily guarded by sandbagged, ack-ack batteries, the de Havilland aircraft factory that produced the Mosquito fighter bombers which have been strafing the German defences since first light this morning.

From Hatfield, the swing eastwards past Epping Forest and the clay-tiled and thatched rooftops of rural Essex towards our crossing point on the Suffolk coast at Orford Ness. And suddenly, twinkling specks in the skies high above us, the comforting presence of the RAF Spitfires and US Mustangs and Thunderbolts – almost nine hundred in all – come to see us on our way.

How much of this magnificence I really saw, though, is a moot point. For one thing, much of the early part of our journey was swathed in thick cloud. And for another, I spent most it with my nose buried in a bag of vomit.

God, they really are the very worst things to go to war in: built on the cheap for one flight only, with no concern whatsoever for the comfort or convenience of the poor buggers who have to spend two or more hours stuck helpless in the back, seeing little, hearing nothing, fearing absolutely everything.

Price's way of dealing with it is to pretend it's not happening. He just sits there with the Sunday papers on his lap, smoking cigarettes, doing the crossword (my mother taught him how) very, very slowly.

Wood and I, on the other hand, are keen to see what's going on. So we take turns to freeze our bollocks off, sitting as close as we dare to the glider's large side door, which – against all regulations – we've kept open. The whistling wind does tend to inhibit conversation but at least it helps get rid of some of the nauseating oil and petrol fumes from the cargo.

We've been flying for about twenty, extremely bumpy, minutes and I've just gone to light a cigarette off the end of Price's so as to take away the taste of all the vomit I've recently expelled, when Wood starts shouting and beckoning me to come right now.

'Hang on!' I say.

'Quick, sir, quick!' he yells back, his face drawn and ashen.

Steadying myself on the rope we're using to shackle one of the jeeps, I edge my way down the bucking fuselage towards the large hole in the aircraft's side, grab a tight hold of what seems to be a firmly anchored canvas strap, and very cautiously stick my head out.

The wind rush makes my eyes start watering and I'm about to ask Wood what the devil he's on about when I catch something moving about 1,000 feet below. Several things moving, in fact, big ones and small ones, tumbling out of the sky. The small ones – my God! So many. Count 'em. Twenty-one? Twenty-two? – are waving their legs and kicking their arms, and none of them has a parachute on, and everyone is screaming. The big ones are the broken segments of their glider.

I stare open-mouthed.

'What – WHAT HAPPENED?' I yell to Wood.

'The tail, sir. It just fell off.'

'Don't be ridiculous. Tails don't just fall off.'

'This one did.'

Wood stays where he is, transfixed.

I can't bear to look any more. Nor listen either. I'm sure, from 2,000 feet, with all the background noise of the engines and the wind, you're not going be able to discern the sound made by twenty-two bodies when one by one they smack into the ground at speeds of around 150 mph. But I'm not hanging around to find out.

'Heavens, Price,' I gasp between drags of my cigarette. 'I've just seen something DREADFUL.'

Price continues carefully to fill in the crossword clue he's just solved.

'Told you you should have kept the door shut,' he says.

Price doesn't look up till the Dutch coast when the first flak hits our aircraft. Nothing major – just two sudden flurries of rattling, like a handful of pebbles thrown against a window, the first forward and the second mostly aft of where we're sitting.

He's about to go back to his crossword when he notices me staring at the small hole in the floor between my feet. Another few inches and it could have been very painful.

'Sit on your helmet, I should,' says Price, who's already doing likewise. I suppose when you've only one ball left, it does tend to make you more careful.

'And what's the betting as soon as I do I'll cop a packet in the head?'

'Then you'll just have to ask yourself which you'd rather spill: your brains or your John Thomas.'

I think for a moment about how demoralising it would be for

my men to set off without their section commander. Then, for by no means the first time, I think of the unfinished business with Gina, whom I haven't seen once since our tryst on the Mound. I think of the taste of her mouth, and the sweetness beneath the smoke-sour tang of cigarettes and champagne. I think of her heavy breathing.

I unstrap my helmet and sit on it.

Price breaks into a ragged, wolfish grin, as if a mischievous thought has just occurred to him.

'Still reckon she's worth it then?' he goads.

Of course, I absolutely refuse to rise. He's fishing, that's all. Trying to find out whether or not I still hold a candle for Gina. I've not brought up her name once, for this very reason, but I expect he has heard rumours through the household-servant network. Our disappearance into the night after the Brecon Abbey dinner is bound to have set tongues wagging. But I'm not giving the game away that easily.

'I don't. I'll tell you that for nothing,' Price goes on.

Ignoring him I light up a cigarette and stare impassively into space, for all the world as if he didn't exist. Wood, fortunately, is asleep.

'Easy enough on the eye, I'll give you that,' Price muses aloud. 'Goes like the clappers, too, I'm sure, but there's half your problem. How're you going to keep a filly like that satisfied? Where will you get the experience you need to stop her bolting?'

I draw deeply on my cigarette, rather pleased by how well I'm taking it. A lesser man would have had Price on a charge by now. Or pushed him out of the aircraft.

'Anyway, if it's a bit of harmless fun you're after – and at your age it's all you should be after – I could point you to plenty of easier options round our neck of the woods. That skinny land girl you took a shine to, a few months back. Bet she'd happily teach you a thing or two. I know she did me,' he says.

Calm, Dick. Calm. As with drunks, dogs and children, the sooner you ignore them the sooner they'll leave you alone.

'Or if it's a bit more upmarket you want, how about young Mrs Ashenden. Never ungrateful for a bit of attention now her husband's six feet under, so they say. Adventurous, too. Play your cards right, from what I hear, and she'll sometimes make it a double with Lavinia Crumblebeech.'

'Price, you're babbling like a lunatic; do stop,' I say, trying not to smile at the absurdity of this unlikely combination. Caro Ashenden, lovely though she is in her demure floaty way, is widely reported to be so tragically undersexed she couldn't even deliver the goods to poor Lt. Ashenden on his wedding night. As for Lavinia Crumblebeech, I know she has a reputation as a man-eater, but I rather doubt a fox-hunting girl as down-the-line as her has ever essayed anything more exotic than the jumping position with one single and very terrified male.

'All I'm saying, Mr Richard, is—'

'Well, don't say it,' I snap, for my patience is finally at an end. 'I will not sit here and have you traduce my friends' names with these vile and baseless calumnies. Least of all Gina's. What the devil has she ever done to you, anyway?'

'You don't know?'

'No.'

'You really don't know?'

'NO.'

'I'm stuck here, in this flying coffin, on the barmiest suicide mission since Cardigan said, "Let's have a pop at them Russian guns," and you still DON'T KNOW what my beef is with Gina Bloody Herbert.'

'Less of the bloody, thank you.'

'I'll bloody that girl all I like, because I see now what's happening. It's like Normandy all over again. There I was, thinking

78

the reason I was here was so as to help you get your medal and save Great Meresby and my future livelihood with it. But it's not, is it? Yet again, it's just so's you can get your end away with a flighty prick-tease who'll string you along till kingdom come, then ditch you like a shot the moment something better comes along.'

'I'll have you know Price that that "flighty prick-tease" and I are engaged to be married.'

'Contract written in blood, signed in triplicate and witnessed by the Lord Chancellor, was it? Because if it's anything less, I'd say a promise from Lady Gina ain't worth the paper it's written on.'

Far too cross to think of a suitable riposte, I rise from my seat, put on my helmet and stomp disgustedly up the fuselage in search of some air. Price calls something after me, which he seems to think is frightfully clever. Something about pips and stars, which I'm not going to attempt to understand because I know whatever it is it will only make me crosser.

Having gazed out of the glider doorway at the flooded polder below for a while, I feel a whole heap better. I've been thinking about the coming op, which isn't what a soldier normally does to cheer himself up, but this show is different. I feel it in my bones. We all do, I think. Those of us whose surnames don't begin with P and end in 'rice', at any rate.

Yesterday, the OC called us all together for a final pep talk. 'Gentlemen,' he says, 'today is my forty-third birthday. Tomorrow, you are going to get me my best present ever – and I don't mean a bunch of tulips or a gaily painted pair of clogs. What I want from each of you boys is a dead German!'

You should have heard the cheers that greeted that. It's not that any of us have anything personal against Jerry. More that we're quite sick to the teeth of training and waiting, training and cancellation, and all we want to do now is get this business over with, finish off Hitler, return to our loved ones and get on with the rest of our lives without having to worry every few seconds whether the next minute's going to be our last.

This op is calculated to do exactly that. Code-named Market Garden it's split into two parts. Market consists of dropping over thirty-four thousand British, American and Polish paratroops and glider troops either side of a fifty-mile stretch of a highway which heads north-east through occupied Holland. These shock troops – forming what Monty calls an 'airborne carpet' – will guard this corridor from attack while the ground forces of XXX Corps, led by the tanks of the Guards Armoured Division, push up it as quickly as they can. This phase of the operation, a sort of blitzkrieg in reverse, is known as Garden.

The key to the operation's success will be the capture of the various bridges crossing the rivers and canals en route. If any of these are held for too long, or worse still blown, then clearly XXX Corps will be unable to complete its advance, creating great difficulties for the lightly armed airborne units awaiting relief. The task of capturing the southernmost bridges has gone to the US 101st Airborne Division; the middle bridges are to be captured by the US 82nd Airborne Division; the honour of capturing the furthermost bridge at Arnhem has been granted to Britain's 1st Airborne Division, to be aided by a brigade's worth of Poles.

Obviously, we like to tell ourselves that the reason we've been given the toughest objectives is because we're the best. But it probably owes more to politics. An operation planned by a British field marshal ought necessarily to expose British troops to the greatest risk. And also, it goes without saying, to the most kudos when everything turns out right.

Once XXX Corps reaches the top, which we expect it to do in about two days, we shall cut the Germans' Western Europe forces in half, loop round their most formidable defences – the notorious Siegfried Line – seize their industrial heartland in the Ruhr Valley, wipe out their means of production and generally give Jerry such an almighty kick up the arse that come Christmas we'll be chomping our turkey drumsticks in the snowy ruins of the Reichstag.

Down below, the polder – deliberately flooded by the Germans to try to stymie operations just like this – has given way to higher, drier ground and the first few settlements. From almost every rooftop, excited civilians are waving – the bolder ones proudly fluttering the strictly verboten orange flag of the Free Netherlands.

By all accounts, they've had the most dreadful time under the Nazi jackboot. Much harder than the French. Indeed, if reports of the liberation of Antwerp are to be believed, our biggest problem won't so much be the Germans as the overwhelming gratitude of the newly free Dutch men and women, swamping our troops with flowers, drink and kisses and God knows what else.

It's going to be tough, very tough. Especially when those young blonde Dutch girls start closing in, eager to make up for the four long years in which all their eligible menfolk have either been cooped up in prison camps or slaving as German 'guest-workers'.

You'll say I've no business thinking of such things when I've got so perfect a girl waiting for me back home. But the way I see it, it would be jolly poor form to deny the nubile, female citizenry of the Netherlands the opportunity to thank their saviours in whichever way they see fit. Besides which, as Price reminded me just now with his characteristic delicacy, the last chap a sophisticated girl like Gina wants to marry is a sexual innocent. Not, of course, that I am. But I do concede that the more notches on the side of my Spitfire before Gina and I tie the knot the better it will be for both of us. We don't want any awkward repeats of what happened on the Mound, do we?

She was very understanding at the time, and none of the three delightful letters she has sent me since has given any indication that she has been getting cold feet. But I've become a mite concerned all the same that Gina may secretly have marked me down after my performance; that, heaven forfend, she might even be casting around for some old roué better capable of satisfying her needs.

That Jim Gavin, say, with his deceptive baby-face, his airborne swagger and his fancy-pants major general's stars.

Stars.

Oh my God. That's what Price was talking about. He was saying a lieutenant's pips are no match for a major-general's stars. Damn his eyes. Damn both their eyes. What does he know that I don't?

'Price?'

Price doesn't look up from his crossword.

'Price, damn it, I need to know. What have you heard about Slim Jim Gavin?'

Price grins.

'Fearless chap. Leads from the front. Biggest cock in the US military.'

'Has he been seeing Gina?'

'I wouldn't put it past her.'

'Less of the innuendo. Tell me what you know.'

'What I heard is that the General's been to stay at Brecon Abbey a couple of times.'

'Literally a couple?'

'Two or three, maybe.'

'Does that include the dinner I attended?'

'What else do you want? Dates? Train times? Toothpaste brand? Number of times he had a dump?'

'Price, this is not funny.'

'Do you see me laughing? Do you not think I might have better ways to spend a sunny Sunday than flying fifty miles behind enemy lines to battle the might of Jerry's massed panzer divisions with nothing but pea-shooters and pop guns – and all so's you can get your end away with your blue-blooded strumpet?'

It was precisely this kind of defeatist talk which threatened to sour the OC's final briefing yesterday. Price, I'm sorry but not wholly surprised to tell you, had picked up some idle tittle-tattle about German tanks having been spotted in the woods in the Arnhem region. Of course, sly bugger that he is, he got one of the other ranks to pop the awkward question.

'And is there any sign of any armour, sir?' I remember Hughes, our wireless op, asking in an innocent voice.

'Barely a whisker, our intel says,' says the OC.

'Would that be Tigers' whiskers or Panthers' whiskers?' jests Darkie.

At which point, the OC shoots me a quick, sharp look, for of course it hasn't escaped his notice that these doubting Thomases belong to my section.

'If there's armour, so much the better! I'm damned if I'm going to lug our PIATs and Gammon grenades all the way to Holland and not get a chance to use them!'

This last remark comes from Lt. Randall, the Squadron's carrot-topped goodie-two-shoes, his usually bright-red face turning a rich shade of purple as it does whenever he's excited. He's so keen and patriotic he makes me feel like a shirking Bolshevik. But then, young officers often are when they've not seen much action before. Perhaps this is why the OC has detailed his section to spearhead the assault. You gallop faster when you've never yet taken a tumble.

It earns a big cheer from Lt. Randall's loyal section, anyway. And also from that half of the audience which has never had to use a PIAT or a Gammon grenade in anger before. Everyone else keeps their thoughts to themselves.

'So would that be a "no armour", then, sir? Or a "maybe just a bit of armour, if we're unlucky"?' asks Bleackley.

'I'd be lying if I said it wasn't a possibility,' says the OC. 'There have been unconfirmed reports from Dutch underground sources of Mark Threes and Mark Fours possibly awaiting refit; most likely in transit back to Germany. But given what we know about the Abwehr's penetration in the Netherlands, I'd be inclined to take all local intelligence with a hefty pinch of a salt.'

There are nods and murmurs from the audience. German counter-intelligence in the Netherlands has been particularly effective and vicious. Rumour has it that any Dutch agent who hasn't been hanged or shot by the Nazis is most likely now working for them as a double agent.

'But even if there are tanks, remember, our task is not to engage them. Merely to contain them until they can be dealt with by 30 Corps,' the OC says.

'How long will that be, sir?'

'Best guess is forty-eight hours. Three days, if we're unlucky. Four, if we happen to encounter one of their ear battalions which hasn't heard the order to retreat,' says the OC, searching his audience for signs of mirth. Without much success.

The OC decides to pick on one of the faces in the front row, a jug-eared fellow from A Troop.

'Stickings, that was supposed to be a joke. Why aren't you laughing?'

'Sorry, sir. I don't think I know what an ear battalion is?'

'Well, why didn't you ask? Can anyone here tell me what an ear battalion is?'

I stick up my hand.

'Yes, Mr Coward.'

'It's a special unit for German soldiers who have one or more ears missing.'

There is much laughter at this hilarious notion.

'Go on.'

'Quite often they'll be minus an arm or a leg, too.'

Louder laughter still.

'Keep it down, chaps. I want you to know about the sort of opposition you'll be facing,' says the OC, beaming.

'You wouldn't laugh if you saw them,' I say. 'They're some of the bravest men I've ever scr—'

'Fought against, I believe you mean, Mr Coward,' says the OC with a smile. He realised I was about to say 'served with'.

'Quite so, sir,' I say, blushing. 'But their operational efficiency does tend to be compromised by two significant handicaps. The first being that they can't hear orders: you have to communicate using hand signals, which is fine so long as you can first get their attention –'

I'm really not trying to be funny. Problem is, as far as the Squadron's now concerned, I'm the brightest new star of comedy since George Formby first strummed his ukulele. It's all I can do to make my last lines heard.

'And the second is, they can't generally hear incoming shell fire. Which means—'

But the Squadron don't need to hear what it means, they've worked it out already, and they're going to be laughing about it all the way to Arnhem.

Wood yawns awake and stretches, then focuses blearily on Price and me.

'Are we there yet?' he asks.

'Why don't you go and ask the driver?' says Price.

Wood toddles down the fuselage towards the pilot's cabin,

still half-asleep, with a guilelessness even Price seems to find affecting.

'Poor kid,' he says. 'Doesn't know what's about to hit him.'

'And I suppose you do?' I say testily, for a little of Price in Cassandra mode goes a very long way with me.

Price contents himself with one of his wise, meaningful grimaces, which I find more annoying still.

'Look, if you're so convinced it's going to be a disaster, why didn't you stay at home?'

'And who'd have got you your medal if I'd done that?'

'Er, myself, perhaps?'

'Don't make me laugh.'

'Remind me who it was flying my Spit when I won my DFC.'

'You've had nothing since, though, have you? And not for want of trying.'

'I'd hardly say I've been *trying* to win a medal. Only shits like James do that.'

'Then maybe it's about time you did.'

'Oh really, Price —'

'You're here for a reason and one reason only and if you don't realise that yet you don't deserve Great Meresby or Lady Gina or anything, because they're all connected, you know, and they all depend on one thing.'

At the front of the glider there's a sudden loud bang. Right in the cockpit it sounds like. The aircraft dips ominously. Then rights itself.

Price strikes up another cigarette and offers one to me.

'Where did that come from?' I say, once I've had a couple of good drags. Shakes you up a bit, a near miss like that.

'For a minute I thought the pilot had copped one.'

'Me too. Now what was I saying?'

'Damned if I can — Jesus, whatever's happened to him?'

By him, Price means the figure now stumbling back towards

us from the pilot's cabin. His face is pale, his eyes are wide, the front of his Denison smock is dripping so much gore I'm surprised he isn't already dead.

'Mr Coward,' gasps Wood. 'You'd better come quick . . .'

6

Happy Landings

If it weren't for the co-pilot's blood splattered on the perspex, the view would be rather lovely. Below us the shimmering Lower Rhine, to our right the curving steel skeletons of those two soon-to-be-very-famous bridges; ahead, just before the railway line, a broad expanse of starkly geometrical arable land bordered by long straight roads and thick woodland dotted with strange little crosses.

As we glide lower, the crosses begin to reveal themselves as gliders, their black-and-white invasion stripes like zebras amid a dun-coloured savannah. It ought to be green but looks worryingly like mud to me. Freshly ploughed mud.

'It's very good of you to help,' croaks Lt. Verney, his voice growing ever weaker, blood trickling from the shrapnel graze across his temple. You may have gathered, he's not in the most ideal of states to land a glider. Still less so, the co-pilot, lying outside the cockpit.

'I do have a vested interest,' I reply tersely, scanning the ground for a suitable landing spot. There are far too many gliders, it seems to me, vying for far, far too few spaces. Nor do I much like the look of those woods at the end, especially when there's virtually no headwind to slow us down.

I try subtly steering us towards the much more suitable area to our left, but Lt. Verney notices and corrects with his rudder pedal.

'Yes, that nice clear patch does look awfully tempting,' he chides, his voice now barely a whisper. 'But we were asked expressly to keep it clear for tomorrow's lift.'

'Listen, you silly, brave bugger. If I'm flying this kite, it'll be a case of beggars not choosers. Now remind me again what the drill is for landing these things –'

The glider's nose has suddenly and unexpectedly dropped.

'Pat?'

A glance at my neighbour and the problem becomes immediately apparent. Lt. Verney has slumped, unconscious, with his hand resting forward on the joystick.

'PRICE?' I call.

Sgt. Price, who has been hovering anxiously, appears at once.

'Pull him back from that joystick, then get back and strap yourself in. We're in for a tricky landing.'

For once Price does as he's told, but no sooner has the pressure eased than the glider's nose suddenly jerks upwards – the very last thing you want to happen on your landing run. By the time I've corrected it, we've already missed the spot I was aiming for. There's another gap a bit further on, which I'm set fair neatly to plug when – BUGGER! – some sod in a ruddy great Hamilcar comes swooping in far too fast and far too steeply from my left and bags it for himself.

'*Scheißkopf!*' I swear, then immediately feel rather a heel, for now the Hamilcar's nose has caught in the unexpectedly soft earth and executed a complete backflip, damn nearly taking me out with its tail. As I fly past, I can hear the brittle crunch of splintering wood and perspex, and the awful rending groan of shattered chains and cascading tons of metal – jeeps? 17-pounder anti-tank guns? – which I try hard not to imagine mashing the poor soldiers next to them. Any moment now the same thing could be happening to us.

'Keep it shallow. Not too hard on the brakes!' I say to myself, as the cold sweat drips down my face, my hands tense white round the joystick, and the woods at the end of the landing ground rush faster towards me than Dunsinane to Macbeth.

I see khaki figures diving for cover. I see the driver of a jeep backing out of the tail of a Horsa directly in my path staring at me in horror. I see a ghostly group of figures dressed in white – asylum inmates? – dancing and waving and smiling at me as if it were all just a delightful game.

At the very last second I skip over their heads, then, moments later, I feel a light bump as the glider makes its first tentative contact with Dutch soil. Then another, much more substantial one as the nose threatens to bury itself in a furrow.

'Oh God, oh God, oh God!' We could die so easily. Just the slightest mistake. The merest hint of too much pressure on the brake and that will be it: over before we've even begun.

Ahead, racing towards us still much too fast, is the wood, now discernible as individual trees. Beech. Oak. With horribly thick trunks.

'Jesus!'

Now I've overcompensated. Instead of bogging it, I've taken her too high. We're going to hit those trees! We're going to—!

In my nightmares I hear it still. The awful crunching and ripping of wood on flimsy canvas; the shrieking protest, like demons screaming to be released from hell, of the chains which are all that stand between 4 tons of heavily laden jeep and the back of my head.

When I come to, I'm unable to move. My mouth is full of leaves and blood, there's a spear-like branch not an inch from my forehead, the cockpit is a tangle of foliage and splintered wood. I try to wriggle my hands. Then my feet.

From the other side of the cockpit, through the leaves, I hear a cough, then –

'I say. Are we there?'

I spit out the leaves. My mouth's so dry it's all I can do to speak.

'Not quite what you'd call a textbook landing.'

'Bollocks is what I'd call it,' comes a voice from the back.

'What's the matter, you ungrateful sod, I got you down, didn't I?'

'Depends on your definition of down,' says Price.

'Bugger!' I say, looking up at the trees between whose trunks our glider is sandwiched, suspended by its shattered wings about 10 feet above the ground.

'Oh, I dunno. Could be worse,' says Price, with a smirking nod towards our neighbour – a Horsa, possibly from the same serial as ours – which has crash-landed even deeper in the woods than us. Its rear door is so badly buckled and twisted that the crew can't let down the ramp at the back.

A red beret with sergeant's stripes, almost apoplectic with desperation, is hacking away furiously with a hatchet. Thump, thump, thump, THUMP. It sounds especially loud because the rest of the landing zone is almost completely silent. Eerily so. No flak. No machine guns. No sign of enemy resistance whatsoever.

'Isn't that Sarnt Nutter?'

'Why do you think I'm smiling?' says Price.

Nutter is Lt. Randall's section sergeant. Lt. Randall has been given the honour of leading the assault on the bridge. Price rather feels that, we being the Squadron's most experienced members, that honour should have gone to us instead.

I look back at our glider. Though the wings have been smashed to smithereens, the fuselage and contents appear to be intact. But there's an awful lot of debris to be cleared first.

'How are we going to get them clear?'

'Leave that to me, Mr Richard. You get yourself over to the RV asap – take Teddy Bear along to get his fluffy broken head looked at – make sure the lads are ready to mount up just as soon as Wood and I can bring in the jeeps. Till then, see how far you can wiggle your tongue up the OC's jacksie. "Ready to move when you are, sir. Jerry never hangs about so nor should we, sir. Poor Mr Randall's transport stuck hopelessly up a gum tree, sir.'"

In the distance a low rumble, building in slow crescendo. The paratroops are on their way.

'Price, I am not going to lie just so that we can be first to the bridge. Besides I need to be here, supervising the jeeps' extraction.'

'Pardon me, Mr Richard. But do you want them out before the bridge is taken or after?'

Before I can think of a suitable riposte for his impertinence, Price's eyes have swivelled towards five lost-looking infantrymen – glider-borne troops from 1st Border Regiment – who've chosen just the wrong moment to wander into view.

'Oi, where did you think you're going?'

'Looking for our RV, Sarge.'

'Your RV's here, son,' says Price. 'Least till you've helped me unload this glider.'

They look up towards the glider then – in dismay – back towards Price.

'But we—'

Quite unnecessarily, it seems to me, Price points his Sten towards them and cocks it menacingly.

That decides it. The last thing I want to face is the wrath of the 1st Border Regiment officer when he discovers his men have been held captive. Anyway, the less I know of Price's devious machinations the better. Just before I leave, I overhear him talking to Sgt. Nutter, who has come over to ask whether he can borrow one of our 22 wireless sets. Both his have been damaged during the landing.

Price reassures Sgt. Nutter that he'll happily pass on any message he needs relayed. Sgt. Nutter, poor fool, believes him.

Lt. Verney is sitting with his back against a tree, apparently

92

much improved by the mug of tea I had Wood brew for him. With the bandage wrapped round his head, he does indeed resemble a teddy bear with which a child has just been playing doctors and nurses.

'Capable fellow, that sergeant of yours,' muses Lt. Verney, raising his voice so as to be heard over the din of the approaching aircraft. 'Have you known him long?'

'Since the beginning.'

'The same as myself and Bob.'

'Bob?'

He runs a hand fondly over the gas cape next to him. Beneath is the cold, lumpen form of his co-pilot.

'We volunteered together for glider training. We were stuck in Northern Ireland with a training battalion. We were beginning to worry the war would end before we heard a shot fired in anger.'

'Be careful what you wish for, eh?' I say, or rather shout, for the noise of the aircraft overhead is deafening.

We both look upwards. The sky is now speckled with tiny black dots. Hundreds of them; thousands of them. You've never seen so many men in the air at one time and you probably never will, for no one is ever going to launch a parachute landing on this scale again. For reasons which will shortly become apparent.

As in those extraordinary nature documentaries where speeded-up flower buds explode suddenly into bloom, each dot erupts in a burst of silken colour. Down they all drift like a vast school of jellyfish – khaki, blue, yellow, white, orange, on and on, until your neck hurts from craning and you wonder whether it will ever end.

Then the last planes pass. The final men drop. And the skies are empty once more.

By now every bit of heath within a two-mile radius will be swarming with paratroopers, shrugging off their chutes and their jump overalls, hauling in the jump bags strapped to their legs, retrieving drop canisters, inspecting equipment, forming up in twos and threes then setting off in search of their unit.

A couple of them land just ahead of us.

'Piece of cake,' one yells at the other as he dusts himself down.

'YMCA drop,' agrees his mate, which is to say it feels more like an exercise on Salisbury Plain where there's a YMCA canteen dispensing tea at the end than it does a genuine operation.

'Come on, come on, you ruddy northern layabouts!' Price is barking in the distance, as his Border Regiment slave gang pulls on the rope attached to one of the fallen trees blocking our jeeps' exit route.

Near by, Sgt. Nutter and his glider crew are making steady progress with their hatchets and saws.

'Come on, we'd best get weaving,' I say, helping Lt. Verney to his feet.

It's only about a mile's walk from our landing zone to our rendezvous point and it feels like a stroll in the park. Quite literally. A park on one of those sunny bank holidays when everyone's out and about and no one can quite believe their luck at being blessed with such glorious weather.

By the roadside, Dutch men and women from the nearby farms stand waiting to cheer us on.

One lanky young man with an orange armband round the sleeve of his jacket has a sack at his feet.

'Welcome, Tommy,' he says to every soldier who passes, reaching down and handing each bemused man a carrot.

'Did you know that if it hadn't been for the Dutch, carrots would be purple?' I say, wiping the dirt off mine and taking a bite.

Lt. Verney's mind is clearly somewhere else. From beneath his bandage, rivulets of sweat are trickling down his dust-coated features. I did suggest that he didn't bring his bulging, glider pilot's backpack – much more unwieldy, it seems to me, than the small packs and webbing the rest of us wear. Price would bring it up in the jeep, I said. But, as we learned back in the glider, Lt. Verney never seems to choose the easier route when there's a harder one available.

Suddenly in the distance I hear the most marvellous and unexpected sound.

The sweet, clear notes of a horn blown by a huntsman summoning his pack.

'Goodness gracious,' says Lt. Verney.

'That'll be 2nd Battalion, I expect. Do you know, they communicate using the same bugle calls Wellington's men used in the Peninsular War.'

'But that's a hunting horn, not a bugle, isn't it?'

'Yes, their OC, Johnny Frost, is a hunting man. A former Master of the Royal Exodus, I believe.'

'Is that one of the Exmoor stag packs?'

'Jackals mainly. They hunt out of Baghdad.'

The horn sounds again and I'm reminded of a wondrous Wednesday morning's cubbing about this time of year four seasons ago, on one of the very few days out I've been able to enjoy in this long and wretched war. It was a small field – Price, myself, Lavinia Crumblebeech, Caro Ashenden and two or three others, and we'd just topped Lord Hereford's Knob when the sun burst through the clouds and illuminated the valley below. We looked down on the Wye and the leaves just beginning to turn orange, red and yellow and the flocks of sheep grazing in fields of deep green, and I remember looking across to Price and saying, only half in jest, 'This is why we're going to win this war. Because we hunt and Jerry doesn't.'

'Do they not have foxes in Germany?' said Price.

'No, worse, Hitler banned it,' I told him.

'I knew he was a wrong 'un,' said Price. 'But I never realised quite how much of a wrong 'un till now.'

Ahead, two Dutch girls of about eight or nine are kneeling on a discarded parachute, trying to fold into it a manageable size. A third is lifting one they've just folded onto a child's handcart already piled high with coloured silk. Their dresses are threadbare, their arms thin as sticks. As we draw near, they watch us with the wariness of rats startled in the grain cellar. But when we smile, they smile back brightly enough. Lt. Verney hands the youngest and scrawniest one a bar of chocolate. Shortly afterwards, the girl comes running after him, with a posy of wild flowers she has just picked for him.

'We seem to have caught Jerry napping,' says Lt. Verney, twisting the posy distractedly in his hand.

'What were you hoping for? Armageddon?'

'A chance to pay them back for poor old Bob, at least,' he concedes with a sorry smile.

'Then it's Sarnt Price you should be talking to, not me,' I say. 'I'm sure he could supply just the bleak prognosis you're after.'

'How so?'

'Oh, you know, the usual gripes. By landing too far from the bridge we've lost the element of surprise. What if Jerry has tanks? That sort of nonsense.'

'It might not be nonsense,' says Lt. Verney, a sudden glimmer of hope in his voice.

'Perhaps, but I should warn you that Price ain't exactly the new Nostradamus. He lost ten guineas backing Rommel at Alamein. Came damn near to making it a double at D-Day, till I talked him round by pointing out that even if his bet came good he wouldn't be alive to collect his winnings.'

More notes on the hunting horn. Much sharper and closer now. Then all of a sudden, from a field of tall, nodding sunflowers they emerge, in line abreast – damn near a battalion's worth of red berets, gimlet-eyed, firm of jaw, bristling with arms and ammo, with their moustached commander Johnny Frost.

We know each other, vaguely, from the hunting field, and I'm unable to resist a feeble quip.

'I hope you'll not be blowing "Gone away", sir,' I say. I forget whether or not you've ever hunted, Jack, but 'Gone away' is when you've lost your quarry.

'Well, if the hunting's no good, Lieutenant, I've come prepared. I've got my driver coming from Nijmegen tomorrow with my clubs and my guns.'

'Very sensible, I'm sure, sir.'

After a discreet exchange of salutes – not really encouraged in the field at this stage of the war, because it rather too easily enables Jerry to pick out our officers – we head our separate ways.

'You don't think he meant that, about the clubs and the guns?' wonders Lt. Verney.

'I'd be most surprised if he didn't. Why so shocked?'

'Well, if battalion commanders are bringing their golf clubs, we really must be in for a dull old time.'

'Oh you never know, it might just be for show. A desperate attempt to keep the morale up when the brass are predicting disaster.'

'Now you're just humouring me.'

'Look, if it's any consolation a pushover isn't quite the arrangement I would have chosen either.'

'But I thought you were sick of fighting?'

'Oh I am but that's not quite the point. You see – well, you must promise you'll keep this to yourself, for it's not the sort of thing that makes a chap popular –'

'You have my word.'

'All right. Well, the thing is, I need to win myself a VC.'

Lt. Verney lets out a whistle.

'I say. You have set yourself a task.'

'Haven't I, though? Eleven thousand paratroopers landing on

the German equivalent of the Home Guard. It's not exactly the sort of encounter from which VC legends are made.'

'Must it really be the VC, though? Surely, with a DFC already, an MC would more than do the trick. Whatever the trick is. A young lady, perhaps?'

'That's part of it, certainly,' I say, before lightly treating Lt. Verney to a résumé of what you already know: James, the inheritance, my father, Lord Brecon, Great Meresby, Gina and the rest.

Lt. Verney laughs sympathetically.

'I'd say you were the one who really needs an Armageddon.'

'No thank you,' I say with feeling. 'I've had quite enough of that already. Burma. Stalingrad. D-Day. No, I'll tell you what, Pat, do you know what I'd really like?'

Lt. Verney beams back, with that wonderful, open, friendly curate's face of his. Funny, how quickly in war you get to know people, how ready you are to treat chaps who till so recently were strangers to the innermost secrets of your heart.

'Well, it's like this,' I say. 'Do you play tennis?'

'Rather. It's my sport. Give you a game if you like, when we get back to Blighty.'

'You're on. Tell me, though, when you're playing someone feebler than you – as I fear you'll find with me – do you find yourself almost unconsciously lowering your standards so as to make it more of a game?'

'Absolutely. Hate being too far ahead. A match is so much more fun when you're coming from behind and there's everything to play for.'

I smile. Pity he never got to fight in the early war years, I'm thinking. It would have been right up his street.

'I have a similar weakness. If it is a weakness. Sarnt Price certainly thinks so. He'd kill them all at once if he could, by whatever means necessary. Bomb 'em. Shoot 'em. Burn 'em. Fry 'em. Just get the damned thing over, that's his view.

Whereas for myself, I don't know what it is – squeamishness maybe? – but I've never felt so comfortable about killing the enemy en masse. Unless they're Japs, of course. Never had much difficulty there. But the Germans, well. My grand-mother's from Bavaria and I had some jolly times in Germany before the war. Speak the lingo. Scratch the surface, add a sense of humour, and you could almost be dealing with ourselves. Do you catch my drift?'

'I think so,' says Lt. Verney. 'What you'd like if you could is for Market Garden to be like the best sort of tennis match. One you win in the end, obviously, but not so easily that it takes all the pleasure out of victory.'

'Does that sound awfully frivolous?'

'No, it sounds rather the sort of thing I'd choose for myself, if I could. But tell me, you've seen a fair bit of action. Is that ever how things actually play out?'

'Um, not often, no. Usually it's much more like that,' I murmur, jerking the barrel of my Sten towards a body lying at the edge of our path. It belongs to a German soldier – not the scowling *Übermensch* of popular Allied myth, but a sweetly oafish-looking fellow with round glasses and a chubby face.

Lt. Verney steps to take a closer look, no doubt wondering, as I am, how so innocuous a chap met so sudden and pointless an end. Looking up, we see a pair of bored riflemen from the King's Own Scottish Borderers standing guard by what's left of two gateposts. We must have wandered slightly off course, for we're now in front of what's left of Wolfheze asylum. Whether the Germans had been using it as a position I don't know, but our bombers have taken no chances. The place is a shambles: deep craters, collapsed walls, shattered glass, and a pervasive smell of sweet raw meat which suggests that there have been casualties.

One of the KOSBs points us in the direction of what he thinks is our RV. He's seen quite a few jeeps heading that way, in any case.

I glance past the shredded remnants of what were once clearly some very attractive landscaped gardens towards the asylum building. A nurse is coming towards us up the pathway, wearing a distinctly frosty expression.

'*Goedemorgen*,' I say.

She bustles determinedly through our group so that we all have to step aside to let her pass.

'Miserable cow!' mutters one of the KOSBs.

'We didnae have ta liberate ye, ye ken,' says the other. Then his expression darkens and he raises his rifle.

Now I'm all in agreement that rudeness should be made a capital offence, but I do rather draw the line at killing sisters of mercy. Before I can respond, though, there's a sharp crack, and something sings past my ear. Then there's another louder crack as the KOSB discharges his weapon and I whip round to examine the appalling thing he's done. There's the nurse, juddering on the ground as if she's receiving electroconvulsion therapy, and I'm thinking, I'll see you hanged for this, you murdering Jock!

Fortunately, before I articulate this thought, I notice the handgun on the ground beside that convulsing body. And I remember the mysterious shot I heard so lately, whistling past my skull.

'Why on earth?' I hear myself muttering.

'I wud ask her for ye, sir,' says the Jock who shot her. 'But I dinna think she's in a condition to say.'

The Squadron's rendezvous, on the corner of a large wood 750 yards south of the Wolfheze level crossing, is a scene of feverish activity. PIATs, Bren guns and 2-inch mortars are being hauled from kitbags, inspected and made ready. Red berets form up for departure by section and troop. From all directions, stream in a succession of Willy's jeeps, some pulling Polsten guns, some pulling trailers of supplies and ammo, some packed with tense young men itching for the off. HQ Troop's wireless ops kneel hunched over their sets, trying to establish contact with those parts of the Squadron which have yet to turn up.

Fortunately, my jeeps are among those that have recently arrived. Price and Wood are in their respective driver's seats, enjoying a self-congratulatory cigarette, while the rest of the section under Cpl. Cholmondeley's direction are loading up the last of our kit. Near by, watching them rather as impatient hyenas watch lions when they're gorging themselves on the best bits of a kill, stand Lt. Randall's section. They don't look best pleased that their arch-rivals' jeeps have turned up while their own ones haven't.

There are cheers when I join the men, Lt. Verney by my side. Knowing Price, he has already briefed them as to the possibility that we might yet be leading the assault on the bridge.

'We'll have to move sharpish, though,' says Price, *sotto voce*. He's got my pair of binoculars round his neck. Earlier, I saw him intently scanning in the direction of our glider's landing zone.

'And why would that be, I wonder?'

'Surely, Mr Richard, you know better than to ask a question like that.'

In the heart of all the mayhem stands our jovial OC, maps spread out in front of him on the bonnet of his jeep, tufts of white hair poking from his ill-fitting beret, beaming like Akela at a Cubs' jamboree. You'd never guess that we were in the middle of a battle zone, still less that there was any urgency to our predicament. In twenty minutes' time we're supposed to be leading the assault on the bridge, yet still nearly half our jeeps and men haven't arrived.

'Ah Dick. The hero of the hour!' booms the OC, prompting smiles from most of the troop and section commanders around him, and a seriously dirty look from Lt. Randall.

'Really, sir?'

'No need for false modesty, your sergeant has already spilled the beans. Carry on like that, and we might have to think about finding some vertical stripes to go with your diagonals.' As he says this, he's looking at the thin, slanting black-and-white stripes of my DFC ribbon. What he means is that he's considering me for an immediate MC.

'And might I have the honour of putting myself forward as a witness, sir?' says Lt. Verney, who was insistent that he met the OC before getting his medical treatment. Now I know why.

'By all means, Lieutenant. Did an all-right job, did he, in a GP's professional opinion?'

'Sir, that he got us down in one piece was little short of miraculous,' says Lt. Verney.

I appreciate what he's trying to do but I rather wish he wasn't. To judge by their expressions, one or two of my fellow officers are finding it difficult to keep their breakfasts down.

'Sir, Mr Verney's being too kind but my taking the controls was an act of preservation, no more than that. And the fact that we saved the jeeps was pure fluke.'

'We gather that Mr Randall's weren't so lucky. Any chance they might make it here in time, you think?'

I get a look from Randall which conveys everything from suspicion and resentment to pleading desperation.

If I'm honest, I think there's every likelihood that his jeeps will make it. When I left, Sgt. Nutter and the crew seemed to be making perfectly good headway, and Sgt. Price's shiftiness just now would appear to have confirmed this. On the other hand, that Lt. Randall really is such a frightful tick . . .

'Sarnt Price would be the one to ask, sir.'

'Ah, that settles it then,' says the OC, with a sympathetic shrug towards Lt. Randall. I dread to imagine how blatant a lie Sgt. Price must have told them when he radioed in. 'Sorry, Kim.

Looks like you shan't after all be going point. Which rather begs the question—'

'But surely, sir, it's not definite yet!' says Lt. Randall, cheeks flushing, clearly quite unable to bear what the OC is about to say – viz. that someone else will now have to lead the assault. 'We've still twenty minutes.'

The OC consults his watch.

'Seventeen now, actually, old man, and if your jeeps make it the job is still yours. But we'd better find an alternative point section just in case. What do you reckon, David?' – This last addressed to our troop commander, Capt. Fisher. 'Shall we ask for volunteers?'

Capt. Fisher agrees. And, of course, every one of the section commanders in the designated lead troop, myself included, puts up his hand.

'Not you, Dick. Didn't I say I wanted you back with your troop HQ, where I can keep an eye on you?'

'With respect, sir, if I was nearly worth an MC a minute ago, I'm worthy of being your point man now.'

'Oh touché,' says the OC, mulling it over for a moment. When he speaks, he sounds – as he so often does – very amused by the puckishness of his decision. 'All right, Dick. The job's yours, so long as you have no objections, David.'

'None at all,' says Capt. Fisher.

The other section commanders don't look too miffed, thank goodness. None of them, that is, apart from Lt. Randall.

After the OC has given us our final briefing – we already know it backwards and it's all very simple: part of A Troop and a small Squadron Rear HQ will stay here in reserve on the drop zone; the rest of us, with my section at the head of the lead troop, will make hell for leather for Arnhem bridge and seize it by *coup de main* – we repair to our various sections.

'So sorry you can't come with us,' I say to Lt. Verney, who's going to stay and have his head looked at by one of the medics, before trying to hook up with the rest of his squadron.

'Not half as sorry as I am,' he says. 'And may I wish you the very best of luck in your extraordinary endeavour.' He means the VC, of course.

'And may your battle prove as lively as you'd like it to be – but not an ounce more lively than that,' I reply.

My men are all ready in their jeeps, engines running. Price is still peering anxiously through the binoculars. The others look intently at me, apparently scanning my expression for signs and portents.

'Right, chaps. We're in the driver's seat!' I announce, to put them out of their misery.

The resultant cheer sends a great big shiver down my spine. Truly, I feel privileged to be leading these men into battle. And if a certain economy with the truth was what was needed to put us there . . .

'Quick,' hisses Price, leading me gently away from my jeep so that none of the others can hear. He casts an anxious glance towards Lt. Randall's section, then looks back conspiratorially at me. 'It's now or never!'

'We can't.' I check my watch. 'Not for another ten minutes.'

'Course you can,' he suggests. 'Your watch wasn't correctly synchronised. You misheard the start time. You thought the OC had already given the signal . . .'

'No, Price. I've pushed it far enough, but I'll go no further. Now get back to your jeep and await my signal.'

'Very well, Mr Richard,' he says, with that marvellously imperious huffiness I've seen him use even on my father sometimes, when he wants to say in so many words he's a damned bloody fool, unfit to own a hovel, let alone a large country estate.

Taking my seat next to Wood, I fondle the stock of my Vickers K.

'Everyone, OK?' I say, smiling at the chaps in the back. Darkie Beckford. My wireless man Hughes. Dour, square-faced Cpl. Cholmondeley.

Before they can answer, Wood has let out a sudden surprised yelp.

'They're off, sir.'

'Who—?'

I'm halfway to asking when the number one jeep in our section accelerates past ours. It's being driven not by the driver/mechanic Meadows, but by Sgt. Price. And you only need one glimpse of those set, glowering features, to tell that he's not going to stop, come hell or high water.

7

Bash On!

'Where to, Mr Coward?' asks Wood.

'After Sarnt Price, of course!'

'Only—'

'Step on it, man!'

Wood slams down his foot and, like a jumpy starter at Aintree, the jeep bucks then surges forward.

'Oi!' yells Hughes from the back, one hand clinging for dear life to the side of the jeep, the other onto his threatened wireless set.

'Bash on, Recce!' yells Beckford.

'Mouth shut. Eyes peeled,' barks Cpl. Cholmondeley, miserable killjoy that he is. He's quite right, though. It may feel like an exercise. But we are fifty miles behind enemy lines. And all it would take to stop us in our tracks is one burst of well-aimed MG fire.

We're passing through broad, open heathland which an hour ago was alive with soldiery. Now it's almost empty again, save for a few stragglers, the various Rear HQ units, and those companies which have been charged with guarding the landing and drop zones, ready for the arrival of tomorrow's reinforcements.

Our forces appear to be making good headway. Twice now, we've had to swerve round the smoking wreckage of German motor vehicles – a Kübelwagen and a motorcycle/sidecar combination – the bodies of their crews sprawled unburied by the road.

What puzzles me is the identity of the unit causing all this mayhem. If I had to put money on it, I'd guess it was most likely those thrusters at Johnny Frost's 2nd Battalion. Except, from what I can remember of the overall battle plan, they were going to come at the bridge via a more circuitous southern route skirting the north bank of the Lower Rhine. Our job, on the other hand, is to approach the bridge by the much more direct northern route, following the line of the railway track leading almost straight from our RV point into Arnhem.

Talking of which –

After a puzzled look at the map billowing in my lap I lean across to Wood. I have to shout to make myself heard against the roar of the engine and the rushing of the wind.

'Oughtn't we to have crossed the railway by now?'

'Yes, sir.'

'Then why haven't we?'

'We're heading in the opposite direction.'

'WHAT? WHY DIDN'T YOU SAY?'

'I thought you knew, sir. When I said, "Where to?" and you said, "Follow Sarnt Price." Shall I flash him to slow down, sir?'

'No, not here,' I cry, with an uneasy glance at our surroundings. Heathland has now given way to woods dense with spindly beech trees and leggy conifers. It comes almost to the edge of the road and you can't see more than ten yards into its murky, menacing depths. Anything could be hiding in there.

I feel my grip instinctively tightening on the stock of the Vickers K. Looking back, I see Cpl. Cholmondeley has had the same idea. With a forking gesture of his fingers to his eyes, he indicates to Beckford and Hughes that they should keep an extra-careful look-out. Darkie squints tentatively down the barrel of his Bren. Cpl. Cholmondeley tautens the strap on his Sten.

'Fast as you can, Wood,' I say, eyes flicking agitatedly from one side of the impenetrable wood to the other, grateful for every second that passes without a deadly volley of shots.

As second jeep in line we're bound to catch the brunt of it.

'Keep up, damn it, or we'll lose him.'

'I'm trying, sir, but he's driving like a lunatic.'

Then, quite suddenly, the landscape changes and with it the general mood. Where before we were on the edge of our seats, hearts racing, knuckles white, eyes on stalks for the first signs of the seemingly inevitable ambush, we now find ourselves amid scenes of almost absurd gentility and calm. Like taking a wrong turn mid-race at Brooklands only to end up at a Pimm's and tennis party *chez* Miss Joan Hunter Dunn.

'Bloody 'ell,' declares Wood, looking about, amazed. 'We're in Tunbridge Wells.'

Somewhere like that, certainly. The tall trees and the detached thirties houses set back from the road behind lawns abundant with laurel, rhododendrons and dwarf conifers remind me rather of the A4 in Surrey. But there's also an orderliness, a neatness, a retirement-home reserve that calls to mind Bournemouth, or Cheltenham, or anywhere, really, with a stuffy lawn bowls club and a lavishly funded municipal gardens department.

You'd never dream of fighting a battle in such a place. It would be like crapping in your grandmother's drawing room.

We've turned left and are heading down a road which, if I've got my bearings right, is called the Utrechtseweg and will take us directly into Arnhem. There's no great sense of danger any more because we've now caught up with one of the advance foot battalions. They're strung out, in single file, either side of the road for a good half-mile ahead – giving us the thumbs-up (or is it a lift they're jokingly asking for?) as we rocket past.

Price is only a couple of jeeps' length ahead of us, having slowed to skirt round yet another shot-up German vehicle. He's about to drive past it when an officer steps out from the trees, where he has parked his jeep, signalling for us to stop. We do so, just behind the German vehicle – a staff car, no less, with at least one ugly-looking body hanging out of the door.

'Recce Squadron? We've been looking for you,' says the officer briskly. He's a captain from Divisional HQ.

Behind his wheel Price stares ahead, ignoring my quick, angry look.

'General Urquhart's been trying to contact your OC but something's playing havoc with our signals. No idea where he is, I suppose?'

'Half an hour ago, he was at our RV near the Wolfheze level crossing about to follow the line of the track to Arnhem. Is there a problem?'

'Slight change of plan. Look, if you bump into him, can you get him to contact Div HQ as a matter of urgency?'

'Yes, sir.'

Before we go, none of us can resist having a peek at the car. There are four bodies inside, riddled with bullets, all a frightful mess. Worst is the man in the leather overcoat, with half the top of his head missing.

'Who's this beauty?' I ask the Captain.

'One General Kussin. Commander of the Arnhem garrison, we believe.'

'Jerry really is having a rough day.'

'So far,' says the Captain, with a certain edge in his voice. At the time I put this down to typical staff officer's cautiousness. Later, though, it does occur that perhaps this fellow knew more than he was letting on.

My eyes keep straying back to the General's head. Not from

prurience, I don't think. More from puzzlement. The cut's too regular and clean for it to have been done by a bullet. It has been hacked with a knife, presumably after death. In fact he looks as if – yes, that's it –

'Fuck me, 'e's been scalped,' exclaims Wood, causing Hughes, who has already been looking a touch green at the gills, to bend over and begin noisily decorating our jeep's rear tyre.

'Rather looks that way,' agrees the Captain.

'Not by our chaps?' I say, mildly aghast.

'Not if they know what's good for them. We think more likely it was Dutch boys, having fun.'

'Funny idea of fun,' mutters Hughes.

'For how long have you lived under Nazi occupation?' asks Cpl. Cholmondeley coldly.

'Never, actually, Corp but—'

'Then do not judge!' says Cpl. Cholmondeley.

Before we head off, the Captain warns us to be careful ahead. Besides several sniping incidents, there have been reports of anti-tank guns, even unconfirmed rumours of self-propelled guns.

'SPs?' wonders Wood, as we drive on, our jeep in front this time. 'Are you sure you wouldn't rather have Sarnt Price's jeep going point, sir?'

Delightful spot this, I think to myself, as we speed on into town. If you have it in mind that the Netherlands is a dull, flat, marshy, featureless place with nothing to write home about but dykes, windmills and clogs, think again. This part, at any rate, is wonderfully civilised, with its lush greenery, attractive villas with tall windows and patterned shutters, and neat gardens ablaze with late-summer blooms, surrounded by country I'll bet is ideal for riding and golfing and cycling.

There's a particularly handsome white building we pass, set like an English country club in its own spacious, landscaped grounds, which I earmark for future stays. 'Hartenstein Hotel' it says in big black letters.

HARTENSTEIN, HARTENSTEIN, HARTENSTEIN, I repeat to myself, for otherwise the name's bound to go clean out of my head.

There are friendly locals everywhere, of course. A bit drawn and bony, after four years of deprivation, but all of them scrubbed and smiling and neatly dressed in their Sunday best.

As we draw closer to the centre of Oosterbeek, these crowds thicken to the point where it becomes almost impossible to continue our advance. Some want to give us flowers, others jugs of milk or lumps of cheese or flasks of fiery alcohol. Still others simply want to touch or embrace or kiss their first Allied liberator.

'If this is a dream, please, no one wake me!' crows Beckford, as a pair of dark-haired twins vie to feed him titbits from their aprons. Most of the locals having never seen a black face before, the dirty bugger is getting far more than his share of adulation. It's at times like this you definitely want to be one of the men, not an officer. Officers have to stay aloof. NCOs too.

'I don't like this, sir,' growls Cpl. Cholmondeley, standing up to get a clearer view over the sea of heads. He's right. The streets around us may look a picture of Continental bliss – cafés, bakeries, groceries, sweet little hotels – but behind every window a sniper could lurk, behind any wall an 88 waiting to blast us to kingdom come.

'No, quite. Any bright ideas?'

I'm remembering the intelligence warnings we got at our briefings that not all the natives are friendly. The Dutch have provided a higher percentage of young volunteers to the SS than has any other occupied nation. How easy it would be for any of these people, in the guise of presenting a gift, to drop a grenade in our laps!

There's a couple of Dutch youths whom I don't trust one bit. They're both about fifteen, dressed in greasy, ill-fitting suits. And though they have orange bands round their arms, I'm not sure I believe they are genuine members of the Resistance. One, brandishing an ancient pistol which probably last saw action sometime during the era of William of Orange, has a pale face more pockmarked than the surface of the moon. The other, carrying nothing more dangerous than a dirty leather bag, is tall and gangling with a particularly long neck and a pronounced Adam's apple, which gives him the appearance of a giant newt.

Their compatriots, I notice, tend to be giving them a wide berth.

'How about a quick burst over their heads?' suggests Cpl. Cholmondeley.

'Or why not have done with it and just shoot a couple,' I say. This is the problem when you've been with Price as long as I have. His sarcasm can be terribly catching.

Wood sniggers. Cpl. Cholmondeley does not.

'Might it not make us unpopular?' he asks.

'Joke, man! Joke!' I explain quickly, before he takes me up on my suggestion. 'No, we need to find ourselves a civic leader. Someone in the Resistance, maybe. Look out for orange armbands.'

'Them?' he says, jerking his Sten towards the grisly youths. King Newt has pulled something from his bag and is waving it in people's faces with the macabre glee of a schoolboy brandishing a dead rat in the girls' changing room. Not sure what it is, exactly, but it's dark and horrid and it's making everyone recoil.

'I think we can do better,' I say.

'I'll say you could, Mr Coward. Look at her!' says Wood.

As soon as I do I wish I hadn't. Her eyes are like Carrara marble in the midday sun: so blindingly intense you're forced to look away. It's not that she's young, blonde and pretty, though she is very much all those things. It's the sexual frankness in her stare. The look a woman gives you when you're lying on top of her and she's about to . . . well, never mind that right now. My point is that she's putting into my head thoughts which a responsible section commander really doesn't need in his head when advancing to contact.

Averting my gaze quickly, I'm rescued by a fat-faced Dutch matron with her hair in a bun and tiny, red, worm-like veins threading her cheeks, who interprets my panic-stricken look as an invitation. She waddles to my side of the jeep, seizes me in a python embrace, says, 'Welcome, Tommy!' and kisses me once on each cheek.

'Um, thank you, madam,' I gasp, once I've recovered my breath. 'Do you speak English?'

Out of the corner of my eye, I notice the pretty blonde girl trying to get closer. Before she can do so, the twins who were flirting with Beckford step in to block her path. They hiss something at her in Dutch.

'*Moffenmeid!*'

The girl tries to push past them and this time one of them slashes at her face like an angry cat. Only by pulling back quickly does the poor girl escape being scratched.

'*Moffenmeid!*'

Sexual jealousy, I suppose. I dare say things get quite competitive when you've spent the last four years bereft of suitable menfolk, and suddenly five thousand of them drop down all at once from the sky.

'I speak English good!' says the woman with the bun.

'Then please could you ask all these people to disperse. Tell them that it is very dangerous.'

'Winston Churchill, good!' says the woman.

Suddenly the crowd on my side of the jeep parts and Sgt. Price is standing at my side, wearing a face like thunder.

'At this sodding rate it will be 30 Corps who get to the bridge before we do.'

'I appreciate that, Sarnt, so what do you propose we do?'

'We ask them politely to bugger off.'

'And how do we do that?'

With one bound he is standing atop our jeep. He cups his hands and yells something very loud at the crowd in what sounds like remarkably fluent Dutch. To judge by the expressions on the faces of the older and more genteel members of the crowd, it is also very disgusting Dutch. I remember a tall tale Price told me once, about all the odd jobs he'd had to do during the Depression when he'd had some sort of falling-out with my father. One of them, so he alleged, was working as a pimp in an Amsterdam brothel. But I never believed him till now.

'Ask them nicely, did you, Sarnt?' I ask, as the crowd begins to disperse, clucking whatever the Dutch is for: 'And I thought the English were supposed to have good manners . . .'

'I did say please at the end.'

I watch our well-wishers' retreating backs. The matron with her hair in the bun, the twins, the old man who'd put on some campaign medals from a war I couldn't recognise. Such lovely people. Such a damned shame.

Wonder what's happened to my little blonde moppet? Ah, there she is. Seems she's a friend of those two frightful Dutch youths, now walking either side of her.

'She's a fast one and no mistake,' muses Wood. 'Did you see what those two lads she's with had in their bag?'

'I couldn't make it out.'

'You remember old General Kussin back there, with his scalp missing?'

'No! Surely not?'

'A right Burke and Hare, them two, I should say. 'Ere, look. What are they up to with young blondie?'

It's not immediately clear. Perhaps it's just horseplay. The boys at any rate are laughing as if it's all the most uproarious joke. But the girl has raised her voice and she doesn't sound altogether content with the arrangement. Is she trying to get away?

'Price, I don't suppose you know what *Moffenmeid* means?'

She's struggling harder, now. Definitely trying to escape.

'I think *Moffen*'s what the locals call Jerry. *Meid*? Probably means those tarts who've been sleeping with Jerry. Wouldn't want to be one of them right now. Why do you – oh, I see. Yeah. Bad luck. Poor girl.'

'What do you think they'll do to her?' I ask. Not that I don't have my suspicions.

'Shave her hair off, if she's lucky.'

The girl lets out a yelp. She's trying to twist her head round, to call for our attention. No one else is going to help her, certainly. All those smart, God-fearing Dutch folk. They're all looking pointedly elsewhere. Hasn't any of them heard the story of Mary Magdalene?

'The full Kussin chop, let us hope,' says Cpl. Cholmondeley.

I glare at him with disgust. He glares back, with grey-eyed defiance.

'What shall we do, sir?' says Wood.

'The right thing, of course!'

'Sir, we haven't the time!' says Price.

'She is a collaborator!' says Cpl. Cholmondeley.

'Sarnt, catch us up. Wood, step on it, now!'

A roar, a scream of tyres and the jeep takes off. Within seconds we've caught up with the scalpers. Once we've indicated at the point of our guns that it's the girl we want they release her immediately. On their faces is that bewildered, mildly hurt expression pet cats adopt when relieved by the owners of a half-dead fledgling.

I try to maintain an expression of dignity and command. But

it isn't altogether easy when you're blushing like mad and you've got an hysterical seventeen-year-old girl soaking your collar with her tears.

'Could I have a private word, Mr Coward?' says Sgt. Price.

Sensing danger, the girl tightens her limpet-like grip. She's looking up at me, trying to make eye-contact, which I mustn't allow for it would be fatal. The sweetness of her breath, and the faint, not-at-all unpleasant musky smell from under her arms are already doing damage enough.

'Beckford. Would you mind looking after this young lady for a moment.'

'My pleasure, sir,' says Beckford with a delighted grin. He hops off the jeep and, after a bit of a struggle, manages to hold the girl off long enough for me to wriggle clear.

'Just remind me, Mr Richard, because I'm getting a bit confused,' says Price when we're out of earshot. 'Did we come all this way to chase skirt or to capture a bridge?'

'We've come here to do the right thing by these people. If we don't we're no better than the Germans.'

'And if she'd a face like a plucked broiler's arse, would you feel so strongly still?'

'I'm presuming you didn't call me aside to discuss ethics?'

'Just wondering really what you planned to do with her.'

'I shan't just abandon her, if that's what you mean. Not with those two malcontents in the vicinity.'

'Thought you'd say that. And we can't take her with us, because it's too dangerous and there isn't room. So what I was thinking was . . .' Price cups his hands around his mouth, lowers his voice still further and mutters his unorthodox suggestion in my ear.

'No.' I study him aghast, trying to work out whether he's joking. Apparently not. 'They're on our side. It would be murder.'

'No one would know. Casualties of war, and all that. I'll be discreet. Pop off with them round the back of that hotel, maybe. It'll only take five minutes.'

'No, Price. I've a better way. You're going to find out from the girl where she lives and see her safely home. We might well pick up some intelligence.'

'And don't you half need some, Mr Richard.'

The girl's name is Annette and thank God her home is close by for I'm not sure I could have borne the embarrassment much longer. No one says anything, of course. But while neither Beckford nor Hughes seems unduly concerned at having a pretty girl sandwiched between them in the back, it's quite clear from Cpl. Cholmondeley's huffy silence he thinks his section commander is a complete bloody nincompoop.

Her home is a large villa with an enormous garden a few blocks below the Hartenstein Hotel, on a promontory overlooking the Rhine. Protruding from the roof is a tower with a 360-degree viewing window, which looks like it might make a very useful OP. It all belongs to the wealthy uncle and aunt with whom Annette has been staying for several months, apparently because her parents back home in Eindhoven thought Oosterbeek the place least likely to be involved in any fighting.

The men conceal the vehicles behind laurel hedges and stand guard, while Price and I escort Annette back inside. Her uncle, Jan and aunt, Christina – a handsome middle-aged couple: he with a neatly trimmed beard, she resembling a riper version of her niece, both speaking reasonable English – are almost hysterical with gratitude. It seems they've been up all night scouring the streets for Annette, who went missing during yesterday's horrendous bombing raid on Wolfheze, and had come to fear the worst.

Jan leads us into a large drawing room, resplendent with fine old furniture, rare-looking books and teak cabinets housing ethnic objects presumably collected on his ancestors' travels. The wallpaper is printed with a very striking toucan motif.

'Please,' he says, breaking open a bottle of firewater. 'We must drink to the health of your king!'

It seems rude not to, so once he's poured out the measures – large ones for the chaps, smaller ones for the womenfolk – we raise our glasses in a toast to His Majesty the King. Price and Jan drain theirs in one so I follow suit.

Unfortunately, a toast to our king requires a reciprocal one to the Queen of the Netherlands, with an even bigger-looking measure than the first.

'We should be getting off, shouldn't we, sir?' says Price, completely unaffected.

I'm reeling, though, and could do with a few moments to get myself straight. A splash of water on the face, at least.

'Might be worth a look from that tower, first, so we can get our bearings,' I say.

'Annette,' says Jan to his niece, followed by something in Dutch, which I imagine means, 'Show him upstairs.' Annette looks very pleased at this prospect.

'There are German positions she can show you,' says her uncle.

'I'll bet,' mutters Price.

Annette entwines her fingers in mine, in a way you could either interpret as guileless or forward. Her uncle mutters something else to her in Dutch, something admonitory. Annette responds with a weary sigh, and a roll of her eyes. She lets go of my hand. A fat, rather disgusting-looking ginger cat follows us, purring loudly.

As soon as we're out of view, though, she takes hold of it again. Her palm is warm. Neither of us looks at one another, or says anything. But there's an intimacy here as thick as my throat. If only she were less alluring. If only I didn't have a job to do. If only that bloody cat weren't watching like a witch's familiar.

From the drawing room, the conversation carries up the stairwell.

'You are going to Arnhem bridge?' asks Jan.

'Might be,' says Price.

'Which route do you intend to take?'

'Now that would be telling,' says Price, ever cautious.

'This is important. Go the wrong way and you will die.'

I'd like to hear more but we've now passed through a narrow doorway – the ginger cat too, unfortunately – and are climbing the narrow, creaking staircase which leads into the tower itself. It's cramped and musty – not much larger than a dovecote. Running round the edge underneath is a bench with a faded floral cushion. Whoever built this place was no doubt fully aware of its romantic potential. Instead of 'etchings', a view of the Rhine.

Annette perches on the cushion and, smiling up at me, she pats the space next to her. The cat jumps up next to her and she strokes it absent-mindedly, the look in her eyes suggesting it isn't puss she'd most like to play with. I pretend to be preoccupied with military business. With the sleeve of my Denison smock I polish the dust and cobwebs from one of the panes facing south-east and then peer intently towards the river. In the fading light you can make out one of the bridges – the railway one – our chaps were supposed to capture and probably have done by now. The Arnhem road bridge is hidden round a bend in the river, but you can see roughly where it is because of the church spires jutting out just to its north.

Bet Lt. Randall's there now, the ruddy show-off – crowing to the rest of his section about how they'll go down in history as the First Men To The Bridge.

'Dick,' says Annette softly. Oh God, did I tell her my name? How stupid of me!

I study the bridge through my binoculars, fine-focusing on the figures advancing towards the centre. Ours or theirs? Red berets. Ours!

'I like you, Dick,' says Annette. The way she says it, it sounds more like a proposition.

Concentrate, man! Concentrate! You're here to do a job, remember. You are an officer in His Majesty's Armed Forces. You have men to command. A mission to fulfil.

'Do you know what I would like to do to you?' Jesus, how come she suddenly speaks English? She's more lethal than a battery of Nebelwerfer, this one.

'Um . . .'

'Now, Dick. Right now, I would like to—'

BOOM!

With a startled screech the cat leaps from Annette's lap.

'Cripes!' I say, swinging my binoculars back round towards the source of the almighty explosion. Even from a mile and a half distance we can feel the vibrations. They're coming from the cloud of grey-black smoke billowing up from where the railway bridge used to be. The sky above it is alive with spinning debris – steel girders, wooden sleepers, stretches of track, lumps of stone, unidentifiable bits, which I hope to God aren't human . . .

'You must go?' says Annette.

'I must go!' I say.

'You will come back?'

'Hope so,' I say, with feeling.

'Find out anything useful?' I ask Price as we make for the jeeps. Bleackley has already been dispatched to fetch the others.

'Quite a bit,' says Price. 'She's being treated as an outpatient for a severe nymphomaniacal disorder at the Wolfheze asylum. She's already worked her way through half the German garrison. Now her uncle and aunt are worried she's about to do the same with the 1st Airborne Division and are wondering whether we're up to the job.'

'I meant, Sarnt, about the disposition of our forces.'

Price spreads out our map on the bonnet of his jeep.

'He reckons if we want to get to the bridge, our best route is this one,' he says, jabbing a finger at the southernmost road, which our planners have designated Lion. 'In fact, he says it's our only route.'

'And how would he know?'

'Says he's in touch with the local underground. They say all the roads north of here, including Utrechtseweg, are already blocked.'

'A likely story. They're such bloody pessimists, these Dutch. Anything else?'

'Still nothing from Squadron HQ, but Hughes did manage briefly to raise Div HQ.'

'And?'

'Here he is now, you can ask him. I'll brief the men. I take it we'll be taking the southern route?'

'I've not yet decided, Sarnt,' I say, mainly to put him in his place. His joke about sweet little Annette strikes me as having been in very poor taste.

Hughes has little to impart. All Div HQ wanted to ask him was the whereabouts of Maj. Gough. Before Hughes could find out what the news was from their end, he got cut off.

Shortly afterwards, Cpl. Cholmondeley returns with the Bren team, the recce patrol and further dismal tidings. Not five minutes ago, a jeep screeched up beside him and whom should it be carrying but the Divisional Commander Gen. Urquhart and one of the Brigade commanders, Brig. Lathbury.

On seeing Cpl. Cholmondeley's 1st Recce, they say, 'Where's your OC, we've been looking for him everywhere.'

Cholmondeley says he doesn't know.

'Who's your section commander?' Urquhart asks.

Cholmondeley tells him.

'Well, you can tell this Lieutenant Coward from me that we need his jeeps at the bridge, not here, piddling about in no-man's-land. And that if he's not there in half an hour, you and he can swap jobs, Corporal. Do you think you can remember all that?'

'So that's what he said, sir, and now, I'm telling you,' says Cpl. Cholmondeley.

'Thank you, Corporal.'

'My pleasure, sir,' he says.

8

I Will Stand at Thy Right Hand

'Bloody 'ell, sir. How did we manage that?' gasps Wood.

'I was going to ask you the same question,' I say, staring up in amazement.

Before us, quite unheralded, looms the bridge we were beginning to think we'd never see. The Arnhem road bridge. The Bridge Too Far.

You'll no doubt have seen it in those aerial reconnaissance photos – a brutally pragmatic, single arch steel structure curving in a shallow semicircle high above the Lower Rhine. But until you've seen it up close, nothing can quite prepare you for how massive it is, how imposing, how –

I was going to say ominous but that wouldn't be quite true. After the events of the last ten minutes, there's no room in any of our fizzing, reeling, punch-drunk heads for fear or apprehension. Only for blessed relief that a) the bridge is there, intact and apparently unoccupied by the enemy, and that b) we're still alive to see it.

Up until the railway it was all going very well. On the advice of Jan, the bearded Dutchman, we took the southern route code-named in our operational plan as Lion and soon found ourselves speeding past the tail end of Johnny Frost's 2nd Battalion, who grinned and warbled their encouragement with the eerie, wailing battle cry they picked up in North Africa that sounds like a muezzin's call – 'Waho Mohammed'.

The middle route code-named Tiger – straight into town down the Utrechtseweg – would have been more direct. But Jan told Price this would be suicide. He'd spoken to friends less than an hour ago, who had told him the Germans were already starting to prepare ambush positions all along that road.

'I suppose we should try to get a message through to Fitch's lot, just in case,' I said, meaning 3rd Battalion, the unit tasked with that particular route.

'Hughes has already tried. No use,' said Price. 'There's something in the air here that seems to be buggering our wirelesses.'

I shrugged. Bound to be a load of old nonsense, anyway, I remember thinking to myself. Crummy line-of-communication troops are hardly going to be a match for one of our parachute battalions.

'So what do you reckon? Are we going to take Jan's detour or carry straight on?' I said.

'Tough one,' said Price. 'If we take Tiger and get ourselves killed, we'll feel right bloody berks. And if we take Lion and survive you'll be crowing ever after about how if you hadn't done your knight-gallant act with that blonde nympho we'd all have ended up dead for want of Jan's advice.'

'Gosh, I hadn't thought of that.'

'Sorry I mentioned it, then. Let's take Tiger. I'd much rather have me dead than you right.'

'Lion it is, then,' I said with a grin.

Anyway, as I say, up till the railway bridge it all went fine – a pleasant, late-Sunday afternoon's motor through one of those picture-perfect Dutch villages so neat and clean it could have come from the side of your grandpa's model train set. Small, tidy gardens; smiling Dutch; a pretty church in dark-red brick; cows grazing on the far bank of the Rhine; a distant windmill. Really, about the only indication that we weren't on our hols was the dirty plume of smoke from the remnants of the railway bridge and the sporadic crackle, pop and rattle of small-arms fire from the north.

Then we saw the first casualties retreating back towards us either side of the road, so we knew there was trouble brewing. What we didn't appreciate – you rarely do – was how soon it would hit us.

Ahead the road ran through a tunnel underneath a railway embankment – an invitation to an ambush if ever I saw one. Fortunately, our chaps had cleared it by the time we nosed cautiously through. But only very recently, for the bodies hanging over the lip of the German machine gun-nest on the far side were still smoking, and the German wounded had yet to be cleared – as we discovered when one of our wheels bumped over the field-grey leg of a corpse in the road, and the corpse let out a yelp.

I remember leaning over the side of the jeep and looking back the way we'd come, idly curious to see what had become of the poor fellow and whether our number two jeep would run over him too, when I became aware of whooshing and a brief but intense pressure-wave roughly where my head would have been if I hadn't bent round.

At almost the same moment, the number two jeep burst through the tunnel with, rather bizarrely, everyone aboard wearing exactly the same expression, as if part of some synchronised mime ensemble: skin blanched Marcel Marceau-white, eyes open as wide as can be, bottom lips forced against upper lips to make a heartfelt and very emphatic 'F' sound as they all simultaneously registered whatever it was I hadn't seen yet.

The crew of my jeep were yelling much the same expletive, so I guessed before I turned round that it wasn't some particularly fine example of Dutch vernacular architecture to which they were trying to draw my attention.

Ahead, side on to us in the middle of the road, was a German armoured car, with its turret swivelled towards us and its 20-mm cannon flashing an angry orange. Fanning out from behind it were about a half-dozen troops in spotted camouflage smocks, who must have been travelling on the back. They were deploying more like seasoned combat infantry than the garrison troops they were supposed to be but this wasn't the moment to stop and ask.

It's lucky I had my Vickers K to cling on to because, if I hadn't, I'm sure I would have been thrown into the road, so sudden was Wood's screeching evasive swerve. There was a jarring bump, in which my eyeballs seemed to meet the top of my cranium, then several more as we veered off the road and began carving a destructive path through a succession of neat surburban plots, well-tended lawns, and lovingly maintained herbaceous borders.

Wooden fences crunched and splintered, clods of earth and plants went flying, a potting shed collapsed and a charming Dutch tableau featuring a miniature windmill, a scallop-studded grotto and two merry gnomes fishing in a pond exploded against our bumper in an eruption of plaster, sea shells and bright paint.

'Was that really necessary, Wood?' I yelled down from my wobbly standing position as I tried to swing the Vickers K round to cover our rear. The armoured car had now turned its attentions to the second jeep, whose fate I feared, unless its driver could pull off something very clever indeed.

'Someone had to do it, sir,' said Wood.

I probably would have smiled, except that the elation of our dramatic escape had now given way to a sudden melancholy. We'd lost the armoured car, by this stage. But we'd also lost Price.

The bridge is so quiet you'd almost think it were deserted. But as soon as we've come to a halt underneath, at the bottom of one of the road ramps leading up to it, red-bereted figures emerge warily from the gloom, Stens at the ready. An officer appears. Tall, slim, aloof he carries a major's crown on his shoulders, and in one hand, instead of a weapon, he's holding a furled umbrella.

'Well done, Recce,' he drawls, with an edge of sarcasm. 'Better late than never. What kept you?'

'We're surely not the first?' I say. 'Where's Lieutenant Randall?'

'Am I supposed to know who Lieutenant Randall is?'

'He was leading the – oh, never mind.' Suddenly I feel rather bad. I can't think of many things that would stop an annoying young thruster like Lt. Randall in his tracks. Only one, in fact.

The Major leads me up the ramp, careful not to poke his head too far above the top, and says in a low voice, 'Now you ought to be aware that the bridge isn't ours yet. Just before you arrived, we had a section shot up by that pillbox. See it? About a quarter of the way across. Until we can get a bit more back-up, I plan to consolidate our bridgehead with what forces we have by occupying the houses either side. You can take that one there.' He points towards a tall, residential building with his brolly. 'You'll find a courtyard to the rear where you can harbour your vehicle. Any questions, Mr, er—?'

'Coward, sir. Dick Coward.'

He shakes my hand.

'Digby Tatham-Warter. Officer commanding A Company, 2nd Parachute Battalion. Bagged fifteen brace on your father's estate, once. Ajax Coward's boy, right?'

'Yes, sir.'

'Like shooting, do you?'

'Very much, sir.'

'Lucky, that.'

The house we're about to occupy is an elegant, three-storey residence built in the grand Parisian style. Its long-term-survival prospects have, unfortunately, since been jeopardised by the erection in its back garden of perhaps the most strategically vital bridge since Horatius.

Like the house, the well-dressed lady of a certain age who answers the door, clutching some manner of lapdog, has an air of faded distinction.

'*Goedenavond*,' I say. 'We are British soldiers. May we come in?'

'We have been expecting you,' says the lady, beckoning us inside. The walls are peeling and the antique carpets are threadbare. The paintings – seascapes, warships, admirals – speak of a more illustrious past.

A balding, red-cheeked man in a blue blazer with too many shiny gold buttons glares down from the staircase.

'*Goedenavond*,' I call up sheepishly. 'So very sorry to disturb you.'

The man makes a disparaging comment to his wife. 'If you're really so sorry then why don't you bugger off,' would be my educated guess.

We introduce ourselves. The couple are called Mr and Mrs Kock. (Cue a stifled snigger from Wood.) 'But my maiden name is Van Ghent,' adds Mrs Kock, grandly gesturing towards the largest painting, which shows a wigged naval officer clutching a roll of parchment, while in the background sailing ships burn.

She reminds me rather of my Aunt Matilda, who always refused invitations to Buckingham Palace garden parties on the grounds that Windsors were below the salt.

'We caught you napping, is that the phrase?'

'Oh, you did, you did, Mrs Kock,' I say with one of those strained laughs you put on when you don't get the joke but daren't ask for an explanation. I study the picture for clues. Late seventeenth century? Early eighteenth?

'But I see your men are puzzled, Lieutenant. Perhaps you had better remind them of the story.'

'Mrs Kock, I believe his descendant ought to have the honour.'

'Sir,' protests Cpl. Cholmondeley, 'We really—'

'All in good time, Cholmondeley,' I say.

'You are too kind,' says Mrs Kock, turning to address my half-section in the slow, hyper-enunciated manner schoolmistresses adopt with halfwits.

'Gentlemen, it was my ancestor, Lieutenant Admiral Willem Joseph van Ghent, who commanded one of the squadrons responsible for, how does one say this politely, your *abject humiliation* in the famous Dutch victory of June 1667.'

The men look back blankly. Wood stifles a yawn. Hughes fiddles with the strap of his Sten. Cpl. Cholmondeley casts an appraising glance at the various entry and exit routes.

But I do think that if one is going to commandeer an upstanding lady's fine old house, one ought at least to observe the preliminary courtesies.

'When our ships sailed up your River Medway, captured the town of Sheerness, destroyed the pride of your fleet, and carried away your royal flagship?' prompts Mrs Kock.

Still the men look blank.

'But every child in the Netherlands knows of this famous victory,' protests Mrs Kock, a shrill note of indignation in her voice.

'Ah, but the thing is, ma'am, in England we win so many battles – Waterloo, Agincourt, Crécy and the rest – we don't have the time to learn about the odd one we lose,' says Beckford. You can tell by his shy smile and the gently apologetic way he says it that he's just trying to be helpful.

But Mrs Kock feels provoked.

'You did not win those battles,' she snaps.

'Not me personally, no,' agrees Beckford. 'But me ancestors did.'

'But you are – they were – they cannot have done because the people in those times they were . . . white,' says Mrs Kock.

There's an awkward silence. Hughes whistles softly through his teeth. Beckford looks glumly at his boots.

'You need to do a bit more reading up on your English history, missus,' chips in Wood. 'You never heard of the Black Prince?'

'So, anyway, Mr and Mrs Kock,' I say with my best diplomatic smile. 'If you don't mind, we'd like to borrow your house.'

'For how long?'

'No more than two days.'

'Two days!'

'Well, quite possibly less. Depends on when Second Army gets here. They shouldn't be long. That racket you can hear on the other side of the bridge: that'll be them coming now.'

'They are coming from Nijmegen?' asks Mr Kock from the staircase.

'I'm not at liberty to say.'

'Then I will tell you. They are coming from Nijmegen. And they will fail.'

'That may be your opinion as a civilian, Mr Kock. But as an officer, let me tell you—'

'Not so long ago I was an officer, too. In games before the war we tried to do what your Second Army is trying to do. It does not work. It cannot work.'

'Says who?'

'Lieutenant, believe me, it gives me no pleasure to tell you this. My command was the armoured unit whose job it was to spearhead our advance. With speed and determination I was convinced we could make it. But every time the problem was the same. As you know, the ground in this part of the Netherlands is soft – too soft for tanks to manoeuvre in. And the roads that pass over this ground are built on high, narrow embankments. In such conditions you can be as brave and fast and determined as you like, but you can only advance as fast as the lead vehicle. If the enemy should first destroy that vehicle with an 88-mm gun or a Panzerfaust, well –'

As if to emphasise his point, there's a large explosion, really quite near by, which causes the whole house to shake and the windows to rattle. Then a Spandau opens up. And a Bren stutters in reply.

'Sir?' pleads Cpl. Cholmondeley.

I give the nod and the men are off like greyhounds out of a trap. Mr Kock stands stiffly watching them as they thud past.

'You will ask them to be careful, won't you, Lieutenant?' says Mrs Kock.

Once I have seen to it that the Kocks have everything they need in the cellar they will be sharing over the next one or two nights with their dog and a maidservant named Rita, I head upstairs to check on Cpl. Cholmondeley's progress.

He has done much as I hoped he would, but was too embarrassed to ask in front of the Kocks. Every bath, basin and bucket has been filled to the brim with water; every pane in the tall Dutch windows has been smashed with the zeal of a Leveller encountering his first stained glass. Now, from each room comes a rhythmic thumping, followed at intervals by the thud of cascading plasterwork and fallen brick, as the men prepare their loopholes and rat runs for the coming battle.

In a large upstairs bedroom offering the widest field of fire over the bridge, I find Beckford firing short, aimed bursts with his Bren.

'Cease fire!' I command, for there's no evidence of any stuff coming our way. 'What are you shooting at?'

'Jus' testin', sir. Can't seem to get me rangin' right. I think it's the polish on this table that's the problem. My bipod keeps slipping – see?' He fires another quick burst so I can see how the metal legs skip across the surface, leaving ugly little grooves in the antique walnut.

'Enough, man! We haven't the ammo to waste.'

'You don't think that Dutch bloke was right, do you, sir?' says Hughes, as he moves his 22 set from spot to spot, trying in vain to get some reception. 'About Second Army, I mean.'

'Chaps, you're not to worry. That man Kock is talking balls.'

Hughes and Beckford laugh, whether out of politeness or genuine mirth one can never truly be sure with one's men.

'I just wondered whether maybe he knows something that we don't,' says Hughes.

'Go on then. Name me five great Dutch military victories. Three even.'

Hughes racks his brain.

'Now do you see my point? It must be nigh-on three hundred years since the Dutch last had a victory worth savouring. So, of course they're going to look at every prospective engagement with a different perspective from ours. The perspective of born losers.'

As I tramp back down to inspect Beckford's work on the ground-floor defences – we've not nearly enough men to repel a concerted assault – it occurs how much I miss Price. He's good, Cholmondeley. Very good. But he still doesn't know me quite well enough to overrule my wilder idiocies. Letting Mr Kock shoot his mouth off like that, in front of the men. Pricey would never have allowed that to happen. He understands, as all the best NCOs and officers do, that a soldier is only as good as the purblind faith you instil in him that everything is going to turn out OK.

On the half-landing, I meet Mrs Kock and the maid. Mrs Kock is clutching a pile of sheets, the maid holding up a tray with a silver teapot and five china cups.

'Lieutenant Coward, I wanted to apologise for my husband's rudeness –' she begins.

'Mrs Kock, I assure you no offence was taken. But please, for your own safety, would you both return to the cellar.'

'Yes, of course, Lieutenant, but could I ask you a favour? Your Negro, as he comes in and out of the house with those bags of soil, he is forgetting to wipe his feet first.'

'Mrs Kock, I shall remind my – er – Trooper Beckford at once.'

'Thank you, Lieutenant, I knew I could rely on you. My husband laughed when I told him. "These are not *Moffen* soldiers," I replied. "They are English soldiers. And English soldiers never forget their good manners."'

'Thank you, Mrs Kock,' I say, smiling weakly. 'Now if—'

'One more thing. These sheets are to protect the furniture. Especially the table with polished walnut in the master bedroom, which you should know belonged to the Admiral himself. My husband says we should have thought of this earlier, but we have not been used to the war in Arnhem. For four years, it has been a quiet place, and that is how we imagined it would remain.'

'I'm sure it will all be over very soon, Mrs Kock.'

'The tea. I insist you let us serve you the tea. It is very special. We had been saving it for the day of liberation,' she says, trying to sidestep past me.

'Thank you, Mrs Kock,' I say, blocking her passage in the nick of time. I retrieve the tray from the maid.

Mrs Kock, sensing defeat, heads back towards the cellar. The maid follows.

At the bottom of the stairs, Mrs Kock stops and calls up to me, 'If you could just ask your men to be careful with those cups. They belonged to my great-grandmother.'

I'm woken by the sound of my name. The air is foul with the smell of burnt paint, rubber and oil, and the room, almost unpleasantly warm, flickers with an orange glow. My gorge rises;

I'm now horribly awake and ready for immediate action. But then the panic subsides, as I remember the cause of the heat and the flames. It's not our house which is on fire but the bridge itself.

Last night, at about 21.00 hours, a fighting patrol was sent to neutralise the stubborn concrete blockhouse which held up yesterday's advance across the bridge. With them, they took a flame-thrower, which they tried directing into the embrasure, only to miss and end up hitting a neighbouring ammunition shed instead. The fireworks were spectacular and the blockhouse was cleared. But it put paid to any immediate attempts to capture the far end of the bridge. Attackers and defenders alike would have been roasted alive.

I glance at my watch. 03.30 hours.

03.30 hours? I distinctly asked Cholmondeley to wake me up at 02.30 hours, so as to give me plenty of time to make ready for stand-to – the hour in the run-up to dawn, when the Germans most commonly launch their attacks.

That's his voice I can hear outside, I think. What's he saying?

'. . . better for all of us if he was out of our hair.'

'Oh, you did, did you, Corporal?' says a soft, well-spoken voice instantly recognisable as Maj. Gough's. 'And you imagine it's your place to make these command decisions, just when we're expecting a major enemy assault?'

'It's not that, sir, it's . . .'

'Corporal, you've said your piece and to my ears it sounds little short of mutiny. Now get upstairs and have the men clear the decks. We've a busy morning ahead of us.'

I just have time to pull myself out of the armchair and brush off the worst of the plaster dust coating my uniform when the OC strides in, looking more than ever like a rumpled uncle, with tufts of white hair poking from beneath his beret.

'Dick, my dear fellow, good to see you,' says the OC. 'I should think we both deserve a drink, don't we?'

'Probably, sir.'

'Only probably?' he says, pouring two measures from a hip flask. 'You made it here in one piece, didn't you?'

'Minus Sarnt Price and half my section.'

'And I've just lost 90 per cent of my squadron, but I'm not putting on the sackcloth just yet. It's horrid. But we've got to make the best of it. Chin, chin!' He downs his drink in one. I down mine. Cognac, I think.

'I would have come down earlier but I was tied up at Brigade HQ,' he says. 'How are you getting on with your new comrades?'

He means the platoon from 2nd Battalion which Brigade HQ sent to reinforce us a few hours ago. They seem a decent enough lot, led by a subaltern named Mills so fresh-faced he makes Wood look like Methuselah. Claims to know me from school, though I don't remember him because he would have been four or five years below me.

'Very well, thank you. Of course, the chaps were all of the view that being Recce men they could quite easily have held the house by themselves.'

'But of course,' says the OC with a laugh.

'And I think their platoon sergeant has rather put Cholmondeley's nose out of joint. He was enjoying being senior NCO.'

I only mention this, you'll gather, in order to draw the OC out on that worrying conversation I overheard.

'Ah. That might explain his bolshiness just now,' says the OC. 'Behaving himself generally, is he?'

'If I'm honest, sir, I fear he does not love me as he ought.'

'But I'm presuming all's well with you and that you're feeling up to the job.'

'Of course, sir.'

'Sorry. Impertinent to have asked. But I can't stress enough how important it is, when we're fighting alongside show-offs like 2nd Battalion, that we acquit ourselves in our finest traditions.'

135

'I understand, sir.'

'Thought you would. And it's just as well you do, for you might as well know now, this op isn't turning out to be quite the pushover we'd hoped.'

The OC fills me in on what happened. Turns out, as I feared, that shortly after they crossed over the railway line at the Wolfheze level crossing, and turning right down a farm track running parallel with the railway, Lt. Randall ran slap bang into an ambush.

'Were there many casualties?' I ask.

'We were still trying to clear them when I left. Not exactly helped by Jerry. When the MO went in with his Red Cross flag clearly visible, he damned near got his head shot off.'

'That's not on.'

'Never were, though, the Waffen SS.'

'SS?'

'Ah. Allow me to break the good news. Turns out that, contrary to earlier reports, we shall not after all be playing the village B side. Instead, Jerry's decided to field the full County XI, including his 9th and 10th SS Panzer Divisions.'

'But that can't be right, surely. They were wiped out in Normandy.'

'Well, for ghosts, they fire pretty solid bullets.'

I remember the whoosh of the 20-mm cannon shell over my head and those fit, eager men in spotted camouflage leaping from the back of the armoured car.

'And they've armour, too, presumably.'

'Not too much, we hope.'

'We *hope*?'

'Not a word of this to the men, old boy, but strictly *entre nous* this operation's starting to look like Pandora's box.'

9

Gräbner's Last Stand

'Quick, Mr Coward! Quick! They're here! They're bloody here!' yells Wood, bursting breathlessly into the large, top-floor bedroom which we Recce men have bagged for ourselves, leaving the rest of the house to the 2nd Battalion platoon.

His inane grin is so infectious that, at first, in my dulled, numb, tired state, I think he means Price and co.

'Are they all all right?'

'Hard to tell from a distance. Come and see for yourself.'

'Who's here? Grassy? Tiger? Bleackley?' calls back Beckford from behind his Bren. Like me, he's distracted because his new temporary number two – a chap named Chalky White on loan from 2nd Battalion – was in the midst of reading aloud to us all the good bits from *Lady Chatterley's Lover*. They found it in a locked study, beneath a portrait of Adolf Hitler, which served the most useful purpose of assuaging our guilt over what we'd done to Mr and Mrs Kock's home.

'Not our lot. Second Army.'

'Second Army? That all?' says Beckford, in mock exasperation.

'Yeah, talk about coitus interruptus,' grumbles Hughes, who has also been enjoying the reading. Chalky does a very good gamekeeper accent, and has a particularly expressive way with all the expletives. In fact the only one of us who hasn't been enjoying the show is Cpl. Cholmondeley – which is the main reason I've been encouraging it.

'Want me to go, sir?' says Cholmondeley.

'No, I suppose I'd better,' I say, with a certain affected languor.

Of course, underneath, we're all just as thrilled as Wood. It means our job is almost done and the battle effectively won. But, when you've been keying yourself up for the fight to end all fights, it's hard not to feel a sense of mild anticlimax.

Besides which, there's the terrible, unnecessary destruction. I'm thinking not just of all the lovely old houses like this one which have been trashed to no purpose, and of all the families rendered homeless, but also of the innocent victims like the fellow who made the grave mistake just now of trying to do his Monday morning round in his dustbin lorry.

An ordinary Dutchman doing his job caught out and annihilated by an accident of history. Did he have any idea, I wonder, of the danger he was in, before the bullets ripped into his cab from a dozen windows and turned him into a human colander? Did the men who did the shooting – and Beckford was one, I'm afraid – even stop to ask themselves what threat he posed, before they opened up?

I clamber up the ladder which leads through a hole in the attic floor and up to the rooftop observation post we've made by removing some tiles. There's a Bren team too; and a sniper; and a chap with a PIAT, which I doubt would have been much use against armour at this range so it's just as well he now has no need to try. Lt. Mills, who has arrived just ahead of me, is peering through his binoculars towards the vehicles whose clinking tracks and grinding engines are clearly audible at the south end of the bridge.

'I don't know, Walker,' he muses to the private standing by his side. 'Without seeing the markings it's hard to—' He looks round and smiles when he sees it's me. 'We need a second opinion, Dick. Theirs or ours?'

I squint through his binoculars. (I've a lovely pair of Zeiss at home, borrowed from a German officer. But I prefer not taking them into action because of the attention they attract from snipers.)

Even through the smoke and predawn murk it doesn't take very long. The motorcycle/sidecar combinations are the giveaway: we don't really go in for them. And half-tracks, if they were Allied, would be much more likely in a US unit than in Guards Armoured Division. As for the armoured cars, they bear rather too strong a resemblance to the ones that spoiled our afternoon yesterday.

'Bollocks!' I say with feeling.

'Oh dear, are you sure?' says Lt. Mills.

At the far side of the bridge, there's a whoosh of incoming and the approach road erupts. A motorcycle and its sidecar leap into the air, its rider and passenger shooting even higher above them, before spinning back downwards, their bodies black against a wall of orange flame. Men run for cover. A half-track explodes.

'Our artillery is,' I say.

'Second Army is?' yells Lt. Mills.

'Rather looks that way,' I say.

'I say, Dick. You don't mind me calling you Dick, do you?'

'Not at all, um, Tom, isn't it?'

'Tommy, if you like.'

'Tommy then.'

'What I was going to – phew, that was a big one! – I brought a bottle of fizz, especially for this moment. It was a devil to fit in my small pack, but I'm jolly glad I made the effort because, well, an occasion like this calls for a toast.'

'Perhaps not just yet.'

'No?'

'Well, if you had an armoured division coming at you on one

side, and five hundred or so lightly armed paratroopers on the other side, and you were Jerry, which way would you head?'

For about a minute it looks as if they've got away with it. The two lead armoured cars thread their way round the smouldering wrecks of some lorries that we shot up on the bridge last night, and over a necklace of mines which one of our patrols stretched across the road.

'Jammy beggars!' someone exclaims as the rope linking the mines catches under the wheels of the lead car, dragging behind it for several yards without anything actually detonating.

Then the second car bumps over the mines, also without effect, and after that we've had enough. Almost simultaneously, from every roof, window, slit trench and mortar pit in the rooms and grounds of at least twenty different houses spread either side of the bridge, every man opens up with whatever weapon he has to hand. Brens stutter in short, aimed bursts, Stens and Tommy guns crackle, rifles pop, spitting such a quantity of concentrated lead at the approaching vehicles that you'd imagine nothing could possibly survive.

And as it turns out, very little can. Thanks to a fiendish bit of foresight from one of our gunners, we've preblasted a V-shaped nick into the parapet of the bridge. This means the 6-pounder anti-tank gun we've concealed in the street below can pump round after round into the approaching vehicles with virtual impunity.

Quite literally, they don't know what's hit them. The next armoured car slews to a halt with an armour-piercing round through its engine, and the one behind slams into its back and almost immediately bursts into flames. Only the commander manages to escape before the thing brews up, and he's quickly cut down by bullets from so many different directions his corpse doesn't know which way to judder.

After the armoured cars come the half-tracks, the lucky ones covered, but most of them open-topped with the men sitting in ranks in the back quite horrendously exposed to the fire being poured down them at near point-blank range. One or two make a hopeless attempt to climb out and run in search of cover (of which there's little, if any), but the majority don't even have time to move, packed so closely together as they are, and no doubt staying put in the vain hope that their driver can somehow steer them a way out of this mess.

One half-track, reversing out of trouble, topples backwards over the parapet and lands upside down on the road 30 feet below, crushing all the men in the back. Another gets as far as the exit ramps only to tumble down a bank, where its men are cut to pieces in a hail of bullets and grenades. Most simply pile into one another, in the central killing zone packed with flaming vehicles and burning, screaming men.

It's the screaming that haunts me most. Death by fire is such an awful, ugly way to go – the one I've feared more than anything since my days as a flier, and only reinforced by the time I spent in tanks in the desert. God knows, I've heard that awful animal wail often enough through my RT headset as yet another of my friends shrieks his last, but at least on those occasions it's only one or two men you can hear dying.

Here, the Germans are being burned alive by the two or three dozen simultaneously, and it's like listening to a chorus of harpies, some screeching and shrill, some giving a deep bellowing roar, some quite inhuman, each registering a different note of fear, agony, desperation, or appalled recognition that this is how it ends, this is how it's to be, not with nobility or dignity but as a bubbling, fizzing, spitting mass of hissing, blackened pain.

There's a rifle going spare. I lean out of one of the window-frames, elbow on the ledge, not caring overmuch how exposed I am, for it seems such a one-way contest. I aim for the heads to put them out of their misery.

The others appear to be enjoying the whole business much more than I am.

'Fuck me, this is fucking brilliant!' yells our temporary recruit Chalky as he changes the barrel on a Bren gun sizzling from overuse.

'How many?' calls Hughes, blazing away with his Sten. It's a close-range weapon, but at this distance, with the targets so concentrated, its pretty impossible not to miss.

'Two dozen?' says Beckford.

'I meant kills not barrels,' says Hughes.

'Ha ha,' says Beckford.

'Less talk, more shooting,' says Cpl. Cholmondeley, taking careful aim.

I pull back from the window, for a moment quite unable to continue. It's not just the piteous wails – '*Mutti*', some of them are shrieking, '*Mutti*' – it's that terrible, sweet barbecue smell of charring pork, which fills the nostrils and coats the back of the throat. I take a sip from my canteen. Still the taste won't go away. I feel as if I might be sick, but something prevents me.

Cpl. Cholmondeley is observing me.

'Bit rich for you, Mr Coward?' he says, slotting another magazine into his Schmeisser.

'Don't mind me, Corporal. You go ahead and enjoy yourself.'

'Oh I am, sir. But then, these people are not my friends,' he says.

On the bridge my eye is caught by a lone figure who has burst suddenly from behind a burning half-track, like a grouse breaking cover, and is running in a panicked zigzag from one side of the bridge to the other. He has cast aside his weapon, and removed his helmet so that you can clearly see the determined expression of animal desperation on his drawn features.

I follow his progress through my sights.

He wants to live, God, how he wants to live. I know the feeling. The difference between this chap and his comrades is that, for the moment, his wish is staying true.

There's more lead in the air than there is on the roofs at Hampton Court, yet Aryan wonderboy here seems quite impervious to it. Wherever he runs, the bullets either end up just in front of him, just behind him, or a fraction above him.

'Will you look at that!' declares Hughes.

'Drop him, Beckford!' orders Cpl. Cholmondeley.

'Give us half a mo, Corp. We've got a jam,' says Beckford, working with Chalky to clear the obstruction from his Bren.

Cpl. Cholmondeley shakes his head and empties his magazine in the German's direction. Not one of the bullets strikes home.

'Get on with it!' he shrieks at Beckford.

'We're trying, Corp,' says Beckford.

'Seems a shame, though, in a way,' muses Hughes. 'I mean—'

'Kill him!' snaps Cholmondeley as the bullets from his long next burst spark and ricochet harmlessly off the tarmac by the German's boots and the concrete parapet behind his pounding torso and heaving head.

Hughes's burst is even further behind. Rather as if he wasn't even trying.

'You missed!' says Cholmondeley.

'Well, he is only a sparks, Corp,' says Beckford.

'You missed *deliberately*!' says Cholmondeley, in thunderstruck disbelief.

The SS man has now disappeared from view, quite possibly still alive, which for at least some of our contingent has been a cause for celebration. I'm sure those were cheers I heard coming from the other side of the mousehole leading to next door's room when he clambered over the parapet and launched himself off into heaven knows where.

Cpl. Cholmondeley, however, is taking it personally.

'You deliberately disobeyed my order, Hughes. You'll be punished for this.'

'Not without my say-so, Cholmondeley,' I say.

He glares at me, on the verge of saying something I intend to make him regret.

'There he goes!' shouts Beckford.

'Where?' says Hughes.

'On the roof of that lorry down there. It's broken his fall.'

'Fuck me. He's got the luck of the devil,' says Wood.

'Nobody shoot,' says Cholmondeley, clipping another magazine into his Schmeisser. 'He's mine.'

When I lean out of the window for a better look, I notice that the men in the room next door are following his progress with equal interest. The chaps on the floor below, too.

'"*Run, rabbit, run, rabbit run run run!*"' some joker begins to sing, in a quavery, rustic Bud Flanagan voice.

Then they're all at it: '"*Run, rabbit, run, rabbit run run run!*"'

On the bridge, young men burn, scream and writhe. But for the moment, all anyone in our household at least seems to care about is the fate of this solitary young German, now pulling himself unsteadily to his feet after his jump from the lorry roof.

'"*Don't give the farmer his fun fun fun!*"'

He wasn't quite so lucky with his fall this time, for he's now limping heavily, head jerking this way and that in search of somewhere to hide. Seeing nowhere, his eyes alight on the front door of our house. In a final act of desperation, he directs his gaze piteously upwards towards the laughing men of the Flanagan and Allen chorus regaling him from the upper floors.

'*Kamerad!*' he says, hopefully raising his arms.

'Too late for that, my friend!' snarls Cholmondeley, right beside me, steadying his Schmeisser against the window-frame.

I catch his forearm with my elbow only just in time to prevent his long, careful burst hitting its target. Only when I'm sure his magazine is empty do I stop disrupting his aim.

'Hughes, Wood, get down there quick! I want him brought in alive.'

'I knew it!' hisses Cholmondeley, his mouth contorted with a hatred you normally only see on chaps who are trying to bayonet you. '*I knew it!*'

'Whatever it is you knew, Corporal, I should keep it to yourself.'

'Nazi-lover!' he spits.

'You'll retract that remark, Corporal.'

'Do you deny that it is so?'

Interesting that – the way, whenever he gets angry or stressed, his colloquial English seems to become so much more stilted.

'I asked you to retract that remark, Corporal.'

'Remember, Lieutenant, I have seen your tattoo. I have heard also the story of how you acquired it.'

'Idle rumours.'

'Then you deny that you once fought for the Wehrmacht against our Soviet allies?'

'*Bist du Deutsch, vielleicht?*' I ask him suddenly, to throw him off balance.

He doesn't reply but he doesn't need to. I've already caught that brief flicker of comprehension in his eyes.

'*Und Jude, auch?*'

Again he doesn't respond.

'*Oder Kommunist?*'

Yes, of course. That'll be it. He'll be one of those fanatical German Communists who got out just in time.

I would have had a lot more sympathy if he'd been Jewish, I must say. From what I've seen of the Reds in action – and that's rather too much – they're quite as unpleasant a shower as the Nazis. Still, I suppose one has to accept that they are on our side. More or less. For the moment.

'Tell you what, Cholmondeley. How about I stop rattling your skeletons and you stop rattling mine? We'll get on with our jobs and say no more about it. Hmm?'

Cholmondeley regards my extended hand with no less distaste than if I'd been offering him a curl of dog turd.

'Come on, Corporal. Now Price is gone we'll need a good section sergeant.'

'Yeah, go on, Corp. Kiss and make up. It's so much nicer when we're one big happy family,' yells back Beckford between stuttering bursts of his Bren.

'Belt up, Beckford!'

'Yes, Corp.'

Finally, warily, Cholmondeley reaches out his hand to mine, pauses mid-air for a brief wrestle with his better judgement, then clasps my palm hard.

'Very well, Mr Coward,' he says.

The German's name is Otto Schweizer, he's eighteen years old and he's a *Schütze* – a private soldier – in the Reconnaissance Battalion of the 9th SS Panzer Division Hohenstauffen.

'Did you get that, Wood?' I say.

'All sounded German to me, sir,' he says.

'He's one of us. A Recce man!'

We're conducting the interrogation in Mr Kock's study, because being on the opposite side of the house to the bridge it's less exposed to the gun battle still raging outside. I've left Cpl. Cholmondeley in charge of the section.

Wood is sitting in with me guarding the door with his Sten.

Schweizer cups the mug of tea Wood has brewed him in his burned, heavily bandaged hands. His face is blackened, his baggy, camouflage combat jacket singed and stained with oil and blood, his body trembling all over like that of a rabbit with myxomatosis. No doubt he has been well-briefed by his older comrades on what the Red Devils do to captured SS men.

'You speak German well,' he croaks in a small, pathetic voice.

'Thank you,' I say.

'Did you study in Germany?' he asks. No doubt that's another thing he's been advised: in the unlikely event that your captors haven't immediately shot you, try to make them your friends.

'I'm asking the questions,' I remind him.

'Do you mean to kill me?'

'That depends on how well you answer the questions. Cigarette?'

'Thank you.'

Schweizer only joined his unit from training camp a week ago and found the veterans in good spirits, despite the pasting we'd given them in Normandy. The Dutch were not all unfriendly, the countryside was beautiful, and their commander Hauptsturmführer Viktor Gräbner a truly inspirational leader whom his men would gladly have followed to the ends of the earth.

Not four hours ago, Schweizer and his comrades had watched proudly as their divisional commander Lt. Col. Walther Harzer had hung Germany's highest military honour – the Knight's Cross – around Hauptsturmführer Gräbner's throat.

When Hauptsturmführer Gräbner ordered the assault on the bridge, not one man doubted it would succeed. A canny tactician, he knew well how to exploit our lazy habits. Instead of attacking at stand-to, when we would all be on full alert, he would time his assault for just afterwards. '"When Tommy always makes his tea," Herr Hauptsturmführer Gräbner said.'

The minutes before the assault had been the most tense and exciting of young Schweizer's life. A bit nerve-wracking, of course, but since none of his comrades was showing any fear, Schweizer decided that he mustn't either. Was it not for this that he had volunteered for the elite SS rather than the lowly Wehrmacht?

As the armoured cars and half-tracks warmed and revved their engines and the air began to fill with choking, silvery-grey exhaust fumes, Schweizer was reminded of that thrilling day in 1937 when his father had taken him to the Nürburgring to watch the late, great Bernd Rosemeyer – 'another good SS man' – win the German Grand Prix. And when Muller, the unit's hoary Sturmscharführer, who'd famously lost his arm on the Eastern Front to the sword of a Cossack he'd simultaneously shot with a Luger, offered him a cigarette his happiness was complete. Schweizer thought to himself, 'I'm a man!'

With this stirring thought in his head, Schweizer found it easy to withstand the shock of the sudden, violent artillery barrage which obliterated the crew of the motorcycle combination barely 3 metres from where he sat waiting in the back of his half-track. They knew because one of the wheels flew right over their heads, and because a motorcycle gauntlet dropped into Otto's lap with the owner's hand still inside.

Everyone went very silent at that, till Muller picked it up and said, 'Ah. Just what I needed,' and pretended to try to fit it onto the end of his stump.

That's how they began the assault, roaring with laughter and with tears in their eyes.

'*MARSCH! MARSCH!*' they heard Hauptsturmführer Gräbner yell from the Humber armoured car he'd captured from us in Normandy, as he punched the air with his fist.

Forward they accelerated, not as fast as they would have liked, for fully laden half-tracks are underpowered and slow. But at least now that they were on the bridge, the artillery had stopped. 'The British are afraid of destroying the bridge,' someone said. Schweizer found himself secretly wishing they had done. The half-tracks were nearly at the other side now and still the British hadn't opened fire. The pent-up tension was starting to make his skin crawl. He felt himself subconsciously trying to shrink his body so that when the shooting started he'd offer the smallest possible target.

Schweizer was lucky enough to be blown clear by the same high-explosive shell that killed most of his comrades in the back of the half-track, and just quick enough to outrun the snake of burning fuel that hissed across the road, burning the wounded survivors alive. He looked around for someone to give him orders and saw Muller striding calmly through the wreckage. Muller signalled for Schweizer to follow him forwards, which he did for 15 or so metres before Muller was cut in half by a burst of heavy machine-gun fire and Schweizer took shelter behind a parapet.

Schweizer cowered and watched in appalled fascination as, almost to a man, his battalion was wiped out. He saw dashing Hauptsturmführer Gräbner die and prickly Untersturmführer Hink die and foul-arsed Scharführer Buttlar die and kindly Schütze Schmidt who only yesterday morning had helped him catch a fish from beneath this very bridge die and all those other men in his troop who he hadn't yet got to know but fully expected to over the coming months, yes, he watched them die too. And what he learned in those ten or twenty or thirty minutes of hell is that death does not discriminate between the good and the bad, the noble and the cowardly, the friendly and the unfriendly, the pessimistic and the optimistic. It does not care whether you belong to Herr Hauptsturmführer Gräbner's Reconnaissance Battalion or the most miserable unit of conscripted Ukrainians. When your time is up, it will destroy you with no more compunction than a schoolboy squashing a snail beneath his boot.

'Talks a lot, don't he, sir?' observes Wood in the contemplative silence that follows.

'Yes, but it's quite moving actually. He's talking about how it feels to have your whole unit annihilated.'

'Whatever happened to name, rank and number? I thought they were supposed to be tough as old boots, these fanatical, baby-eating SS killers.'

'Ha!' Schweizer has recovered from his slump and is sitting bolt upright in his chair. Wood's disparaging remark has given him a new sense of purpose.

'*Dann verstehst du Englisch?*' I ask.

'*Natürlich,*' says Schweizer. He glares fiercely at Wood. 'You think I tell you these things because I am not strong, *ja?*' His blackened features suddenly crack into a smile. And definitely not a friendly one. 'No.' He shakes his head. 'I tell you because I want you to know that what has happened to me and my comrades will also soon happen to you and yours.'

'Sir, what's the German for, "Piss off, Fritz. You don't know what you're talking about?"'

'Sorry to disappoint you, Schweizer, but that barrage that made such a mess of your motorcyclist chums just now. Where do you think that came from?' I say.

Schweizer shrugs.

'From the west somewhere? I do not know. It is of no consequence.'

'From the south, you mean. Don't play silly buggers. You know it came from the south.'

'You think it came from the south?' says Schweizer, cracking that rictus smile again. 'That is funny. That is very, very funny.'

'Fuck me, sir, if it makes a German laugh, it must be the funniest thing since Buster Keaton!'

'I'm not sure that I get the joke,' I say.

'You think it came from the south because you want it to have come from the south. From your forces in Nijmegen, no?' says Schweizer.

I shrug.

'You tell me.'

'With pleasure I will tell you,' he says. 'Between Arnhem and Nijmegen there is an island called Betuwe, yes?'

'What is this, sir? A geography test?'

'Before your forces can relieve you they must cross that island, yes? So, yesterday, when Hauptsturmführer Gräbner sees your *Fallschirmjäger* come down and hears reports that American *Fallschirmjäger* are landing to the south, he guesses at once what is happening and what we must do to stop it. Last night, we race from Arnhem to Nijmegen across Betuwe island. And do you know what we see?'

'Proper little Sphinx, isn't he, sir?'

'Germans. Everywhere Germans. Not Americans or British but Germans!'

'Go on. Tell us the punchline. They're all dead, right?'

'Joke now if you wish, for you will not be joking much longer. Your relief forces are not coming. They are never coming. They are stuck on the south bank of the River Waal, bunched up like cattle in the market so that our artillery may more easily slaughter them. And you are stuck here, surrounded. You are trapped. You will die here like dogs just as my battalion died like dogs. That is why I tell you my story. And now, if you wish, you can kill me. I do not care. For as I am, my friends, so you soon shall be.'

Later that afternoon, I take advantage of a lull in the fighting to visit the OC a couple of blocks away at Brigade HQ. Wood comes with me for back-up, for in the ebb and flow of street fighting, you never know quite who you are going to bump into next. Schweizer, I entrust to the tender cares of Cholmondeley, who has become much more amenable since our hand-shaking entente. 'You can reminisce about the good times in Germany,' I very nearly say, for, like most of the men, I'm feeling decidedly skittish after this morning's achievements.

I return, rather later than I would have liked, in a much more sober frame of mind. And also – as we shall see, with unfortunate consequences – a slightly more jittery one.

The sobriety is the result of the conversation I've just had with Maj. Gough. We talk about this and that – the intelligence I've gleaned from Schweizer, the worrying shortage of ammunition, the decreased likelihood that any of the other parachute battalions will reach us tonight – when he gives me one of his avuncular smiles and says, 'Well, Dick. I've got some good news and some bad news. Mind if I give you the good news first?'

'If you like.'

'The good news, old bean, is that you've just become odds-on favourite to inherit the Coward family estate.'

'Has something – has something happened to my brother?'

'Eh? Lord no. Or if it had we certainly wouldn't know. We've heard nothing from 30 Corps since we landed. No, I meant rather your arrangement with your father.'

'Ah.'

'Look, you can always say no. It's volunteers-only, this mission. Colonel Frost – you know he's been promoted to Brigade Commander? Major Jackson's taken over Second Battalion – is calling it a "flying column". Unofficially, we're his "suicide squad". But it's top gongs all round if we pull it off.'

The mission is indeed pretty dicey. Tomorrow morning, before dawn, Maj. Gough and myself will attempt to perform a reverse Hauptsturmführer Gräbner. With us commanding the two lead jeeps, and a Bren-gun carrier chasing behind, we shall zoom across the bridge, shooting up anything that moves, and somehow capture the far end in a *coup de main*.

'How does that sound?'

'Optimistic?'

'Think of it as common courtesy. We've got the Poles landing

152

tomorrow and you know how upset they'd be if there was no one there to greet them. You game?'

'But of course.'

'Good man. Knew you would be.'

I try to comfort myself with the thought of Price, sitting on his heavenly cloud, or wherever he is now, nodding his grumpy approval. 'Never, never, NEVER volunteer,' he always used to say to me. But the way he's been banging on about that wretched VC this last couple of months, I'm presuming he would have made an exception in this case.

Then I remind myself of those stories I used to read as a child about impetuous young ensigns in the Peninsular War volunteering to lead the Forlorn Hope in the charge against the enemy ramparts. And how much I envied and admired the ones who miraculously survived, and were rewarded with instant promotion, high honour and eternal glory.

But there's still a part of me that wants just to slink off, there and then, and put a bullet in my head. At least I'd have the business over with.

By this stage there seemed to be Germans absolutely bloody everywhere. First time Wood and I tried leaving Brigade HQ, we were delayed by a pair of German Mk III tanks clanking past, spraying the buildings either side with their machine guns until some brave soul put a PIAT up their arse and sent them packing. Then, after we'd waited what we thought was a decent interval, we were just on the verge of leaving a second time when we heard an English voice calling from the other side of the front door.

'Quick mate, let us in,' it hissed.

'All right, chum, we're just leaving,' replied Wood, pulling the door open.

Soon as he'd done so, there, bold as brass, stood a man in German uniform holding some sort of cloth package which he proceeded to lob inside our entrance hallway.

Wood was so shocked he didn't even think to close the door, which was just as well, since it gave the experienced Sergeant who had been standing just behind him the chance to give the package a flying kick-back in the direction it came from. Only then did Wood have the presence of mind to slam shut the door, after which, almost immediately, there was a very loud crump from outside.

'There's been a lot of that going on recently,' said the Sergeant to me, quite unfazed, as we cautiously poked our heads out to inspect the result. There wasn't an awful lot of the German left. 'Take my advice, sir. If you don't hear them use the password straight away, shoot the buggers.'

We return to find our position in a considerably worse state than we left it. The walls are all riddled with bullet holes, there are chunks of plasterwork dangling precariously from the ceiling, and everywhere there's dust which clogs your eyelids, fouls your throat and thickens your nostrils with dry, scabby bogies.

'What the hell did this?' I ask, inspecting a gaping hole in the outer wall. Armour-piercing, I'd guess. You can see the exit hole on the other side of the room. Damned lucky no one was standing in the way.

'We think it was a rat, sir, after Darkie's chicken stew.'

'Chicken stew, eh? You kept some for me, I hope?'

Cpl. Cholmondeley and the men all study the floor. Selfish swine have scoffed the lot, and all we've left now of the tinned rations is bloody Spam. I knew there was something shifty about their manner.

'And apart from proving yourself a bunch of greedy swine, any other developments?'

Again, an exchange of shifty looks – the men deferring to Cpl. Cholmondeley.

'Not especially, sir.'

'And you're all clear on the new position regarding ammo?'

'Whites of their eyes, sir?' says Beckford.

'Smell of their breath, more like. We were far, far too profligate this morning. From now on, unless you can be sure of a kill, don't shoot.'

'We have been doing our best to hold back, sir. Problem is, Jerry's cottoned on,' says Hughes.

'Been taking the piss, in fact,' says Chalky White.

'Yeah, till he gets to within a hundred yards he doesn't bother even trying to keep his head down,' says Beckford.

Wood seizes the cue to regale everyone with the tale of our narrow escape at Brigade HQ.

'Gave you a nasty turn by the looks of it. You especially, sir. You're all pale,' says Cholmondeley. I'm not sure I like this exaggerated concern for my welfare. Particularly since he's probably right. The thought of tomorrow's suicide mission has rather unnerved me.

'Nothing that can't be resolved with a bit of Spam and some tea,' I say. 'Wood, do you want to see to it?'

'Right away, sir.'

'Has the prisoner been fed yet?'

'Sir?' says Cpl. Cholmondeley.

'Schweizer. Has he been fed yet? I did ask you to take care of him.'

'Yes, sir.'

'Where is he?'

Cpl. Cholmondeley's hard grey eyes settle on mine just long enough to deliver their challenge. Then they look away. His Adam's apple bobs in his throat, but he doesn't speak.

'Well?'

'We took care of him, sir,' he says, in a flat, matter-of-fact voice.

At first I think he's being stupid. Or insolent. Or that he's mis-heard me.

'Yes, of course you did. That's what I –' I begin. Then it dawns.

I take a long deep breath.

'I see.' I'm trying to maintain an aura of calm until I can be absolutely sure that he means what I think he means. 'And where is he now?'

'In the study, sir.'

'You'd better show me.'

The study appears to be empty. But it's in a terrible state. The bookshelves have collapsed and their contents have formed a pile, like a loose pyramid, on the floor by Mr Kock's writing desk. Then in the fast-fading light, I notice the dark pool spreading out from underneath.

Cpl. Cholmondeley stands impassively beside me.

'Clear those books, will you, Corporal?'

'Yes, sir.'

When he's done, he steps to one side, the better that I may admire his handiwork.

Schweizer's skin is a bluey-white, except for the long, deep, crimson gash across his neck.

What galls me most is the arrogance of the gesture. The death of an SS prisoner I can more or less take. Not least after what they did to us, that time in Dunkirk. But the cold-bloodedness, the cynicism, the arrant disregard for my orders – now those are something else. Damn it, Cholmondeley hasn't even tried to make it look as if Schweizer has been shot while trying to escape.

'Corporal, did you give any thought to what Jerry might do if he finds Schweizer's body in this condition?' I say, surprised by the calmness of my voice. I suppose it's because I'm trying to behave not as I feel like doing – viz: fly off the handle, threaten him with demotion and court-martial – but rather to behave as

I think Price would have done in a situation like this. Pragmatism before emotion.

'Jerry's not going to find him, is he, sir?'

'What, you think he might be foxed by your cunning books-pyramid tomb, do you?'

'No, sir. Because I wasn't planning on ever surrendering our position. Were you?'

In the end Cholmondeley and I reach a shabby compromise with which I can't pretend I'm happy. We wrap Schweizer's corpse in a rug and I help him lug it downstairs, through the back door and into the yard where we've harboured our jeeps and where, in the gathering darkness, we're less likely to be observed.

'Don't think this is the end of it,' I snap, furious with myself for not having dealt with the matter more firmly.

But what was I supposed to do? Have him put under close arrest? Demote him? Until XXX Corps relieve us, we're going to need all the good fighting men we can spare. Besides which I was relying on him to take over command of the section while I'm engaged on tomorrow's suicide mission.

As we heave the rolled rug through the back door, the sentry from 2nd Battalion guarding it says, 'Good idea, sir. Them carpets was looking far too shabby.'

'Right. Bit further. You drag. I'll cover,' I whisper, as we venture further into no-man's-land. Though the sniper risk has diminished with the fading light, this is just the time when Jerry likes to send out his patrols to probe our defences.

The streets have gone quiet for the moment, which only adds to the menace. Your ears conjure from the silence all sorts of ominous noises: the clack of a hobnailed boot; the squeak of a tank track; the click of a rifle bolt. And in the smoke and flickering shadows cast by the burning building Brigade HQ has ordered set alight so as to illuminate the bridge, a thousand

and one Germans appear to scurry, crawl and take slow careful aim.

Cholmondeley's breathing as he drags the body sounds as loud as a steam train.

'Shut up, you bloody fool, you'll get us shot,' I think, pointing my Sten now this way, now that. My nerves really are in shreds. Hunger, probably. Should have eaten that Spam before I left.

A few more yards and I've had enough.

'This'll do,' I whisper, pressing myself against a wall.

Cholmondeley unrolls the rug and then pushes Schweizer's body into the gutter with his foot. He crouches down, about to pull the pin from a 36 grenade, which he's going to leave beside Schweizer's neck, when I signal for him to stop.

I've heard a noise. Coming from between us and our house.

Or am I imagining it?

We remain frozen for a few seconds.

Cholmondeley indicates that he's seen something. He jabs a finger towards a pile of rubble. Nothing. All is still. Then suddenly a head pops up. The figure is so busy investigating the rear door, inspecting our defences, that he hasn't seen us.

I wait for the sentry's challenge.

The sentry hasn't seen him.

He's nearly at the door, his weapon ready.

'Halt,' I yell.

He wheels round in surprise to face me.

'AIR,' I call out.

'BORNE,' he's supposed to reply, but if he does, I certainly don't hear him and he's got a submachine pointing straight at me. I think it's a Schmeisser.

I fire before he does. A very short burst but it's enough. The figure crumples to the floor.

There appears to be no more movement.

'Grenade!' hisses Cholmondeley.

We sprint back to the house, yelling to the sentry, 'It's us. 1st Recce. Don't shoot.'

Behind us the grenade explodes.

'AIR?' calls the sentry.

'BORNE,' we yell back, leaping over the slumped body and bursting through the back entrance.

'What was that all about?' says the sentry, once we've recovered our breath. All now seems to be quiet outside.

'Some cheeky bugger, trying to creep up on us.'

'You get him?'

'Yes, but I think he caught one of ours.'

I look askance at Cholmondeley. What has he noticed that I haven't? Cholmondeley replies with a quick shake of his head, raising a forefinger to his lips. It's for my eyes, not the sentry's. I still don't understand what he's getting at, but I resolve not to say anything till I know.

'Should I have a butcher's, sir?' says the sentry.

'Go ahead.'

Cholmondeley and I keep him covered, while the sentry slips cautiously through the door.

He bends down by the body.

'Fuck me!' he says.

'What's the matter?'

'It's our OC. Major Jackson. That fucking German's gone and killed him.'

With a terrible lurch in the pit of my stomach, I look across, aghast, at Cholmondeley.

IO

Twinkle Twinkle

Do you still have those stars above your bed, Jack? The luminous yellow ones stuck to the ceiling that form a Milky Way to entrance you when you turn off the light? They never used to entrance me, I'm afraid.

I never mentioned this when you were younger and I hesitate to bring it up now. But what they've always made me think of is the charnel-house scene in the cellar on the Tuesday after the landings.

The stench down there is something else – as you can well imagine of a dank, crowded, windowless chamber crowded with dead, dying and wounded men. Excrement blends with stale sweat, urine, burnt flesh, vomit and the cloying smell of rotting meat to form an aroma so powerful you'd probably gag if it weren't for the medicinal notes of iodine and the revivifying whiff of cordite.

It's not the smell I remember most, though, nor the pitiful groans, but the flecks of brightness speckling each prostrate form. They glow in the men's hair, on their exposed raw flesh, on their bandages and even from within their wounds, as if they've all been sprinkled with fairy dust. But it's not nice fairies that did this. It's the phosphorus from the shells which the German tanks have been firing at us all day, trying to reduce all our positions to rubble.

And they've been doing a damned good job of it, too. On Sunday, we held round about eighteen houses at the north end of the bridge. Now we're down to ten, the rest having since either fallen to the enemy, or been burnt to the ground or been blasted by tanks and artillery to a pile of bricks. This has been helpful in a way. The debris means their tanks are having great difficulty manoeuvring close enough to finish us off. Plus, of course, it affords our chaps plenty of cover for ambushes. But there's only so much you can do when you're outnumbered, low on rations, sleep and ammo, and your casualties are mounting by the hour. If XXX Corps don't turn up soon, we're beginning to suspect we might have to start rethinking our holiday plans.

'FUCK,' gasps a private, as one of the orderlies, Minns, yanks a splinter from his arm.

'Less of that, son. There's ladies present.'

'Sorry, Corp, but if they hurt as much as that fucking did they'd fucking understand.'

'Don't worry, Corporal,' says Mrs Kock, as she changes the dressing of a man propped against a nearby wall. 'I have heard much worse from my husband. And Rita, she fortunately speaks no English.'

Rita looks up briefly at the mention of her name then back at the pallid, shaky boy whose limp hand she is holding. She has been whispering to him over and over again in Dutch. The Lord's Prayer.

'Then I hope she don't start learning here, ma'am,' says Cpl. Minns.

'"Worse from my husband?" This cannot be true!' says Mr Kock, not unjovially, pausing to take a breather from his waste-and-filth-cleaning duties. The less of his house there is left, I've noticed, the more agreeable he seems to become. It's as if he's found his purpose at last.

'You are a soldier, my dear, and like all soldiers you swear without even being aware of it,' says Mrs Kock in English, to much appreciative laughter from those men well enough to hear.

'Amen to fucking that, missus!' declares the private to louder laughter, which very abruptly dies in all our throats as from upstairs we hear an explosion followed by a brisk exchange of much-too-close-for-comfort gunfire.

At the top of the stairs, the cellar door is kicked open. Those of us who are capable look anxiously upwards and, as our eyes try to adjust to the light streaming in, we see two figures silhouetted in the door frame. One is holding a machine pistol, the other a small length of wood with a thick metal protrusion at the end. Both are wearing coal-scuttle helmets.

I fumble for the Colt .45 in my holster – stupidly I hadn't thought to bring my Sten – but it's far too late for that. The stick grenade has been tossed downwards, the Schmeisser has started to chatter, sending sharp, popping echoes all round the cellar walls. But not before two remarkable things have happened, almost simultaneously, which ever since have brought tears of pride and amusement to my eyes.

The first is Cpl. Minns bounding suddenly forward to place his heavy six-foot frame at the base of the cellar steps, arms open wide like an England goalkeeper trying to put a German striker off his penalty.

The second is Mr Kock, hands spread like a fielder in the slips ready for his catch. This strikes me as odd, given that as a Dutchman he can surely never have played a game of cricket in his life. What's odder still, though, is that he succeeds in catching that grenade.

And what's truly miraculous – a miracle to which perhaps a dozen of us owe our lives – is that he has the time and the skill and the confidence to lob the grenade he has caught right past Cpl. Minns's ear, up the cellar stairs and back through the open door where it lands in the hallway and explodes, killing both Germans.

But not, unfortunately, before the one with the Schmeisser has loosed off that first deadly burst, all of which ends up in the chest, groin and face of brave Cpl. Minns. Minns tumbles backwards, landing directly on top of Rita, who in turn is forced down on top of the dying boy she is trying to comfort. Rita lets out a winded yelp; the lad being crushed beneath her rasps a ghastly death rattle; but I'm already halfway up the stairs by then, pistol in hand, for if there are any more Germans where those two came from, we're all in a bit of a pickle.

Just as I'd feared, the two men who were guarding the front entrance are dead, as we'd all be by now if there'd been more Germans around to press their advantage. But here they are now. You can hear their boots and heavy breathing and their scream-ing cry of 'Waho Mohammed!'

Ours, then. Thank heaven.

It's the patrol that was supposed to recapture the house across the road which one of the other platoons abandoned this morn-ing. And little wonder for of all our remaining positions it was by far the most exposed. Unfortunately, it has been deemed of such importance to the integrity of our defensive perimeter that it must be regained at all costs. The dazed, appalled expressions on the first men through the door do not augur well. Nor yet does the sight of their platoon sergeant coming through on a stretcher, contorted face the colour of lead, bloodied rags wrapped around his chest, from which a grisly sucking noise comes every time he tries to breathe.

'And Lieutenant Mills?' I ask the next ashen-faced private through the door.

' 'Ad it,' he croaks.

Then Lt. Mills is brought in, preceded by a waft of roast pork so sweet and pungent I've never been able to enjoy a barbecue since.

Someone must have pumped him with morphine. An awful lot of morphine, for he couldn't not scream, let alone manage a smile as beatific as the one he's got on his charred, cracked face, with burns like the one I can see he's got the length of his naked body and which he, thank heavens, can't.

I think he wants me to come closer. Something in his eyes tells me he does and his eyes, I'm afraid to say, are about the only part of him that are still almost recognisable. Even the blond hair, eyebrows and eyelashes have been burned off, giving him the appearance of one of those desiccated grinning mummies at the British Museum. It takes a considerable effort of will for me to do as I think he wants.

The smell! The purples and oranges and crimsons and charcoal blacks of that mottled, scorched, weeping skin.

I kneel beside him and bring my ear close to his mouth, so he can say what he wants to say and I don't have to look. (Even though part of me wants to.)

The whispery rasp that emerges from his rictus mouth is quite unintelligible.

'Sorry. Didn't quite catch that.'

He tries again.

'No good warm, anyway,' it sounds like.

I don't get it at first, thinking it must be some typically stoical English reference to the flame-thrower tank, which, I'm guessing, is what did for him.

'No, quite,' I agree, with a laugh which sounds to me horribly false, though with luck he'll be too far gone to notice such nuances.

Then, I realise. It's the champagne he means. That champagne he wanted to share with me when XXX Corps arrived.

I try, quick as I can, to think of a more apposite response. You know how annoying it is when one says something witty and the listener pretends to have heard though he clearly hasn't, thus quite wasting one's joke? Well, I don't want this poor man's last thoughts to be, 'Damn it, I made a joke and Coward didn't get it. He didn't get it at all.'

Something about always having liked Glühwein, maybe? Except he might not know what Glühwein is and then I'll have to explain and a joke explained is a joke lost.

Or a pun involving the word 'chill' maybe. 'Chill' as in 'cool', but also as in the surname of one of the German divisional commanders we're currently up against. Bit obscure maybe.

Or some play on the idea of hell freezing over. Except, is it really helpful mentioning hell to someone who has just been burnt to a crisp?

Then I think of it. It's brilliant. Absolutely brilliant. Though I say it myself, one of the wittiest ripostes I've ever dreamed up, and well worth the thirty seconds' mental strain I've put into it.

'Though you could say, Tommy—' I begin cheerily, only to be cut off by a long, dry, papery rattle from Mills's throat.

I look into his dimming eyes, willing him back to consciousness. But the light has gone.

Through the mousehole leading to the next-door room I can hear snatches of Maj. Tatham-Warter's pep talk to my reluctant fighting patrol.

'Battle of Britain . . . Western Desert . . . Stalingrad . . . no officer more experienced in the whole of the British Army . . .'

'Excuse me, sir, but if he's that ruddy good, how come he's still only a subaltern?'

'Ah well,' barks Tatham-Warter. 'You see –'

But I miss his explanation because now Maj. Gough is offering me one of his precious last cigarettes and saying, 'They're terribly good, those 2nd Battalion fellows. I'm sure you needn't worry.'

'Oh I wasn't. Not about them.'

'Cholmondeley?'

I nod and take a deep drag of the cigarette. They taste truly foul on a throat desiccated by dust, thirst and fear. But before a mission like this you can't not have a last cigarette, can you?

'Dick, I know he's a bastard, but at least he's our bastard.'

'Is he, though?'

'You're worried about that German thing?'

'Not that. He quite clearly hates his own people far more than we do.'

'Jewish, is he?'

'Communist, I fear.'

'Well, they are theoretically on our side.'

'Yes, but I don't think he likes what I got up to on the Eastern Front.'

'You think he might try and avenge his Red comrades by putting one in your back, that it?'

'Freddie – do you mind if I tell you something in the strictest confidence?'

'Fire away.'

'I think it was me who shot Major Jackson.'

I keep my voice low as I explain to the OC how it happened. He nods sympathetically, especially when I tell him about not hearing Maj. Jackson give the password. It turns out that he was so notoriously unintelligible that his men used to nickname him 'Mumbles'.

When I'm done, the OC has a good long scratch at one of the tufts of white hair poking from his beret, his expression a mix of pity, confusion, despair and – to judge by his next remark – macabre mirth.

'I could say that to bump off one battalion commander is a

misfortune, whereas to bump off two begins to look like carelessness,' he says eventually. 'But I shan't, for that really would be in poor taste.'

'Yes, sir.'

'Does anybody else know, apart from Cholmondeley?'

'No, sir.'

'Then I think you can at least stop worrying about him putting a bullet in your back.'

'Do you think?'

'Well, all he has to do is let slip to one of the 2nd Battalion chaps what he saw you do to their OC and I expect one of them will do the job for him.' Maj. Gough goes on. 'Still, look on the bright side. At least you and I never had to go through this morning's stunt.'

By this, of course, he means the planned charge in our jeeps across the bridge. It was called off because the Polish drop on the far side of the bridge was cancelled.

'You think we wouldn't have pulled it off?'

'I'm certain we wouldn't. Whereas with this new mission you've a halfway decent chance of coming back smelling of roses. Your friend Mills is up for an MC. Imagine what he might have got if he'd managed to take that wretched position and hold it.'

How the house hasn't collapsed yet I cannot understand, for there's the most enormous great hole on the ground floor where Jerry hammered it earlier with one of his 10-cm guns, and it goes all the way through to the far side where there used to be another house and now there's just a heap of bricks, beams and girders.

Behind the house, in what's left of its garden, are the remnants of the men who tried to hold it – some half buried in their collapsed slit trenches, some quite messy, but the majority of them eerily unscathed with only their stillness and the coating of dust on their bodies to indicate that they're no longer alive. Their weapons have all been taken – by Jerry, one presumes. Things have now got so messed up that, when you hear a Sten burst or a Bren, you instinctively flinch, for the likelihood is it's a German doing the shooting. With the number of Schmeissers and MG42s we now have in our possession, I suspect Jerry has similar difficulties when he hears ours.

Stealthy as rats, we pick our way in Indian file through the debris, alive to every sight and sound: the fat, motionless field-grey arse poking from a bed of miraculously unscathed marigolds; the crackle of burning timbers and the pop-pop-pop of cooking-off rounds; the groans of an uncollected wounded man in no-man's-land; the burnt-out half-track with the ranks of human-shaped lumps of charcoal tumbling out of the back; the crack –

Bugger me, that was close!

– of the sniper's bullet which has just smacked into a wall past my ear.

The private behind me isn't so lucky. Next shot he collapses, drilled straight through the head, so obviously dead it's not worth pausing to check. I don't know his name. The Recce names I know, of course – Cholmondeley, Hughes, Wood, Beckford and his new mate White – but not those of the six 2nd Battalion men who've been volunteered to come with us. Five, rather, now, so that's one less to learn.

We don't know whether or not the house is occupied and the safe way is to check with grenades but Cpl. Cholmondeley isn't having it.

'Cold steel,' he insists and I'm not going to fight him on it. He may be right. It certainly works wonders in those tense moments before we set off.

'Fix bayonets,' I hiss, and sagging shoulders lift and tired, despondent faces suddenly light up with an unholy mix of fear, excitement, menace and vengeful glee. Though I do find it a frightful bore when feminists bang on about men and violence, I suspect that on the issue of bayonets they probably have a point: slotting 12 inches of razor-sharp steel onto the end of your rifle is like having an uncontrollable erection – all you can think about is where you're going to stick it.

In the garden where the slit trenches are, we pause among our dead comrades to regroup and listen. From one of the ground-floor rooms comes the sound of low murmured conversation. Cpl. Cholmondeley, who has been taking point, signals that he's going to go forward alone. I notice two of the 2nd Battalion boys exchanging glances, as if to say, 'Well, this arrangement isn't working out so badly.'

Cpl. Cholmondeley pads carefully forward, keeping low, the sound of his tread masked by the strips of cloth I've had everyone bind round their feet. He disappears through a hole in the wall, holding a fighting knife.

There's a wait which I time as lasting only two minutes, but which feels much longer, after which he re-emerges, wiping his knife on his arm. He beckons towards Wood. Wood points at himself questioningly, to indicate, 'Who, me?'

Cpl. Cholmondeley's brusque response suggests irritation.

'Yes, you, you bloody fool, who do you think I meant?'

Wood goes forward. Hugging the wall either side of the hole, they exchange further signals. I watch him reach down towards the dagger he keeps strapped round his leg. They both disappear into the house.

Next thing I hear is a German voice, saying, quite loudly and clearly, 'Quick! Quick! Downstairs!'

I'm about to call out that they've been spotted, and lead the others to their rescue when, thank goodness, I have the presence of mind to realise that the voice is Cholmondeley's, beckoning more Germans to their doom.

Sure enough, the clatter of boots on the stairs is followed by a strangled gurgling noise, one or two thumps, then a long silence.

Wood and Cholmondeley reappear in the doorway and signal the thumbs-up.

The position is ours.

There's never a dull moment when a tank brews up, and this Flammpanzer is more spectacular than most. The black-clad commander comes rocketing from his turret like a cork from a champagne bottle, pursued by glowing, screaming machine-gun rounds, and a tongue of flame so tall it damned near singes our noses, while in the hell down below his crew howl like tortured tomcats till the petrol tank mercifully explodes with a kettle-drum boom, and all is silence save for the groans of the burning panzer-grenadiers crawling for cover, and the hissing, and crackling of the roasting crew as they melt into fat like boars on a spit.

For the men of my fighting patrol peering cautiously through their loopholes and over their window ledges, it's no doubt a scene to be relished. It was a damned good throw of Cholmondeley's, the way he lobbed that explosive charge through the open turret as the commander stood there with his head and shoulders poking out, discussing his battle plans with the panzer-grenadier NCO. And it's certainly no more than they deserve for what they did earlier to poor old Lt. Mills.

All the same, I'm afraid, the stinking pyre below – now belching oily, rubbery black smoke foul with the tang of paint, petrol, high explosive, burnt electrical circuits, and death – fills me with rather more dread than joy. It means that the period of grace during which we've been able to occupy this position unnoticed is now over.

We are no longer the hunters but the hunted.

Knowing full well what's to come I rest the men by turn in

groups of four for a brew and half a tin of stew and a cigarette. For some, I suspect, these will be the last such pleasures they'll enjoy.

Meanwhile, I take a tour of our defences. Being only eleven in total, we've had to spread ourselves pretty thin. But we do at least have two Bren teams, enabling us to punch above the weight of a normal infantry section. God knows, we need all the help we can get.

Behind one of the Brens is the ashen-faced private who told me Lt. Mills had ''ad it'. He doesn't look up, though his number two, who has a pleasant, freckled face, at least manages an embarrassed grin.

'Thanks for doing this,' I say, for want of anything better.

'Didn't have a choice, did we?' he snaps.

'Leave him be, Alf. It's hardly the Lieutenant's fault that Mr Mills copped one,' chides his freckle-faced neighbour. He looks up at me. 'Don't come down too hard on him, sir,' he pleads. 'He's been taking our casualties very personal.'

'Is it true, sir, you got the bastard who got our new OC?'

'Er, yes.'

'Pity you couldn't have brought him in alive. Then we could have all taken our turn with our bayonets.'

'If we did that, Private, we'd be no better than the SS.'

'Better at fighting, sir? Or better people?'

Leaving Private Grim to his vengeful thoughts, I inspect the upper floor, where all the Recce men are, save for Beckford who's downstairs with White among the dead in the slit trenches, covering the rear entrance.

I find Cholmondeley alone perched on an old sofa, cleaning his spare Schmeisser. With his close-cropped, prematurely grey hair, dark stubble and air of cool assurance, he looks every inch the 'alter Hase' – the wily 'old hare' NCO – who makes every German battlegroup such a formidable prospect.

It's the first time since the shooting incident that we have been alone together. I take a seat next to him and offer him a cigarette. He shakes his head, but does take the square of chocolate I offer instead.

'You did well with that tank,' I say in a soft, low voice.

'Ach. They were too cocky.'

'They won't be next time.'

'We Germans do not make the same mistake twice.'

'Then I guessed right,' I say to him in German.

'Was it so difficult?' he replies, also in German.

In the corridor outside, something creaks.

'Actually, you know, it's probably safer if we don't,' I say, returning to English.

Cholmondeley nods. There's an awkward pause which I fill by lighting my cigarette.

'Did you wish to ask me something?' he says.

'Probably,' I say.

'I have not told anyone,' he says. The 'yet' is left clearly hanging.

'Nor have I,' I reply, meaning, of course, his killing of the prisoner.

'Then we are quits,' he says.

'Not really,' I say. 'Mine was an accident that could have happened to anyone. Yours was an act of premeditated murder.'

'Murder?' He smiles sneerily to himself, as if at a private joke. 'Do you think so?'

'And then to go round boasting afterwards.'

Cholmondeley's expression darkens.

'No more would I boast about such a thing than about killing a rat.'

'Everyone seems to know. Even the 2nd Battalion men.'

'I see no harm in that. Perhaps it will, how shall I say, stiffen their sinews?'

Now it's my turn to get cross. Quietly cross, obviously.

'Since when, may I ask, did airborne troops need their sinews stiffening? We're a *corps d'élite*. We fight as determinedly as any British troops have ever fought. You're saying, what, that if only we could take a few lessons from you Germans, then we might actually cut the mustard?'

'*Leck mich am Arsch!*'

'Never mind that.'

'Your tattoo. You got it by fighting with a German machine-gun *Truppe* on the *Ostfront*. That is the story I heard. Is it not true? You can tell me now.'

'All right. Yes.'

'Then you are in a position to tell me what I know to be true, and what you also, I think, know to be true. Germans fight with more conviction, do they not?'

'You do generally when you know the enemy doesn't take prisoners.'

'It is more than that. You know it is. It is a question of spirit. Discipline. Willingness to take casualties. If you English fought like we Germans do, you would have won the war by now.'

'Perhaps. But at what cost to our national character?'

'Ach. Such concerns are a matter for your poets and your philosophers. As soldiers, it is not our job to think of such things. It is simply to fight battles and win. Just now you congratulated me for destroying the tank. But for me this was nothing. This is my profession. So long as you remember that it is yours, too, you have nothing to fear,' he says.

The last part is delivered with a hard meaningful stare, which I presume constitutes some sort of threat.

From not all that far away, we hear a noise that reduces both of us to immediate silence: the ominous clank and squeak of caterpillar track on cobbled surface.

And it's getting louder.

Moments later Wood appears. He's been keeping lookout from what's left of the roof.

'Sir, sir –' he whispers urgently.

'Have you seen it yet?'

He nods. I've never seen him this jittery.

'Well?'

'It's a T-t-t –' he begins. 'A T-t –' he tries and fails again, though I've a fair idea by now that he doesn't mean tomtit, trout stream or Tiller girls taking tea with the 50th Tyne Tees. 'Better come and look, sir.'

I follow him up the ladder, across the precarious eaves, to the hole he's made in the slate roof. They're taking no risks this time. All you can see protruding from the rubble is the angular bulk of the thick frontal armour, and the long, menacing barrel of its 88-mm gun. We've nothing in our armoury that could scratch it at this range, especially not when commander and crew – uncharacteristically for Germans – all appear to have their hatches battened down.

'It is one, isn't it, sir?' asks Wood.

A lot of chaps are so in awe of the beast they won't even say the name. If you'd ever found yourself staring down the barrel of one – like gazing into the splayed arse of hell, it is – you'd most likely find yourself speechless, too.

I don't say anything in reply. Instead, I reach an arm across his shoulder, and give him a quick hug, as you might to console a nervous son whose 1st XV debut just happens to be playing a team of visiting Maoris.

'Do you mind if I ask you a question, Mr Coward?'

The turret is swivelling.

'Nothing to do with tattoos, by any chance?'

Wood smiles.

'That was going to be my second one, if I felt like pushing my luck.'

174

The massive gun barrel is slowly elevating. They have all the time in the world to play with that tank crew.

'Tell you what, Wood. When all this is over, I'll give you and the rest of the section an exclusive private screening, with champagne, canapés and an organ recital from no less a personage than Mrs Ethel Price, nimble-fingered meloditrix of the Hereford Odeon. Till then, tell me your other question.'

'I was just wondering, sir, of all the actions you've fought in, how does this one—?'

Suddenly, though, Wood isn't there any more. He has vanished and I am falling through space. Everything seems to be happening in the wrong order. I feel the impact seconds after I've landed. And I hear the thunderous roar as the shell which hurled me through the floor obliterates the roof and presumably poor Wood with it, seconds after that.

Looking up, I see flames licking an empty sky. Either side of me are two huge beams, one of them burning with an unholy white-hot glow. I'm coated in chunks of plasterwork and a thick layer of dust which seem to have cushioned the blow of the bits of slate and brick which landed on top of them. But though I don't appear to be injured, this is no time to lie around revelling in the miraculousness of my escape.

The questing 88-mm barrel has already reduced the rooftop level to nothingness. Next in line for destruction is the upper floor on which I am now lying.

'CHOLMONDELEY!' I wheeze, as loudly as I can, though how loudly this is I can't possibly tell with that gun still blasting and my ears ringing.

There's no answer.

I stagger to the room where I think it was I last saw him. It's empty, or seems to be from what I can make out through the smoke and swirling brick dust. But in the chaos and noise and immediacy of the moment, nothing is certain save the imminence of our house's destruction and the urgency of our need to escape.

'Men, we're pulling out. Everyone, PULL OUT.'

I mean to check all of the rooms, except that some – including the one Hughes was occupying – have already disappeared under the merciless volley of shots. To hasten the position's demise, the gunner has aimed for the corner of the building, making a huge section of the house suddenly collapse in one go.

With a frantic leap, I manage to dive downstairs just as the next massive shell from the traversing gun blasts through the floor above my head with the roar of an express train, and the breath-sucking, rib-crushing, brain-scrambling power of a thunderbolt. If there was anyone still left alive on Cholmondeley's floor, they're not any more.

'Out. Everyone out. We're pulling out!'

On the next floor down two dazed figures stagger towards me, coughing and choking. With the dust on their faces I don't even recognise them, and before I can make a stab, they're cut down in an instant, blood spurting from their mouths and chests, by a terrible raking burst from the tank's machine gun. By diving to the floor, I only just manage to avoid being hit myself.

There I wait, gasping amid the filth, splinters and debris, for the shooting to stop but it never does. On and on the firing goes, belt after belt of ammo, tearing the walls to shreds, macerating an old upright piano, which for an eerie moment sounds as if it's playing by itself, smashing what little glass there is left unsmashed, ricochets pinging and whining and zipping, while chips of brick and nasty splinters are sent flying like tiny missiles into every exposed part of my quaking body.

Crawling on my belly, I only just manage to escape the house before the whole central section collapses, leaving only two corners standing like the towers of a ruined castle.

'Crikey, Mr Coward, we thought you were all goners,' says Beckford, pulling me into his slit trench.

'Did you see anyone else get out?'

'No one,' says White.

'Pity,' says Maj. Tatham-Warter once I've cleaned up, had a swig of our now carefully rationed supply of water, and been debriefed. 'Now we'll have to waste another platoon trying to recapture it.'

'Sir, with respect, there's nothing left to recapture.'

'With respect, Mr Coward, I told my men you were the sort of fellow who died where he stood.'

'Steady on, Digby. My chap did his best,' chips in Maj. Gough.

Maj. Tatham-Warter sighs. His sharp tone softens slightly.

'Yes, all right, I'm sorry. It's just that with that position gone that Tiger's now going to have a clean run at us. Such a bugger you couldn't have had a bash at taking him out.'

'Sir, if we could have got nearly close enough with our Gammon grenades—'

'It's all right, Coward. All further excuses unnecessary. You did your best—' Maj. Tatham-Warter cuts himself off mid-flow to address a breathless runner from our rooftop OP. 'Yes, Walker? Is it on its way?'

'Not yet, sir. But there seems to be firing coming from inside the abandoned position.'

'German, surely?'

'Not unless they've started killing their own men, sir. We saw a troop of them forming up outside, bold as brass. Next thing we know they're being mown down like ninepins. Bren, we think, sir.'

'But that can't be right,' says Maj. Tatham-Warter, throwing me a quick, sharp look.

From outside there's a sudden very loud boom. It's coming, more or less, from the direction of the abandoned position. Or rather, it would now appear, the not-quite-so-abandoned-as-I-had-unfortunately-thought position. The boom gives way to a series of sounds not dissimilar to those when Cpl. Cholmondeley took out the Flammpanzer: the crackle, whizz and popping of cooking-off ammo. A kettle-drum ka-boom.

We're all peering through every available ground-floor loop-hole now, weapons at the ready. Is this the prelude to another assault?

'Sir?'

'Yes?'

It's another runner from upstairs.

'Sir, you're never going to believe this, but there was a blooming great Tiger coming straight up our way just now, and now there ain't,' says the runner.

'Sir, men coming this way,' calls one of the men watching the rear entrance.

'Shoot 'em.'

'They're shouting "Waho Mohammed".'

'Don't shoot 'em then,' says Maj. Tatham-Warter.

As the four men file in, Cholmondeley conscientiously covering the rear, there are gasps, then claps, then cheers and ululating cries of 'Waho Mohammed' from the assembled men and officers.

I stare dejectedly at the floor, self-disgust mingling with burning injustice. Only a German, only a bloody German, I'm thinking, could have found his way out of that *Götterdämmerung*, and then destroyed a near-indestructible Tiger tank with a Gammon grenade.

'Cheer up, Taylor,' says Maj. Tatham-Warter to the miserable private. 'I shouldn't be surprised if there isn't at least an MM in it for you, after this handsome escapade.'

'Thank you, sir, that will suit me very nicely,' he says. 'But I'll tell you all for nothing who won't be getting a gong,' he adds as an afterthought to his crowd of admirers.

Then he looks straight at me and says, 'The man who shot Major Jackson.'

11

Nijmegen

The Lower Rhine is cold and foul with oil and floating bodies, the banks are crawling with Germans who could spot me at any moment, and even with my boots and heavier clothes bundled in a waterproof sheet and pushed out to form a float in front of me, my progress against the powerful current is painfully slow.

But none of this matters. I'd much rather be here than in a house full of men who loathe me for a quitter and a coward, and would more than happily see me take a bullet because of what I did to their OC.

Not long ago, just before I slipped out of our defensive perimeter, Darkie Beckford and Maj. Gough bade me a somewhat embarrassed farewell.

'No one should have got out of that house alive. No one. I know you did the right thing, Mr Coward, even if no one else does.'

'Thank you, Beckford. I appreciate it.'

Maj. Gough extended a large, pudgy hand.

'You may be a Coward, Dick, but you're certainly not one of the yellow variety. Though I expect I'm not the first to make that pun.'

'No indeed, sir.'

'It's true all the same. You're not a bad soldier. Just a damned unlucky one. I pray for all our sakes this final mission will be the exception to the rule.'

I'm not sure I like his use of that word 'final'. Then again, I suppose it's marginally preferable to 'suicide', which is what it is really. First I'm to swim across the river, then I'm to make my way incognito through twelve miles of enemy territory, then I'm somehow to find my way across another, even broader and faster river called the Waal, there to make contact with XXX Corps and impress upon its commander Lt. Gen. Horrocks the urgency of our need for immediate relief.

Though it's nearly midnight, the surface of the river is shining almost as brightly as if it were broad day. The only difference is that the whole landscape has been drained of all colour save the flickering bronze imposed by a combination of burning buildings and lingering smoke. It's as if the whole world has been transformed into one giant sepia photograph.

With my head at water-level every sound – from the crump of incoming shells to the laughter and banter of those Germans disposed on the relatively safe southern riverbank – is distorted and exaggerated so that it seems as if the whole battle is being directed personally at me. Each kick of my legs feels as if it's going to be my last, for if I can see everything around me so clearly – the reflections of the buildings, the red arcs of tracer, the bulk of the road bridge now receding as I'm carried inexorably downstream in the direction of the rail bridge – how can it be possible that no one has yet spotted me?

But if they do spot me, what does it matter? What does anything matter any more? I've let down my squadron; I've earned the undying hatred of all but two men at Arnhem bridge; and I've blown probably my only chance of achieving the one thing dear old Pricey reckoned I was here to achieve.

A near cert for the VC, they're saying of Cpl. Cholmondeley's actions. If only I'd hung round for just half an hour longer, and been prepared to risk the minute's worth of reckless pluck needed to plant the Gammon bomb on the Tiger, that gong might have been mine. As would the estate. As would Gina.

I could have gone home to a hero's welcome. Rogered Gina senseless. Rogered her again. Then again just for good measure. And lived happily ever after, presumably.

Instead, here I am, in the middle of a dirty great river with starshells bursting over my head, Jerries to the back of me, Jerries to the front of me, and nary a toothpick to defend myself with when I eventually wash up on the far shore. The idea is that, if I encounter any of the enemy, I'm to use my fluent German to talk my way out, aided and abetted by an SS-issue camouflage smock which we've looted from one of the dead.

Of course, if I'm captured dressed in German uniform, I face being summarily shot. But the way feelings are running on both sides after three days of remorseless slaughter, I'm not sure that the same wouldn't happen to me whether I were caught in a frock, a sailor suit, or the full ceremonial fig of the Hussars.

In any case, as we shall see, if Jerry threatens to get too inquisitive I do have one more trick up my sleeve. A bit kill-or-cure though it may be.

Here's an odd thing I've noticed about war, Jack. Whatever it is that you are expecting to happen next, you're 90 per cent certain to be disappointed. Look at Market Garden: sunny day, perfect landing, everyone convinced it was going to be a pushover. Then – well, I don't think I'm spoiling the ending when I tell you that the frog didn't turn into a handsome prince and that the footmen stayed as mice.

Sometimes, though, quite the reverse is true. You'll be setting off on what you're quite convinced is going to be the most arduous mission of your entire military career, only to find yourself being carried to your destination on palanquin by liveried servants, while bare-breasted maidens pop sweetmeats onto your tongue, heavenly choirs sing 'Ave Maria' and England regain the Ashes with eight wickets to spare.

My passage from Arnhem bridge to the north bank of the Waal is a case in point. I wash up in a reed bed, sufficiently remote from any German positions to be able to dress at my leisure; when I do hear a challenge from my darkness and I reply briskly in German, 'Belt up, you stupid idiot, it's only me!' my challenger doesn't think to question who 'only me' is; and when I've successfully circumvented the German positions and reached the Arnhem–Nijmegen highway, what should I find waiting for me at the edge of the road, its engine idling, but a dispatch rider's motorcycle.

The rider himself is squatting near by, trousers round his ankles, with a very audibly bad case of the squitters.

I don't even deliberate – for such is my confidence born of having so much luck. I stride right up to him, which of course is the last thing you want anyone to do when you've been caught short.

'Nice bike,' I say, quite meaning it. The BMW R/75 is a chunky, capable, powerful machine, much better than anything we have on the Allied side. 'Can I sit on it?'

Well, he doesn't know what to say, does he? Just wants me to go away. He grunts something irritably which I take for a yes. Then before he knows it, I'm sitting astride his motorcycle, kicking it into gear and roaring off south.

Only to run just 200 yards on into a bloody German check-point. Run by typically Teutonic sticklers, who, despite my gesticulations that I'm on a very urgent mission which will brook no delays, seem determined to make me halt all the same. A large NCO in a heavy greatcoat steps forward into the road with his palm thrust out flat towards me. You'd think, with all the excitement going on not half a mile away, he'd have better things to do than bother solitary dispatch riders. But that's the Hun for you.

There's a barrier across the road, which I might just be able to nip round, I suppose. No sooner have I glanced sideways to see whether it's viable – a bit steep because this is the point where the embankment begins – than the German corporal reads my intentions and makes to point his Schmeisser at me.

I slow down, heart sinking, quite ready to believe my luck has run out for the very last time. Apart from the barrier and the increasingly suspicious corporal, there's a sandbagged sentry post containing two more guards to negotiate. And behind me, I can hear Klaus Thunderarsen yelling blue murder and catching up fast. 'My bike,' he's yelling. 'He has stolen my bike.'

'*Was?*' says the Corporal, sharply.

Which, fortunately for me, is the last word he says because, at that very moment, a huge, deep, sucking sigh announces the arrival of a large incoming shell. It lands directly on top of the sentry post, completely obliterating it and the two guards, and sending a shard of shrapnel straight into the Corporal's upper body and killing him stone dead.

'Better late than never,' I think to myself, for this is the 'final trick up my sleeve' I mentioned earlier: a barrage Maj. Gough most kindly arranged to have ordered in from our battery at Oosterbeek to keep the Germans' heads down while I exfiltrated their positions.

Whenever I watch that marvellous film *The Great Escape* – on which, as you probably know, I acted as technical adviser – I always look forward to that splendid scene where the Steve McQueen character roars off on his powerful captured motorcycle. In real life – how typical of Hollywood to change him into an American! – that character was me. I didn't try to leap over any fences on this occasion. (That was another incident, which I'll no doubt tell you about in due course.) And as you know, I wasn't wearing a tight, muscle-revealing T-shirt but an SS trooper's smock. The delighted grin on his face is pretty accurate, though.

I'm through! I'm thinking to myself as I bump over the collapsed wooden barrier, and then twist my hand on the throttle, strangely oblivious to the shells landing really quite close all around me. I'm bloody well through!

On the twelve miles of road from Arnhem to the north end of Nijmegen bridge my luck continues to hold. There's plenty of German traffic in both directions – half-tracks, supply lorries, the odd panzer, troops on foot, troops on bicycles – but it's dark, they're tired, and they're heading off to one or other fronts, so the last thing on their minds is to question the identity of the solitary dispatch rider weaving swiftly past them.

About half a mile before the River Waal, I decide on the spur of the moment to follow a narrow track that heads off left at right angles to the main highway. My luck's in again, for there's nobody on it, and better still, it curves southwards to within 50 yards of the river. I make a mental note of just how sparse are the German defences on this section.

I abandon the bike near a bed of reeds, wondering what the hell I'm going to do next. I'm far too enfeebled by cold, exhaustion and hunger to try swimming across. What I really need is a boat, but I'm hardly going to find one of them, now am I? Not in the dark. Not when every floating vessel on the entire Betuwe island will either have been destroyed or requisitioned and put under guard?

It's at this moment, not unlike those shimmering, distant oases one used to see in the desert whenever one was feeling most parched and desperate, that my eyes decide to play a cruel trick on me. Poking from the reeds barely 6 feet in front of where I'm sitting, mulling my position, is a shape that my eyes deceive me into imagining is a boat. A rowing boat, apparently intact, and with what might be a pair of oars sticking out of it.

This, it turns out, is what it is. It doesn't appear to have a hole in it. Otherwise that stagnant pool of water I've just found in the bottom of it would surely have drained away. And it doesn't seem to have been booby-trapped because if it had I'd be dead by now.

Having glanced all around me one more time – there's part of me convinced this is some kind of trap – I rest my right shoulder against the heavy varnished stern – 'Mathilde', it says in gold letters picked up by the moonlight – and, gasping with the effort, heave the boat from its reedy hidey-hole, across a stretch of shingle and into the water.

No sooner is it afloat than *Mathilde* begins taking off downriver and I have to leap precipitously aboard to stop her drifting off without me. The thudding and scrabbling and creaking as I land heavily in the hull, pull myself upright and wrestle to get either oar in is enough to waken the dead.

Taking a long, deep breath I try to force myself to be calm and not think how desperately exposed I am out here between two opposing armies, both no doubt convinced I belong to the other side. 'You're on the lake at Great Meresby,' I whisper to myself. 'You're rowing a picnic to the island and Gina's there waiting for you. It's a lovely summer's evening. Very warm. So warm that, while she's waiting, Gina decides she'll have to strip off for a cooling dip . . .'

What's ruining this fantasy, apart from anything else, is the current. There are no currents on the lake at Great Meresby, whereas the one here is so strong it's like being in one of those Tarzan films where the river's carrying you inexorably over the waterfall – but with no Johnny Weissmuller to save the day.

My plan, in so far as I had one, was to skip straight across to the other side of the river, landing a comfortable 1,000 yards away from Nijmegen Bridge. But at this rate, I'm going to end up landing directly beneath it – a sitting target, for perhaps two or three battalions' worth on either side of itchy-fingered snipers, machine-gunners, tankers and mortar men.

God, it's an ugly bastard. Heavier, longer, taller, more menacing. And I thought the Arnhem bridge was a pig but compared to this brute it's prettier than Venus emerging from the waves on her cockleshell. I don't envy the poor sods who are going to have to take it, as take it they must very soon if they're to have a hope of reaching Arnhem before our positions are overrun.

Now I'm about halfway across the width of the river, I realise I definitely shan't be making landfall this side of the bridge. I shall be forced to row directly underneath, raising a new difficulty: someone up above is bound to challenge me. Whatever answer I give is unlikely to satisfy. Death will swiftly follow.

Unless –

Yes, why not?

Unless I can persuade them that I'm no longer a threat.

Ideally, I'd stow the oars to stop them being lost but I fear this won't look realistic enough. I'll just have to rely on the current carrying me on to the southern bank rather than the northern one, as I suspect it will, judging by the way the river bends. So, here goes.

I keep rowing, but much more slowly so I can listen carefully and react quickly. What I'm listening out for is a burst of small arms fire, from which I might plausibly have taken a stray shot.

There!

'Aarggh!' I cry as I jerk my head backwards, arch my spine, and fling out my arms. As an impression of someone being shot, I doubt even Olivier could do better, and as I lie there, looking sightlessly upwards into the night sky, I think, Well, I jolly well hope someone was watching.

From this point on, time passes very slowly. I'd thought about dying face down and that would have been even duller, no doubt. But even the way I am – face up, arms and legs akimbo, the back of my head in that pool of stagnant water I foolishly neglected to bail – I find that playing dead is only narrowly more eventful and interesting than actually being dead.

The stars are out, but mostly obscured by the foul-smelling plumes of oily smoke which collect like vultures over a battlefield. Sometimes, a broken line of red tracer arcs overhead or a distant airburst illuminates the sky like a giant camera-flashbulb. Then all goes quiet and darkish again and I float on, increasingly nauseous as the boat spins and eddies, desperate to adjust into a more comfortable position, but unable to do so because I've just no idea how close I am to the bridge and all those people watching me for signs of life.

On and on the boat drifts, and still I haven't reached the bridge. This is ridiculous. Last time I looked it was too close. How come it's now so far away?

Then just when I least want or expect it it comes all at once: the blinding brightness as a parachute flare bursts almost directly overhead, the dark, massive girders of that gargantuan bridge towering menacingly above me, and shadowy figures whispering to one another, some in field grey, others in spot camouflage peering down from ladders and walkways, their weapons trained on my face.

They'll have sniper scopes, some of them. That flare that went up, that will have been for my benefit: so they can focus right up close on my eyes to see if they blink, on my nostrils to see if they flare, on my lips to see if they twitch. How many cocked loaded guns are there pointing at me now? All of them just waiting for the tiniest excuse to fire.

'What the hell does he think he's doing?' says one.

'Was doing, you mean. He's dead,' says another.

'A deserter, perhaps? A Dutch spy?'

'Bet you ten marks I can take his head off, first shot.'

'Do that and you'll get us all killed. There are Americans all along that shore, waiting for your muzzle flash.'

'They're crap shots, the Americans. Even worse than the British.'

'Risk it, if you want, Reinhard. But just give me time to get away first.'

The tension is almost too much to bear. Maybe it would be better just to get it over with. End the agonising uncertainty. Move. And die. I wouldn't be the first chap in war to have made that decision. Survival can be such an exhausting business you begin to wonder whether it's worth the effort.

But it's not just for my sake I need to stay alive, I remind myself. What of Gina? What of the comrades I abandoned at Arnhem bridge? I owe it to them to get to the other side, and get to the other side I will. I can stay still for five minutes. I'll stay still for five hours if that's what it takes.

At last a glimpse of sky tells me I've reached the other side, but I daren't move just yet. Preferably not till the boat has beached itself.

Next thing I'm aware of – I must have fallen asleep – I hear more murmured voices. English ones this time, or rather American, to judge by the shape of the helmets popping briefly in and out of view above the lip of the boat.

'Not your 45, you jerk. Finish him off with your knife.'

'But I just sharpened it.'

'So now you can test it.'

'Screw you, I ain't wasting it on a dead man.'

'We're all dead men, Jarecki. This is the last chance you'll get.'

'Um, excuse me, you chaps,' I say in my brightest, breeziest, most quintessentially English Bertie Wooster drawl.

'Move an inch and you're dead, Mister.'

'Lieutenant, actually. Dick Coward. 1st Airborne. I take it you fellows are with the 82nd?'

'Don't tell him, Jarecki.'

'You think I'm stoopid, O'Brien.'

'So what are we going to do?'

'Kill him, I guess. Better safe than sorry.'

'What if he's who he says he is?'

'Why would a Limey be dressed as a Kraut?'

'OK, so maybe he's a Kraut. Couldn't HQ use some intelligence out of him?'

'If he's a Kraut, he double-dies with sugar on top.'

'Now, gentlemen, if I may say so, that really isn't cricket.'

'Aw, he's bound to be a Kraut, for sure.'

'How do you know?'

'Limeys only talk like that in the movies.'

'Lieutenant General Browning talks like that.'

'Lieutenant General Browning's a friend of mine. And Major General Gavin. We had dinner only last month,' I say.

'Can you believe the stones on this guy? I say we better kill him now.'

'With you, Jarecki.'

There's not even time for a 'but' or even a squeal, let alone an explanatory subclause: O'Brien's already on me, knees on my chest, knife poised at my throat, eyes staring purposefully into mine, as if to say, 'I don't feel bad about this any more, Kraut scum.'

I glare back. Then make it quick, bastard! runs my very final thought. Or my semi-final one. The actual last one is the one that goes, Well done, old chap! We'd always hoped you'd die like a Roman, but you can never quite be sure, can you?

Rather to my irritation, though, O'Brien has lost his nerve.

Bugger, it's going to be like one of those awful botch-job executions at the Tower, where Mary Queen of Scots is running round with her head still dangling by a thread, screaming, 'Will ye no do the job properly, the noo?'

'I can't do it,' says O'Brien, withdrawing the blade from the neck.

'Why the hell not?'

'This guy. When you look at him, up close,' says O'Brien. 'It would be like killing the Cap!'

'Tea, Lootenant?' asks Capt. Richard Du Croix of 3rd Battalion, 504th Parachute Infantry Regiment.

'Coffee's fine if that's what you're drinking.'

'Your tea's better than our coffee,' says Capt. Du Croix, signalling with two raised fingers and a T gesture to a private, who reaches immediately for the canteen on the portable stove. 'Your field rations generally beat the hell out of ours. Mighty fine fighting knives, too. The rest of your equipment, with respect, Lootenant, you can keep.'

I smile at the odd mix of directness and politeness, so characteristically American, I find. We're the mother country. It ought to be us teaching them how to behave. But I've often found there's more old-world courtesy in your typical US infantry officer than there is in the whole brigade of guards.

'Dick, please. Cousins surely ought to be on first-name terms.'

'Especially cousins named after the same guy: our great-grandfather, I believe.' He smiles.

'It's the damnedest thing, though. Meeting here of all places.'

'It might get stranger. Somewhere in a tank hereabouts is my brother James.'

'Sheesh. We could have had a fine old family reunion.'

'Maybe we yet will,' I say, catching the mournful note in his voice.

'Maybe,' he agrees with a sad smile.

We're sitting on the lip of his hastily constructed dugout, on the reverse of an embankment maybe 1,500 yards from the edge of the river. He doesn't expect his company to stay here long, he told me when Jarecki and O'Brien brought me in and we'd first made our thunderstruck acquaintance. Nor live long, either, is my impression.

'My men didn't treat you too rough, I hope, Lootenant?' was the first thing Capt. Du Croix asked me after he'd dismissed my former would-be executioners, both of whom slunk off looking appropriately sheepish.

'Like a prince,' I said with a grin.

'Like a prince in the tower, knowing those guys,' said Capt. Du Croix. 'If you knew where they were going, though, I think you wouldn't judge them too badly.'

'Where are you going?' I asked.

Capt. Du Croix just gave a pained smile and jerked a hellward gesture with his thumb.

Our tea is brought, together with a can of beef stew and another one of fruit pudding. Capt. Du Croix waits in sympathetic silence as I devour them, one after the other. It's the first proper food I've had in two days.

When he sees I've nearly finished, he says, 'I powerfully appreciate it, your spending time with me when I know you're hot to get on to Corps HQ. Pretty unprofessional of me to detain you.'

'We're family. No one's going to begrudge us ten minutes.'

'What I was thinking,' says Capt. Du Croix, nodding seriously. 'Would you think it strange if I said your turning up like this feels like a sign from God?'

'A good sign, I hope.'

Still smiling – as I do when I'm really nervous: must be a family trait – he sniffs non-committally.

'It's good to be with family at times like this, that's for sure,' he says. Then he pulls himself upright, drains his tea and snaps, 'Come on. You need to get to Corps HQ. I'll brief you as we go.'

Our destination in Nijmegen's wooded suburbs is only a short distance away as the crow flies. But the log jam of traffic in its bombed-out, rubble-strewn streets – still under sporadic shell fire from the north bank of the river – makes the journey slow, tortuous and mildly nerve-wracking.

Because my cousin chooses to drive me there himself, he can afford to be frank. His company has been detailed to lead what soldiers generally regard as the bloodiest and most desperate form of assault in the tactical handbook: an opposed river crossing.

'They can't be serious,' I say, once he's explained the plan.

'Hey, don't feel sorry for us. Major General Gavin came up with the idea. We volunteered. It's nobody's problem but our own.'

'B-but –' I flounder for a moment, quite lost for words as I remember how utterly exposed and helpless I felt crossing the river last night. The idea of paddling against that current under fire strikes me as pure suicide. 'Is there no other way?'

'We've been through the other options.'

'And?'

'There weren't any. If your tanks are gonna relieve your guys at Arnhem bridge, we've got to take this bridge first. Our frontal assaults aren't working. Our parachute infantry have been trying for the best part of two days, with full armoured support, and if they can't do it, no one can.' Capt. Du Croix smiles. 'And you've got to admit, Dick, the new plan does have one thing in its favour.'

'Really?'

'It's so damned crazy, the Krauts are never going to see it coming.'

Lt. Gen. Browning has commandeered as his Corps HQ an elegant woodland villa in Nijmegen's wealthy suburbs. The grounds are dotted with slit trenches occupied by his personal guard – a detachment of glider pilots who, so the general feeling at 1st Airborne Division runs, would have been better used carrying more men and supplies to the sharp end in Arnhem, rather than ferrying His Nibs and his entourage to Nijmegen, where for all the difference they're making to the battle they might just as well be in Surrey.

As an old family friend, I feel quite saddened by this widespread caricature of Boy as a remote, stuffy figure – Eton and Guards personified – with woefully insufficient battle-command experience and next to no understanding of how to talk to his men.

As one of his junior officers, though, I'd say his critics have a point.

Unless, perhaps, that critic happens to be American.

'That's your Lieutenant General Browning's billet and you know why it's so big?' says Capt. Du Croix, *sotto voce*, as we stride up the drive. He indicates an imperial-size caravan on the lawn, protected by sandbags. 'So they can fit all his changes of uniform.'

'Excuse me, Richard, but your Slim Jim is hardly a slouch when it comes to fancy dressing.'

'Our Slim Jim, I'll have you know, Dick, was offered a caravan like Lieutenant General Browning's and turned it down. He says if his men are going to live in foxholes than so will he. Carries a carbine. Does his share of night patrols. Now that's what I call leadership.'

'That's what I call showing off,' I say, a picture springing unbidden into my head, of Gina, her face flushed and her eyes bright, giggling uproariously at one of Slim Jim's no doubt dismal attempts at a joke.

At the front door a very spruce young ADC asks our business. When we tell him we need to see Lt. Gen. Browning in person, he casts a thoughtful eye over my greasy, blood-matted hair and my ripped, filth-spattered Denison smock.

'Best if you have a wash and a shave first, old chap.'

He means well but it's too much for my American cousin.

'This Lootenant has come straight from Arnhem bridge. Every

second you keep him waiting another Red Devil dies,' he explodes, his fingers fumbling towards the Colt .45 tucked in his belt.

The ADC pulls a pained, slightly desperate face.

'A shave, at least?' he pleads.

Almost instantly, an NCO materialises at his shoulder brandishing a razor, some soap and a bowl of steaming water.

'Thank you, that's very kind.'

'No. Thank you, Lieutenant Coward, for being so understanding,' replies the ADC. 'I'll have Sarnt Cooper bring you some tea.'

'Tea. Tea. TEA!' cries Capt. Du Croix, when we're back out on the drive. 'Is there ever a time when you guys don't think it's time for more tea?'

Shortly afterwards, we're led into a drawing room, where a group of senior officers including three generals and their aides are gathered around a large table covered with maps. We exchange salutes.

'Gentlemen,' announces Lt. Gen. Browning with a twitch of his neat moustache. 'Allow me to introduce Lieutenant Coward, come direct from Arnhem.'

'Lootenant *Dick* Coward?' says Maj. Gen. Gavin, with gratifying astonishment.

'General Gavin, delighted to see you again, I'm sure.'

'You know one another?' says Lt. Gen. Browning.

'We have common interests,' says Maj. Gen. Gavin, slyly. 'Though I had no idea that one of them was fighting.'

That last remark, I think, is meant as a backhanded compliment since, as he says it, he tips his fingers to his forehead in a light salute.

'Some in-joke I'm missing? All the Cowards I know are the bravest of the brave,' says the third general – clean-shaven, grey-haired, aquiline nose, cleft chin. He's a bit scruffier than the others but with a much friendlier, more approachable manner. 'Ajax's other boy?' he says, looking askance at Lt. Gen. Browning, who nods. 'Brian Horrocks,' he says, stepping forward to clasp my hand warmly. 'Knew your father in France and your brother's one of the finest squadron commanders in my corps. A pleasure to meet you.'

'And you too, sir.'

Maj. Gen. Gavin turns to Capt. Du Croix and says abruptly, 'Have the boats still not arrived, Captain?'

It's a rhetorical question since, if the boats had arrived, clearly my cousin wouldn't be here – he'd be down by the river commanding his company. It's also a very pointed one. The boats, provided by Lt. Gen. Horrocks's XXX Corps, were supposed to have been here last night.

'Latest ETA is 11.00 hours, sir.'

'You're good to go as soon as they're here?' asks Maj. Gen. Gavin.

'Yes, sir.'

'You're not thinking of crossing in daylight, surely?' says Lt. Gen. Horrocks.

'If it's your boats you're worried about, we promise to buy you some brand new ones when we're done,' says Maj. Gen. Gavin.

'You know very well that's not what I meant.'

'General, I don't need to tell you of the special bond that exists between airborne soldiers. If there's anything humanly possible my parachute infantry can do to relieve your Red Devils, then do it they will. Isn't that so, Captain?'

'Yes, sir. Certainly, sir,' says Capt. Du Croix.

'That's decent of you, gentlemen. More than decent. But I'm sure I don't need to tell you, General, of the aversion developed by those of us who saw service in the First War towards needlessly sacrificing the lives of our best fighting men.'

'Indeed, General. I have become aware of that,' says Maj. Gen.

Gavin in a voice that says he could wish things were otherwise. The general feeling in the American camp is that we British are perhaps just that little bit too careful with our manpower. And so would you be, we tend to mutter, if you'd had to spend the first three years of the war fighting Hitler on your own.

'What do we think, Frederick? Can we really risk an assault in daylight?'

Lt. Gen. Browning doesn't immediately reply, and I can guess what he's thinking: 'I've already lost one division. But can I afford not to take the risk?'

'I think we should consult Lieutenant Coward,' he says.

Gosh, thanks, General, thanks a lot, I think to myself as all eyes turn to me. It's not a pleasant feeling being asked to send five hundred men to their deaths, still less when one of them's a cousin to whom, in your brief acquaintance, you've grown rather attached.

'Should this really be his problem?' says Maj. Gen. Gavin, making me like him slightly more than I did.

'I'm not asking him for a yea or nay. We just need to hear from the horse's mouth how things are at the bridge. Can Johnny Frost last another night, that's what we need to know. Well, Richard?'

Calling me by my Christian name. Now there's a worrying development.

'I say to hell with it. Soon as the boats arrive, we go!' says Maj. Gen. Gavin.

'And I say a daylight crossing will be sui—' Lt. Gen. Horrocks corrects himself quickly. 'Inadvisable.'

Then beside me, I hear my cousin's voice.

'Just tell them what's what, Dick. No more. No less.'

So, awkwardly at first, I tell the senior officers all they need to know about the state of our defences at the bridge. How we're so short of ammo we can only afford to fire aimed shots, not the bursts we need if we're to stop the enemy advancing under our noses; how the wounded in the basements are at constant risk of being burned alive; how the German tanks have been firing at us at almost point-blank range, reducing our positions to rubble, floor by floor; how our initial strength of five hundred has been reduced by at least two-thirds; and that the opposition outnumber us by a probable four to one.

I try to keep things as matter-of-fact as I can. Indeed, I half hope, as I describe our force's predicament, that I'll suddenly remember some telling detail which proves things aren't quite as bad as they sound. Apart from, 'Morale remains astonishingly high and there's not a chap there who doesn't want to see this one through right to the end,' I can't think of any. As I finish speaking, I'm aware that there's only one conclusion that can be drawn from my account: no, Johnny Frost most certainly won't last another night. If there's to be any chance of getting to them in time, we must force a crossing today.

In other words, I could scarcely have consigned my cousin and the rest of 504th PIR to death more effectively than if I'd put a gun to their heads and personally shot them one by one.

12

Blade on the Feather

On the south bank of the Waal, near the power station, is a concrete factory tower whose summit affords a panoramic view of the obstacles that lie ahead of 504th Parachute Infantry Regiment. My cousin takes me up there with his regimental commander Col. Tucker and the battalion commander Maj. Cook, who'll lead the assault, for a last look.

Directly below us is the stretch of shingle, completely exposed, across which the men must manhandle their boats into the water under enemy fire. Next is the river, about 300 yards wide, whose current is likely to make the actual crossing distance almost twice as far. Those men who survive the crossing will then have to charge across 800 yards of river flats, still with no cover whatsoever, before pausing for a breather at the base of a dyke embankment about 15 or 20 feet high.

It's here that their real work will begin. They'll have to clamber up the bank and, taking care not to have their heads shot off as they crest the rise, destroy the numerous enemy positions we can clearly see lining the road atop the dyke. Then after that, it gets harder. About 800 yards beyond the road is a squat, ugly and very impregnable-looking fort, marked on the map as Fort Hof van Holland, with thick walls, a moat and embrasures concealing heaven knows how many machine guns.

It strikes me as unlikely at this point that there will be any men left from the first waves. But if there are, their job will be to dash on and take first the railway bridge, then the road bridge. And if there aren't, this task will be taken on by the second, third and fourth waves – always assuming that there will be sufficient boats left from the first wave to ferry them across.

'Well, Lootenant,' says Col. Tucker, a small, tough man, rippling with pent-up energy and with a constant expression of mild amusement. 'You still wish you were coming with us?'

I did volunteer to join my cousin, of course, but the Colonel refused me permission. He said my local knowledge would be put to much better use once the bridge had been taken, guiding our tanks on the final stretch of road to Arnhem. It does nothing to allay my terrible, gnawing guilt.

'Sir, it would have been the greatest honour of my career,' I say, with a crack in my voice.

'Come now, Lootenant. It ain't exactly like you've missed out on much of the action these last five years, from what I hear.'

'Puts guys like us to shame,' agrees Maj. Cook. 'Makes us kind of nervous whether we'll ever have time to catch up.'

'Oh really,' I say, blushing.

'See, your cousin's gone red,' says Maj. Cook to Capt. Du Croix. 'Let's see if we can't make him redder. Why don't you tell Lootenant Coward what you told me that time in the foxhole in Anzio?'

'Sheesh, I couldn't,' says Capt. Du Croix, turning possibly even redder than I've gone.

'Then, damn it, I will because it sounds like something your cousin needs to know,' says Maj. Cook. 'Now, as you may remember, Lootenant, Anzio wasn't always the easiest of battles. There were times when some of us began to question what the hell we were doing there. All of us, in fact, except Colonel Tucker, whose one abiding fear was that the Rangers might get to Rome before we did.'

Col. Tucker laughs throatily.

'So we're in this foxhole in the mud one cold, cold night, Richard and I, and it's the first time all day the shelling has died down long enough to hear ourselves speak,' continues Maj. Cook. 'And the conversation turns to what it was that made us join Parachute Infantry when, face it, there are many more comfortable ways for an educated American to do his bit for Uncle Sam. Especially a guy who doesn't exactly need the fifty dollars a week jump pay.'

More laughter from Col. Tucker. It's a running regimental joke, I would imagine. The Du Croix are one of the richest families in America so it's quite true: the extra money a US officer is paid for being a parachute infantryman is but a drop in the ocean for my cousin Richard.

'And Richard starts telling me about this cousin he has in England. Guy he's never met but wishes he could because he's done so many of the things he wishes he could do.'

'Ah, now let me stop you there,' I say. 'The cousin he's referring to must be my brother James. He's the one with all the medals.'

Richard slowly shakes his head.

'Was James the guy who won a DFC in the Battle of Britain? Was it James who escaped the SS massacre in Dunkirk? Did James fight in North Africa with the Long Range Desert Group and the SAS?' asks Maj. Cook.

'Oh all right,' I agree, reddening again. 'But how on earth do you know all this?'

'Your mom wrote my mom,' says Capt. Du Croix. He smiles at the memory. 'I think Mom kind of wished she hadn't. "Why can't you join the Navy, like your brothers? You look so good in white," she'd say. But she knew the reason I wouldn't. I wanted to go to Europe. See the places my cousin Dick had been. Maybe, who knows, even bump into him one day. Yeah, right, I said to myself. Like that's ever going to happen.'

'Well, I'm flattered,' I say. 'I just wish I were more worthy of your admiration.'

'Jeez, don't tell him that or he'll forget how to be brave,' says Col. Tucker.

'Yeah, that's the other thing he told me that night in the foxhole. I asked him how it was that he never seemed to be afraid. "Oh I do get afraid. All the time," your cousin said. "But whenever I do, I just ask myself, What would Dick Coward do?"'

The assault is due to begin at 15.00 and the boats arrive barely twenty minutes before. Just as well: the last thing these boys need is time to dwell at length on the almost comical inadequacies of the leaky old vessels supposed to ferry them through the gates of hell.

'Jesus H Christ, then I won't be needing these,' exclaims one young second lieutenant when he glimpses the first of the collapsible boats being unloaded. And he purposefully begins to divest himself of all his personal items – cigarettes, lighter, family photos, wallet – which he stacks up in a pile on the bank, ready to be forwarded to his soon-to-be-grieving relatives.

If you think this unduly fatalistic, you clearly haven't seen those boats. We'd been expecting them to be reasonably large and solid, at least to have an engine. But these flimsy canvas structures – just 19 feet long, and with gunwales no more than 18 inches above the waterline – I'd barely consider fit for a carp-fishing expedition for two on the lake at Great Meresby, let alone an opposed crossing on a fast-flowing river with a compliment of nineteen heavily armed men. Oh, and they're propelled not by engines but by paddles – which could be awkward given that there are only two paddles per boat, and that the majority of the men have never rowed before. Why should they have? They volunteered to be parachute infantry not marines.

'I can't swim, I can't swim, what the hell am I going to do?' says a panicked young PFC.

'First thing you can do you can stop making me jealous,' says his buddy. 'Least for you it's gonna be quick.'

Standing around like a lemon, with little to do to help, with nothing to say that can be of any comfort, what I'd like to do is slink off and hide till they're gone.

But I'm afraid someone might notice and take it amiss. Several times during our wait for the boats, I've had men spot my red beret, come up to me and say, 'Red Devils, right? We're going to get you out of there, don't you worry, sir. We're the 504th and we never leave our buddies behind.' This, of course, makes me feel even more guilty than before.

Perhaps I'd feel more optimistic for them if I hadn't peeked over the lip of the embankment just now to watch the Typhoon attack. In our fighters went, machine guns blazing, rockets streaking. What most struck me, though, wasn't the damage those rockets did to the enemy positions, but rather the stuff the Germans put up in response.

'*Bam bam bam bam bam!*' The air was so thick with black puffs of flak, those aircraft had no need to fly, they could have just put down their wheels and driven on it. In twenty minutes' time that same concentration of artillery is going to be brought to bear on the river. And this time its targets will be paddling at rather less than 400 mph.

Now our tanks are having a go, about thirty of them lined up on the reverse of the embankment, pummelling those German defences with high-explosive shells. It won't be enough to dislodge them though. With the Germans it never is.

There's a thump in the small of my back, hard and sudden as shrapnel.

'Hey, Lootenant,' says Jarecki, the tall paratrooper who nearly murdered me in the small hours of this morning. 'You coming to join the party?'

'I'm afraid your Colonel won't allow it,' I say.

'Well, in case this is the last time we see each other, can I apologise for what happened this morning. See, O'Brien, he really didn't mean you no harm. But you Brits know how it is with the Irish,' he says, tapping a finger to his forehead to indicate extreme stupidity.

Shortly afterwards, O'Brien appears.

'Lootenant, about this morning. I just wanted to say how sorry I am, you being the Cap's cousin and all.'

'That's quite all right. I understand why you were suspicious.'

'Yeah, but Jarecki, he didn't need to be quite so heavy-handed. Problem is, as you may have noticed from the name, he's a Polack. You know how dumb Polacks can be.'

Ten minutes till H-Hour now and the boats have mostly been assembled. There are twenty-six of them in all, each of which will carry thirteen paratroopers and a crew of three engineers who understand at least the rudiments of paddling and steering. The men, formed up in squads next to the boats, have gone quiet now. What is there left to say? Some are kneeling in prayer, some bent double as they void their stomachs, most just gazing blankly into space with their own thoughts.

'Excuse me, but did I overhear you saying the Colonel had refused you permission to cross?' says a kindly voice. Its owner, a captain, is wearing the insignia of an Army chaplain.

'Yes, and I do feel the most terrible heel.'

'If that's English for feeling bad, then I'm in just the same boat. So to speak. Name's Kuehl. Delbert Kuehl. Regimental Chaplain. If ever the boys need my services, I'd say that time is now, wouldn't you?'

'Sir, I would. I'm Coward by the way. Dick Coward. I'm—'

'Captain Du Croix's cousin, I know. He's spoken of you often.'

'It's awful, Chaplain, that there's nothing we can do to help.'

'There's always something, Lootenant. Do you remember that

wonderful story about the man who helped Jesus carry his cross to Calvary?'

A whistle blows. As one we surge forward and upward, out of cover and on to the embankment. The useless boat digs into my shoulder. It smells of mould and neglect. I hate it with a will.

Roaring, grunting, cursing, making whatever damn noise we can to drown our screaming thoughts, we stagger up to the top of the bank. Our stomach knots tighten in anticipation of the first enemy shots. We're skylined. We're like ducks in a shooting gallery. Why haven't they opened fire yet? Are they toying with us? Are they slow? Are they—?

Such noise, all of a sudden, as you can scarcely imagine. Bullets pinging and ricocheting beside and beneath us; airbursts above; clattering, tearing, burning shrapnel; cries as the first men crumple and drop; yells of renewed determination, as we stumble downwards, the boats growing heavier the more men get hit.

Across the spitting, tormented shingle – more screams, more men down – we drag the boat the last few yards and thrust it with defiance and hate into the river. Almost immediately, as happened to me last night, the boat starts drifting off. Those few men who've managed to climb aboard thrash against the current with the paddles. Two men grab the stern and are pulled along behind it in the water.

'Let go! We can't steer it,' yells one of the engineers aboard.

'I can't. I can't swim!'

One man has waded too deep and got stuck in the mud.

'I'm stuck!' he screams. 'Someone help me, I'm stuck.'

No one has time to help him. We're trying to stop the boat floating off, running parallel with it along the shingle, hoping the engineers can manoeuvre it back to shore further downriver.

The artillery is getting fiercer, louder, more accurate.

Not a single boat has been successfully launched. Everywhere it's the same problem: men floundering, the current dragging, men dying, paddles splashing in frenzied futility.

'Get me out someone, please!' screams the man who's stuck.

I'm about to help him when the man beside me says, 'What the hell are you doing here?'

'Saying goodbye!' I say to my cousin.

'You've said it. Now go!' says Capt. Du Croix, immediately turning his back, making for his boat which the engineers have now successfully beached. His men clamber heavily aboard, some falling head first and getting trampled as their comrades pile frantically on top of them.

'Sweet Jesus, can't someone help me?' says the man stuck in the mud.

I want to help the man. I want to cross with my cousin. I want to get off this beach and back behind the safety of the bank.

Which?

There's room in my cousin's boat. I know there is because they've just turfed a dead paratrooper over the side. If only I can get aboard that boat, I've a feeling I'll make it across the river in one piece. If I don't, then it will be a sign that I must turn back.

Almost there. Except this mud, this terrible mud, it's threatening to suck my boots off – or worse, leave me stranded like that poor man, I wonder what's happened to that poor man.

Looking up, about to reach for one of the hands now extending towards me from the boat, I see the barrel of an automatic pistol pointing straight in my face.

'Goodbye, Dick,' shouts Capt. Du Croix, with a half-smile and a rueful shake of his head.

'Good luck,' I shout, converting my reaching gesture into a final wave.

So there's my sign then and it's surely for the best. God knows what possessed me to want to follow them across.

Price would not be impressed. 'What did you go and do that for, you bloody young fool?' he'd say. 'Do you think your father will give two hoots for a Purple Heart or a Silver Star? It's Crimean bronze he wants, not some shiny Yankee gewgaw.'

Something like that, anyway, and he'd be right. There's nothing in it for me, in this action.

But do you know what? I think that's the thing which most attracts me to it. Everything I've done on this operation so far, I've done with half an eye on Price's preposterous medal-winning scheme. Here for once, my motives can remain unsullied and properly true to the motto on our family crest. *Semper Audax*: 'Always Bold'.

Still, I've made up my mind. If I'm not going to cross with my cousin, then there's no reason for me to cross at all.

'Hey, Lootenant. Lootenant Coward. Over here.' Still stuck, near the bank, are seventeen desperate men in a boat with just three oars between them. Some of the others are using the butts of their rifles, but to little effect. Each time they manage to escape the shore, the combination of poor steering, inept paddling and the vicious current sends them bumping back onto the sand.

'Can you use a paddle, Lootenant?' calls a man leaning towards me from the prow. It's O'Brien and next to him is the huge form of his buddy Jarecki.

'I rowed for my college,' I yell back. Then I notice – and if this isn't a sign, I don't know what is – that floating past just a few feet from where I'm wading is a loose paddle.

Jarecki leans further over, almost capsizing the boat. The men on the other side lean back to compensate just in time. Then I'm aboard, wet and gasping.

Did I mention how much stuff Jerry has been throwing at us all this while? The noise is quite atrocious. The crack and pop and whizz of rifle shots; the tearing and buzzing of the MGs; the judder and boom and deafening blast of 20-mm cannon and 88 high-explosive shells bursting all round and about, seems to have merged into one great terrifying überdin, such as Wagner might have written for an audience of deaf people on a thundery day when he was feeling especially cross.

What really brings it home is the state of the river: the whole surface is alive, boiling, as if ravaged by a tropical thunderstorm. It hisses and spits and sputters with a malevolent fury quite terrifying when you consider that each splash represents a bullet or a twisted shard of metal. And what you can't help noticing is just how very small the gaps are between them.

At this point we are, I should say, no more than a third of the way across the river. The three engineers at the stern are doing their best, but the other men's rhythm's all wrong with arms becoming entangled, raw knuckles being bashed by flailing rifle butts and eyes damned near poked out by barrels, crabs being caught, strokes too shallow or too deep, the result being pretty much total chaos. I haven't intervened so far because I'm not sure it's my place, but when we start spinning in circles yet again because another paratrooper has gone over the side and unbalanced the paddling, I decide enough's enough.

'Do you mind –?' I begin, leaning across towards the 1st Lieutenant who's in charge of the boat, for I think it's only courteous to ask permission before sticking my oar in. But just as I lean forward, a 20-mm shell which presumably had my name on it passes over my bent back and through the Lieutenant's head.

The force ought to have carried the body overboard, but unfortunately the Lieutenant's feet have got themselves jammed in the boat and, like a hosepipe snaking under high water pressure, his convulsing torso begins spraying us with bright red arterial blood. Much of it ends up soaking the man in the middle of the boat, who's holding all the spare weapons and, with his hands thus occupied, is unable to wipe the warm, salty gore from his face. To his credit, he manages to project his resultant vomit over the barrels of the rifles and the BAR – any minute now, they're going to come in rather handy – so that it lands instead on a surprised and disgusted Jarecki, who's busy trying to free the Lieutenant's feet, which eventually he does, heaving the body overboard with a, 'Sorry, Lootenant!'

I, meanwhile, am now trying to signal to those three engineers. No sooner have I done, than something of very high calibre and very high velocity – an armour-piercing 88, I decide afterwards, though at the time I don't pause to deliberate – simultaneously removes all three of them in one whooshing rush.

It's at moments like this that even the best-trained men fall to pieces. I feel like doing so myself, because it's abundantly clear now that we're not going to make it. Glancing upwards, my eyes meet those of another man in a boat maybe 20 yards beyond ours, whose mood so clearly echoes mine it's like gazing into a mirror. His expression is one of the most unutterable despair. Doomed, I think, but maybe that's because I've recognised him as the officer who was piling up his belongings in the sure knowledge that he wasn't going to survive the day. Or maybe, subconsciously, I've plotted the trajectory of the incoming shell, which hits the boat the very next second, folding it like origami and quickly sinking it beneath the water.

'Men!' I shout.

Odd looks: 'Who the fuck is this guy?'

'Men, listen to me. I sound English but I'm one quarter American, I'm the ranking officer and I rowed at Oxford so you're jolly well to do as I say!'

'Hey, listen to the guy, you sons of bitches! Listen up!' calls Jarecki.

'Men, we're going to sing a song and you're going to paddle to the rhythm. Smooth, even, in time. Ready?'

If you've seen *A Bridge Too Far* or read Cornelius Ryan's excellent book of that name, you'll know what they were saying in some of the other boats. For Maj. Cook, a devout Catholic, it was, "'Hail Mary, Mother Of Grace . . .'" And for Chaplain Kuehl, who, like me, couldn't resist the temptation to join the crossing, it was, "'Thy will be done . . .'" In my boat, however, the words that got us across the hell of the River Waal went like this:

"'*Row, row, row your boat —*'"

My voice is hoarse and raw. It sounds more like an ailing wolf than a popular nursery rhyme.

"'*Gently down the stream —*'"

The first signs of recognition from the men. Mostly puzzlement, perhaps even a measure of disgust at such levity in their time of trial.

'Fucking Limey!'

"'*Merrily merrily merrily merrily —*'"

Now at least Jarecki has joined in. That's something.

"'*Life is but a dream!*'"

Wry, reluctant smiles at this. The blood, the fear, the friends already gone, the fighting to come – this about as far from a dream as any man has ever been.

'All together now!'

'And in rhythm, you sons of bitches. IN RHYTHM.'

"'*Row, row, row your boat —*'"

Another boat has taken a direct hit. Bodies splash into the water just ahead of us. Some are still alive, most of those will be wounded, but we can't stop to help.

"'*Gently down the stream —*'"

A third, maybe half, of the men are croaking along now. More important, everyone's pulling more or less in rhythm.

"'*Merrily —*'"

Jesus. Under my feet, below the waterline, I actually felt the force of a bullet, no, a stream of bullets, smacking into the boat, coming out the other side, just missing me.

"'*Merrily* —'"

Another man gasps and goes floppy and stops paddling. Before he can drop his rifle, one of the men in the middle snatches it, swaps places with the wounded man, and begins paddling.

"'*Merrily* —'"

We're moving faster. We're definitely moving faster.

Merrily.

But we're taking in water. At this rate we're going to sink before we get there. I'm about to give the order but two men are already on the case, bailing for all they're worth with their helmets.

"'*Life is but a dream* —'"

If only. The fear is so thick you can chew it and choke on it. We're like prematurely buried men trying to scrabble from our coffins: that's how desperate we are to reach the other side. But we know we're not going to, not unless we keep singing that song. The words will protect us. The words will get us there. Keep singing those words and the words will get us there. And when we get there, nothing is going to stop us.

Nothing!

As we draw closer to the far bank the singing grows louder. It's the singing of men who are beginning to come to the terms with the idea that maybe they're not going to die after all. No, more than that, it's the singing of men who are preparing to kill.

The song's not an innocent song about boating any more. It's not even an innocent song about boating in murderously inapposite context. All the song is about now is what we plan to do when we get to the other side.

Kill, kill, kill and kill.

Kill and kill and KILL.

Kill and kill and kill and kill.

Kill and kill and KILL!

It's not what we're singing but it's what we're thinking.

Nothing personal, Jerry. But you can't expect to torment men the way we've been tormented without expecting some form of payback. You've terrified us within an inch of our lives. You've killed our friends. You've thrown everything you've got at us without stint or mercy. So you mustn't be surprised if we want to do the same to you.

Just as soon as we get to that bank.

Just wait till we get to that bank.

Just wait.

13

A Hard Rain

You'll have this image in your head of fit young American para-troopers – devils in baggy pants, the Germans called them – storming onto the north shore of the Waal, guns blazing. The reality more closely resembles arthritic pensioners trying to disembark from a coach on a busy road on a windy day in Skegness.

Our arms are leaden; we're completely out of breath and soaked to the skin; the boat keeps threatening to capsize as we gingerly negotiate our exit over the moaning wounded and cold, wet dead; and all around us mortar bombs are falling, shrapnel is screaming and airbursts are tearing apart the welkin while machine-gun bullets zip past our ears. It's carnage, utter carnage. Bodies on the shingle. Bodies piled high in crewless boats floating downriver like some grotesque, bargain-basement parody of a Viking-longship burial. Dying men being comforted by Chaplain Kuehl. Wounded men being dragged by medics onto the few boats still afloat to be ferried back by the few engineers still alive. Medics being wounded and then attended by other medics, before they in turn get wounded or killed. Screams of agony. Screams for Mother. Surprised yelps. The horrid dull thump of bullet into flesh.

Unless we can take out those enemy positions, we're all goners. There's fire coming down on us from the top of the embankment; more immediately, there's fire coming at us from machine guns in the marsh flats below the embankment. To charge them is madness; but to stay where we are is suicide.

Where the beach meets the plain, there's a bank just high enough to keep us protected while our vomit-coated armourer hands round the weapons. Jarecki retrieves his Browning Automatic Rifle; I grab a spare M1 carbine slimy with sick, blood and viscera.

'FIX BAYONETS,' I hear a surprisingly resolute voice order the five paratroopers from the boat who remain unwounded.

Too late, I remember that I don't have a bayonet to fix.

With a grin Jarecki hands me his.

I spread my fingers and thrust them towards the men, to indicate that we should all fan out.

A Spandau is sweeping our section of the beachhead. We wait until its latest arc of bullets has passed over our heads, with a buzz like a swarm of angry bees.

And over the top we go.

Now you'll hear a lot from British soldiers about how gung-ho and trigger-happy American infantry are; how they're too reliant on artillery, how they lack initiative and finesse, how the only way they can dominate the battlefield is through sheer weight of firepower.

It's a particular hobby horse of that whippersnapper Max Hastings – who only reported on skirmishes like the Falklands and Afghanistan, so what does he know about a proper shooting war? – and he's just as scathing about the British. Namby-pamby citizen-soldiers too reluctant to die, that was the Western Allies' problem, he says. Not like those magnificent, well-trained, ruthlessly efficient Germans with their splendid blond hair, Michelangelo torsos and refusal to surrender however hopeless the odds against.

Well, I grant you, I've witnessed plenty of occasions where

young Max's thesis was proved right enough. But the crossing of the Waal wasn't one of them.

We beat the enemy because we outfought the enemy.

I don't remember being remotely scared. Well, you're not, generally, when you're in the thick of an action – far too many other things to think about. But in this one in particular I felt something much closer to exhilaration. Exultation even.

If you'd come up to me with a wand at that moment and said, 'Dick, you can either be here or on a South Pacific island, smeared in coconut oil, high on rum and straddled by three Tahitian lovelies,' I wouldn't have even paused to consider.

Damn it, I was enjoying this.

'Damn it, I'm enjoying this,' I actually hear myself mutter, as we advance across those 800 yards of exposed ground in line abreast. Myself, Jarecki, O'Brien, and all those other men whose names I don't even know and perhaps never will before they die.

We move forward in bounds, firing from the hip. The ground is squelchy and uneven, with tough little tussocks of marsh grass which threaten to trip us up but somehow never do, such is our confidence and sure-footedness. There are enemy machine-gun positions everywhere, but we swat them aside like flies.

Soon as one of them opens up, Jarecki keeps the crew's heads down with suppressing fire from his BAR, while the rest of us surge towards their flanks to pick them off. Often we're on to them so quickly they're still lying prone on the ground, staring ahead, wondering where we've got to. Some of them have just enough time to look up in wild terror, or even half rise up, preparing to raise their arms in surrender, before we finish them off.

By the time we've reached the base of the embankment, only four of my group are left. Normally, you'd take a breather, but there isn't time and the adrenalin flow's too powerful. This is how berserk warriors must have felt when they rushed forward, mad as wolves, biting their shields, killing their enemies at one blow. The red mist has descended.

I glance meaningfully towards the top of the embankment, 20 foot above us.

'Grenades,' I command.

With a grin, Jarecki unclips one from his chest and hands it to me.

Up over the crest, the German gun positions are easy to identify because of the tracer streaming above our heads towards our comrades on the riverbank. So long as we stay on the bank, though, we're immune to their fire. We clamber purposefully up the embankment. In the two or three hundred yards either side of us, little, self-contained groups just like ours are preparing for similar, private engagements.

Jarecki takes the rear with his BAR. The rest of us fan out ahead, each of us choosing our own machine gun to engage.

I pull the pin from my grenade – not using my teeth as they do in films because that jolly well hurts – and release the safety lever. The others, all watching me, follow suit. The grenades are now live and dangerous but these boys are so disciplined that none of them throws just yet.

What we're doing is something risky but necessary called 'cooking off'. This will reduce the time our grenades take to detonate after they've been thrown. Otherwise, with the enemy so close, there's a chance they'll have time to pick them up and throw them back.

'One thousand and one; one thousand and two,' I'm carefully counting to myself, when the ghastly thought streaks through my brain that these are American-issue grenades, not the British ones I'm used to, and that the fuse length may be shorter than our standard four seconds.

I get rid of mine quickly in a near-vertical lob, which with any luck will explode mid-air directly above the enemy position. Immediately afterwards, I flatten myself against the embankment, my face buried in the soil. Almost simultaneously a tremendous blast wave thumps across my back, followed by a shower of unidentifiable lumps, which I think may have wounded me, for when instinctively I reach behind to feel my hand comes back red and sticky. No time to investigate. From just over the lip of the embankment there are screams and moans. We must press our advantage before the enemy recovers.

We crest the embankment firing from the hip. The crew of the gun pit in front of me are already dying or dead. I empty my magazine into their bodies just in case. Twenty yards to my left, Jarecki is spraying another gun pit with his BAR. Beyond him, another paratrooper is wielding his rifle like an axe, smashing it down so furiously and frequently that its bloodied butt has begun to splinter. The length of the embankment, small groups like ours are fighting similar actions with grenade, rifle, machine gun and bayonet. There are Germans everywhere.

Just to my right, a dazed lad in a forage cap is clambering from his foxhole with his arms raised. He's young, not much more than sixteen, I'd say, with classic Hitler Youth looks – dirty, blond hair, blue eyes which are looking straight into mine, half confused, half imploring.

He mouths something at me. '*Kamerad*', I'd guess, though I'm not properly taking things in. My ears are ringing. My thoughts are racing. Nothing quite connects. It's all just rushing at me in a series of random, impressionistic gobbets.

Some of them exist in the present, like the paratrooper who has commandeered a Spandau and is mowing down Germans mercilessly, as like ants whose nest has been scalded with boiling water they clamber in stunned zigzags from their subterranean hidey-holes.

Some of them are flashbacks to the river crossing: the 1st

Lieutenant's head exploding, the sense of helplessness; the intense desire for escape and revenge.

Some, I'd rather not know what they are, like the image I have of a blond boy's face crumpling in surprise as a bayonet enters his belly and twists. It's the lack of judgement in those that haunts me most. There's no bitterness, there. No recrimination. It just seems to say, 'Oh. So that's what you've decided to do. I thought somehow you wouldn't and now you have; well, there's not really an awful lot I can do.'

When I want to feel better, I persuade myself that it must have been someone else who did it. Killing unarmed boys just isn't my style. But every time I try that, I remember the garlicky sausage smell which emerged with the boy's last gasp, and the passage of his blond, wavy, rufflable hair down my chest – almost as if he were a child who'd come to his father for a snuggle – as he slumped forward onto my shoulder, and dragged face-first down the length of my body, before collapsing at my feet.

Next thing I know, Jarecki's tugging at my sleeve, yelling, 'We gotta move, Lootenant.'

Behind and below us on the plain, wounded paratroopers are crawling past more bodies towards the medics on the shore. In the eleven surviving boats, the next wave is already halfway across the river.

The top of the embankment is littered with bundles of what looks like discarded laundry, some of it olive drab, but most of it field grey. Eyes stare from dead sockets. Splintered bone gleams white from blackened wounds.

But I shall spare you the details, Jack. Suffice to say that the rest of that long, bloody, exhausting afternoon continues much as it has done before: with small bands of paratroopers taking on much larger bodies of entrenched Germans and overwhelming them by sheer force of will.

The Fort is typical of this. Its walls are many feet thick, it has a deep moat running round it. All military logic tells you that this is not the sort of place which will crack without intense artillery bombardment and a lengthy siege. Having neither the materiel nor the time, we stumble up to it, Jarecki and myself, and just hope a solution will present itself.

I can't remember how we took it in the end. What I think happened is that we didn't bother – we just left two or three machine-gunners to keep the Germans cowering inside pinned down, while the bulk of us swept on to our next objective.

Rather, the reason that fort sticks in my mind is because of the very strange sight Jarecki and I saw emerging from the moat. It was covered in dripping weed, like some creature from the swamp, its eyes glistening white through a wall of green.

'Jesus H Christ!' says the swamp monster on seeing Jarecki and me.

'Good God, Richard, I'd feared you were dead,' I exclaim.

'Damn it to hell, Dick, I seem to recall ordering your ass to stay put.'

'I did try to stop him, sir,' says Jarecki, quite untruthfully.

'Try isn't good enough, Jarecki. If you catch him doing anything this dangerous again, you got my permission to shoot him.'

'Consider it done, sir,' says Jarecki.

'Er, Jarecki, you do realise he's joking?' I say.

'I ain't that dumb, Lootenant. Jeez, have you been listening to O'Brien?'

'God, that's a point, what happened to him?'

'You really want to know?'

'Well, it's odd. He just seemed to disappear.'

'No, no, Lootenant, he's much closer than you think.'

'Where?'

'Right behind you. Can't you feel it? That's him stuck all over your back.'

*

God knows how many Germans we ended up killing that day, but on the north end of the bridge alone – we took it in the early evening, after a short, sharp engagement – we later counted over two hundred bodies. Jarecki had gone by then, stumbling back to the river's edge with a bullet in his arm. One of the two remaining paratroopers in my group quickly took over his BAR and from then on, we fought alongside my cousin and the seven surviving men from his boat.

It's an odd sensation when you've spent four or five hours expecting to die any second suddenly to find yourself still alive and with a reasonable prospect of staying that way. I remember, not long before the last leg of the assault, catching Capt. Du Croix's eye and both of us shaking our heads, then grinning, then laughing out loud in disbelief at this extraordinary turn of events. And then having to put on very straight faces again, because the Other Ranks had started to look worried.

'We must do this more often,' I say.

'We must,' he agrees, putting on a mild British accent.

They're the first words we've exchanged since the Fort, which gives you an idea how intense the fighting has been. There's only time to talk now because we're waiting for some more ammo to arrive, while taking shelter in a farmhouse on the edge of an orchard littered with delicious apples and German dead.

I offer him a cigarette from my silver case. My hand is so black and red with dirt and congealed blood it looks more like a demon's claw.

He declines, raising an apple to his lips with a, 'This'll do me more good.'

'Do you really think so?' I say, lighting up. I exchange a conspiratorial grin with the two paratroopers by the window, both of whom, as most soldiers do, are sucking on cigarettes as if their lives depended on it.

'They say tobacco can be injurious to a man's health, you know.'

'Well, someone clearly neglected to tell your president.'

'Your prime minister, too.'

'My point entirely. Our leaders smoke like chimneys. The opposition's leader can't bear tobacco. Ergo, for any member of the Allied forces, smoking ought not to be considered a vice but a bounden patriotic duty.'

Capt. Du Croix smiles and takes another bite of his apple.

'Is it really true, that story about you and Hitler?'

'The pissing incident, you mean? Why, certainly.'

'Would you rather not, er—?' says Capt. Du Croix, sensing, as I have, that the men have suddenly become very interested in our conversation.

'Captain, it would be my pleasure,' I interrupt and, for the room's general benefit, launch straight into the heart-warming tale of how it was I once accidentally on purpose came to hose down the Führer's leg with a voluminous stream of British urine. Till the goon beside him in the leather coat chose painfully to intervene, that is.

Jack, I shall tell you the full story one day, I promise. But if you don't mind I'd rather do so in context, lest I turn into yet another of those dodderers who repeat the same yarn quite oblivious to their audience's discomfort.

I've only just got to the end – the men are laughing their socks off – when the ammo arrives. There's no mucking about with these US airborne chaps. Barely have the boxes touched the floor, than everyone's stuffed their pouches, wiped off their smirks and stiffened their sinews ready for the last and possibly most dangerous leg of the assault.

'Richard, I just want you to know that this has been a pleasure and a privilege,' I say softly.

'Dick, the pleasure and privilege have been all mine,' replies my cousin. And with that, he's off issuing clear, concise orders for the final stage of the attack, to be covered by smoke from the white phosphorous mortar bombs which have just been delivered.

*

The attack has gone pretty well. By the time we regroup at the foot of the bridge, near a gun pit smeared with German dead, only one of our number has gone missing. There's still some work to be done in the middle of the bridge – as the frequent zinging shots from high in the girders testify – but it shouldn't be much more than a mopping-up exercise. What's important is, with both ends of the bridge now in our hands, our tanks in Nijmegen have a more than halfway decent chance of pushing through to Arnhem before it's too late.

Capt. Du Croix points towards the lower road which runs parallel with the river underneath the bridge.

'Sergeant Maddox, take four men and check the underside, especially round the supporting columns. Anything that looks like a wire, cut it. The Krauts could try to blow the bridge at any time.'

The rest of us follow Capt. Du Croix very cautiously up the flight of concrete steps which leads onto the bridge itself. The silence is eerie. At the far end, a battle royal is still raging. Up at this end, you could hear a pin drop. Well, you could if your lugholes weren't ringing something rotten from all the noise.

For the moment we shan't attempt to capture the bridge. Rather, the idea is to consolidate the fairly lengthy stretch of road – perhaps a thousand yards – which extends north-west from the road bridge and passes beneath the viaduct of the railway bridge we captured earlier. It's near this viaduct that an incident occurs for which the Americans have never quite forgiven us and in which Cowards play no small part.

We've just passed under this viaduct when, from the direction of the road bridge, there comes an ominous creaking and clanking.

Armour.

Most likely German.

Either way, there's no point hanging around to find out. We all dive for the cover of the ditch that runs either side of the road, while two of the more enterprising troopers make ready with their gelignite charges.

And only just in time, too, for through the viaduct the tank roars, machine guns blazing bright in the dusky half-light and only narrowly missing the heads of the troopers who've leapt up to throw the charges.

Whomp!

Whomp!

Neither charge has found its mark and the tank trundles on, its turret gun now swinging towards us. Instinctively, desperately, hopelessly I flatten myself harder against the soil. To move is to invite immediate destruction from the tank's coaxial machine gun; to stay still will mean eventual death by high-explosive shell instead. Our only remaining chance is if some enterprising soul with another gelignite charge can somehow creep up on the tank from its blind side and then –

'It's ours!' someone yells.

'American! American! We're American!' calls someone else.

Now the tank has stopped firing, and from either side of the road, shadowy figures are rising from the ditches. A head pops up from the tank's turret. It's a Sherman, I now recognise, as no doubt I should have done earlier had it not been so dark. The paratroopers are swarming all over it, some kissing the armour, another with his arms clamped in a bear hug round the neck of the bemused tank commander.

'All right, lads, that's enough of that,' he says in his embarrassed English way.

'God save the King!' replies the paratrooper, planting a huge smacker on his cheek.

Another tank has pulled up behind his now, followed by a third. Soon the paratroopers are crawling jubilantly over theirs, too.

'I say, do you mind?' calls a voice from the turret of the third

Sherman, cutting through the gloom. It's drawlingly confident and upper class as of course one would expect of the Guards Armoured Division. The squadron commander's, presumably.

'Richard, he's right, if they come under fire it could get very messy,' I murmur to my cousin.

'Men, come away from those tanks! They need to get to Arnhem.'

'Arnhem, he says,' I hear the first tank commander calling down to the head poking from the driver's hatch below. 'I'll give him full marks for optimism.'

I don't think any of the US paratroopers hear. Or if they do, perhaps they've mistaken it for quirky English humour. It certainly hasn't occurred to any of them yet that what they are witnessing is the very furthermost extent of the British armoured breakout from Nijmegen bridge.

On either side of the road, the paratroopers have formed lines, like guests at a wedding waving off the bride and groom. If there was confetti, they'd be throwing it.

'Way to go, guys! Over to you!'

'Give 'em hell!'

'Send the Red Devils our love!'

When the tanks stay resolutely immobile, the paratroopers begin to make sweeping gestures with their arms in the direction of Arnhem. Still the tanks refuse to budge.

'Aw, c'mon, guys, what's the problem?'

'They haven't had their tea break,' someone jests.

'Sweet Jesus Christ, they ARE having a tea break,' observes another.

And sure enough, there are the crew of the middle tank, huddling by the roadside over their billycan and stove. It isn't long before the crews of the other tanks follow suit.

The mood is turning nasty. The American paratroopers have started to jeer, while the British tankers are affecting to pretend they don't exist. This insouciance, of course, annoys the Americans no end. They've begun to close in on the tank crews, standing round them in menacing, jeering circles.

'We'd better sort this out,' I say to my cousin.

'Let them go to hell,' he says.

'Look, Richard, I know you're angry . . .'

'For Christ's sake, Dick. I did not sacrifice half my company so that your guys could sit around here drinking tea,' says my cousin, turning puce. In battle he was so calm. But you can't keep all that rage, frustration, pain, aggression and despair bottled up for ever. 'Nor will they!' he adds, lurching suddenly towards one of the tank crews.

I try to grab him by the arm, but he's too quick and determined. With a flying kick of his paratroop boot, he has sent the crew's billy can hurtling into the ditch. To cheers and catcalls from the surrounding paratroopers, the tank crew scuttle for the safety of their Sherman and batten down the hatches.

'I say, you. Yes, you!' calls the squadron commander. His crew, too, have now fled inside their tank. The squadron commander, whose voice sounds oddly familiar, is talking down from the top of the turret.

'Jeez, Dick, what did I just do?' mutters a shamefaced Capt. Du Croix in my ear.

'You'd better let me do the talking,' I mutter back.

We approach the tank side by side.

'Try anything like that again, Captain, and I shall not hesitate to use my guns,' says the voice. I know it. I definitely know it.

'If you'll allow me to explain, sir –' I begin through gritted teeth, for this officer – I'm presuming he's senior to me – is quite clearly a prick of the first water.

'And you are?' Ah the contempt. The sneering, preening hauteur. It's too dark now to see his face, but there's only one person in the world who talks quite like that.

'Your brother.'

'Dick? Good God, man! What on earth are you doing with this rabble?'

Beside me, Capt. Du Croix bristles. If I'm not careful he's going to charge that tank single-handed and I know just what my brother James would do if he tried.

'This rabble, James, have just crossed the Waal.' I try to keep my voice matter-of-fact, free from hatred or simmering rage. But of course my brother, being my brother, detects both qualities instantly.

'Funnily enough, so have I,' he says.

'But not in a flimsy collapsible boat under fire,' I say, though God knows why, for the 504th PIR's achievement hardly needs special pleading.

'Very impressive, I'm sure,' drawls my brother. 'But, with all due respect to your American friend here, if his chaps had done what they were meant to and taken both ends of the bridge on day one, the heroics wouldn't have been necessary, would they?'

Yet again I sense that – not altogether surprisingly – my cousin is preparing himself for a suicidal charge.

'Allow me to introduce your cousin Richard, James,' I say, quickly. 'Capt. Du Croix, meet your cousin Major Coward.'

'My American cousin, eh? What a rare pleasure.'

'If only, sir, I could say that the feeling was mutual.'

'I say, Dick, I think our dear coz is trying to insult me.'

'He's just lost half his men, James, trying to save our backsides at Arnhem. I think he's perhaps a little puzzled as to why our tank commanders aren't quite so committed.'

'And what, exactly, are you insinuating?'

'Nothing that I haven't insinuated before when you so gallantly "won" that first MC, brother dear.'

Red rag to a bull, that one. I'll tell you the full story when I get round to recounting my Western desert adventures. Suffice to say that it was not the most shining example of a chap getting his just deserts.

'That's Major to you, Lieutenant,' snorts my brother. 'And I'm damned if I'm going to have to justify my actions to a mere sub-altern.'

With a contemptuous toss of my head I turn to my cousin and say in a stage whisper, 'Are you familiar, Captain, with the term "windy"? Here's a textbook example.'

'Damn it, another word like that, Lieutenant, and I'll have you court-martialled for insubordination. My orders were to advance no further than this viaduct. Those orders I intend to obey.'

'Those orders are a death sentence for your comrades at Arnhem bridge,' says my cousin.

'If you feel so strongly, why don't you take it up with Lieutenant General Horrocks? It's his command decision,' says James.

'In parachute infantry our officers are trained to show something called initiative. Ever heard of that, Major?'

'You're saying that in my shoes, you'd press on willy-nilly, in the dark, with just three tanks on an exposed road through twelve miles of enemy-held territory bristling with Panzerfausts and 88s?'

'I am.'

'Then you'd be an even bigger fool than I thought you were, Captain. Without supporting infantry, you wouldn't last a hundred yards.'

'Is that your only concern, Major? Jeez, why didn't you say so? I've got thirty good men here who'd be more than happy to give you infantry back-up. All the way to Arnhem, if needs be.'

'That's a very kind offer, Captain, but you must know I can't accept.'

'Why can't you accept?'

'Because as I thought I'd made quite clear, my orders were—'

'So radio back, explain the position and get the orders changed,' says Capt. Du Croix.

'I'm sorry, Captain, but I can't do that.'

'Why can't you do that?'

'Because he's a cunt, is why,' I confide to my cousin, just a little more loudly than I meant to.

'What did you just say, Lieutenant?'

'I said couldn't you just give it a go?'

'That is not what you said. You know it's not what you said.'

'All right, brother dear, fair enough. But if I retract, could you at least have a stab? I agree HQ will probably say no, for any number of reasons, but it's surely worth a try. You might even go down in history as the man who saved 1st Airborne. Father would definitely give you the estate for that.'

'Unless I'm much mistaken, he already has. Now are you going to apologise for what you just said?'

'I'm sorry.'

'How sorry?'

'Very sorry.'

'Sorry enough to understand that there's not a snowball's chance in hell of my acceding to your ridiculous request?'

'What?'

'You heard me. No one calls Major James Coward DSO MC and bar a cunt and gets away with it. Least of all a disinherited, passed-over lieutenant.'

14

Home

No one who was at Oosterbeek will easily forget the 'morning hate', the banshee chorus of shells and mortar bombs with which Jerry, in his inimitable way, would insist on bidding us *guten Morgen*. But I must have slept clean through it on the night of my arrival, because the first thing I remember as I re-emerged into vague consciousness – cold, shivering, damp and thoroughly downcast – was the sound of 'The Teddy Bears' Picnic' crooned by Hal Rosing to the jaunty accompaniment of Henry Hall and his orchestra. "*If you go down in the woods today you're sure of a big surprise . . .*"

You couldn't escape that song in the thirties, blaring as it always did from the gramophone at some point, at every children's birthday party you ever attended. So you'll imagine the psychological effect it has on all us chaps holding the perimeter at Oosterbeek. Here we are, doing our best to be big, brave and manly, and there's Jerry – one of his specialist propaganda units, no doubt – doing a horribly effective job of turning us back into sobbing schoolboys, clinging on to Mummy because we didn't win pass-the-parcel.

It's certainly how I feel, anyway. I'm tired and I'm upset and I want to go to bed. That's proper bed, with cotton sheets, a reading lamp, Mummy to kiss me goodnight and, in the morning, that glorious view over our parkland, down to the Wye and up to the hills beyond. Definitely not this foul, smelly ersatz version in the shallow trench I've scraped myself by digging through the rotten floorboards of an old garden shed, before covering myself, for a semblance of warmth, with a couple of hessian sacks reeking of benzene. And definitely not with all that endless rat-a-tat-ing, screaming and booming going on outside of which I've had enough now. I've damned well had enough!

After 'The Teddy Bears' Picnic' comes something more poignant still. It's Gracie Fields, at her most powerfully nostalgic and tear-jerking, warbling her way through 'Home'. "*When shadows fall and trees whisper day is ending, my thoughts are ever wending home,*" she trills, voicing sentiments which in the past I've tended to dismiss as saccharine. But this morning, oh my, never has cheap music sounded more potent. It's ridiculous, but I can actually feel the tears welling in the corner of my eyes. I think it's only the voices that have started chuntering outside which stop me from breaking down completely. They belong to four men who, unfortunately, I will never see alive.

'Treacherous cow!' says one.

'Wash yer mouth out,' says a Lancastrian accent. 'She's a Rochdale lass is our Gracie.'

'Then what the fook's she doing batting for the Opposition?'

'Maybe Jerry's taken her as a swap for "Lili Marlene".'

'Shh. Lads. I can see it!'

'Where, Corp?'

'There! See? T'other side of that track. Underneath the laurel.'

'Fook. Ent much cover, is there?'

'Why do you think nobody's retrieved it yet?'

'Maybe they have. Maybe it's empty. Maybe it's a trap.'

'If you don't like it, Cobb, there's still time to piss off back to your slit trench. We'd rather divide the spoils three ways than four, wouldn't we, lads?'

'I'm still game, Corp. I'd just feel happier if I knew what it was I were risking my neck for.'

'What do you think is in it, Corp?'

'That's the fun of the fair, ain't it? It's a lucky dip.'

'Fags, I'm hoping.'

'Aye, then we can chuck 'em over to Jerry and hope he smokes hisself to death.'

'Grub, I want. Corned beef, for preference.'

'Oh, you do surprise us, Fatty.'

'And you're hoping for grenades, .303 and a gross of PIATs, I suppose. So you can burrow your way even further up Major Pritchard's arse?'

'Not wishing to spoil your fantasy, Fatty, but were you aware we're in the midst of a fooking great ruck wi' Jerry, with fook all left to chuck at him?'

'Lads, if you go on bickering, we're never going to find out what's in that basket.'

'All right, Corp. What's the MO? You'll be wanting me to go in first, I suppose.'

'Sounds like you're volunteering, Johnson. Well done, lad.'

'Do you reckon there's snipers?'

'Bank on it. Soon as you get to the laurel, you'll be safe, I reckon. It's the fifteen yards of open ground beforehand you need to worry about.'

'Oh heck, Corp. Where's the blooming smoke grenades when you need them?'

'In that basket, probably. Good luck, lad. I'd say take the rope but it'll only weigh you down. Soon as you're across, we'll chuck it to you. Go on, then. What are you waiting for?'

'Nothing, Corp. Just catching me breath.'

'Don't catch it too long or the war'll be over.'

231

From the not too far distance, the sound distorted by a whistling, over-amplified tannoy, come once more the hissing, crackling introductory bars to 'The Teddy Bears' Picnic'.

I hate the song more than ever now, because it's making it harder to hear whether or not Johnson has made it. Though I have no intention of making my presence known to these four brave men, I now feel intimately involved in the success of their mission.

The next thing I hear is a tense but exultant 'YESS!' so I presume Johnson has crossed the open ground without difficulty. If you realised just how many German snipers there are out there, you'd appreciate that this in itself has been no small feat. They infiltrate through our perimeter in the dark, tie themselves to the tops of trees, wait for the dawn and pick us off at their leisure. Of course when we catch them, we show them no mercy. It's the catching them before they kill you that's the hard part.

'" *YOU'RE SURE OF A BIG SURPRISE –*"'

'Right, Arbuckle. Reckon you can throw him that rope from a crouching position?'

'If it's corned beef in that basket, I could do it prone and blindfolded.'

'" *BETTER GO IN DISGUISE –*"'

'Want me to have a look for you?' I can hear Johnson calling from across the track.

I can now see the top of the laurel bush too. Grim fascination having overcome my depressed lethargy, I've pulled myself out of my shallow trench and found a bullet hole in the shed's wooden wall affording a reasonable view of my surroundings. You can identify the bush by the collapsed parachute draped on top of it. Beyond it is the expanse of woodland in which the snipers, if there are any snipers, will be hiding. And beyond that, is enemy territory.

If I'd known how close this shed was to the perimeter when I blundered into it last night, I certainly wouldn't have chosen it as a hiding place.

'Don't, Johnson,' calls the Corporal. I can't see Johnson but I can see the bush rustling as he does something with the drop canister. 'Leave – oh fuck!'

The crack of the rifle and the Corporal's expletive tells me all I need to know.

'Is he dead, Corp?'

'"*TODAY'S THE DAY –*"'

'As a doornail,' the Corporal confirms.

'"*HAVE THEIR PICNIC –*"'

'Who –?'

'It's all right, lads. I'll choose the short straw this time. Now for God's sake, keep your heads down.'

'"*THE LITTLE TEDDY BEARS ARE HAVING A LOVELY TIME TODAY –*"'

CRACK!

I think I saw the muzzle flash this time.

'Fook!'

'The Corp's not bought it?'

'Fooking 'as, 'n' all.'

Part of me – the old part – wants to go and tell them, help them, do anything to stop them getting killed. The new part is incapable.

But they'll die, protests the old part.

No they won't. They'll see sense and give up, says the new part.

'"*THEY LOVE TO PLAY AND SHOUT, THEY NEVER HAVE ANY CARES –*"'

'Now what?'

'What do you think what? I'm going meself. Give us the rope. You'll never throw it from the crouch.'

'"*AT SIX O'CLOCK THEIR MUMMIES AND DADDIES WILL TAKE THEM HOME TO BED –*"'

'You sure?'

'Just give it us, will you?'

'"*TIRED LITTLE TEDDY BEARS –*"'

A long, anxious pause.

Then:

'You made it!'

'Give us a second. I'm going to tie the rope to the basket then chuck the other end to you. Got that?'

'Got it.'

'"*SAFER TO STAY AT HOME –*"'

I'm watching the treetops now. Just the treetops.

Yet the two survivors are well aware of the danger by now. They surely won't expose themselves unnecessarily.

'You ready?' calls the man on the far side.

'When you are,' calls the man on my side – Fatty Arbuckle, isn't it?

'"*WATCH THEM, CATCH THEM UNAWARES –*"'

'Bugger. Too short.'

'It's OK. Think I can reach.'

'I'll throw again.'

'No, it's OK –'

CRACK!

Definitely saw the muzzle flash this time. Ten o'clock. Second from top branch of the big beech tree.

'Fatty? FATTY? Oh fook! You fooking German bastard! Lads. Lads? Anyone still alive? Arbuckle? Johnson? Corporal Fisher? Fook. What the fook do I fooking do now?'

He gibbers to himself in this way for some time – sometimes angry, sometimes fearful, sometimes tearful – and with each new outburst, I inwardly writhe.

Help him, damn it! Help the poor man! says my old voice, the one belonging to the Dick Coward you know best, but who sadly exists only 95 per cent of the time.

But what can I do. What can I do? says the snivelling, hateful new man I've become, for it's the 5 per cent we're stuck with now.

Create a diversion. Have a pop at him – you know exactly where he is now, says old Dick.

With a Colt.45? says new Dick, reminding old Dick not unreasonably that we lost our Schmeisser during yesterday night's fraught river crossing – the one with a boatload of gallant Poles, under fire damn near as petrifying as we experienced over the Waal, from the southern bank of the Rhine at Driel to the northern bank, which now forms part of our defensive perimeter. Against a German sniper rifle? You'd get killed instantly.

After your behaviour just now, maybe death's what you deserve, says old Dick.

New Dick stays quiet. He knows in his heart that old Dick is probably right. His behaviour is quite inexcusable. But when your nerve has gone, what can you do?

'"Our Father, which art in heaven –"'

Oh God, please get on with it and hurry up and go! says new Dick.

You heartless bastard! says old Dick.

There's nothing we can do for him, says new Dick.

The prayer diminishes to a whisper. It's not difficult to work out what's going through poor Johnson's mind. If that sniper's good enough to get my three mates, what chance do I have getting across the 15 yards of open ground that separate me from safety?

CRACK!

And there's his answer.

Thank Christ for that, mutters new Dick, not that he doesn't feel awful about the man's death, of course. But at least it means the slate is clean: now there can be no possible witnesses to his cowardice.

Old Dick is at first so disgusted he can't even respond. Then, from perhaps 100 yards to the rear, he hears the unmistakable 'tonk' of a discharging mortar, followed shortly afterwards by an explosion at the base of the beech tree. A camouflaged figure falls from the upper branch, where it dangles and swings from a rope.

Come on, says old Dick.

What? Where? says new Dick.

Outside. We're going outside!

A phrase you'll hear often used in military memoirs, Jack, is 'Courage is a wasting asset.' But I don't think that's the only reason I behaved in the shoddy way I did during those last few days of Market Garden. Nor can I wholly blame physical exhaustion, battle weariness or lack of sleep, though no doubt they played their part.

I think what had really driven me to the edge – and perhaps beyond – on that miserable cold dawn of Saturday, 21 September 1944 was fathomless despair. Despair at the final realisation that the lives, limbs and liberty of eleven thousand of the world's best and bravest men were about to be sacrificed in vain.

When exactly did I realise this? Good question. It came to me not in one single blinding revelation. But slowly, drip by drip, like the Chinese water torture.

I suppose the first drip would have been that scene with my brother near Nijmegen bridge. Was that single hasty expletive beginning with 'c' and ending in 'unt' the real reason why Guards Armoured Division never advanced the final twelve miles to Arnhem bridge, I've sometimes wondered. Was the failure of Market Garden all my and my brother's fault?

Well, no. Even by the Coward family's considerable standards of paranoia, self-hatred and egotism, I think it would be stretching it to suggest that we were personally responsible for adding an extra six months onto the end of the Second World War.

For the record – though, of course, it took me many years to accept this, clouded as my judgement was by my foaming hatred for James – I've since come to appreciate that Guards Armoured Division were quite right not to continue their advance that night. On that narrow, high-banked exposed track, with room to deploy, it would have been suicide.

Could Market Garden still have succeeded once that decision had been taken? Well, I personally still thought so, yes. Which is why, as soon as the bridges had been cleared by my GI friends of their last-ditch defenders, I made my way back early on Friday morning across to Nijmegen and Lt. Gen. Browning's HQ, there to offer myself as a guide for whatever rescue mission XXX Corps now had planned.

'Do you not think you've already done enough, Dick?' says Lt. Gen. Browning when miraculously I've secured my audience. (I only got it, I reckon, because in the garden on the way I happened to bump into Jim Gavin, who had apparently decided to take me more seriously after my crossing of the Waal with his boys from 504th PIR.)

If a man as formal as Boy is using my Christian name, things really must be dire.

'But, sir, with my intimate knowledge of our positions at the bridge –'

'I'm sorry, Dick, but it's too late for that. The bridge has fallen.'

'What?'

'They sent their final signal not half an hour ago.'

'And the rest of the division?'

'They've formed a defensive perimeter in Oosterbeek.'

'Then to Oosterbeek, sir, I must go.'

Even at this late stage of the operation – on the day subsequently to be christened 'Black Friday' – there were still a good many of us, perhaps even the majority, who yet believed that triumph could be snatched from the jaws of disaster.

Certainly, I don't recall feeling unduly downcast that evening as I hitched a lift north in the back of a supply lorry belonging to 5th Duke of Cornwall's Light Infantry, my belly full of food, my webbing and small pack crammed with cigarettes, rations and ammo for our beleagured troops, and with a personal message from Lt. Gen. Browning to Gen. Urquhart. I dozed most of the way, anyway.

It was when we reached our destination – a village called Driel on the bank of the Rhine directly opposite our forces in Oosterbeek – that I started to feel the first intimations of hopelessness.

No doubt I'd been expecting too much. But what I'd hoped to find when I hopped, groggily, off the lorry's tailboard, was a hive of fruitful activity like something from an heroic Victorian etching called *The Relief of Oosterbeek*. I thought I'd find engineers in the midst of extending a Bailey bridge over the Rhine; tanks hull down in extended line offering fire support like they did at the Waal; artillery blazing; battalions of infantry forming up for the assault which would carry Second Army across its last river obstacle, and finish the job we had left undone at Arnhem Bridge.

What I found instead was chaos and frustration: a brigade of tense, chain-smoking Poles itching for some contact; a furious Gen. Sosabowski; a tall, languid Household Cavalry captain named Lord Wrottesley relaying increasingly desperate messages to and from Corps HQ from his armoured scout car; and a gaggle of DUKWs all stuck in the mud on the steep banks of the river approaches, their wheels spinning hopelessly, their back ends slewing wildly from side to side, surrounded by nervous, shattered men trying to push them out of trouble while being shelled and machine-gunned from the German positions on the north bank.

This, I dare say, was the point when I should have recognised that our predicament was beyond repair. The major rescue operation I'd envisaged was clearly no such thing. But with my message from Lt. Gen. Browning, there was no turning back now. Like it or not, I would have to make yet another river crossing in a flimsy boat under heavy fire, this time in the company of Polish paratroopers.

If they hadn't been Poles, I'm not sure I could have coped. Any other race – Americans, British, even Germans – and the collective (and, I might say, wholly justified) fear and anxiety would have unnerved me beyond reason. But the Poles, as you may know, are mad. Or so it seemed to me on that terrifying river crossing in those useless little rubber dinghies.

The weight of fire being poured on us was almost intolerable. The boats fore and aft of us in the line disappeared without trace. Yet all the Poles surrounding me would do – those that weren't pulling across via the rope which had been stretched across the river – was yawn, and grin, and crack presumably very unfunny Polish jokes, and pick their teeth with their bayonets and chain-smoke foul-smelling cigarettes. When one half of your country's been ravaged by Stalin and the other by Hitler, your wife and daughters raped, your sons murdered and your home destroyed, I suppose an adventure like this counts as light relief.

Our boat took a hit and quickly sank, forcing those of us who were capable to swim the last 20 yards. In order not to drown, I had quickly to jettison my machine pistol, my small pack and my webbing containing the ammo, food and cigarettes which would have no doubt won me so many new friends.

The only thing I didn't lose was the envelope, wrapped in oil-skin, containing the personal message for Gen. Urquhart. A shame, really, for this I fear was what finally tipped me over the brink. Not the message itself – it was for the Divisional Commander's eyes only – but the expression on his face as he read it.

Div HQ, as you'll know if you've visited Oosterbeek, was located in what is now the town's Airborne Museum, but which at the time was still that attractive, whitewashed country-club style hotel I'd admired on the day we landed: the Hartenstein Hotel.

It has changed quite a bit in the intervening week. Those handsome landscaped grounds are now are an ugly warren of foxholes, slit trenches and bomb craters. No verdant lawns any more, just an expanse of well-trampled mud; no leaves on the tree branches or bushes either, for those which haven't been stripped by our men for camouflage or cover for their dugouts have long since been shredded to nothing by shrapnel. And strewn everywhere, the debris of war: cartridge cases, chunks of twisted metal, dud shells, discarded bits of kit, empty cans, and unmentionable bits of flesh, some fresh and raw, some black or green and very high.

To complete the effect, each successive horror is revealed to you in flashes – not unlike when you trundle through the dark on a fairground ghost train – as the dark is illuminated by shell bursts.

Guiding me through all this shambles is a glider pilot whose name I don't catch. It's far too noisy for chit-chat and you wouldn't feel much up to it, anyway, what with the constant fear that the next incoming shell will be the one with your name on it, and the vile, pervasive odour of cordite and rotting corpses which makes you want to gag with each step.

At the Hartenstein, an aide with blackened face and puffy, red-rimmed eyes leads me down into the basement. The Divisional Commander's door is open and, before Gen. Urquhart pulls himself upright, I catch him by the yellow flickering light of his hurricane lamp slumped forward on his desk, face buried in his hands. After a brief word with his aide, he beckons me in. We exchange salutes.

He's a tall, slightly stooping, moustached man with a gentle manner and a shy, friendly smile. I hand him the package.

'From Lieutenant General Browning?' he asks.

'Yes, sir.'

'Nice to know we're still in his thoughts,' he murmurs, as he opens the letter.

He tries to force his expression to one of studied neutrality, but from the slump of his shoulders and the blankness of his mournful stare I know the game is up.

'May I ask, Mr Coward –' he begins, choosing his words carefully. 'Did Lieutenant General Browning indicate to you at all his sense of the urgency of our predicament?'

'Well, sir, he knew you were low on ammo and food. But he seemed bucked to know that your morale was sky high.'

Gen. Urqhuart and his aide exchange despairing glances.

Gen. Urqhuart turns to his aide.

'You'd better fetch me Colonel McKenzie,' he says.

This means nothing to me at the time. But I'll later learn that Col. McKenzie represents Gen. Urquhart's last-ditch attempt to get his division's plight taken seriously. He'll be paddled across the river at dawn and try to speak to Lt. Gen. Browning in person.

The aide disappears.

'I gather you were at the bridge,' says Gen Urquhart.

'Yes, sir.'

'Did well to make it out. Only one that has, so far as I know.'

'Yes, sir.'

'I expect you'll be wanting to join your squadron. They're positioned just to the north-east of here. Shall I have someone guide you?'

'Thank you, sir. But I'll find my own way.'

The rest you know, pretty much. Rather than attempt to rejoin the squadron – what use to them could I possibly be in my current mental state? – I wander aimlessly into the night, so little sure of anything any more that I can't even decide whether I'm trying to save my skin or get myself quickly killed.

All I do know is that everything I have done in the last two months has been a complete and utter waste of time: all the training I have endured, all the bonds I have forged, all the expectations I have built, all the agonies of fear and hunger and thirst I have suffered – all of it quite, quite worthless.

When you're in this frame of mind, all you really want to do is crawl into a hole and die. And this, more or less, is what I do. I stumble upon the shed, discover that it is unoccupied, fashion a slit trench of sorts beneath the rotten floor and lie down to sleep. Next morning, I awake to the sounds of 'The Teddy Bears' Picnic' and the chatter of those four men.

But there must be at least some tiny vestige of the old Dick Coward left, for once I've heard the last man die and witnessed the sniper being mortared out of his tree, I find that curiosity overcomes my suicidal despair, and drives me to crawl from my hiding place to investigate.

The bodies are sprawled where they were shot. Still warm, I feel when I roll the first one over. 'Fatty', this one nearest me must be, though in fact he's quite skinny. But with a name like Arbuckle, what other nickname are you going to be given in the Army? His right hand is stretched out towards the end of the rope, nearly touching it. You can see why he thought he could get away with it. He was mostly concealed behind a low hedge at the time. Clearly he underestimated the extent of the sniper's field of fire.

Mind you, that sniper was good. Very good. Every shot a clean head shot. You can't legislate for opposition like that. If you're up against an enemy like that, that's fate's way of telling you your number's up.

Now, of course, I want to know what's in the wicker basket. So – very cautiously, for there's no guaranteeing that that sniper was alone – I stretch out my hand so that it just touches the tip of the rope. Not enough. I shall have to risk exposing myself that little bit more. Slowly, slowly –

Gotcha!

The basket won't budge. No reason why it should – especially if it's laden with something heavy like ammo.

I give it another brisk tug, in case it's merely snagged in the bush. But when you're lying prone on the ground, it isn't easy to get a proper purchase.

'I say. Need a hand?'

Mortifyingly, the voice is coming from directly above me. It belongs to a small, brisk, chirpy-looking fellow with a scrubby little moustache, a twinkle in his eye and a nasty cut down the side of his face that he really ought to get looked at. The crown and three pips I see on his shoulder when he bends down to help me confirm my suspicions. It's our 4th Brigade Commander, Shan Hackett.

Shamed, I pick myself off the floor onto my feet and together we haul the wicker drop basket towards us from the far side of the track. It's not as heavy as I'd first thought. In fact, now that we've got it moving, it feels disconcertingly light. As if it really might, after all, be empty.

Once we've got the basket safely on the other side of the shed, out of prying range of anyone hiding in the wood opposite, Brig. Hackett says to me, '*A toi l'honneur, mon brave.*'

God, now I feel even worse: to be called brave by Shan Hackett is a privilege granted few.

Quickly I undo the heavy leather straps binding the drop basket together. I lift up the top.

Brig. Hackett and I stare into the basket for some time, both of us quite lost for words.

Then he jerks his head in the direction of the four dead men. 'Know them well, did you, Lieutenant?'

'Not very, sir.'

'More a spur of the moment thing then? I've seen a lot of that these last few days. Chaps who've only just met fighting side by side like long-lost brothers. But you must tell me your name, for I'd hate your efforts to go unrewarded.'

'Sir, I'd rather not. I had really very little to do with it.'

'Funny, I had a GP say exactly the same thing to me yesterday. Just after I'd seen him single-handedly dispatch two Spandau nests and an SP gun, with one arm in a sling and a shell splinter in his eye. Now are you going to give me your name, Lieutenant, or shall I have to beat it out of you?'

'Coward, sir. Dick Coward.'

'Thank you, Lieutenant Coward. And thank you for furnishing me with the opportunity of witnessing so splendid an act of gallantry. I'm only sorry – for the sake of your dead comrades, especially – that it couldn't have had a more fruitful outcome.'

We both look dejectedly back at the contents of the drop basket. If only Price were alive to witness it, he'd surely have come up with the appropriate blacker-than-black joke.

They gave their lives so that others might enjoy a consignment of brand, spanking-new headwear.

Red bloody berets.

15

Old Salts

'Price!'

'Mr Richard.'

And that's about as effusive and teary as our reunion gets. Well, there isn't much space for emotional melodrama in a smashed-up, shrapnel-scarred room rancid with unwashed, nervy, battle-weary killers who've been fighting non-stop for over a week and barely expect to survive another day.

'What kept you then?' says Price.

'Got to the bridge. Held it for a while. Lost it. Went to Nijmegen. Came back here.'

'That's more variety than we've had,' says Price.

'And the lads, sir?' asks Trooper Meadows, our section's number two driver. 'Any news of them?'

I tell them what little I know.

'I suppose, after all that, you think you've earned a cup of tea,' teases Lt. McKay, one of my fellow section commanders, as he cleans up a captured MG 34. He acquired it, I'll later learn, during a patrol he led not half an hour ago, by shooting both German machine-gunners in the back of the head.

'Normally, sir, we'd have to say "Hard cheese". We've not had a block of char in four days,' rasps a stocky, very muscular sergeant named Veale in a voice so croaky it borders on the unintelligible.

'But our Trooper Robbins, who you can see over there, has had a lucky find, haven't you, Red Red?'

'I should say so,' agrees Trooper Robbins, tending two cooking pots on top of a fire. One contains a whitish pasty mess, the other a tea-coloured liquid. 'Not just the char and the oats, but the sugar 'n' salt to go with 'em.'

'Bleeding miracle is what I call it,' says a machine-gunner from behind his Bren.

'Fuck of a sight more useful, too, than that angel they had at Mons.'

'And thus a legend was born,' intones the gunner, in mock-reverent tones.

'The Magic Porridge of Oosterbeek,' says his number two.

'I think we're ready. Where's Cheeky? Someone call Cheeky. He's never tried proper English char before,' says Robbins.

Cheeky is summoned from his firing post upstairs. He's a Dutch boy, too young to shave, whose real name is Ruud. The boys have kitted him out in full British airborne kit, including a red beret, which he is wearing at an angle he presumably considers raffish and piratical.

'There you go, Cheeky,' says Robbins, about to hand him a mug.

'Better wait,' says the Bren-gunner, suddenly serious. 'The Girl Guides are back.'

'Oh, they're bloody not?' says Lt. McKay.

'Stupid sods,' croaks Sgt. Veale, readying his weapon as he moves determinedly towards the doorway. 'Right, lads,' he adds to his section. 'You know the drill.'

Lt. McKay and the three men follow him through the door. Sgt. Price indicates that I should stay put. Outside there are a series of explosions. The Bren gun stutters. There's a sharp exchange of fire. Price's only concession is to raise his voice a little.

'You all right?' he says.

'No,' I say.

'You don't look all right. What's the matter with you?'

I'm not sure how much I dare tell him for fear of being overheard. If I'd had any choice in the matter, I wouldn't be here at all. I'd be lurking in the relative safety – though nowhere's safe anywhere any more – of Div HQ, pretending to make myself useful; or better still, hiding in the cellar of one of the unoccupied houses. Problem is, when you've got Brig. Hackett personally taking it upon himself to escort you, in his jeep, to your unit's position, there's not an awful lot you can do to get out of it.

'I'm not sure exactly. I just seem to be in a bit of a funk.'

'Who isn't?'

'No, but I'm not sure I can go on. Not sure I can—'

A stray bullet sings past me, and cracks into the wall a foot above my head. The way I flinch, you'd think it were more like half an inch away.

Sgt. Price looks at me thoughtfully for a second, then reaches into his webbing.

'You need one of these. Maybe two, to be on the safe side,' he says, opening a grubby palm streaked with pale sweat lines.

'Amphetamines?'

'They'll perk you up in moments.'

'It's an MO I need, not pills.'

'Suppose you found one that wasn't up to his neck in offal. What do you think he'd say?'

'Excuse me my duties. Till I'd recovered.'

Price laughs grimly.

'Dead men don't get excused anything.'

The firing stops. Lt. McKay and the men file back in, exhausted but cheerful.

'Well, they won't get their merit badges for that,' says Sgt. Veale.

'Now let's get the char down before that effing SP rolls up again,' says Lt. McKay.

'Quite agree, sir,' says Sgt. Veale. He looks upstairs and bellows, 'CHEEKY?'

The Dutch youth reappears.

'Have a taste of that and tell us what you – will you listen to that! What the hell is that racket?'

The racket – an awful keening, like a calling tomcat – is coming from the direction of the recent confrontation.

'One of the Girl Guides has got herself left behind,' says the Bren-gunner.

'Where?' says Sgt. Veale, rushing over to the barricaded window for a better look.

'Must be hurt,' says the Bren-gunner.

'Doesn't look very hurt,' says Sgt. Veale, having looked through some binoculars. 'I think she's scared shitless her mates have left her to our tender cares.'

'Shall I finish the job?'

'Naah. I've a better idea. Keep me covered, will you?'

Sgt. Veale darts out of the building. There are one or two shots, quickly silenced by a burst from the Bren. Then Sgt. Veale appears with, hanging over his powerful shoulders and wriggling and screaming like a stuck pig, a skinny youth in SS uniform.

Being dropped on the floor like a sack of coal takes the wind out of him for a moment. The SS youth's eyes roll in terror round the room, horrors multiplying in his brain as he glimpses blackened face after blackened face of grinning Tommy malevolence. Then the screaming resumes, even louder and more desperate than before.

By now, Sgt. Veale has managed to drag his trousers round his ankles and slip off his SS belt, which he uses to deliver six hefty thwacks to the lad's bony buttocks. His punishment over, the lad picks himself warily off the floor, eyes darting around the room as if in search of the particular Tommy he knows will surely kill him.

Everyone just laughs, me included, and I'm in no mood for laughing at anything.

The SS boy stumbles off with his trousers round his ankles.

'Now for the third time, can we have our tea?' says Lt. McKay.

'Kids first,' says Sgt. Veale, handing Cheeky his mug. 'Now what do you reckon. And speak the truth. Ain't that the best cup of tea you've ever had the privilege of tasting?'

Cheeky takes a sip and forces a smile.

'Good. Very good,' he winces.

'He doesn't like it. He doesn't bloody like it,' says Trooper Robbins.

'How do the Dutchies like their tea then? Served in a clog or something?'

'If he doesn't want it there's plenty here that do,' says the Bren-gunner. 'Pass it over, will you.'

The mug is snatched from a not-altogether reluctant Cheeky and handed to the Bren-gunner.

'Laarvely,' he says in delighted anticipation. Then, after one sip, 'Bleeeeeuch!' He glares at Robbins.

'Bloody 'ell, if Jerry doesn't kill us, that stupid bastard will.'

'What have I done now?' protests Robbins.

'Only used salt instead of sugar, you ruddy great—'

WHOOOMPPHHH!

By the time we hear the first shell, it has already demolished part of the upper floor.

Nobody needs a second invitation to leave the house. You don't muck about with SP guns.

A number of slit trenches have been dug into the front lawn for precisely this eventuality. Better to take your chances outside than be crushed by falling masonry.

All this I well know but in my dulled, morbid state I'm slower to react than the others, with the result that I'm last through the door, there to find myself face to face with what looks from the front like a mobile hedge – one with a ruddy great steel tubular protrusion in the middle pointing straight towards my head.

I cover the last few yards in a desperate leaping dive. I'm still mid-dive, my head safely inside the trench, but my flailing boots airborne, when a raking burst of machine gun fire thwocks dully into the trench's earthen parados, only narrowly missing my legs.

I land bodily on top of a cursing Sgt. Price, who in turn crushes both a gasping Sgt. Veale and someone even further below I can't identify into the muddy, rain-sodden floor of a narrow trench designed to accommodate two men at most. I'd like to be able to help him, I really would. But with the SP sending all that stuff a few bare inches from my sticking-up legs and arse, I'm buggered if I'm going to jeopardise myself further till the shooting has stopped.

Since this doesn't happen for several minutes – the SP clearly relishing his invulnerability and our discomfort – the man at the bottom is in an awful state by the time we're able to drag him clear.

The house we were occupying has been completely levelled, but there's enough left of the one next door to offer a modicum of protection from mortar stonks and sniper fire. We lay Trooper Robbins on his back in the front room. The late Trooper Robbins, I rather suspect as I kneel beside his limp, battered, mud-coated form attempting to feel for a pulse. Before I can find it, Sgt. Veale has snatched both Robbins's arms by the wrist and pulled them above his head, before lowering them and pressing them against Robbins's chest. He repeats this process two or three times, after which Robbins, with a sudden cough, opens his eyes and begins breathing again.

'What was it, Sarge?' he gasps.

Is it my imagination or does Sgt. Veale give me an accusing look before he replies.

'That bloody SP again, wasn't it?'

'We'll have to stop it,' says Robbins.

'Someone will,' agrees Sgt. Veale, again seeming to glance at me as he says so. But this could be what you nowadays call paranoia.

All around my crotch there's a warm, wet patch. I don't remember doing it, though I do remember how scared I was. More scared than an officer has any right to be in the middle of an action. Fair enough before it starts, but definitely not during, for it endangers all the lives of your men. Suppose, instead of mere mischief-making with that solitary gun, the Germans had pressed home the assault with infantry. With me frozen on top of that slit trench and the others trapped below, we could have been shot like fish in a barrel.

'Don't suppose anyone has a cigarette?' I ask weakly. I need something to try to stop my shakes.

'Crocker might spare you one if it's an emergency,' says Sgt. Price.

'Any idea where he is?'

'Nowhere you'd want to be, old boy,' says Lt. McKay, who has just wandered in, grim-faced. He jerks his head towards a slit trench near to the one where he was concealed. There are three men still in it, upright and apparently alert. But they no longer have their heads attached.

'I'm sure he's not going to mind, now,' says the Bren-gunner.

'Bet he ruddy would and all,' says the Bren-gunner's number two.

'I think what Mr Coward needs is one of my Brazil specials,' says Sgt. Veale.

'Do I?'

'Oh definitely, sir. Proper man's cigarette is the Brazil special. Puts ink in your pen, hairs on your chest –'

'Nails in your coffin.'

'Less of that, Robbins. Mr Coward, I'm quite sure, is a man of discernment.'

'Very well.'

'Give us a moment. Probably best if you don't look, or it'll spoil the surprise.'

I turn away, slightly worried that I'm about to fall victim to some awful practical joke. Problem is, I really am desperate for a cigarette.

'There you are, sir. Tell me what you think of that.'

I can tell without even lighting it. It's rolled in toilet paper, sealed with what looks like jam. As for the contents . . .

Out of duty I accept Sgt. Veale's proffered light, take a drag, and break immediately into a dry, wheezing, hacking cough which seems as if it's going to last all eternity.

'Powerful medicine, eh, sir?' says Sgt. Veale as he thumps me hard on the back.

I try to speak, but it only leads to more coughing. It tasted like burnt, stale, dried-out coffee. It *is* burnt, stale, dried-out coffee.

'It gets better once you're used to it,' croaks Sgt. Veale.

'There's a general feeling you're not entering the spirit of things,' says Price when we next manage to snatch some time alone, early that evening amid the eaves and shattered tiles of our latest roof OP. After a day of sporadic skirmishes, and numerous mortar bombardments, we've occupied a house not dissimilar to the one we had to abandon this morning, only a street further back. Our defensive perimeter is shrinking as our losses increase. A day or two more and we'll have been driven into the Rhine.

'Says who?'

I say it automatically. But the truth is I've long since stopped caring what the others think.

'No one. But it's what they're thinking. You've sat around all day, shivering and sniffling and feeling sorry for yourself. You didn't laugh at Sarnt Veale's Toreador –'

This afternoon, during a lull in the fighting, Sgt. Veale put on a frock coat and a tall top hat he'd found in a wardrobe. For some reason, he decided to perform for our benefit a version of the Toreador's Song from *Carmen*. 'Into the bullring jumped the fucking bull', it began, causing everyone to collapse in tears of mirth. Everyone apart from me.

'It wasn't that funny.'

Price sighs and passes me a cigarette. A proper cigarette.

'Thanks,' I say, my spirits momentarily lifting. 'Where –?'

'Where do you think?' says Price.

Somewhere to our west, the mobile propaganda unit has raised the curtain on its evening show.

'"*IF YOU GO DOWN TO THE WOODS TODAY . . .*"'

Price says, 'I don't suppose you remember that birthday when your mother had me give you a good proper tanning?'

'My seventh. I've never forgiven you. Nor her.'

'Then you'll remember why she had you beaten.'

'Some terribly unfair reason. Piers Waghorn was taunting me with the ball he'd won in pass the parcel so I chucked it into the moat. And serve him right, too. My birthday, not his.'

'And you remember what your mother said.'

'Yes, yes. The usual stuff about it being the duty of our class to be affable and willing even when you don't feel like it, especially when entertaining guests, and yes, I know exactly the point you're trying to make, Price.'

'You sure you don't want one of these?' says Price, proffering his filthy amphetamine pills once again.

'After what happened last time?'

'That was your fever, not the pills.'

I lower my voice to a whisper.

'I did it again, you know. At the bridge.'

'What? Who?'

'Major somebody. New acting OC of 2nd Battalion. By mistake, in the dark.'

'Anyone find out?'

'Everyone. It's why I had to leave.'

'Bad luck.'

'Do you think? I think, for me, it's normal luck. I think it's my destiny never to get any of the things I want. Every step I take forward, along comes fate with his great clunking boot and kicks me two steps back, and I'm sick to death of it, Price.'

'Try expecting less. Then you won't be disappointed.'

'Oh Lord, you're not going to start quoting Plato.'

'If that's what Plato said, he was right. You ask too much of the world.'

'All I ever wanted was my due.'

'Great Meresby, a life of privilege and the hand of the prettiest, dirtiest, most eligible girl in all England? You'll be a bloody marvellous, deserving fellow, won't you then, Mr Richard?'

'If you don't think I deserve it, why did you drag me here?'

'Don't expect such big things to come so easy, is all I'm saying. If you could have heard yourself this time last week —'

'Yes, all right, I got it wrong. Happy now?'

'Happy? Hmm, now let me see. Jerry's surrounded us, we've no food and almost no ammo—'

'I don't need your sarcasm, Price.'

'Let me finish. We've no water, save the rain and what we can drain from the radiators. The enemy are fanatical and merciless. Our boys – all but one of us, anyway – are still cheerful in the face of adversity. Seems to me the conditions could scarcely be better.'

'Have you lost your mind?'

'For that VC of yours, I meant. Why, it's Rorke's Drift all over again. And if that GP can get one, why not you?'

'What GP?'

'You know, Teddy Bear who brought us here from Tarrant Rushton. Took out an SP with a bullet in his arm and a splinter in his eye. If you'd been here yesterday you'd have seen for yourself: there's a section of them, holding the line next to D Troop. Most impressed was Brigadier Hackett. Put him up for the Big One there and then, so I'm told.'

'I could never take out an SP.'

'I'm sure no one would mind if it were a Tiger instead.'

Outside it's raining again. Water drips through the many holes in the roof, some into the buckets and pans we've put underneath, some onto our helmets, from where it trickles down the back of our necks. Whatever day of the week it is, it feels like Sunday.

I pass my tongue over my cracked, sore lips, wanting a drink, but knowing there's not enough water in the buckets yet to make the effort of stooping worthwhile. Everything's an effort now. Everything's too much trouble.

At least the rain has dampened, slightly, the overpowering stench of death. Creeping tantalisingly through are the notes of wet earth and the lush foliage which, in this sector at least, hasn't yet been totally shredded by enemy fire. Even after all we've been through, I don't think any of us can quite get over how neat and tranquil and suburban it all looks. Only when you focus on the burnt-out jeep in the middle of the road next to the ruined 6-pounder, or the bodies strewn like wet rags in the gutter, or the sinister grey shapes flitting in and out of the buildings opposite, do you get the true picture. But it's all wrong. A place like this should be for freshly baked bread, and cups of coffee served with cinnamony apple cake and cream on pavement cafés, and happy family gatherings, and sunny days on bicycles, not violence and noise and foul smells and sudden death.

From the propaganda broadcast vehicle, the sound of 'The

Teddy Bears' Picnic' has given way to a silken female voice telling us our position is hopeless and that if we surrender we shall be well treated.

A croaky voice from below tells her in no uncertain terms what she can do with her offer.

'You know 30 Corps isn't coming,' I say after a time.

Price snorts.

'Thought for a moment you were going to tell me something I didn't know.'

'Do the others?'

'We've filed it next to politics and religion under "Subjects not to be talked about in polite company".'

'Then if we all know it's hopeless why aren't we surrendering?'

'You surprise me, Mr Richard. Whatever happened to Dulcie Decorum and Mr Midshipman Easy and Biggles and Titus Oates and all them other folk you've been banging on about since you were knee-high?'

'Maybe I've finally come round to your way of thinking.'

'Funny that. You've come round to mine and I've come round to yours. See, I know it goes against everything I've ever said to you, but there comes a time, I reckon, when last man, last bullet is the only – well, for want of a better word – the only honourable path to take.'

Price looks a bit awkward as he says this. I think, under all that filth, he might possibly even be blushing. He fumbles in his webbing and removes a bent cigarette.

'Here,' he says. 'Do you fancy sharing this last one?'

This isn't the Price I know at all. The Price I know would have kept it to himself and smoked it craftily later.

He offers me my first drag – again most unlike him. Then I pass it back to him. And so we carry on, single puff by single puff, till within moments we're halfway down and the progress of that glowing butt-end has become as highly charged and nervous-making as the fuse that hisses its way towards a barrel of gunpowder.

I take another drag, torn between the desire to keep it short – and thus prolong the cigarette – and the desire to make it long, for this, despite the dryness in my parched throat, despite the acid reflux that comes with slow starvation, is among the sweetest, and saddest, cigarettes I've tasted.

'You're a stupid bugger, Mr Richard, and you've always been wrong about almost everything,' says Price amiably. 'But there's things we have in common, more perhaps than you'll ever know. And the first is we both of us know a life without Great Meresby is a life not worth living.'

'We'll rub along, I dare say.'

'You say that now but have you thought it through? You'll come out of the bag when the war's over – always supposing we win and Jerry hasn't shot you first – and what will you find? James prancing round the estate with his funny young men friends; James wondering which bits he should sell off first to pay for his drink and his gambling, should it be old Mrs Daintree's tied cottage or his brother's favourite hunter Paddy; James going home to give his new wife Lady Gina one up the—'

'Thank you, Price, I take your point.'

'Then you'll know what's required of you,' he says, seizing both my wrists and squeezing them so tight his hands begin to shake. It makes me wonder how many of those pills he's been taking.

'Do I?' I say. His eyes won't leave mine for a moment. It's as if he's looking right inside my head, reading my thoughts.

'Oh you do, you do, my fine brave lad,' he says, prising open my fingers, his eyes still fixed intently on mine. There are tears in them now, as in each of my palms he places a heavy ovoid chunk of cold, grooved iron. 'There's only two ways out of here now and it's up to you which one you choose,' he says in a soft voice.

'There's one,' he says gently, closing my fingers for me so that they wrap around the first grenade. 'And there –' he says, repeating the process with the other hand – 'is the other.'

Once, when we were very drunk, I did pluck up the courage to ask Price what he'd meant that night when he gave me those two grenades.

'What do you bloody think?' he said.

Personally I've a suspicion that he was rather embarrassed by the incident. As you know, Price has never been much enamoured of the futile gesture, the noble self-sacrifice or the mortally wounded young ensign in the ragged square gasping, 'Play up, play up and play the game!' But I think – surrounded as he had been for a week by so many suicidally brave men performing so many damnably heroic deeds with no more fuss or self-consciousness than if they were putting out some milk for the cat – his head had been turned.

Pressed further, Price claimed that his intention had been kill or cure. He never seriously thought I'd go out and kill myself. He just hoped the ruse would jolt me out of my snivelling lethargy so that once again I was prepared to have a stab at winning that medal. If so, he had misjudged my mental state completely. I was beyond shock tactics. Beyond redemption.

That's why, soon as it got dark and there wasn't too much stuff flying around, I slipped out of the house and began heading in the rough direction of the German propaganda vehicle. Several of our chaps saw me go. But Price had tipped them the nod that I was setting off on some kind of personal vendetta mission, so no awkward questions were asked. We didn't exchange any last goodbyes. Maybe Price didn't want to upset himself. I know the reason I didn't was because I felt too guilty.

My plan was to surrender to the nearest vaguely friendly Germans. Yes, I suppose there might have been better options –

swimming back across the river, hiding myself in the house of that lovely Dutch girl Annette for a day or two till I'd recovered my strength, both physical and mental – but these involved more effort and more peril. All I wanted was a quick, reasonably safe exit.

And where better to find one than with the crew of that Mobile Propaganda Unit? Well, I couldn't imagine the prerequisite for joining an outfit like that was savage ruthlessness. Besides which, having spent the whole day reassuring us how well we were all going to be treated when we surrendered, they were hardly likely to start shooting prisoners on the spot, were they?

'Pssst. Where do you think you're going?' says a voice as I pass what I think might be the rear HQ of the Border Regiment, who are holding the north-west section of the perimeter.

'Recce,' I reply.

'I'll save you the trouble, mate,' says the private, not realising I'm an officer, for like almost everyone I've long since removed my badges of rank. 'Ahead of you – see that hedgerow – there's about sixty of our lads. And fifty yards beyond, there's about six hundred of theirs.'

'And "The Teddy Bears' Picnic"?'

'Oh, you're here for that, are you? Just there, somewhere in those trees. I expect they'll start up again in a moment. They usually do about this time.'

Once I've established from him the best way to negotiate 1st Border's forward positions without being shot, we wait in silence for a minute or so, just listening. Then the music starts up. It's Gracie Fields warbling 'Home' again.

'What did I tell you?' he says.

Fortunately because we're stretched so thin there are big gaps in our defensive line, through one of which I am able to crawl in the direction of the music.

"'*Always wending home . . .*'" trills Gracie, as if personally urging me closer.

Fear not, Gracie. I'm coming as quickly as I can.

Elbow by elbow, I leopard-crawl my way tortuously forward across the exposed no-man's-land of mud and low-growing foliage towards the cover of the trees. The blaring of the propaganda vehicle should muffle any noise I make, and the rain will help disguise my movements, but still I don't want to take any chances.

I'd been worried about stumbling in the dark into the wrong German position, but I now realise there's no danger of that. During gaps in the propaganda broadcasts, when they're changing the gramophone records, you can hear dozens of them, everywhere, making more noise than the monkey house at feeding time. They rattle their mess tins, and raucously laugh, and yell to one another with an indiscipline which would have them court-martialled on our side of the lines. The cocksureness that comes with imminent victory, I suppose.

Anyway, it makes my job easier. The propaganda vehicle is dead ahead now – a large-ish van with an oversized, trumpet-shaped loudspeaker on top, its outline masked by camouflage netting and foliage. There are no crew members visible, but a rectangle of flickering yellow light indicates that at least one of them is inside. He – unless it's that she with the sexy voice – has just slipped an old favourite onto the gramophone.

"'*IF YOU GO DOWN TO THE WOODS TODAY–*'"

I pause for a breather with my back against a large trunk, suddenly aware that this will be my last experience of freedom for a very long time. 'It's not too late to change your mind,' I remind myself. But if I go back, what use will I be? There'll be no use at 1st Airborne Recce's last heroic stand for an officer who has lost his nerve.

Still, it's not going to be pleasant. They'll probably rough me up a bit as they pass me down the line. Rifle through my possessions, steal anything worth stealing. And it'll be ages before they give me anything to eat and drink. Then there'll be the interrogation – perhaps more than one; and the long, tedious train journey to one of their *oflags* in the east; then the delousing, and the cold and the hunger and the boredom and the routine degradation of prison-camp life. Maybe a quick death would be preferable after all.

Perhaps that's why I brought those two grenades with me. So I can keep my options open.

"'*PICNIC TIME FOR TEDDY BEARS . . . THE LITTLE TEDDY BEARS ARE HAVING A LOVELY TIME TODAY.*'"

Beside me in the shadows a sudden movement. Too late, I recognise the shape of a soldier with a machine pistol pointed straight at me, and another two or three men crouched near by. That's my war over then.

Their leader moves closer to me so that he can see my face, and I his. He has one arm in a sling and he's wearing a patch over one eye.

'DICK?' he mouths.

'YES,' I mouth back, uncertain at first as to who on earth it can be. His glider pilot's cap badge is the obvious clue. Then I remember Price's and Brig. Hackett's account of the heroic destruction of the SP gun. 'PAT?'

He nods and points meaningfully to the propaganda vehicle. Then, even more meaningfully, he draws his hand across his throat.

I nod.

Then he points first at his forehead, then at my forehead, before making a thumbs-up gesture.

'Great minds think alike,' is what I think he's trying to convey.

He pats me on the shoulder, before indicating that it might be rather handy if I primed those two grenades he can see dangling from my webbing. When I'm ready, I gesture that he should lead the assault.

He shakes his head.

'After you,' he mouths with a gracious nod of his head and an elegant sweep of his uninjured hand.

We move forward at a rush, five of us in all, each with at least one grenade.

The teddy bears' picnic comes to a sudden, highly explosive halt.

We don't hang about.

16

In a Hole

'Oh, stop mithering. Worse things happened at Passchendaele.'
This is the sort of thing Price would be saying if he were in this
slit trench now with me and Lt. Verney.

A torrential monsoon in Burma where the rain's coming down
so thick and hard even the fish start drowning? It was wetter at
Passchendaele. A concentrated artillery bombardment which
destroys every living thing within a ten-mile radius, bores a hole
through to the other side of the earth, and knocks the planet off
its axis? Ah, but the whizz bangs at Passchendaele . . .

At least at Passchendaele the trenches would have had duck
boards. Lt. Verney and I have nothing and the water's up to our
ankles, seeping through the eyelets in our boots and through our
socks and into our sore, rotting feet, which get colder and colder
and wetter and wetter no matter how often we squelchily stamp
them. I'm permanently shivering now and my nose is like a dripping tap.

The trench reeks of the remnants of its previous occupants.
When they dug it, they didn't do a very clever job. Not only is it
too narrow but it's about a foot too deep, which makes it fine for
cowering in but perfectly useless for firing from because, even on
tiptoes, you can't see properly over the parapet. It's dark, too, for
to conceal our position we've covered it with branches and bits of
debris including the side panel of one of our burnt-out Willy's

jeeps. And to complete the sense of claustrophobic helplessness we're not supposed to exchange one word lest we give ourselves away.

Lt. Verney is the first to break the silence. After two hours' wait, you can hardly blame him. If he hadn't I would have done, especially now that the first of the pep pills Price gave me just before we set off is starting to make me more garrulous.

He positions his mouth about an inch away from my ear.

'You really didn't have to, you know,' he says in a stage whisper. 'I feel I may have put you on the spot.'

'No, no. Not at all,' I lie, for there's absolutely no point at this late stage telling him what I really think, which is, Yes, you did put me on the spot, you stupid bloody idiot, and if this escapade gets me killed it will be ALL your fault. I hate you, I HATE you. I wish I'd never met you and the only thing affording me the merest scrap of comfort in these last minutes of my life is the thought that when I die horribly you'll at least be coming with me.

'Do you know, Dick, I think you're the bravest, most modest man I've ever met,' he whispers.

And even then, I still hate him.

What happened was this. After the destruction of the Mobile Propaganda Unit – and with it my plans of an easeful surrrender – I had no option but to return with Lt. Verney and the other GPs back to our position.

In our absence it had taken another hammering. You can usually rely on the Germans not to attack at night, especially not with their armour, but clearly they'd been getting cockier for the SP had paid us a nocturnal visit. No one had been killed this time, but poor Cheeky had been badly wounded. They were carrying him out on a door doubling as a stretcher just as we arrived, still in his airborne uniform, but so terribly pale, and boyish and frail, now – the little lad who had come a cropper playing soldiers in the woods and now badly needed his mummy.

He was gasping something anxious in Dutch, while clawing feebly at the zip of his Denison smock, but no one was paying him much notice because they thought it was just delirium. Then someone tried to give him a morphine shot and you should have seen him wriggle.

'Kill me,' gasped the boy. 'Morphine kill me.'

'No, it's good, son. Good,' the orderly was trying to explain to him. 'Anyone know the Dutch for "It'll put a smile on your face"?'

'Sarnt Price,' pleaded the boy in desperation.

'We haven't time to piss about – he needs a hospital,' said the orderly.

'Fetch Sarnt Price,' I insisted, for in my experience the dying know best what they need most.

Price was fetched. It was worth it, just to see his expression when he saw that I was back. Then he knelt close to the ashen boy so that he could hear what he was saying.

'He wants changing into his civvies,' said Price at last.

'He's too weak. It could kill him,' protested the orderly.

'If Jerry catches him in uniform he's a goner anyway,' said Price. His eyes alighted on Meadows. 'Off you go, Grassy. Let's not keep the lad waiting.'

Meadows looked pointedly towards the staircase, which presumably once led to plentifully stocked wardrobes but which thanks to the attentions of the self-propelled gun now stopped mid-air.

'Where from, Sarge?' he said.

'Go and look,' replied Sgt. Price, with a gesture towards the dark and not exactly unmenacing street. 'You'll find something.'

'But—' began Meadows, before realising that what he was about to say might best be said out of Cheeky's earshot. He moved back a few paces, beckoned Sgt. Price towards him, and lowered his voice.

'Sarge,' he protested. 'There are some things worth risking your neck for.'

'Suit yourself,' said Sgt. Price, and without another word or a backward glance, he slipped out through the door – just missing Brig. Hackett, chirpy as usual. He was followed by a nervous adjutant – and who wouldn't be nervous having to keep pace with a fellow like the Brigadier – and two RASC men lugging various ammo containers and heavy canvas bags.

'Gather it's your GPs we have to thank for putting a stop to that interminable picnic,' said the Brigadier, sharp eyes searching the gloom. 'I trust one of them wasn't Mr Verney,' he said, having evidently spotted Lt. Verney in a corner, quietly cleaning his Sten. 'For I distinctly remember telling him to put off further heroics till he'd got himself properly treated.'

'Don't worry, sir, it wasn't me,' said Lt. Verney.

'Jolly well was, sir!' protested one of his fellow GPs.

'I can't altogether deny that I played a small part, sir. I just feel that credit ought properly to go to Lieutenant Coward. He did think up the idea first.'

'Where is Lieutenant Coward?'

'Here, sir.' I'd been trying to shrink out of view.

'Well done. Again.'

'Sir –'

'*Please*, Mr Coward,' said the Brigadier, his tone heavily ironic. 'Let's take it as a given, shall we, that of course it had nothing to do with you and that others really ought to take the credit?'

'Yes, sir.'

'Now you mustn't think we've forgotten you at HQ. Indeed, as a token of just how greatly we esteem you, we have decided to bring you Christmas early.'

'Aw. Turkey and all the trimmings. You shouldn't 'ave, sir,' said Sgt. Veale.

'Nearly, Sarnt. How d'you all fancy a nice slice or two of gammon instead?'

To judge by the ensuing languorous sighs, some of the fellows briefly took him at his word. But then the RASC men started emptying the bags and passing round the contents. A PIAT. Three rockets. And what looked as if they might be drinking flasks with screw-on caps and fat, bulbous bottoms made of dark, thick, elasticated material such as might make a sturdy pair of winter stockings.

It's these last – three of them in all – which provoked the Brigadier's rather cruel meat joke.

They're called Gammon bombs, see – named after the chap who invented them, one Capt. R.S. Gammon MC of the Parachute Regiment – and though they do look a touch make-shift, they're very popular with us airborne chaps because they're the most portable and effective defence method we have against armour. As you heard Cpl. Cholmondeley demonstrate earlier with that Tiger.

Very easy to use, too. You just unscrew the cap and inside you'll find a linen tape rolled tightly round the top and a lead weight attached, which you must hold very carefully in place with your finger, or you're buggered because that's how you ignite the fuse which sets off the plastic explosive packed inside. As you lob the thing at your target, the linen tape – pulled by the lead weight – unwraps in flight, and pulls out the pin. The fuse is now armed, with only a weak spring keeping it from contact with the percussion cap, so that the instant it hits the target: boom!

'I'm afraid you'll have your work cut out if you're to beat the divisional record. One of the South Staffs' company commanders has personally accounted for six panzers already,' said Brig. Hackett. 'Major Cain.'

'Ah well, I suppose he would be good at killing with a name like that, sir,' said Sgt. Veale.

'Still no reason why a Coward couldn't do better, sir,' said Lt. Verney.

'What the devil has cowardice got to do with this?' said the Brigadier rather crossly, as you do when someone seems to have said something utterly imbecilic.

'I'm so sorry, sir, I was trying to make a joke. About our Lieutenant Coward,' said Lt. Verney.

'Ah yes. Of course. Very droll.'

From the darkness there came knowing chuckles. It seemed that my fate was sealed. And if it wasn't then, it certainly was moments later when the Brigadier said as an afterthought, 'Coward. Unusual name. Don't suppose you're any relation of Ajax Coward?'

'His son, sir.'

'Didn't someone once tell me an extraordinary story once about some sort of competition you have going with your brother?'

'I'm afraid it's true, sir.'

He picked up the PIAT and placed it in my hands.

'There you are then, Mr Coward. I think you know what to do,' he said.

At 06.30, the 'morning hate' begins.

Lt. Verney shouts something in my ear.

'What?'

'Half an hour early,' he yells.

'Yes,' I agree. Normally the shelling starts at 07.00 on the dot. You can set your watch by it. Perhaps Jerry's trying to send us a message. 'We've unlimited ammo; you haven't,' would be my guess.

But there's no point continuing this conversation, for even

when you're shouting you can't hear a ruddy thing. The shrieks could scarcely be shriller were the entire celestial choir to be simultaneously raped by the hordes of hell; the impact of each distant shell and heavy mortar round makes the earth shake and send clods of mud tumbling down our backs and onto our faces; the close ones churn, jar and melt you like ice in a cocktail shaker. And that's the nicest of it. What's worse, far worse, is when your ears detect – as they unerringly do – the scream of a round heading directly towards you, and your empty stomach dances its queasy little jig in anticipation of the direct hit which will reduce you to nothing.

Then as suddenly as it came, it ends and the silence which follows is even more nerve-wracking than the shelling. For we both know, Lt. Verney and I, what will sooner or later be filling that silence. It will start with a squeak, then a clank, then a rumble. And then it will come to the crunch: him or us.

'Do you think it's fair now?' murmurs Lt. Verney in my ear.

'What?' I say testily, for I'm listening out for that bloody SP.

'I'm sorry, I'm being frivolous, I'm sure. But do you not remember our conversation last week? About the game of tennis?'

'Oh God, *that* one! Yes. What can I have been thinking?'

'Oh, I don't know. I think it was a rather noble conceit. Still do. When we win this one now, it will be SO much more satisfying.'

'You still think we're going to win?'

'Of course. Don't you?'

I'd like a cigarette, but there are no cigarettes, and even if there were I couldn't smoke it lest we give away our position. I'd like to eat but of course there's no food. I'd like to drink – my throat feels hard and dry as a block of wood – but the only water is the filthy mire beneath my feet. So for want of anything better to put in my mouth, I take another of Price's pills. With any luck it'll perk me up sufficiently to curtail my current intense urge to beat my trench-mate to death with the PIAT.

It's not a large pill but in a throat as parched as mine it feels like an ostrich egg.

By wringing my sodden scarf, I manage to squeeze out two or three drops of sweat-tinged rainwater.

'You're thirsty. Why didn't you say?' says Lt. Verney, offering me his canteen. By the sound and feel of it, there's only a mouthful left.

'Don't be silly. It's yours.'

'Take it, or I shall feel most hurt.'

Blithering romantic fool, I think, as the nectar trickles down. Then, Christ almighty, I'm turning into Price.

Is that a good thing?

If we were all like Price, it would forever be stalemate, wouldn't it? No one would volunteer; every order would be squashed with an 'If we do that we're going to get ourselves killed'; no one would talk about '*Dulce et Decorum Est*' except in tones of the most exquisite sarcasm. Everyone would be so bored and miserable and pessimistic the only option would be to pack up and go home. War would cease and eternal peace would reign.

Would it, my arse. We'd just be overrun in a second by all the countries that didn't take that attitude: the Germans mainly; if not them the Russians; the Japs and Chinese in our Eastern territories of course; and the French: let's never underestimate the knack of the French for kicking us when we're down.

That's why we need idiots like Lt. Verney. Idiots like I was a week ago before despair and exhaustion and bitter reality took their toll. Idiots prepared to go on believing, against all the evidence, that we still stand a chance of winning this battle. Idiots who think nothing of hiding themselves in a cold, muddy pit, armed only with a PIAT and a Gammon grenade, in the vague hope that a German self-propelled gun will somehow move in close enough for them to hazard their first and last pot shot, knowing that if they miss it's certain death.

That's why I take a handful more pills. Because I want to be an idiot again. Because at times like this, if you don't think like an idiot, you'll go stark, staring mad.

The enlarged dose does the trick rather nicely. Almost immediately, I feel a surge of confidence and elation. The hunger pangs have gone, and so has the tiredness. I'm fizzing with energy and a new sense of urgency. If someone ordered me to clamber over the top now and bayonet-charge the entire German army single-handed, I'd more than happily do it. What's more I'd survive and win.

'I say. Better not,' whispers Lt. Verney.

'What?'

'Stamp your feet like that. It's making quite a din.'

'Sorry. Do you want one?'

'What?'

'Pep pill. Benzedrine. Marvellous stuff.'

'Don't they give you a funny turn?'

'I don't think so.'

'Can do, I believe. Some of the chaps have been having visions.'

'Oh dear.'

'Depends on the dose, I suppose. I'm sure you'll be fine if you stick to just the one.'

'Oh dear.'

No, not oh dear, actually. I'm enjoying this. I feel alive, strong, invincible. My hearing's so much sharper. Every bullet, every mortar round, every shell, every grenade – I know exactly where it has come from, exactly where it's going, when to flinch, when to gloat, when not to give a damn. And Jerry – not only can I hear his officers and NCOs issuing orders, and the men hissing warnings, jokes and words of encouragement to one another and clumping their boots as they form up for the next assault – but it's as if I can read his thoughts.

I know that soon, very soon, will come the probing attack to inspect how our positions have changed in the night, and which ones are in most urgent need of savage reduction. And that shortly afterwards will come the main event: the sound and light show courtesy of our old friend Sturmgeschütz III – the SP gun.

A right bastard of a weapon it is, your StuG III. Its standard armament is a 75-mm gun, but the one that has been making our lives a misery this last couple of days carries a 105-mm howitzer, designed for hitting targets up to seven miles away. You can imagine the sort of damage it can do at close range. Well, you don't need to imagine, do you? All those men you've seen die as the houses they were occupying collapsed about their ears – it was mostly StuGs that were responsible. And the awful thing is, there's next to nothing we can do about them. You need an anti-tank gun to penetrate that 80-mm-thick frontal armour, and most of our 6-pounders have long since been put out of action. The only remaining option is to do what Lt. Verney and I are doing now. Try to get up close to it, one way or another, and see if you can't hit one of its weaker spots with your PIAT. Has to be a direct hit and in exactly the right place, mind. Otherwise you're buggered.

First things first: the probing assault. God, they come close, some of those German infantry, as they clatter across the cobblestones, and thud past our hidey-hole, their Schmeissers burping and captured Stens chattering, grunts and Teutonic curses and screams of pain erupting above our heads, as they try to overrun our positions. At one point, a cascade of spent cartridges falls down into our trench like the winnings in a penny arcade, from a machine pistol whose owner shortly afterwards gets himself shot. There's a yell, immediately followed by a thud as he hits the ground, then a series of sharp little gasps as, in evident pain, he pulls himself towards cover.

Problem is, the nearest cover is our slit trench, which we're rather hoping to keep secret for the main event. And a wounded Jerry is a dangerous thing. Has a nasty habit of reaching for his stick grenade, and taking an *Englischer Schweinehund* or two with him, so it's imperative we don't give him the chance.

All this I know as his grunts draw closer. Lt. Verney has noticed too, for he taps me urgently on the arm. I'm sure I shouldn't but I'm finding our predicament quite stupidly exciting, as the myriad options rush through my head in a flash flood of possibilities.

Kill him or stun him? Drag him inside or deal with him where he is? And with what? Knife? Gun? Water bottle? The PIAT? Oh, cripes, the PIAT. We've got it resting on the parapet of our trench, hidden by some branches, because there's really nowhere else to put it, and if he's seen it, as he might from his crawling position, he'll guess what we're up to and have his grenade ready and—

Bloody hell, there he is. Eyes staring down at us through the crack he's made in our covering and

CRACK!

The detonation, in so confined a space and so close to my ear, is deafening.

I can't see. Can't see a bloody thing. My eyes are full of something not at all pleasant.

I wipe my eyes. Lt. Verney is holstering his .38 Webley and mouthing something like: 'Sorry old chap!'

The dead German stares down at us, a big black hole where one of his eyes was. I wouldn't mind so much, except that, with his face directly above where I'm standing, he keeps dripping on me, like one of those bathroom taps with a broken washer that stops you sleeping.

I experiment with various positions to try to avoid it. When I'm standing fully upright, it drips onto my helmet with a very faint pit-pit-pit, all the more irritating for being irregular, the precise sound it makes depending on whether it has hit the scrim, the netting or the helmet itself. If I lean forward, it makes my back ache, and leads to drippage down my neck. And I don't want to move any closer to Lt. Verney, for I find I loathe him more with each passing second. It's his fault the German's there dripping on top of me, his fault my ears are ringing, his fault I'm in this hole.

'Shouldn't be long now,' says Lt. Verney.

What a stupid thing to say. Is he trying to cheer me up? Does he think I'm nervous? I'll give him nervous!

'I'll fire the PIAT,' I say.

'If that's what you want to do,' he says in that maddening, friendly, even-tempered voice. In doing so, he has condemned himself to by far the worst of our two jobs. While I fire the PIAT, he will have to crouch underneath me in the stagnant mud, serving as my platform. I'd respect him far more if he made more of a fuss about it.

'It's what I'm going to do,' I declare, full of bitterness and venom.

He doesn't speak after that. Good.

No, not good, actually. It means I've no more excuse to snap at him.

Squeak.

What was that? What was that?

I look up. With his good eye, the German gives me a slow, deliberate wink.

More squeaking. Engine noises too.

'I think he's coming,' says Lt. Verney.

'You don't say?'

Why couldn't it have been him who took that bullet, and not the nice Dutch boy.

Poor Cheeky, whimpering as Price cut him out of his borrowed British uniform, the dressing round that thin, quaking midriff saturated with dark blood. No one wanting to catch anyone else's eye. Everyone thinking, Why him? Why not me? Why did we let him?

Price gently, very, very gently, buttoning Cheeky into an oversized white shirt. Sgt. Veale lifting Cheeky's legs, while Price pulls up the black pinstripe trousers with the waist about 20 inches too big. Another little gasp, when Price accidentally jars his wound.

'Nothing more to worry about, son,' says Sgt. Veale.

Sgt. Price whispers something to the boy in Dutch. The boy smiles and closes his eyes.

'He needs a belt,' someone notices.

'Not any more,' says Sgt. Price, as he feels, unsuccessfully, for a pulse on Cheeky's neck.

'*Seid still!*' I snap.

'I didn't say anything,' murmurs Lt. Verney.

'Not you. Him,' I say, indicating the German looking down into our trench.

'He's dead,' says Lt. Verney, a note of concern in his voice.

'Oh yes.' Another upward glance confirms that Lt. Verney is right. That hole through the eye: you definitely couldn't survive a wound like that. So how come just now, I distinctly heard him whisper, 'As I am, so shall you be.'

The voice was familiar too. It was the voice of that SS reconnaissance trooper that I know can't possibly be here because he died, a lifetime ago, at the bridge. Killed by Cpl. Cholmondeley. Who's also dead, now, no doubt. They all are: Wood, Beckford, Hughes, those boys I never really got to know from 2nd Battalion; most of the Americans with whom I crossed the Waal, perhaps even my cousin by now; the men who were trying to retrieve the drop canister; the Germans from the Mobile Propaganda Unit; the Germans who burned on the bridge, with their terrible screams, and that odious barbecue smell like the one that emanated so strongly from that delightful paratroop subaltern who remembered me from school, now what was his name, oh Lord, this is awful, such a splendid, brave chap and I can't remember his name.

He's right, though, that German, whether he said it or not.

I will be dead soon, for we're all dead men, now here at the *Hexenkessel*. That's what the Germans are calling it, apparently, so we learned from one of their prisoners. The witch's cauldron.

'He's getting close!' says Lt. Verney, quite unnecessarily, for not only can you hear the growl of the engine and the squeak and clank of the tracks on the cobbles, but you even feel the vibration through the earth.

'I'd better look then.'

'Better had,' says Lt. Verney, and for the first time since I've known him, I hear a slight catch in his voice, a hint of trepidation and doubt. Given what he's about to do, I'm not sure I altogether blame him.

Without another word, he drops onto his knees into the mire. As I step onto his shoulders, he wobbles at the initial pressure. Then manages to steady himself.

I peer cautiously over the parapet. To get a proper view I have first, very slowly so as not to attract any notice, to shift a couple of small branches. The StuG is perhaps 200 yards away in the middle of the street, engine idling, no doubt assessing the scene. He's guessed, probably correctly, that he's in no more danger from our 6-pounders, and that PIATs and Gammon grenades are all we have left.

About thirty yards to my left, a movement catches my eye. It's a Bren-gunner, with his number two, waving at me from their slit trench. They've been detailed to cover me, I suppose, in case the StuG attacks with infantry support.

WHOMP!

Behind me a crumble of falling masonry.

Then, after about five or six seconds –

WHOMP!

More instantaneous destruction. At this range there's nothing we can do. He needs to be at 100 yards, minimum, for a PIAT to have any effect.

Now the Bren-gunner has opened up. I can see what he's trying to do, but he's a bloody fool.

WHOMP!

Still more of the building behind me collapses and, for a moment, it seems the SP isn't going to play our game. Why should he? He's doing quite enough damage where he is.

Doggedly, the Bren-gunner continues to fire in short bursts at the self-propelled gun. Of course, .303 bullets are no use against 80 mm of armour, but their impact doesn't half make a terrible din when you're stuck inside, and as any tanker will tell you there's only so much you can take.

The SP has had enough of this nonsense and starts to swivel on his tracks with the slow, calm deliberation of one who knows there can only be one winner from this duel.

With a low belch, the 105-mm gun unleashes another high-explosive round. It tears up the ground perhaps ten yards behind the Bren-gunner's position.

The Bren gun has fallen silent, but it's only a ruse, for no sooner has the SP started busying itself destroying the houses behind our positions again, than the Bren gun opens up on it once more.

This time the SP is taking no chances.

It turns again, launches three more high-explosive shells in the direction of the Bren-gun team's slit trench, and rakes the ground with so long a burst from his MG I'm surprised he hasn't exhausted his ammo.

Then, just to be absolutely sure, he rumbles forward from the cobbled street, heading directly towards the trench, no doubt intending to grind over it back and forth until it has collapsed on its occupants.

Now he's moved closer, here's my chance.

The PIAT, you should know, we primed beforehand. You have to really, for the spring mechanism is so stiff and awkward that it's not something you'd want to do under duress. All I have to do now is load it with one of the three high-explosive anti-tank rounds we have at our disposal, rest the PIAT on its monopod, take careful aim – very careful aim –

'Bugger!'

'What?'

'There's two of them.'

'Are you – quite – sure?' gasps Lt. Verney, sounding at once deeply uncomfortable and highly sceptical.

To be perfectly honest, no I'm not. I'm not altogether sure of anything any more. Something seems to be happening inside my head, something most unhelpful. Not only do I find myself increasingly confused and dislocated and overwhelmed by a rush of emotions that I appear quite unable to control, but it feels rather as if my brain is about to explode.

It's those pills, the pills, don't worry, it's only the pills, the rational part of my brain tries to reassure me. But that's really no consolation, in fact quite the opposite. That pleasantly euphoric feeling I got earlier on, I think that was the first or the second Benzedrine pill taking effect. What I'm now experiencing is the first effects of the ill-advised handful of pills I swallowed more recently in the mistaken belief that it would make me feel even better. And they haven't done so at all.

For one thing they've made the StuG – or StuGs, I can't quite make up my mind – look larger and more menacing than any self-propelled gun has a right to look. The gun barrel is as wide and long as an oil pipeline, the squat, heavily camouflaged chassis resembles a vast chunk of forested slope which has been hacked by giants from the side of a mountain, and the stench of the black smoke from its roaring engine is like the noxious emanations from the bowels of Hades. It isn't just scary, this lowering, questing beast. It's terror and evil and death and mercilessness and murderous intent, all rolled into one frightful, lumbering, squeaking, growling, clanking, rumbling behemoth.

And it wants to kill me.

And unless I kill it first it will.

The thought of this awesome responsibility is almost too much to bear. It IS too much to bear. I've broken out in a cold sweat. My spine is prickling. My whole body is trembling, I can't keep my hands still.

And all the while, that infernal machine is grinding closer to the trench in which that brave Bren-gun team are cowering, if they're not dead already. A second or two more and they'll be crushed to death.

'Still no clear shot?' says Lt. Verney in a strained voice. I've been standing on his back for quite some time.

Yes I do, I do, but dare I take it? The Bren crew are probably already dead and all that will happen if I fire now is make him come after me. Whereas if we stay here, keep our heads low, he's bound to go away after a time. And then we'll live. The Germans will win, sooner or later. We can all surrender. And I won't have to experience what it's like to have your skull crushed like a ripe tomato or your intestines squeezed out of a shattered rib cage or to be buried alive or riddled with machine-gun bullets, or any of the other grisly fates which could so easily be mine within the next thirty seconds if I loose off this useless pop gun with my useless shaky hands and then miss, which I'm bound to do.

But then, cutting through the din of battle, I hear a voice.

'SHOOT, YOU STUPID BUGGER!' it says. It comes from the slit trench about 20 yards to our right. The one in which

Price has been hiding with a Gammon grenade he plans to use if our mission fails. He's thought it all through: SP rumbles over to our trench to crush the idiots who fired a PIAT at it; while it's so doing Price sneaks up and takes revenge with the Gammon grenade.

If it had been anyone else shouting, I'm sure I wouldn't have listened. But over the years I've grown so used to doing what Price tells me that his words manage to bypass the more trepidatious part of my brain and speak directly to the man of action I sometimes can be when the wind's blowing in the right direction.

I aim for the tracks, the weakest part of the SP gun.

I fire.

At the moment the spring hits the firing pin and the anti-tank round flies towards its target, I feel a surge of happiness as great as any I've experienced in my life. I think of Gina and Great Meresby and comradeship and England and the King and all the things worth fighting and dying for. I think of how good it is to conquer fear and do the right thing. I think of how bitterly I would have regretted it if I hadn't taken this risk, and how wonderful it's going to be when it pays off.

And as the anti-tank round slams into the side of the SP gun and explodes in a flash of bright white light, I think –

Bugger!

For it hasn't hit the track, it has gone high and exploded against the gun-mounting, leaving the crew quite unharmed but no doubt exceedingly irked and very determined to take out whoever fired it as quickly as possible – before he has the chance to reload. I could try another go, I suppose. There's a part of me that wants to but my body appears to have overruled it, for already, with no apparent deliberation, I'm using poor Lt. Verney's back as a springboard for a swift and desperate exit, grappling at the parapet and pulling for all I'm worth. You'd be surprised how quickly you can get out of a deep hole when your life depends on it – especially when you're loaded with Benzedrine.

A glance at the SP as I heave myself out and onto my feet tells me I still have a good fifty-fifty chance of finding cover before he completes his manoeuvre. When I hit him with the PIAT round his gun was facing roughly 90 degrees away from me and in the time it has taken me to clear the slit trench that angle has closed to roughly 45 degrees. You'll think this a cruel calculation but I'm afraid this is sometimes how the mind works in extremis: by the time he's facing us dead on and has brought his machine gun to bear, I'm hoping he'll be too busy riddling Lt. Verney to pay me any notice.

I'm making pretty reasonable headway, too, flying across the battle-scarred earth with wings on my heels, eyes peeled for some empty foxhole in which to shelter, for that's my safest, quickest bet, I reckon, when suddenly from beneath my feet like a meerkat from its burrow – and a very ugly meerkat, at that – pops up a brutish head.

'CATCH,' yells Price.

By the time I've worked out what it is I've already caught it, though I wish I hadn't for the thing I am holding is almost live and very dangerous: a Gammon grenade with the white tape at the top already half unravelled as a result of its short journey from Price's slit trench to my sweaty palms.

That split-second pause has done for me, I know it has. The air has filled with an all-too-familiar sound somewhere between ripping canvas and swarming bees and the earth 20 yards to my left dances its mad jig as the SP's machine gun begins the leisurely, murderous arc which is about to cut me in half.

There's no outrunning a gun that fires two bullets a second. Even in my Benzedrine-addled panic I know this, and knowing it induces a strange, sudden and quite unexpected feeling of calm. It's as if, during the crisis point of a fatal fever, someone –

Gina perhaps, or my mother – had pressed an ice-cool flannel against my tortured brow, and before my death I'd been granted one last moment of peace and lucidity.

Near-death experiences can have that effect. Not only do you stop panicking but events suddenly start happening in slow motion. It's part of the body's remarkable arsenal of self-defence mechanisms, so the scientists claim, and what it does is buy you just a few moments' extra time to dig yourself out of whatever hole you've got yourself into. I've had it when trying to extricate myself from a burning aircraft when the cockpit has jammed; I've had it when trying to escape from a tank on the verge of brewing up; and it's tremendously comforting to know it's there, I must say – like having a secret, in-built superpower which only reveals itself when you're in the direst need.

In this moment of calm and lucidity, what I realise is this: that I am doomed, and that since I am doomed it is better that I should die with honour and purpose than like a fleeing rat. So with a sardonic smile I turn to face the enemy. And instead of running away I start running towards it, not directly but at a slight diagonal, faster and faster, in the hope that before the machine gun cuts me down I might just be able to lob the Gammon grenade onto the side armour where it will do most damage.

The SP is now no more than 15 yards away from our slit trench. Lying prone in front of it is that bloody fool Lt. Verney, acting the hero to the very end. He's about to loose off another PIAT round. It'll be a miracle if he doesn't get himself shot first.

But there it goes – whoosh – straight into the front of the SP, where of course it will have absolutely no effect. And after that futile gesture it is now a dead certainty that Lt. Verney's luck has run out. If he doesn't get machine-gunned he'll be squashed.

Not, of course, that I'm exactly in a much better position. I'm amazed the machine-gunner's let me get this close. Why isn't he shooting?

Yes. Why isn't he shooting?

Good God, can this be possible? Has his gun jammed? Is he out of ammo? Did Lt. Verney's PIAT shot perhaps damage his barrel?

Whatever, it has bought me all the time I need.

'Advantage Verney!' I can't resist yelling out, as I pass him. I'm not sure whether or not he's heard, for he has slithered back into the slit trench. A fat lot of good that will do him if I don't put a stop to the SP, which is now almost on top of him.

But thanks to his teamwork, I now think I can.

I don't expect I'll survive this one. I know I shan't survive, for a Gammon grenade is designed to explode on impact and I shall certainly be caught by the blast.

Ah what the hell. I've lived a good twenty seconds longer than I expected.

Advantage Verney? Are those really going to be my last ever words? Surely but surely I can think of something more apposite.

I lob that Gammon grenade upwards.

'GAME SET AND MATCH COWARD!' I shout as I accelerate away from that imminent blast as fast as my legs will carry me.

Which as you know, and I know, just won't be quite fast enough.

17

Heavy Petting

Someone has cloven my head in two with a blunt, rusty axe. My mouth is full of dirt, my whole body aches and I can't see a damn thing. I suppose I must still be alive, -ish.

Wish I could think straight. Wish my bloody head didn't hurt so bloody much. Wish I knew where I was. Better lie still.

Around me I can hear voices, German voices, and that can't be good. But they're calm, conversational, not sharp and urgent, which can only mean that the battle is over. Perhaps the whole show is over. Jerry has won and now he's just clearing up.

No, that can't be right. I hear gunfire, distant but not dramatically so. So the show is still on, it's just my part of it that's over. Our position must have been overrun.

My mouth, the reason it's full of dirt is because I'm lying face down in a muddy area I daren't move to examine yet lest I give myself away. And the reason I can't see is not, thank God, because I've been blinded but because night has fallen. I've been here for some time, then.

Having listened awhile to judge there's no one in the immediate vicinity, I turn my head first one way and see a house, then the other and see a burnt-out self-propelled gun.

Now that rings a bell.

The SP is some distance away, 30 or 40 feet. I must have travelled most of that way in the air. No wonder I'm aching so much.

No wonder I was out for so long. If I hadn't landed in this soft patch – a flowerbed, is it? – I would have broken every bone in my body.

Painfully, slowly, I belly-crawl out of the flowerbed, across a stretch of trampled, muddy lawn, towards the battered front door. It's swinging on its hinges, having evidently been kicked open. The hallway is a mess of broken glass and rubble. I stop and listen for a time. It's clearly empty. I seek out the lavatory. I'm lucky. The cistern is still full. I'm so thirsty I don't bother looking for a drinking receptacle. I just cup my filthy hands and scoop out draught after draught, slobbering it down with all the grace of a dehydrated dog in the midday sun. I don't stop until the cistern's empty. Then I sit on the lavatory, wishing I had a cigarette, and consider what I should do next.

The drawing room with the rainforest-print wallpaper is a frightful mess. Can it really be only a week ago that Price and I stood in this very spot with Jan drinking toasts to our respective monarchs? Did we seriously believe that within forty-eight hours we would have liberated the whole region?

I'm glad it's dark for I'm not sure I could bear to see the damage by daylight. All those lovely, old leather-bound books tossed casually on the floor, the antique prints ripped from the walls, the cabinets of curiosities containing three centuries' worth of artefacts and *objets trouvés* from the East Indies emptied and smashed. This isn't battle damage. This is systematic and deliberate vandalism, done for heaven knows what reasons, though I have my suspicions. It's the sort of thing the Germans might well do in a fit of pique if they knew the owner was a member of the Resistance. That would certainly explain why the house is empty.

Damn!

Flitting through the shadows, cowering behind walls and

under bushes – even in an empty hen house at one point – as German patrols marched by, wincing at the agonising throb of my temples and the shivering pain racking every muscle in my body, I was only kept going by the thought of the friendly reception awaiting me at this house.

I thought, with a fond smile, of pretty young Annette, of course. But mainly I thought of capable Jan and his wife Christina.

They'd give me food, drink, a hot bath, a clean, warm bed to sleep in with crisp cotton sheets. All right: I wasn't thinking straight. In all probability they'd be able to offer me none of those things, but you have to give yourself an incentive, don't you?

But they're not here. They've been taken away, perhaps shot, and I feel awful for them and even more awful for myself. They were my lifeline; my one hope of getting out of this mess; and now they're gone I might as well give up.

I'll search the house for food, very quietly mind, for there's no knowing who might be hiding here. I'll perhaps try to snatch a bit of rest and maybe sleep off this awful, thumping headache. Then I suppose I could either try and slip back through our lines – except it'll probably be light by then and I'll be caught – or take the easier option and just surrender.

Then through the wall I hear it. That hideous ginger cat, perhaps? No, it's definitely human. A faint but unmistakable female sob.

I pad closer. Where can it possibly have come from? It looks like a partition wall. No noise. Perhaps I was imagining it. But I stay stock still just in case.

After a time, the sobbing resumes.

'Annette? Christina?'

There's a pause, then a scuffling. Then part of the partition wall opens to reveal a concealed cupboard.

'Annette?' I address the subdued, shadowy figure that emerges warily from the hiding place. 'It's me. Dick.'

'Dick?' The puzzled way she says it makes me think it hasn't registered. But suddenly she springs forward like a greyhound out of a trap, flings both arms round me and buries her head in my chest, sobbing, 'Dick. Dick. Oh Dick. Dick!'

I remember the embarrassment it caused, last time she pulled that trick in front of the men. And I can't say I feel all that more comfortable with it now.

'Steady on, old thing,' I say, patting her on the back. 'You're all right now. Where are your uncle and aunt?'

This prompts a bout of even more intense sobbing. But eventually she manages to gasp, 'The *Moffen* take them. We hear them coming. They always make too much noise. My Uncle Jan says to my Aunt Christina, "Hide. Hide with Annette." But my aunt says, "No. If the *Moffen* take you, they must take me also." I say, "Then all three of us must hide." But my uncle says, "There is room for only two in the cupboard." Then the *Moffen* come, with Dutch SS who are worse than the *Moffen.* They say my uncle and aunt are traitors and they must be punished. They go. The Dutch SS stay. I hear them talking. They stay to destroy our beautiful house, laughing, joking, happy.'

'I'm so sorry,' I say, giving her an avuncular squeeze. And please, Jack, note the avuncular. I can assure you that, after all I've been through, with my head in the state it is, my intentions towards this vulnerable young girl are purely honourable.

'Will the *Moffen* hurt them?' she asks.

'Probably ask them a few questions, that's all,' I lie. 'There's nothing they can do unless they can prove your uncle and aunt have done wrong.'

'And Elmo and Hendrick?'

'Who are they?'

'The boys. The bad, bad, ugly boys. You save me from them.'

'Ah yes. Them,' I recall with distaste. I've seen some pretty unpleasant sights this week, but still, that gangly giant newt with the German General's bloodied scalp clasped triumphantly in his malodorous paws takes some beating.

'It is them. They are the ones who betray my uncle.'

'What? I thought they were with the Resistance?'

'Hah!' says Annette contemptuously. 'They are with no one. They care only for power. They are bad boys. I know them a long time. From the hospital.'

'St Elizabeth's?'

'Wolfheze. When your bombers bomb the hospital, many dangerous men escape. Elmo and Hendrick, they are the most dangerous.'

'Then I'm jolly glad I stepped in when I did.'

'I also. It is why I always thank you. Always love you.' This last is accompanied by an affectionate squeeze and an upwards look of total and unbridled devotion, such as you see worn by fallen women in sentimental Victorian paintings as they turn their thoughts to Christ. From a favourite old gundog this sort of look is fine; from a girl one barely knows it's a worry.

'Yes, well,' I say, blushing a bit as I pull myself gently free. 'I suppose I'd better, um – shave.'

Shave is the first excuse that comes into my head, though now I think about it it's a not half bad idea. Annette offers to escort me upstairs so we can find her uncle's shaving things but, remembering what nearly happened last time we made this journey, I suggest that instead she goes off to find us something to eat and drink. Now please don't think I'm a prude. I'm not normally in the business of warding off potential advances from blonde seventeen-year old lovelies. It's just that with my headache, my exhaustion and the constant threat of discovery by the Germans the circumstances aren't exactly the most propitious. And besides, there's something – I'm not sure what – that troubles me about this girl.

After various bumps and wrong turns, I find the uncle's bathroom eventually. And after a bit more rummaging in the dark, I find a cut-throat razor, some soap, a shaving brush and a sponge. There's still a finger or so of water in the bath, which I imagine Jan must cannily have filled last Sunday and been rationing ever since, so I treat myself to a half-cupful for a slow, messy, bloody but nonetheless highly rewarding shave. Then, after further consideration – and taking care to lock the door first – I decide it might be a nice idea to strip off all my clothes and treat myself to my first thorough wash since the shower before leaving Nijmegen.

It's just as well I do lock the door for, at the very moment when I'm giving my somewhat encrusted nether regions a vigorous scrub with Jan's sponge – well, I doubt he'll be needing it again, poor fellow – I hear the door click slightly as someone tries to pull it open.

'Dick?'

'Yes.'

'You have all you need?'

'Yes, thank you.'

She tries the door once more all the same. I can see the handle turning. I can even hear the resigned sigh she lets out before she heads back downstairs. That's because my ears are pinpricking with anxiety, ridiculous though it is. If I can survive two SS panzer divisions, what on earth is it that I have to fear from a seventeen-year old girl?

Still, she does seem to have at least one thing in her favour. To judge by the wonderful, fatty aroma wafting upstairs, she's a very accomplished cook. Or scavenger. Which, I don't really care; it smells very edible and very delicious, and if eating whatever it is were contingent on first submitting myself to her advances, well,

I dare say I'd probably do it – though I'm certainly not going to tell her that.

The dining room, where I find Annette waiting for me, has suffered less badly than most of the house. There are several chairs still intact, as is the large, heavy table over part of which Annette has draped a cloth and laid out knives, forks and plates. She has even found a candle from somewhere. A bottle of French wine is open, and two glasses have been half filled.

Annette has somehow found the time to slip into an oriental-looking dress made of dark-red silk, I think, though I'd rather not examine it too closely because the fabric is flimsy and revealing. Her nipples stand out clear as hilltop beacons warning of the Armada.

'To begin, fish,' she announces, manoeuvring a large whole fried fish onto each of our plates.

'There's more than one course?'

'Yes, of course. For you, Dick, the best.'

She picks up her glass and raises it towards me. As she does so, I notice by the candlelight that she has scratches on her arm. They look very fresh, though it's hard to be certain. When I saw her earlier on she wasn't illuminated.

'Proost!' she says.

'Cheers, we say,' I say, raising my glass, still looking at the scratches. They're quite nasty.

'Cheers!' she repeats.

'You've scratched yourself.'

'It's nothing,' she says.

We each have a drink. Though I take only the tiniest sip, my head immediately starts to swim. I must be careful, for I need my senses about me so I can be out of here well before dawn.

Out of manners and habit, I find myself at first trying to fillet the fish elegantly with my knife, but hunger quickly takes over.

'Please excuse me,' I say, grabbing the fish from either end and chomping into it as if it were an ear of sweetcorn. Very bony, greasy sweetcorn, whose scales haven't been removed and whose flesh tastes slightly muddy. But at this particular moment, not even the freshest, most buttery Wilton's *sole meunière* could taste any finer.

'Where did you get fresh fish?'

'My uncle has a pond in the garden. The fish cost him very much money before the war. They are very beautiful.'

'Koi carp, I expect.'

'Yes, koi carp. You are still hungry?'

'Rather.' That bit of protein has perked me up no end, and though it hasn't quite killed the headache, it's dulled it to a bearable level. But more would be welcome. If I'm to make my escape I must build up my strength.

'Wait, I will fetch. It is special meat stew.'

'What special meat or had I better not ask?'

'You will see,' she says with a smile.

As she shimmies off, waggling her pert little bottom, there's a part of me wants to give myself a damn good shake. You'll regret this, you know, says my inner lecher. You'll look back on this moment when you're old and infirm and you can't get it up any more and you'll ask yourself, How could you possibly have turned down so delightful a gift so freely offered?

But as my old Latin beak Clouter Pearson used to say, '*Timeo Danae et dona ferentes.*' In my experience, Jack – and you can take this advice or leave it – the sort of woman who most desperately wants to go to bed with a chap is the sort of woman a chap is best off avoiding like the plague.

And I don't mean to make any moral judgement here, for even if I were that way inclined – which I ain't – I don't believe it's a moral issue. It's more what you might call a sod's law issue. It ought to be the best thing in the world, and every young man's dream: wanton, impulsive lovemaking with a willing stranger.

And it is, it very much is, until the moment comes when, sweating and satiated, you discover that this pleasingly available young filly turns out to be married. To a boxer. Who has just come home unexpectedly early. And very quietly. With an enormous erection. Which he intends to thrust into the first available orifice he encounters on entering the darkened bedroom. With you lying naked on the side of the bed closest to the door. Your buttocks poking perilously outwards.

Or perhaps she's the girlfriend of a German you've just killed and now wants to bite off your manhood and shove a dagger up your jacksie: that actually happened to me, as you know. Or maybe she's a Nazi spy: that happened, too. Or a man: I'm not saying whether that did or didn't happen. Or mad.

Mad. Yes. It's a possibility. We know she was in the Wolfheze asylum when it was bombed; and we know she's acquainted with two of its most dangerous inmates, but is this because she was working there as a nurse or being treated as a patient? Apart from Price's cruel joke about her being a certifiable nymphomaniac, what actual evidence do I have that she's anything other than a sweet, vulnerable girl who wants to thank me for having saved her life?

'*Bon appétit*,' she murmurs, laying a steaming bowl in front of me. She hasn't done one for herself, I notice. Why is that?

I pull the candle closer towards the bowl and peer inside, in what I hope she'll think is appetite-whetting enthusiasm. But what I'm really doing is looking for clues. Watery sauce, with what smells like wine in it. Chunks of root vegetable. And meat, lumps of unidentifiable meat.

'Smells good,' I say, searching her face for clues.

'Thank you,' she says, giving nothing away.

What am I worried about? I've eaten rat. I've eaten snake.

I sip the liquid first. Bit bland, and the alcohol in the wine hasn't cooked off, but it's hot and nutritious, I'm hungry and it's heavenly.

A bit of vegetable next. Turnip. Not quite done, but do I mind? Do I hell. It's chunky, it's filling, it's the first bit of solid, recognisable veg I've eaten in four days, though I do wish she'd stop staring at me like that. I know she's only trying to gauge my reaction, but I can't abide people watching me when I eat.

'You like?'

'Oh very much, but I wish you'd have some too.'

'I cannot.'

'No?'

'Please. The meat. You must try the meat.'

I scoop out one of the smaller chunks with my spoon, and pop it uneasily into my mouth. Nice. A bit tough – as it would be, having had so little time to stew. More bone on it than meat. But a pleasant taste. Quite chickeny.

'You like?'

'Did you think I wouldn't?' I say, keeping the bone in my mouth, rolling it around so that none of the flakes go to waste.

'No. But it is important for me that you like. Then I do not feel so bad that he is dead.'

'Your uncle?'

'Walter.'

'Walter?'

'Walter is my friend. My animal friend.'

'Your pet?' I say, suddenly rather queasy.

'My pet,' she agrees, with a smile which I can't be certain is deliberately sinister, but bloody well looks that way from where I'm sitting.

'Jesus!' I say. Or perhaps something more like 'Jssshhhsss', for simultaneously there's a chunk of half-chewed bone shooting out of my mouth, faster than a shell from an 88.

She tries playing the sympathy card, by looking all hurt and wide-eyed and tearful. This only makes me crosser. To emphasise my disgust I push the bowl sharply away from me, causing it to tip and spread its rebarbative contents over the table.

'Are you quite mad?' I bark.

The question is, of course, purely rhetorical. Too late I've worked out the meaning of those deep scratches on her arm, and why she isn't joining me for this particular dish, and why – most pertinently – there is no longer that revolting, squash-faced ginger cat following her around the house.

'But . . . but . . .' she stammers between sobs. 'I do it to thank you. Because I care for you!'

And I know I shouldn't. She's all wrong in the head. I ought to show her more sympathy. But I'm frankly in a state of shock and I want to give her a piece of my mind.

'Care for me? CARE for me, you stupid, silly girl? And you think – what? – you think that in England we consider cat stew a rare and special delicacy, do you?'

'Walter is not my cat,' she sniffles.

'Do you think I care whose cat he is? Do you think that makes the blindest bit of difference? I do not eat cat. Englishmen do not eat cats.'

'I mean – Walter is my rabbit.'

'Rabbit. Oh yes. Well, of course you're going to say that now.'

'It is true. My cat is Hendrik. I do not give you my cat to eat.'

'Look. It's all right,' I say, in a more gentle tone, for she's still very distressed, the poor mad thing, whereas I'm past the worst of my nausea. 'I forgive you. There's no need to lie.'

'But I do not lie!' she protests.

'Annette –'

'Come. COME!' she insists. With her left hand she picks up the candle, with her right she tugs me by the arm. 'I show you I do not lie.'

With a sigh I follow her to the kitchen.

'There!' she says, holding the light above the sink so I can see for myself its contents.

Sure enough, the furry remains within are fluffy and white with unmistakably long rabbity ears. She keeps holding the candle where it is, her hand trembling with emotion and what must quite rightly be the most tremendous sense of burning injustice. I continue to stare at the bits of dead rabbit for some time, almost willing them to turn more gingery and cat-shaped so that I no longer need to feel quite so guilty.

Never – really never, I don't think – have I felt such a dreadful heel. I'm not sure which is worse: my false and cruel accusation, with its barely disguised assumption that I consider her a complete fruitcake; or my quite inexcusable ingratitude at what must, for Annette, have been the most painful sacrifice. Of course it must have been. Walter was her pet. She loved him. It's why she couldn't bring herself to eat him. But she did it for me because she believed that my need for solid food was greater than her need for a white fluffy bunny hopping about the lawn.

'I'm sorry, Annette,' I say at last, trying to give her a hug.

She pulls away.

'Annette?'

'You think I am mad.'

'No.'

'Yes. You say I am mad. I hear you.'

'No.'

'I think you are different. I think you are nice,' she says. 'But you are the same. The same as them all.'

'Please, Annette, I made a dreadful mistake and I'm sorry.'

'I make you sorry!' she spits. And by George, does she look as if she means it. Her eyes are slits of hatred, the pert nose is like a pig's snout, her pretty little mouth a dark maw of biting teeth, and spittle and malice. If I believed in such things I'd almost say she'd been possessed.

She takes a step towards me, teeth gritted, claws outstretched. And I take an immediate step back, for in this frame of mind there's no knowing what she might be capable of. Perhaps it's all the prelude to one of those explosive rows which can only be resolved by a frenzied bout of passionate lovemaking. Perhaps – quick: hide the knives – she's genuinely intent on doing me harm. Whichever it is, I'll never know, for at this point I receive succour from the most unlikely of sources: a platoon of German infantrymen come to ransack the house.

You'll remember them from the beginning of this adventure. They're the chaps we heard outside, yelling to one another in their raucous Teutonic way, and affording Annette and me just enough time to conceal ourselves, before the first one burst in through the window.

Her response to the new threat is reassuringly immediate. If the girl were really mad, I think to myself, then she'd carry on rowing as if the Germans weren't there and end up getting both of us shot. Instead, her expression lightens as quickly as it darkened, and she seizes me by the sleeve.

'Quick,' she says, leading me swiftly to the built-in-cupboard hidey-hole. We've only just pulled the door shut when the first Jerry blunders in.

Much of the rest, you know, Jack: from the search of the house to the commandeering by a German officer of the room in which we're hiding for use as an interrogation centre. More pertinently, you'll no doubt recall what Annette was doing to me, off and on, during the time all this interrogating was going on; and how increasingly perilous our predicament became as Annette's passions grew more inflamed.

'I did warn you,' laughed Price when eventually I was able to tell him the story.

'Oh, a warning, was it? Sounded more like a joke to me.'

'Well, how was I to know you'd be stupid enough to go back

for second helpings?' said Price, finally repeating to me what Annette's guardians had told him that first day, while Annette and I were upstairs in the tower with the panoramic views.

It seemed that the reason she was living in Oosterbeek was because she'd been sent there for safekeeping by her despairing parents. On the surface a bright, healthy, normal girl, Annette was given to sudden mood swings and impulsive behaviour which had got her into all manner of trouble back home in Eindhoven. Her frequent affairs with the Germans had unfortunately drawn her to the attention of the local Resistance, who had begun making nasty threats. The parents had tried protesting that it wasn't Annette's fault: among the unfortunate side-effects of her mental condition was a strong predilection for dangerous or forbidden sex. But to no avail. Fortunately for Annette, her uncle and aunt had agreed to put her up in Oosterbeek, while she was treated by a psychiatrist friend of theirs who worked at the nearby Wolfheze asylum. The treatment hadn't been going quite as well as they might have liked: Annette seemed, if anything, even hungrier for the Germans of Oosterbeek than she was for those in her native Eindhoven. So it was with some relief that her uncle and aunt had greeted the Airborne landings. If Annette really was going to carrying on dispensing her favours in this wanton way, at least she'd now be making a useful contribution to the war effort.

'We wanted you to know this because your officer seems a nice young man and we do not wish him to come to any harm,' Annette's uncle Jan had concluded his warning to Price. 'Annette is a good girl and we love her very much. But sometimes she can be difficult. And when she is difficult, a man must take great care.'

Well, indeed.

But let us, without further ado, address the conundrum with which I so cruelly teased you at the beginning of this narrative.

Your poor old grandpa – or poor young grandpa as he then was – is trapped in a cupboard with a blonde seventeen-year-old Dutch succubus with the beauty of Venus and the morals of Lucrezia Borgia. The more he caresses her firm and now highly aroused breasts the more she moans and gasps. And the more she moans and gasps, the more certain it is that their hiding place will be discovered by the Germans. But whenever he stops caressing those breasts, the girl gets cross and threatens that if he doesn't keep going, she'll betray him anyway. Looks like Grandpa is scuppered whichever way he plays it.

Unless . . .

Surreptitiously, with the hand that isn't doing the vital bosom work, I reach down towards the knife strapped to my leg.

Outside, as you'll recall, Sgt. Price is being threatened by the Wehrmacht officer.

'Tell us all you know now and we will spare your life. Otherwise I shall have to pass you over to the Hauptsturmführer for further questioning –'

Is the knife sharp enough? Yes. Can I achieve all I need to do swiftly in so confined a space?

'So, Sergeant Price. The choice is yours. Do you wish to live? Or do you prefer to die?'

Sighs. Loud sighs from my cupboard-mate.

'Hmm. The options are so tempting. Let me think that one over for a moment.'

'Enough. Enough of your games!'

I go to work with the knife, in long swift cuts.

Annette screams. I think I must accidentally have nicked her with the blade.

'What was that? What was that?'

Frantically now, for there can't be more than a few seconds left, I cut and slash, cut and slash with one hand, while with the other I try to delay Annette's pushing open of the cupboard. She's panicking, too frightened even to scream, just breathing in sharp little gasps and frantic to escape the man she's convinced is trying to kill her.

Still I need a little more time.

'*Scheiße!*' She's sunk her teeth into my hand, the cow. Christ, it hurts! Christ! But still I've had the presence of mind to shout in German.

'There's a German in there. What the hell is he –?' calls a voice from outside.

Before he can complete his question, I've booted open the door, to find myself staring down the barrels of at least half a dozen Lugers, Schmeissers and Mauser rifles.

'*Heil Hitler*,' I say, clicking my heels as I come sharply to attention and execute a Nazi salute stiffer than rigor mortis. As I do so, I try to keep my gaze focused on that of the officer in the SS uniform. Otherwise, I might run the risk of catching Price's eye as he sits looking up at me from his interrogation chair, and end up doing what he's clearly on the verge of doing – and wet myself with laughter.

Some of the German soldiers have started already. A snigger here, a muffled titter there, the laughter spreading like a barrack-room infection and becoming more overt and helpless the harder the soldiers try to pull themselves together.

I'm not sure which they find funnier: the naked blonde nubile now clinging frantically to the most senior authority figure – viz. one desperately unamused and highly embarrassed SS officer – and squeaking in German, 'Help! Help! He is trying to kill me!' Or yours truly standing in front of him doing the Hitler salute, stark bollock naked save for my boots, which are the one part of my uniform I've been unable to hack off in time.

At the moment I have the advantage of surprise. Most of the guns which were pointing at me have been lowered, and those that haven't been are so trembling with mirth they probably wouldn't hit me even if fired. But this isn't going to last long. Soon someone will notice that my boots are British-Army-issue, not German, as indeed perhaps they have already. So the first thing I do is to make sure I keep babbling in German, in order to sow sufficient doubt that no one tries to shoot me. And the second thing I do, as I yell, '*Entschuldigen Sie bitte, meine Herren.* I will explain everything in just a moment,' is to make a beeline for the door, reverse sharply when I see that the two men guarding it aren't going to let me through, and head for one of the open windows instead.

'Stop him!' commands the SS officer.

'My friends. Wouldn't you have done the same in my position?' I yell, to more laughter. See, they do have a sense of humour, of sorts, our German friends.

Still, it's not quite enough on its own to save me. One of my would-be captors I only escape because Price trips him up with his leg just as he's on the verge of grabbing me. Then, when I'm halfway out of the window – thank heavens there are no shards of glass left in the bottom of the frame or you wouldn't be here now, Jack, listening to these tapes – two more Germans grab a leg apiece and start hauling me back in.

This time – and not for the first time – it's my trusty arse tattoo which saves me.

'*Was sagt es?*' says one, briefly distracted by the writing on my buttocks.

'"*Leck mich am Arsch!*"' reads the other.

Bottom joke. As far as your Hun is concerned, there's simply nothing funnier. Anything to do with poo has them in stitches.

'Ha ha ha!' they go, loosing their grip just enough for me to pull free, launch myself head first onto the soft ground outside the window, perform a nifty roll down the sloping lawn, before darting into the shrubbery, scaling the garden fence and haring off into the cover of the woods.

Quite what I'm going to do next or where our lines are or how I'm going to exfiltrate Jerry's positions and infiltrate ours or how long it will be before the remnants of 1st Airborne Division are overrun, I don't for the moment much care.

18

Double-barrelled

Did I ever tell you about the time I was forced to endure a night of wild, unbridled sex with two randy young Herefordshire girls?

Worst night of my life.

Give or take one or two in Burma, perhaps.

Yes, of course I know what you're thinking, Jack. You're thinking, Yet again, my dear old grandpa doth protest too much.

And I suppose technically speaking you'd have a point. Graceful, brown-eyed Caro Ashenden is silken, yielding, sensuous, sporty, domineering, generously proportioned. Lavinia Crumblebeech has all the braying enthusiasm of a lesbian lacrosse mistress at the inter-house lax finals at Madame Cunegonde's Academy for Exceptionally Nubile Young Ladies and the thigh control of one of those remarkable Asian lovelies who can unscrew Coke bottles without using their hands. The yin and the yang of the perfect *ménage à trois*, you might well say.

For all that, though, I'm sorry to say, my poor heart's just not in it. Nor my poor head. Nor – except sporadically – certain other key appendages further below.

'Giddy up, Caro! Spank his arse! That'll get him going!' Lavinia has to command desperately at one point, clamping round me harder with those extraordinary muscles of hers, dragging me deeper within like a wet rag through a mangle. And that certainly does the trick for a while.

'Oh! Oh! Oh! OH!' gasps Caro when it's her turn, oozing such pure abandon and aching desire and gratitude for anything I can offer – well, she has been widowed two years, let's not forget – that this too works its restorative magic for a time.

Overall, though, I cannot honestly say my performance is one of my better ones. Nor yet that my level of enjoyment is nearly so high as it damn well ought to be on such an occasion.

Part of this has to do with the drink – for I'm about as thoroughly rat-arsed as it's possible to be without waking up tarred and feathered and tied to a lamp post with a carrot up your jacksie. Part, too, to the frustrating fact that neither of these pliant and eager young fillies is Gina. But the main reason, I'm sure, is the difficulty I've had coming to terms with the piece of paper which, without a word of introduction, was thrust under my nose by Father this morning at breakfast.

THE KING has been graciously pleased to approve
the award of the VICTORIA CROSS to:
No: 127351 Lieutenant Richard Owain Devereux
Court Coward DFC
1st Herefordshire Yeomanry
(attd. 1st Airborne Recce Squadron)
[1st Airborne Division] Hambledown Lacey, Herefordshire

In Holland on 17 September, Lt. Coward, commanding a section of 1st Airborne Recce Squadron, was among the first officers to reach the bridge during the battle of Arnhem, and during the next eight days demonstrated outstanding devotion to duty and remarkable powers of leadership while closely engaged at all times and in numerous places with enemy tanks, self-propelled guns and infantry. On 20 September, with complete disregard for his own personal safety, he volunteered to carry a message to his

Corps HQ by swimming across a river, exfiltrating twelve miles of enemy-held territory, then crossing a second river under continual enemy observation. Next, he volunteered to guide the American paratroops of 504th Parachute Infantry Regiment on a heavily opposed, daylight river-crossing, which was achieved despite widespread injury and loss of life. Having been instrumental in consolidating his Corps bridgehead, Lt. Coward determined that he should return to offer support to the remnants of his unit, now occupying part of the perimeter in the village of Oosterbeek. After yet another opposed river-crossing, Lt. Coward found his way back to his unit, moving amongst his men and encouraging them by his fearless example to hold out. During the final days of the defence, Lt. Coward was everywhere where danger threatened and on at least three occasions demonstrated such further disregard for his personal safety as to provoke admiration throughout the Division and contribute immeasurably to its security. On the first, he retrieved the contents of a vital drop canister guarded by an enemy sniper who had already claimed the lives of three of his comrades; on the second, he led the fighting patrol which destroyed an enemy propaganda unit whose broadcasts threatened the Division's morale; on the third, having failed to put out of action a self-propelled gun with a PIAT, he then emerged from cover and crossed 20 yards of open ground under withering fire in order to finish the job with a Gammon grenade. Missing believed dead from injuries sustained during this action, Lt. Coward evaded capture. He went on to lead by further example during 1st Airborne Division's orderly withdrawal across the Neder Rhine from the Oosterbeek defensive perimeter on the night of 25/26 September when he gave up his place in a rescue boat to a wounded man, and chose to swim across the river instead. Throughout the whole course of the Battle of Arnhem, Lt. Coward's conduct was exemplary, his leadership inspirational and his coolness and courage under incessant fire unsurpassable.

Once I've had time to read it through disbelievingly a couple of times, drop my egg spoon, open and close my mouth like a dying fish, and look across to where Mother has been standing, flushed and beaming – having evidently been lurking to catch the moment when her little boy's face lights up with joy – Father grunts, 'Eat up or we'll miss the best of the morning's fish.' And with that, he stomps out of the dining room.

'Does he really mean what I think he means?' I ask Mother, as she pulls me tight to her bosom, showers the top of my head with kisses and calls me her 'brave, BRAVE, darling, clever, SILLY boy'.

If he does, it's a lot more significant than the medal. Never once before in my life – not once, mark you, Jack – has my father ever taken me to his personal River Wye fishing spot, just me and him. In the old days it was usually only John. Or, if Father was in benevolent mood, John, James and me together – with John and James single Spey-casting with effortless grace and catching all the fish, while my function mainly was to be shouted at for getting my line caught up in trees and wreaking havoc with my father's cherished collection of hand-tied flies.

This time, when we're finally standing by the river, and Father has observed me with what I'm convinced must be disapproval, he suddenly says,

'Bugger me. Three casts in a row and not an eye lost yet.'

'Five to two says I'll have blinded the pair of us by lunchtime,' I reply.

A twitch of moustache, a flash of teeth. Good God, I think it's a smile.

'Self-deprecation,' he notes with an approving nod, as though we're still in the midst of my interview for the post of official favourite son. 'You'll need plenty of that when word gets out, as no doubt it will by the time you give your talk.'

'I'm giving a talk?'

'Village hall. 17.30 hours. Wasn't going to mention it till later. Thought it might spoil your fishing. I doubt there'll be more than thirty turning up, and it can't last more than an hour, for you'll need time to change for the formal dinner.'

'I'm not sure you mentioned that, either.'

'All in a day's work for the heir presumptive to Great Meresby.'

'Is that what I am now?'

'Have you reason to believe otherwise?'

'Well –' Apart from the fact that until today you hated my guts and thought I was a cowardly, snivelling toad unfit to lick the ground James walked on, you mean. 'The war's not over yet. Suppose James were to win something similar?'

'Suppose I were to become astronomer general to the King of Siam and find the moon was made of green cheese. Suppose my leg were to grow back. Suppose the estate's books were to balance.'

'I'm sorry?'

'I shouldn't be in your shoes, for it's all to your gain. Your brother has cracked. Let the side down completely at Nijmegen bridge. Might even be the reason the whole operation failed, is what I hear.'

'Father, really, that's complete nonsense – I was there. Any sane armoured commander would have done what James did. To have advanced up that road would have been suicide.'

'Trying to talk yourself out of the estate, what? I knew I shouldn't have mentioned that trouble with the accounts. But a fellow who can take on an SP with a PIAT isn't going to be put out by the odd stiff letter from Higgins of Hereford Lloyd's.

Who's coming to the dinner, incidentally. I'm putting you next to his wife. Lay on the charm and the loans should be good for at least another year.'

'Would these loans be small ones or big ones?'

'That cast you did a moment ago. Show me again, would you? Looked rather unusual, I thought.'

It was a perfectly ordinary double Spey cast, but I take the hint and make no further mention of the estate's financial liabilities.

The fishing goes well. Father's spot is in indeed the most idyllic and fruitful on the Wye, which is why, of course, he'll let no one else near it. By lunchtime, between us, we've landed five very healthy-looking salmon. We sit in the shade of a willow eating Patum Paperium sandwiches washed down in my case with a rather good Chablis, and in Father's with a malt whisky – the silence broken only by the rustling of leaves, the chuckling of the river and the occasional plop of a surfacing salmon.

'I suppose you think you've done well,' says my father.

'They caught themselves,' I say.

'I didn't mean the fish.'

'No,' I murmur, feeling awkward.

'But you won't want to talk about it. I never did. Except one time. The King gave a dinner for a few of us once at Sandringham. We talked then. You can with your own kind.'

Father looks as though he'd like to say more, but then apparently decides better of it and fills his pipe instead.

I light a cigarette to keep him company and keep off the gnats.

Father is agitating his pipe's mouthpiece like a dog gnawing a bone. I'd like to help him out, by giving him some sort of prompt. But the truth is I don't really know how to talk to him either.

'You never can tell, though,' he mutters. 'Who's made of the right stuff. Who's not. Mistakes are made. Nobody's fault. Terrible business, war.'

'Yes, quite,' I say, causing him to flap away my interruption as if it were a swarm of midges. He hasn't finished, apparently.

'Had a fellow shot, once. Name of Thompson. Pederast probably, though that wasn't the reason. One of our fighting patrols brought him back from no-man's-land, three days after his CSM had reported him missing, presumed a deserter. Swore blind he was innocent, of course, as they always do. Some cock-and-bull story about having gone to look for his pal Trowbridge, left for dead after the last assault, but still alive in a shell hole, so he claimed. We might have bought the excuse, too, for it was common knowledge the two were close. Too damn close, in my view. But then the fool went and blew it. Classic mistake. Piled on too much detail, Nonsense about having got to Trowbridge and dressed his wounds and kept him company and tried to bring him back, only to be separated by a persistent sniper, or a Hun patrol, or a sudden barrage, the story kept changing. Well, in the absence of any corroborating evidence at the court martial, there was only one verdict that could be reached. Only one sentence, too. Protested his innocence to the very last moment, as again they inevitably do. Men chuntered for a while but it certainly did the trick. After that, in so far as I'm aware, our battalion had not a single desertion till the war's end.'

'*Autres temps, autres moeurs,*' I murmur, with a sad shake of my head.

Father glares at me sharply. He's still not done.

'A year or two later, I'm in London taking an Armistice parade, when a fellow in civilian dress, but wearing his campaign medals, comes up to me and says, "You're Colonel Coward." "Brigadier General Coward now, sir. Do I know you?" I say. "I doubt that very much, sir, for I was wounded and captured not long after joining your battalion. Trowbridge is the name, sir, and I'll never forget yours. For you're the fellow who ordered the firing squad that killed the pal who saved my live."'

Father's moustache twitches. His face seems to sag for a brief moment and he suddenly looks every one of his sixty odd years. I find myself feeling almost sorry for him.

'Goodness, Father. How terrible!'

'Was it, though?' he barks, pulling himself together.

'Well –'

'Worse than losing half your battalion and your three best company commanders in the space of an afternoon, would you say? Worse than watching your fastest HQ runner drowning in a crater of mud? Worse than gas? War IS terrible, you fool. Thought you would have at least gathered that by now.'

'I meant, Father,' I say, bridling slightly. 'Terrible for YOU.'

'What in the devil's name does that have to do with anything?'

'Oh, I don't know. I thought you might have felt a bit guilty, that's all.'

'GUILTY? And is that the reason I told you that story, do you think? So you could pat me on the back and say "There, there" and we could all have a good blub? Land's sake, boy, if that's the way your generation thinks it's no wonder you're making such a meal of kicking Jerry into touch,' says my father, with a deep exasperated sigh. He frowns at me for a while, as you might at someone so incredibly stupid you're really not at all sure it's worth your while going on. Then he says to me confidingly, 'And I suppose you want to know what I said in reply to this Trowbridge fellow?'

'Sorry; frightful cock-up; *mea culpa*, I would imagine?'

'Nothing,' he says with evident pride.

'Nothing?'

'Never apologise. Never explain!' he declares in triumph.

He thinks I'm going to be shocked by this. He wants me to be shocked by this, the cantankerous old fool, as he sits wobbling on his shooting stick, positively trembling with glee at his own cussedness, at his steely patriotism, at his ruthless expediency, and, perhaps above all, at his defiant, Houdini-like evasion of anything that might smack of the apology he so patently owes me for all the vile, unfair things he has said and done.

Instead, I look him straight back in the eye and, a thin smile on my lips, I hold his stare for as long as it takes – I don't mind, I've got all afternoon if need be. And when eventually he snorts and looks away I know that at least one good thing has emerged from this cursed albatross of a medal. I have lost all my hatred of my father, and with it, all my fear.

'MARKET GARDEN: OUR FINEST HOUR – A TALK BY LIEUTENANT RICHARD COWARD DFC' says the notice outside the village hall. To this a well-wisher has added after my name the letters 'VC'. Someone else, of a more sceptical disposition, has decided to improve on the 'OUR FINEST HOUR' bit by adding the punctuation marks '???!'. It gives you a fair indication of the mixed reception to come.

At first all goes swimmingly. My audience of around thirty tenants, villagers, estate workers and friends – many of them old enough to remember Omdurman with a sense of uncomplicated patriotism to match – listen most attentively, as I recount, in proper Arthur Bryant fashion, the stirring tale of how our gallant Red Berets came so close to finishing the war single-handedly by Christmas, only to be frustrated through absolutely no fault of their own by the devious and exceedingly jammy Boche.

As is expected on these occasions – there are ladies and young folk present, including my dear mama, my sisters, Caro Ashenden, an already-drooling Lavinia Crumblebeech, Gina's mother the Countess of Brecon (but no sign as yet, I'm concerned to notice, of her daughter) – I am careful not to betray any indication that the battle may have involved unpleasantness of any description. There is plenty of 'biffing' and 'hitting for six', a degree of tight-lipped 'dealing with', but certainly no bayoneting or disembowelment.

But even when it's going well, I can't pretend my heart's much in it. One reason is I'm far too distracted by the absence of Gina. Where on earth can she be? She must have heard the talk's on, for her mother would have told her. Is she ill? Being difficult? Gone to stay with some lover who's appeared on the scene in my absence? The tension of not knowing is unbearable and I wish I'd found out earlier. If I had my way I'd abridge the whole story to a couple of pithy sentences, take one question from the audience, and draw the event to a close. Unfortunately my father's in the front row, monitoring me with his stopwatch. Forty minutes for the talk, he says; twenty minutes for the questions.

The second reason I don't much enjoy it is because, frankly, I feel a bit of an imposter. I can think of dozens and dozens of chaps who did more to deserve a VC at Market Garden than me.

When I lightly skip over all the incidents on my medal citation, I imagine my audience thinks I'm being modest. Really, though, it's because I can't bear to remind myself of the huge gulf between what I purportedly did and what actually happened, between the heroic selflessness which the citation claims was my sole motivation and the squalid mix of fear, cowardice, foolhardiness, drug-induced mania and selfishness which was my real inspiration.

Not one of my supposedly heroic deeds was done for the right reasons, and that includes the final one on the citation, in the small hours of Tuesday 26 September, whose details I shall now relate to you.

I'm huddled in the mud on the north bank of the Neder Rhine, in one of several long, straggly queues made up of perhaps a thousand shattered, battered, trembling men, most of whom would mortgage their souls – those of their loved ones too – for a place in one of the rescue craft which are supposed to be ferrying us to the other side but of which we've glimpsed none for at least half an hour.

We've felt our way there under cover of darkness and pissing rain using guide tapes laid by the glider pilots who now wait at strategic intervals along the route to hurry us along with urgent hisses. As if we bloody need any encouragement. The wounded we have been told to leave behind, though it's an order many have disobeyed. No one likes to abandon an injured mate to the mercy of the SS.

An hour or two ago, before Jerry twigged what we were up to, we might have applauded this sentiment. But now that we're under increasingly heavy mortar and machine-gun fire with nowhere to shelter and with our survival chances decreasing every second longer we stay here, our Birkenhead Drill stoicism is beginning to fray. If it weren't for all the wounded holding up the evacuation, some of us are starting to think, we'd be home and dry by now.

Then, materialising like a ghost ship through the cordite smoke and the plashing rainspray, another boat nudges towards us. It bumps onto the bank.

The engineer piloting it casts out a painter for someone to grab.

'Easy,' calls the engineer to his passengers in a soft Canadian accent. 'Easy, or you'll swamp her.'

These are low-built, flimsy craft. Even when they're empty their gunwales barely clear the water's surface. Now, in their desperation to scramble aboard, down slopes slippery with mud, blood and entrails, and into that crowded, desperately unstable hull, the passengers have damned near sunk her before she's left shore.

'No more. She's full,' says the Canadian engineer, adding, not altogether convincingly, 'plenty more on their way.'

Now his outboard motor has stalled. He tugs the lanyard. The motor coughs and dies. Another tug of the lanyard. And another. And another. But with no more success than the first.

The boat is starting to drift with the current.

'Hold hard there,' calls the engineer to the soldier on shore straining to keep hold of the wet, slimy painter.

He's leaning back at an angle, trying to take the weight by digging his feet into the mud. But his feet are slipping, his hands are slipping. He's flat on his back and the boat has drifted off, the Canadian engineer still yanking at his lanyard, the engine still sputtering without result, the boat overloaded and rocking dangerously.

And still we watch them go with ravening envy bordering on hatred. The lucky swine! They're on they're way and we're still here.

Then, from downriver, where roughly the boat should be by now, there come splashes, and cries, then screams. The boat has capsized. God, I hope not – but is that a hint of *Schadenfreude* I can feel?

'Help me! I can't swim!' someone yells. 'Heellppp!'

Onshore, the knots in our stomachs tighten another twist. Not through empathy, so much, as fear for our own safety. He had his fair chance, that bloke, and fate decided against him. But that's no reason why he should be allowed to jeopardise our future by drawing Jerry's attention to our position.

'If he has to die, why the hell should he make such a bastard noise about it?' grumbles a soldier squatted next to me. Uncharitable, but it's what a lot of us are thinking.

Sure enough, moments later, the earth all around us erupts, and we bite and hug and squeeze the wet mud, as the mortar bombs crash about us, and shrapnel and clods of earth and torn flesh fly above our heads. And as we crawl past the smoking corpses of our neighbours, appalled sympathy vying with guilty gratitude for the fact that we're now several places further up the queue, a pair of MGs opens up – one from the east and one from the west – sending angry streams of fiery tracer zipping inches above our heads, forcing us to press ourselves hard against the earth once more in terror so abject it seems to squeeze out every last vestige of decency or humanity or fellow-feeling. Frightened animals, that's all we are now. Animals who want nothing more than to survive.

Needless to say, I don't mention this to my audience in the village hall. Those who know won't want to be reminded. Those who don't know, are better off not knowing, for they're troubled enough about the suffering of their sons and brothers and grandsons and husbands as it is.

But what I don't do either is tell them the story they want to hear: the one about me giving my place in the next rescue boat that comes along to a wounded man. The bare facts are true enough, but what the bare facts don't tell you is the underlying sentiment.

What in fact happens, as I'm about to take my place in the next boat to come along, is that I take one look at the sea of sorry faces in that jam-packed, wobbling hull, remember what became of the last boat, and think to myself, I don't fancy my chances with you lot. I reckon you're all goners.

And I glance back up the bank, notice a fellow with a bandaged arm looking woeful and envious, and say, 'In you go, old chap. Your need is greater than mine.'

By far my biggest fear at this point is that the chap with the bandaged arm will reply, 'No, really, after you.' That's why, in a gesture of determination and finality – mistaken by those who witness it for bravura heroism – I tear off my bloodied, ill-fitting uniform (which was scrounged for me from some corpse or other, a few hours before, after I'd found my way back through to our lines, stark naked but for my boots), before plunging into the river.

There are claps and cheers as I swim off, not remotely merited in my view, for you know what I think is going to become of all the chaps doing the clapping and cheering.

Do they survive the crossing? Not sure, to be honest. But as I swim across the river, my only regret about my decision is not having taken it earlier. The water's cold, the current reasonably strong, and of course I'm desperately exhausted. Still, I'd much rather court cramp and a quick death by drowning than find myself in the position of those poor chaps I can see in the boat about 200 yards downstream of me, clearly illuminated by the fires burning on either bank, and now being shredded by mercilessly accurate German machine-gun fire. The Waal crossing was enough. Never again.

Surprisingly soon afterwards, I'm being hauled up the far side by two friendly, congratulatory Tommies, one of whom wraps me in a blanket and directs me towards a white guide tape which I'm to follow over the bank towards safety. Further on, as I stumble forward, step by disbelieving step, with a group of similarly dazed survivors, someone calls kindly from the roadside, 'You need some boots, mate.'

I look down at my torn, muddy, numb feet, scarcely recognising that they're a part of me. They don't feel real. Nothing feels real. Any moment now, I'm thinking, I'm going to wake from my dream and find that I'm back in that cellar crowded with wounded at the Kocks' house by the bridge or yelling curses with the boys of 504th Parachute Infantry or deep in a foxhole with Lt. Verney as the StuG rumbles towards us.

I take the proffered boots, just in case. They're a couple of sizes too big, which seems nearer the mark. But then, about a mile further on, like a mirage in the desert, I stumble upon a mobile canteen, and behind the counter, dressed in Salvation Army uniform, a grey-haired lady serving tea. And I know then for certain that I'm imagining the whole business.

A day later, we're in Nijmegen, parading for an address by Lt. Gen. Browning, who thanks us for all we've done and promises that there'll only be one more job after this – the victory parade. It gets a few sour laughs, that one.

The day after that, what's left of our squadron spends the night at a monastery in Louvain on the road to Brussels. Things are starting to feel more normal now, though we almost wish they weren't. To acknowledge reality is to acknowledge just how few of our comrades will be coming back.

It's worse, though, on the Saturday when we get back to England. Our plane touches down in Lincolnshire at seven-thirty in the evening, but it isn't till very late, after we've been served a hot meal, that we get to Ruskington – the village we've come to call home.

Someone says, 'Isn't it funny – it feels like aeons since we were last here, but it was only twelve days ago that we left.'

Someone else, says, 'Yeah. And do you remember how many lorries it took to get us all to the airfield? Ten. But only two to bring us back.'

After that, what we need most of all is a drink to drown our sorrows, but of course the village is dark and silent and the pub's closed. Then with true Recce initiative, some bright spark thinks to knock up the landlord, and soon half the village is up and out of bed to welcome us back with a pint or two at the Leg of Mutton, and to enquire nervously as to the whereabouts of old friends they haven't yet spotted.

'Is there another lorry still to come?'

'Is he one of the wounded, anyone know?'

'What are you having, Mr Coward?'

It's Sgt. Veale, one of the few to escape when our position was overrun. We haven't spoken much since. Everyone in the Squadron has been perfectly cordial to me, but I do get the slight impression that behind my back I'm viewed as something of a

Jonah. Myself apart, only three men from my section have come back in one piece, and though it might just be the shock of battle, or the natural distance between men and their officer, I detect in their behaviour towards me a certain reserve. As if they think, somehow, it's my fault that so many of their comrades are dead, captured or missing. Perhaps because they think I was too reckless; or too intent on personal glory; or just plain jinxed.

'Please, allow me, Sarnt.'

'That's all right. You can buy the next one.'

'A mild-and-bitter then. Thank you.'

Someone yells from a table for Sgt. Veale to come and join them.

'Half a mo,' he calls back.

We go outside where it's quieter.

He nods at my pint.

'That's Gonad's tipple, isn't it?'

Gonad is one of the nicknames Price encourages his friends to use – in reference, of course, to his missing testicle.

I nod, not feeling wholly comfortable. There's a called-into-the-headmaster's-study-for-a-quiet-chat element to Sgt. Veale's approach, I feel.

'Good man, Gonad. One of the best. You bumped into him in the bag, I heard.'

I give Sgt. Veale a short, highly expurgated account of the circumstances in which I last saw Sgt. Price.

'You think he was on his way to getting himself shot, then?'

'Not necessarily. He's escaped worse before now. I'm just trying not to get my hopes up. We go back a long way, Price and I.'

'Save your arse a few times, did he?' says Sgt. Veale.

'One or two,' I say, searching his expression for the faint malevolence I think I can hear in his voice.

'I'll bet,' he says.

'Do you?' I say, my irritation showing now.

Sgt. Veale shrugs and looks away. Then he says, very casually. 'And where do you think you'll be going next?'

'I'm not sure I get you.'

'Oh, did I hear wrong, then? I thought you were only ever with the Squadron on attachment. And what with the OC in the bag now, and most of your section gone, I wasn't sure you'd have much reason for wanting to stay with us.'

'That's something for me to consider, privately, in my own good time, wouldn't you say?'

'Don't take too long about it, would be my advice, Mr Coward.'

'And why would that be, Sarnt?'

'No reason in particular. More of a general feeling, really. Based on what I'm hearing from some of the lads.'

'I see.'

'Not all of the lads, I'll admit. There's some who saw what you got up to with that SP who think you're a right proper fire-eater. Then there's others of us more inclined to wish we'd listened to what Vic Cholmondeley said, right from the beginning.'

'Cholmondeley never was my greatest admirer.'

'No. And if I tell you exactly what he said you'll have me on a charge for insurbordination.'

'Tell me.'

'That you weren't to be trusted and you'd get us all killed. Even had this idea that you might be working for the enemy.'

'You think that?'

'If you want the honest truth, I don't know what to think. That incident with the SP. I was there, I saw it, but I still can't work out what was going on. What I do know is that while we like a bit of eccentricity in the Squadron – and you've got that in spades – what we need most of all is men we can rely on one hundred per cent. With the best will in the world, Mr Coward, that's not something that can be said of you.'

'I suppose I should thank you for your bluntness, Sarnt.'

'That's good of you to say so. I can't say this is a task I've much enjoyed.'

'Put up to it by the men, were you, Sarnt?'

'And one or two of the officers. And don't take it too hard, Mr Coward. We're a tight-knit bunch, are the Squadron. It's not everyone that fits in. We all wish you the best, wherever it is you decide to go next.'

After I've given my talk at the village hall, I take questions from the audience. Most of these aren't so much questions as invitations to reiterate how thoroughly magnificent I am. I try to be modest. Indeed I succeed in being modest. (Rather wasted though I feel my efforts are, without Gina in the audience to witness them.) But it still isn't enough for the young chap on crutches at the back of the hall, dressed in civvies but sporting a red beret.

'So I suppose, all in all, Mr Coward, you think you're blooming marvellous and 1st Airborne won the war?' he says sneerily. I think I can now guess who scrawled in that extra punctuation.

The rest of the audience leaps instantly to my defence, craning round to stare at him crossly and making hissing noises and crying, 'Shame!' Our church verger, a muscly man who served as a stoker on one of the capital ships at Jutland, lurches to eject him, which I don't want at all.

'Let him speak!' I command. And not just because I've recognised the crippled fellow as Valentine Wood, the scion of a large local gypsy family who could make life exceedingly unpleasant for us if they so chose. But also because I know something of how he lost his leg on D-Day, on operations with 6th Airborne Division.

'No, of course I don't think I'm marvellous,' I say.

Sympathetic laughter from the audience.

'As for 1st Airborne, we did our best. But no more than you fellows achieved in Normandy.'

'I'm glad to hear you say that,' he says a bit awkwardly, the wind slightly taken out of his sails. 'Only I wanted to tell you a story, about something that happened to me in the Green Dragon, last weekend. A bloke comes into the bar, not from these parts, and he sees the colour of my beret and he says, "Arnhem hero, eh? Let me buy you a pint." And I looks him up and down and I says, "You can buy me a drink, if you like, but I ain't no hero and I'm damned if I was at Arnhem." "Damned if you weren't at Arnhem?" he says, not liking my manner, I suppose. "Then maybe I'll change my mind." "Well, if you're so ruddy ignorant, maybe I don't want your ruddy drink," I says. "You calling me ignorant?" he says. "I certainly am," I says. "Then you're lucky I'm not the sort to hit a crippled man," he says. "And how is it you think I got to be crippled then?" I says. "I'm not sure I'm interested," he says. "Ever heard of the Merville Battery?" I says. "Rings a vague bell," he says. "It should do more than that," I say. And I tells him all the things our lot did on D-Day. How we took the battery, and never mind the mates we lost and the limbs we lost to mines on the way in. How we took Pegasus Bridge – not just took it, but kept it, too – which is more than could be said for some other airborne divisions I could mention –'

'Shame!' says the verger.

'What's he saying?' bellows my father, who as you know is half-deaf.

'I understand your feeling the way you do,' I say. 'But surely to celebrate 6th Airborne's achievements we don't have to denigrate 1st Airborne's?'

'Just answer me one thing, then. How many VCs did 6th Airborne get for doing their job in Normandy?'

'Er . . .'

'None, that's how many. Not a single ruddy one. And how many do you think 1st Airborne are going to get for failing to do theirs?'

'I say, that's a bit unfair.'

'Unfair, is it? I'll tell you what's unfair. Seeing blokes like you get showered with medals for the biggest cock-up since the Charge of the Light Brigade, while 6th Airborne get bugger all.'

'Get that man out of here!' says my father.

'No, give him a chance,' I say.

Yelling dire curses, poor Valentine Wood is bundled out of the village hall, to a chorus of booing and 'good riddances'. Expensive mistake. I'm sure it was one of Wood's lot who, some years later, relieved our rose garden of an uninsured Canova statue, which a chap from Christie's told me to my horror would have been enough to pay for the estate's upkeep for the next half-century.

Afterwards, my female fan club crowds round the podium to mob me, with Lavinia Crumblebeech to the fore, demanding to kiss the hero's noble brow, my little sister tittering, Caro Ashenden fluttering her doe eyes in that sweet, chaste way of hers, but, damn it, still no sign of the girl I most want to see.

'Richard, my dear, you were perfectly marvellous,' says Lady Brecon, planting a kiss on either of my cheeks. 'Never more so than in your forbearance with that frightful man.'

'Well, I meant it actually, Auntie Margaret, I felt rather sorry for him, you see—'

'Gina, I'm sure, will be most fearfully proud when I write to tell her.'

'*Write* to her? Where on earth is she?'

'Oh dear, did no one tell you? Did Ajax not pass on the letter? Dear me, I *knew* I should have given it to your mother instead.'

My darling, DARLING Dick,

Please forgive the unforgivable haste of this letter, only
I was supposed to have left half an hour ago, and I've a
boat to catch, which the GI driver waiting outside – he's
the most terrible crosspatch – says I'm now in great
danger of missing. Will write a longer one as soon as I get
to where I am going. Promise.

   What you must promise me in return is that you're
not going to be cross with me. I know you will be cross
but you really shouldn't be because I'm doing it totally for
you. Remember that night on the Mound? I think about
it all the time. And the thing I think about most – apart
from that bit where you-know-what so tantalisingly,
thrillingly, very nearly happened and I can't wait till it
does as one day it will, I know, and won't it be all the
better for the wait? – is what an awful heel I was for
sending you off to that frightful battle.

   It sounds horrendous and, of course, if I'd known how
perfectly ghastly it was going to be I would have insisted
you stay safe in Birmingham – and hang the
consequences! (Imagine, me – a Brummagem housewife!
I would have done it for your sake, though, I would.) But
now you've come through it in one piece – and covered
with glory, I hear – I know I mustn't regret it too much,
because it will make your daddy happy and my daddy
happy, leaving the path very much clear for our Plan.
(I shan't say what, for I know how nosy some people can
be. Mummy, if you're reading this, stop!)

   Oh dear, I see I STILL haven't told you my News,
which only goes to show how jolly fearful I am of your
crossness – but Crosspatch is beeping his horn outside, so
I can't delay. Darling, I have been offered some important

war work! With the Americans! The charming General that Daddy sat next to me at dinner a few months ago has pulled strings and I shall be working in his Divisional Headquarters. Doing what, I'm not quite sure yet, but I've been assured it's not dangerous – the Division is soon to be rested in France and I shall be far behind the lines.

Darling, you must admit, it's the sort of exciting offer that doesn't come along often. Perhaps you'll think I should have turned it down, though I hope not. When we do finally come to fulfil our Plan – Mummy, if you're reading this DEFINITELY stop now – ours, I hope, will be a partnership of equals. I believe the best thing we can do before we settle down together is to accumulate as much experience as possible of the world in all its variety. In terms of adventure and service to my country, I have an awful lot of catching up to do. Not for a second would I presume to suggest that there are any areas where you yourself could benefit from more experience, my darling Dick. But if you think that there are any, you have my fullest encouragement to do whatever you feel is necessary to rectify it. This, I am sure, will prove the key to the happiest marriage the world has ever known.

All my love,
Gina

Dinner – attended *inter alia* by the Lord Lieutenant, the chairman of the golf club, the Vicar, our bank manager, the usual compliment of staff officers and their various spouses – is as dull as you'd imagine. Afterwards, though, perhaps by way of a reward for my good behaviour, Father calls me to one side and says, 'If you young folk want to carry on the party, I suggest you repair to the cottage. The fire's laid, the bed has been made and there's plenty more to drink, should you need it . . .'

I think, I could almost get used to this.

By the cottage, what Father means is the Gothic folly one of our ancestors built on the edge of the wood, there to roger stable girls, chambermaids, dairymaids and the like, while his wife entertained her own lovers in her private wing of the big house. It used to belong to Thompsett, the estate manager, now missing in the Far East; more recently, it was occupied by Thompsett's replacement, Price.

Poor Price, of course, will have to live without the seclusion and fairy-tale charm of his private knocking shop till the end of the war now. I wonder how he's getting on. Bloody desperate places they are, POW camps, especially for a fellow with Price's libido. It's true that starvation-induced exhaustion diminishes one's desire to a certain degree, but not completely, I'm afraid. You don't know the true meaning of lust till you've sat in a prison-camp concert hall with five hundred captured officers, some of whom have been behind the wire since Dunkirk, all gazing rapt as a trio of heavily made-up ephebes barely out of public school sashay, trill and pout their way through 'Three Little Maids'.

Never mind. Perhaps I can put his bower of bliss to good use instead. And this I get the distinct impression is exactly what my father wants. Has surprisingly Regency views, does my old man, on correct form for a rakish son-and-heir.

So all of us young 'uns – my sisters Lucy and Isobel, Isobel's fiancé Julius Greene (the Commie intellectual-type from the Army Film Unit), Caro, Lavinia, one or two others – all repair to the cottage, where we amuse ourselves for an hour or so with games of dumb crambo and grandmother's footsteps.

We drink quite a lot, myself more than most, for despite all the supposedly good things that have happened to me these last few weeks I'm not feeling especially happy.

During a lull in the games, when I step outside for a bit of air and a brief respite from Lavinia – who has been all over me, ever since hearing about the stupid gong and its presumed effect on the inheritance – Lucy comes to join me.

'You all right?' she says.

'I'm not quite sure,' I say, lighting up a cigarette.

Before I can close it, Lucy snatches a cigarette from my case.

'Smoking at your age? Outrageous. You're a disgrace to the family name,' I say, lighting her cigarette for her.

'But you are no longer. You must be bucked by that?' says Lucy.

'Not really. I feel an imposter.'

'They all say that.'

'Do they?'

'Every chap I've ever met who's won a gong knows someone who deserved it better. Well, everyone apart from James.'

'Yes, but this isn't any old gong. It matters more, surely, that it should only go to the right person.'

Lucy squeezes my hand.

'You ARE the right person.'

'Have you seen the citation? Bears absolutely no resemblance to anything I did. Seriously, I might be reading about a different person.'

'THERE you are, Dick. Come on. We need you! We're about to play – Lord, Lucy, what is that you have in your mouth?' says Lavinia Crumblebeech.

'A cigarette.'

'Well, I shan't want you in my wardrobe, smelling like an old kipper. Come on, both of you. Or you'll miss sardines.'

'Sardines. Do you mind if I sit this one out?'

'What? And deny the young ladies of Hambledown Lacey the chance of close confinement with the district's most eligible war hero? Such a spoilsport, you are!'

'I'm sorry, Lavinia, but I developed a bit of an aversion to cupboards on the last op.'

'Oh dear, have I been very insensitive?'

'Insensitive, Lavinia? *Toi!*' says Lucy.

'It's perfectly all right, Lavinia, I'm not offended. Think of another game and I shall be along in a moment.'

'Murder in the dark?'

'Lovely.'

'So. Which is it to be? says Lavinia hoarsely, with a dangerous look first to Caro then to me. 'Dare? *Double* dare? Kiss? Cuddle? Or promise?'

The richly lecherous inflection she puts on 'double' leaves little doubt what she means by 'dare'.

Or does it? Despite what Price said to me on the glider, despite all Lavinia's decreasingly subtle hints, despite the fact that there's just the three of us now and we're all sitting semi-naked and tantalisingly close to one another on the rug in front of the open fire with Lavinia's delightfully firm large breasts hovering near me like Twin Zeppelins, I certainly don't intend to count my chickens till the fat lady sings.

What I do know for certain is that we're all quite stinkingly drunk. We've been on the pink gins for a good three hours now, in between bouts of murder-in-the-dark, then spin the bottle, then – after the others had gone off to bed – the game of strip poker which has got us all down to our underwear.

It's that stage of a party where the survivors have tacitly agreed to absolve one another of all responsibility for any behaviour, however outré, that follows. Just as well, really. My father and I are hosting the hunt's next meet in a couple of days' time and with Caro and Lavinia among our most stalwart members it will be the most terrible bore if I can no longer look either one of them in the eye as I hand up their port.

'We haven't finished our poker, yet,' I say, still feeling a little awkward about the increasingly inevitable.

'I'm bored with that game. I think it's time for another. Don't you, Caro?' says Lavinia, with a lascivious yawn.

'Dick should decide, don't you think? It's his night,' says Caro, who I'd still been half expecting up to this point to veto the exercise. Then again, what's that they say about the quiet ones? From the flush on her cheeks I'd say she is at least as up for a bit of action as Lavinia. Good God, if I'm not careful I'm going to get myself eaten alive.

'Yes, but you heard how he wriggled just now. Come on, Dick, make up your mind. Presuming, that is, you're interested in girls.'

'Um, yes. Yes, of course,' I stammer – thinking, Help! Where's a foxhole when you really need it?

'Don't worry, if you're only interested in Caro I shan't be at all offended,' says Lavinia, with a slight tremor in a voice which indicates quite the opposite. Poor thing. Despite that long, equine face, klaxon-voice, and palpable air of man-hungry desperation, she's not nearly as unattractive as she thinks she is. Especially not when you're goggle-eyed with gin and you keep your gaze focused on that magnificent chest, as proud, imposing and primed for action as the main guns on her father's battle-cruiser before Jutland.

As I dither, Lavinia rises from the rug and begins putting on her bra.

'It's perfectly all right. I understand,' she says.

'No, Lavinia. Wait. Please don't go.'

'Well, if you're sure,' says Lavinia. '*Are* you sure?'

'I think so.'

'Sounds like you're not. I'll be off then.'

'No. No. I'm sure. We'll go upstairs and do it now.'

'That's more like it,' growls Lavinia.

Nervous as a tethered goat in a tiger trap, I'm led upstairs to my doom.

Oh all right, I exaggerate. In terms of sheer physical horror, by

327

no stretch of the imagination can my romp with Caro Ashenden and Lavinia Crumblebeech be compared with torture by the Kempitai, stonking by a battery of Stalin's organs, attack by a salt-water crocodile, rape by a female Soviet commissar with the body of a walrus and the face of a camel's arse, massacre by the SS, immersion in a pit full of Japanese dysentry, burial alive in a Cretan drain-hole or any of the myriad other near-death scrapes that contributed to making my war such a lively and memorable one.

Indeed some of it, I concede, is no ordeal at all. The stints with Caro underneath me recall the floaty sensuousness of an opium dream. The ones with Lavinia on top of me are as stirring, lively and sometimes downright hair-raising as a brisk five-mile chase over South Dorset jump country on a frosty Boxing Day. And the ones where it's both of them together, well, it rather depends who's doing what to whom, who's in, who's out, who's suffocating, who's feeling like a spare part – 'twas ever thus, Jack, I'm afraid with troilism – but when it's good it's very, very good and when it's bad, it's never less than different.

'So much more imaginative than his brother!' observes Lavinia at one moment, damned near bringing proceedings to a very abrupt halt.

Then Caro sighs, 'Bigger too.'

And that get me right back on track. Do you know, I think it might be the most wonderful remark I've ever heard anyone make on any subject ever.

You'll be wondering by this stage what on earth I've got to complain about. And after what I've just described to you, I'm beginning to wonder myself. But here's a thing I've noticed over the years. Just as you can experience hell on earth – the bloodiest action, the bitterest disappointment, the harshest pain – and come through it almost unscathed if you keep a positive frame of mind, so too the opposite is true. You really can have too much of a good thing.

Whenever my body looks in too much danger of enjoying itself, my wretched mind keeps dragging me into areas which really I'd rather not visit. And I don't just mean routine stuff like bloated corpses, blackened flesh, severed heads, crying wounded and that horrid rotten smell which lingers with you long after you've left the field of carnage. Nor the ugly thought of Gina off in France doing whatever she's doing with her strapping, all-American war hero, Jim Gavin. Nor even my nagging worry of what might happen if any of the Arnhem bridge contingent manage to make a home run and start spilling the beans about the OC I accidentally shot, and the position I failed to hold.

No, I mean something altogether more oppressive and insidious than that. I mean the sudden, awful realisation that you can be granted your every wish and still be sick to the depths of your soul.

VC! VC! VC! I murmur inwardly, in time to the squeaking bedsprings. But this quickly gives way to thoughts of just how unworthy I am, of all the bolder, braver, better men who deserve one so much more than me.

The estate. The estate. The estate! I silently crow, as I pump away at the perspiring Caro Ashenden. But that's no good either. When I think of Great Meresby now, I see not rolling acres, magnificent views and architectural splendour, but only unpaid bills, obstreperous tenants, dull meetings with the bank manager, and relentless social duty.

You have beaten the General! I think to distract myself, as Lavinia goes to work with those amazing inner-thigh muscles. But when I do, it's not the savour of victory that springs to mind but that brief flicker of doubt, fear even, that I saw in his eyes as his old certainties exploded beneath him like some gargantuan Somme countermine. My father: afraid? Is there to be nothing sacred in this fickle new universe which so reluctantly I have been forced to inhabit.

'*For what shall it profit a man, if he shall gain the whole world and lose his own soul?*' says the Bible.

'Shut up and be grateful, you miserable mithering bugger!' would, I'm sure, be Price's response.

But I'm not Price. I need a mission, a cause, a grail. The war is not over yet. And I know now that, for better or worse, I cannot rest till I have truly earned my spurs.

Editor's Notes

This is the second published instalment of my grandfather Dick Coward's adventures, which, as readers of the first volume *Coward on the Beach* will know, comprise my lightly edited transcriptions of the tape-recorded memoirs he left to me in his will.

As before, many readers will no doubt wonder: how much of it is true and how much poetic licence? My honest answer is: we shall never know. I don't believe that my grandfather was – as some reviewers cruelly claimed of Volume 1 – a deranged fantasist. But I would concede that he may have had the occasional memory lapse and embroidered the odd detail, either to protect the innocent or to make his story more satisfying or perhaps out of general mischievousness.

The following notes will, I hope, help to unpick the fact from the fiction. They are not compulsory. Some of you may feel my grandfather has treated you to far more military historical detail than you needed. And possibly you're right, but I'm afraid I just couldn't resist adding more. Arnhem truly was one of the most fascinating and extraordinary battles of the Second World War, and the more you read about it, I find, the more eager you are to learn about the personalities involved and the whys and wherefores of its disastrous outcome. Besides which, I'm a great fan of George MacDonald Fraser's Flashman books, and the trainspotterish notes at the end are one of my favourite things about them.

But this is not a comparison I wish to stress too far – as

some, less careful readers have insisted on doing. For one thing, Flashman was a cad and a coward and generally rather successful with women whereas Dick Coward, bless him, was none of these things. For another, Flashman was a fictional creation whereas my grandfather was, of course, my grandfather.

Jack Devereux, Great Meresby

Units at MARKET GARDEN – A Handy Guide

1st Airborne Corps: **Lt. Gen. Frederick Browning** (NIJMEGEN)

1st Airborne Division: **Maj. Gen. Roy Urquhart** (ARNHEM)

Polish Independent Brigade
      Group: **Maj. Gen. Sosabowski** (DRIEL / ARNHEM)

1st Airborne Division comprised three brigades (two parachute, one glider), each of three battalions:

1st Parachute Brigade: **Brig. Gerald Lathbury** (landed nr. ARNHEM on Day 1)
1st Battalion: **Lt. Col. David Dobie**
2nd Battalion: **Lt. Col. John Frost**
3rd Battalion: **Lt. Col. John Fitch**

4th Parachute Brigade: **Brig. 'Shan' Hackett** (landed nr ARNHEM. on Day 2)
156 Battalion: **Lt. Col. Sir Richard des Voeux**
10th Battalion: **Lt. Col. Ken Smyth**
11th Battalion: **Lt. Col. George Lea**
1st Airlanding Brigade: **Brig. 'Pip' Hicks**
1st Battalion Border Regiment: **Lt. Col. Tommy Haddon**

2nd Battalion South Staffordshire
                Regiment: **Lt. Col. Derek McCardie**
7th (Galloway) Battalion King's
        Own Scottish Borderers: **Lt. Col. Robert Payton-Reid**

Each Brigade had its own Field Ambulance Unit (Royal Army Medical Corps).

The Division also had support units including:

21st Independent Parachute Company (the 'pathfinders' who parachuted in first and marked the landing zones and drop zones)
1st Airborne Recce Squadron
1st Airborne Divisional Signals
1st Airlanding Light Regiment (Royal Artillery – light field guns)
1st and 2nd Airlanding Anti-Tank Batteries (Royal Artillery)
9th Airborne Field Company (Royal Engineers)
250 Airborne Light Composite Company (Royal Army Service Corps – supplies and transport)

MARKET – the airborne part of the operation – was carried out in conjunction with two US Airborne Divisions:
101st Airborne ('Screaming Eagles') (EINDHOVEN)
82nd Airborne ('All American') (GRAVE; NIJMEGEN)

The ground part of the operation GARDEN
was conducted by:
Second British Army – **Gen. Miles Dempsey**,
who tasked the breakthrough mission to:
XXX Corps ('30 Corps') – **Lt. Gen. Brian Horrocks**. This unit comprised:
Guards Armoured Division
43rd (Wessex) Division
50th (Northumbrian) Division

Page 4. '. . . we could be stuck here for hours. Days even' Such indeed was the fate of another Arnhem hero, the redoubtable **Maj. Tony Deane-Drummond DSO, MC and bar**, 2ic Divisional Signals. Already an experienced and dedicated escaper (he was one of only a handful of British soldiers ever to have made a home run from an Italian POW camp in the days when Italy was still an Axis power), Deane-Drummond was captured again after Arnhem and temporarily imprisoned with a large group of his comrades in the basement of a villa. Noticing a wall cupboard just large enough for one man to hide in, he reversed the lock, hid inside and locked himself in. Shortly afterwards his comrades were transported elsewhere by the Germans, and Deane-Drummond expected that he would soon be able to slip out and make good his escape. Instead, he was appalled to hear the room in which he was hiding being prepared as an interrogation centre.

For the next three days he heard the captured men of 1st Airborne Division being questioned just feet from his hiding place and, like Coward, found himself generally impressed by how little they gave away. Once the interrogations were finished, Deane-Drummond imagined his ordeal would shortly be over. All he had to eat or drink was a canteen of water and a small amount of bread. But his hopes were dashed yet again when he heard the Germans using his room as a billet.

After thirteen days of agonised confinement he had finally had enough. Hearing a German convoy passing in the road outside, Deane-Drummond assumed – correctly – that it would distract the villa's occupiers long enough to enable him to slip away. With help from the Dutch underground he made his way to freedom.

After the war, as Lieutenant Colonel, he commanded 22 SAS during the Malaya Emergency and in 1959 took part in one of the greatest exploits in the annals of the regiment in Oman, when his two squadrons captured the near-impregnable 10,000-foot Jebel

Akhdar from Communist rebels by rope-scrambling up its sheer, unguarded slopes and taking the enemy by surprise. Subsequently, Deane-Drummond rose to the rank of Major-General. He tells his amazing story in *Return Ticket* (Collins, 1953).

Page 5: 'The German Army rank of Hauptmann and the SS rank of Hauptsturmführer are both roughly equivalent to Captain. The SS would have considered the use of 'Herr' before the rank as insufferably bourgeois. The army officer is clearly trying to wind him up.

Page 7: **Airey Neave, DSO MC**, was the first British officer to make a home run from Colditz, and was recruited to the wartime escape organisation MI9. After the Market Garden debacle, he organised Operation Pegasus, which successfully retrieved 138 Allied soldiers, airmen and Dutch Resistance from behind enemy lines. He subsequently became a Conservative MP. In 1979 – weeks before Margaret Thatcher's first general election victory – he was murdered outside the House of Commons by the Irish Republican terrorist splinter group the INLA. They had feared that, were he to be made Northern Ireland Secretary, his no-nonsense approach would bring the Republican movement to its knees.

Page 8: Actually, the Geneva conventions require you to give your name, rank, serial number *and* date of birth, known as the Big Four.

Page 18: 'Marching at the treble'. This is, of course, a rhetorical flourish. Marching at the double is difficult enough.

Page 22: **Daphne du Maurier** (1907–89) was the daughter of debonair actor-manager Sir Gerald du Maurier and granddaughter of *Punch* cartoonist George du Maurier (author of the Gothic bestseller *Trilby*). Her books and short stories include *Rebecca*, *Jamaica Inn*, *Frenchman's Creek*, 'Don't Look Now' and 'The Birds' (not as Coward mischievously misremembers it, 'The Flock'). Menabilly was the house in Cornwall she leased for many years from the Rashleigh family.

Page 27: A former Grenadier Guards officer who had served with distinction in the First World War, **Lt. Gen. Frederick Arthur Montague 'Boy' Browning DSO** was the father of the British Airborne movement. He raised and commanded its first division, he decided its character – many of his sergeants came from Guards regiments in order to maintain the highest standards – and he even commissioned the design of its distinctive cap badge. The famous emblem of the warrior Bellerophon riding Pegasus the winged horse was designed for him by the artist Edward Seago.

Page 29: 'A bridge too far'. Browning may never have actually used this phrase but it is certainly true that he expressed similar reservations after his personal briefing from Monty on 10 September 1944.

Page 30: 'Well-known brand of cigarette'. Coward means, of course, du Maurier brand – named after Daphne's father.

Page 31: An alternative theory is that the Germans named them Red Devils because they were coated in red Tunisian mud.

Page 38: 'Ringway'. Airfield near Manchester where the first parachute-training experiments took place.

Page 38: It is nearly impossible to hit a descending paratrooper though clearly quite sporting to try. It's much easier to get them when they're running round their DZ like headless chickens.

Page 39: The main reason paras are dropped so close to the ground is so they land close together.

Page 44: 'Up the blue'. North Africa campaign veteran slang for 'in the desert'.

Page 44: 'Vickers K'. Originally designed for use in aeroplanes, the Vickers K was popular with special forces including the SAS and the Long Range Desert Group for its lightness (just 19 lbs), its resistance to jamming and its rapid rate of fire (1,050 rounds per minute). It fired standard .303 ammo, fed from an overhead drum of 96 rounds. SAS units in Italy used as many as five per jeep. Maj. Gough asked for at least two per vehicle but was only allowed one to save on ammo.

Page 44: Had 1st Airborne Recce Squadron been equipped with Humber armoured cars – or even, as 6th Airborne Division's Recce Squadron had when it landed in Normandy, Mark VII Tetrarch light tanks – the first day of Market Garden might have turned out very differently. Maj. Gough asked for Tetrarchs but was refused them, again because of insufficient lift space.

Page 46: The Bren gun was famed for its accuracy – much more so than its German equivalent the MG-34 – and was invariably handled by the best marksmen in a unit. Even so, even at 1,000 yards, with the body armour that several men took with them to Arnhem, Tiny is taking quite a risk for his 2 guineas.

Page 47: **Maj. Freddie Gough MC**, forty-three, was one of the oldest commanding officers in the division. Silvery-haired, avuncular, with supremely high standards of fitness, Maj. Gough insisted his men complete a training run-walk of up to ten miles every day with full equipment, arms, ammo and water bottles. He was invariably near the front, accompanied by his Dandie Dinmont terrier Swilly.

In the First World War he had served as a midshipman in the Royal Navy; at the beginning of the Second he went to France with the British Expeditionary Force, where he was mentioned in dispatches for his sterling work organising the perimeter round Dunkirk and facilitating the evacuation from the beaches. In 1943, now in command of 1st Airborne Recce Squadron, he won his MC in Italy.

The Squadron was very much his baby: 'Freddie Gough's prime concern was to recruit officers who had those particular gifts of personal initiative and imagination that he considered most appropriate for the specialised reconnaissance role. As a consequence, all applicants were carefully vetted and scrutinised by the commanding officer, whose criteria of judgement were very much his own, and who knew exactly what he wanted,' says John Fairley in his unit biography *Remember Arnhem* (see below).

Gough was notoriously unpunctual, failing to turn up on time even for the first Market Garden briefing on 12 September. Maj. Gen. Urquhart wrote: 'After the briefing had started, Freddie Gough, a cheerful, red-faced, silver-haired major, turned up with the air of a truant playing schoolboy and I laid into him afterwards for his unpunctuality. It was not the first time he had been very late for a conference.'

Page 47: '30,000 Airborne troops'. A total of 33,971 men (US, British, Poles) went into action by air during Market Garden – 20,190 by parachute, 13,781 by glider – together with 5,230 tons of equipment, 1,927 vehicles and 568 guns (Middlebrook, see below).

Page 48: 1st Airborne Recce Squadron was part of the Reconnaissance Corps – with its distinctive badge of a golden spearhead flanked by two lightning flashes – which was formed on 1 January 1941. Its role was to obtain 'vital tactical information in battle for infantry divisions'. Because of necessity, their job involved going ahead of their own positions and probing the enemy's. It was a hazardous calling. One in ten of those who served in the Corps died in action.

Page 51: The Pioneer Corps was the initial destination for German and Austrian émigrés who wished to serve with the British armed forces but whose loyalties were not yet considered sufficiently certain.

Page 54: Coward's loathing of Evelyn Waugh has got the better of his architectural historical accuracy here. Brecon Abbey is, of course, largely in the Palladian style and could consequently never have been used as a model for the baroque Brideshead.

Page 57: Belying one of his nicknames – Gentleman Jim – **Maj. Gen. James Gavin** could scarcely have come from more humble origins. He was adopted at the age of two out of a New York Catholic foundlings' hospital by a Pennsylvania couple, and was often beaten by his fierce, drunken adoptive mother.

At seventeen, he joined the US Army, where a kindly lieutenant coached him in algebra, geometry and history to help win him a place as an officer cadet at West Point. Though deeply ambitious, Gavin remained popular thanks to his reserved charm and his punctilious good manners. He smiled often but rarely made jokes. At twenty-two he began an unhappy marriage, which, though it gave him an adored daughter, was punctuated by several affairs.

An early advocate of airborne warfare, Gavin got his first combat command as Colonel of 505th Parachute Infantry in Sicily, where he immediately distinguished himself in a messy action at Biazza Ridge, winning a Distinguished Service Cross.

By D-Day – the youngest Brigadier General in the US Army since Custer – he was deputy commander of 82nd Airborne Division. The fighting in Normandy was bloody, and on several occasions Gavin only managed to goad his riflemen into action by heroic personal example. He returned a national hero: the poor kid made very good indeed.

On 17 July 1944 he was promoted to Major General and given command of 82nd Airborne. He hated everything about Market Garden. He despised Browning and had no confidence in the plan. 'The flak in the area is terrific; the Krauts are many,' he wrote in his diary on the eve of his jump. 'It looks very rough. If I get through this one I will be very lucky. It will, I am afraid, do the Airborne cause a lot of harm.'

Page 70: Balancing a glider's load was a fine art and a painstaking process, complicated by the fact that no two glider loads were identical. One might carry two jeeps and a trailer, another a single jeep, a trailer and a Polsten gun. Tiny details made all the difference – even down to the weight of the jeep's engine which sometimes meant that instead of being parked facing towards the tail so that it could easily be driven off on landing, the jeep had to face the front.

In 1st Airborne Recce Squadron, two or three men travelled with each glider load – though it would have been very unusual for a section commander to travel, as Coward does, with his section sergeant.

Page 71: Graffiti on gliders. This graffiti was the subject of much earnest Teutonic speculation in a report sent by SS Sturmbannführer Sepp Krafft for the personal attention of Himmler himself. Commenting on 'We are the Al Capone gang' and 'Up with the Reds', he commented: 'How far this is connected with the political convictions of the troops themselves or whether it is due to Bolshevist or American influences is not known.'

Page 76: 'WHAT HAPPENED?' As old-timer war veterans sometimes do, Coward is remembering an event here which he cannot possibly have seen. Over the village of Paulton, near Bath, a Horsa glider suddenly parted in the middle and dropped out of the sky – killing two glider pilots, five NCOs and sixteen sappers of No. 1 Platoon, 9th Airborne Field Company, Royal Engineers. But to have witnessed this horrible tragedy – probably the result of explosive devices going off prematurely – Coward would have had to have flown from Keevil, not Tarrant Rushton.

Page 83: Price is supernaturally well-informed regarding the presence of German armour at Arnhem. Hardly anyone among the Allies knew about it apart from Browning and his intelligence officer Maj. Brian Urquhart (no relation to the General). Hearing from Montgomery's 21st Army Group that two SS panzer divisions were refitting in the Arnhem area, Urquhart tried, without success, to warn Browning of the danger. In desperation, he asked for a Spitfire to take recce photographs and sure enough on the morning of Friday 15 September – two days before the op – he had visual proof: prints of Mk III and Mk IV tanks lurking in the woods close to Arnhem. Browning's response was to treat Urquhart like 'a nervous child suffering from a nightmare'. He ordered his senior medical officer to have Urquhart diagnosed with nervous strain and exhaustion – and sent home on sick leave.

Browning has often been blamed for this but what else was he supposed to do at this late stage: call the whole thing off? What's far less excusable is his failure to have communicated Brian Urquhart's intelligence to anyone in the Division. Had they known, they would surely have taken more anti-tank weapons and ammunition than they did.

Page 91: Price's uncharacteristic keenness to lead the assault is understandable, given that it was the most glamorous, important and medal-friendly mission of the Arnhem landings, on which all else depended. 1st Airborne Recce Squadron's job was to rush Arnhem bridge by jeep – before the startled Germans had time to respond – and hold it until the paratroops of 2nd and 3rd Battalions could catch up on foot. Major Gough had always disliked this plan, arguing that his men were better suited for reconnaissance than for *coup de main* operations of this sort.

Page 95: Tall, stooping **Lt. Col. John Dutton Frost, DSO and Bar, MC** – OC of 2nd Battalion – was the most dashing commander in the division. After service with the Cameronians in Iraq – where he'd hunted with the Royal Exodus – he was posted to the nascent Parachute Regiment and took part in its first major action, the Bruneval Raid on the French coast. 'I knew that Frost of all people would press on rapidly if it were humanly possible,' wrote Urquhart, explaining why he had tasked him with the capture of the Arnhem road bridge. (The modern replacement – nothing remains of the original, nor, disappointingly for war buffs visiting the battleground, any of the old buildings surrounding it in 1944 – is named the John Frost Bridge in his honour.)

While Frost had severe doubts about the hare-brained decision to drop his men so far from its objective, he was nonetheless convinced the operation would be a success. So much so that he did indeed ask his batman Pte. Wicks to load his shotgun, dinner jackets and golf clubs into the staff car which would arrive with XXX Corps.

Page 109: Rather unfortunately for the commander of an Airborne division, **Maj. Gen. Roy Urquhart** couldn't parachute, loathed flying and was sick on his glider journey to Arnhem. Lt. Gen. Browning had chosen him for the command because he wanted a man 'hot from battle'. Urquhart had seen plenty of action as an infantry commander in North Africa, Sicily and Italy, but his complete inexperience in airborne warfare caused much concern within the division. Later, it was suggested that had he been a paid-up member of the airborne club, he would have made stronger attempts to change the Market Garden plans.

This is unfair. Urquhart did his best to point out the flaws in the plan, asking that the lifts take place over one day rather than two, and urging that landing zones be found closer to the bridge. The first request was overruled by US Air Force Generals Brereton and Williams – probably on the grounds that the mainly American transport fliers lacked the necessary experience, especially in night-flying, to manage more than one trip in a day. The second was overruled by British Air Vice-Marshal Hollinghurst, concerned by reports of German flak battery concentrations near the bridge.

Urquhart's unflappable leadership earned him the huge respect of his men. A soldier's soldier, he was once described admiringly as 'a bloody general who didn't mind doing the job of a sergeant'. At one point in the battle a signalman, not recognising him, asked him to drag a heavy spare battery out of a storage trench to the command trench. Then, after that, another one. All this Urquhart did without hesitation and only afterwards did the signalman recognise who he was and begin thanking him profusely. 'That's all right, son,' the General replied.

Page 109: "'Recce squadron? We've been looking for you.'" Here Coward glimpses the beginnings of one of the greatest tragi-comic escapades of Market Garden: the disappearance for two days of the Divisional Commander.

It began on Sunday evening when Maj. Gen. Urquhart first heard of Recce Squadron's disastrous run-in with Battalion Krafft and realised he must warn Brigadier Lathbury, commander of 1st Para Brigade, that there would now be no British forces there to meet his parachute battalions at the bridge. Unable to contact Lathbury by radio, he impatiently set out in a jeep to find him.

Urquhart caught up with Lathbury as he was paying a visit to Lt. Col. Fitch's 3rd Battalion, just as it was bumping into the same German blocking line that had done for Recce Squadron (see note *Page 136*). After the fight, Urquhart found his jeep had been blown up, his driver wounded, and that it was no longer safe to leave the area. This had the knock-on effect of compromising Fitch's decision-making process: how could he think clearly with two senior officers breathing down his neck?

After leaguering for the night – when some argue they should have pressed on – 3rd Battalion moved forward the next morning. Urquhart and Lathbury were with the lead company which had become separated from the main body, and soon found themselves on the outskirts of Arnhem surrounded by Germans. As they tried to escape over a garden fence, Lathbury's Sten gun accidentally went off, narrowly missing Urquhart's foot. Shortly afterwards, Lathbury was wounded by a burst of Spandau fire and had very reluctantly to be abandoned in a Dutch house. (He was later taken to St Elizabeth's Hospital where he was made a POW.) As Urquhart and his companions were leaving, a German appeared at the window and Urquhart shot him in the face at point-blank range – the sort of close quarters combat almost unheard of for a general officer.

Outside No. 14 Zwarteweg, Urquhart and his two companions met a Dutchman who offered to hide them in his attic. Almost immediately afterwards the street filled with Germans and an SP gun parked itself directly in front of the men's hiding place.

Urquhart was all for lobbing in some grenades, then legging it, but was advised that this would be suicide. Instead, he had to remain stuck in his cramped hidey-hole for another day, becoming increasingly irritated by the enormous handle-bar moustache of one of his companions, Lt. Cleminson. He thought it 'damned silly'.

The next morning, after the area had been briefly cleared of Germans by men of 2nd South Staffordshires and 11th Battalion, Urquhart was able to commandeer a jeep and make his escape.

Page 109: **Gen. Friedrich Kussin** was Arnhem's town commandant. He had come to visit the headquarters of Battalion Krafft at the nearby Hotel Wolfheze and had ignored advice that travelling back by the main road might now be dangerous, with fateful consequences for himself, his driver and his batman/interpreter. There are several grisly photographs of his body, in some of which he has clearly been scalped by persons unknown.

Page 111: The Hartenstein Hotel went on to become famous, of course, as Urquhart's Div HQ during the defence of Oosterbeek. Now it is the site of the excellent airborne museum.

Page 120: The task of capturing the railway bridge was given to Lt. Peter Barry's No. 9 Platoon, C Company, 2nd Battalion. They were very lucky. Having run about 50 yards towards the middle of the bridge, they found themselves exhausted and out of breath and lay down to recover. No sooner had they done so than the bridge blew up, just yards from Barry's nose. Had they not stopped they would all have been killed.

Page 124: 'Buggering our wirelesses'. Wireless communication was notoriously poor throughout the Arnhem operation. Because the sets had been packed and unpacked countless times for the various cancelled operations, they were already in a poor state.

On landing they were often further damaged by the thump of the impact, which often put them 'off net' – i.e., on the wrong frequency. Nor was their performance improved by the dense woodland which considerably reduced their ranges.

In any case, most of them were too weak. The largest 19 set had a range – in good conditions – of twelve miles, but there were precious few of these: only the artillery had them. Next down was the 22 set (as carried by 1st Airborne Recce Squadron on their jeeps and also used at divisional and brigade level), with a maximum range of six miles. However, by far the commonest set – used for communication from battalion level downwards – was the feeble 68 set, with a maximum range of only three miles (but much less in built-up areas or woodland).

Had the infantry units landed closer to the bridge – as had been envisioned in earlier plans – then this might not have been such a problem. But with the LZs and DZs at least eight miles from the bridge, the forward battalions were barely able to communicate with one another, let alone their divisional HQ.

Maj. Tony Hibbert, who commanded 1st Parachute Brigade HQ and Signal Squadron on reaching the bridge, said: 'My first job was to inform Division that we held the bridge. Not one of our wirelesses could pick up the faintest whisper from anyone in Northern Europe except John Frost who was all of 50 yards away.'

Divisional Signals knew all along that it was going to be a problem. They wanted more 19 sets. They realised that inter-unit communications would be extremely dodgy until the Division's forces were concentrated by the bridge. But they also realised that with so little time to prepare there was absolutely nothing they could do about it.

Said Tony Deane-Drummond, 2ic Div Signals: 'There is no doubt that risks were taken by everybody with eyes open. The feeling was we had to get there before the German Army packed up.'

Page 124: There were three main planned routes from the DZs and LZs into Arnhem. Leopard, the northernmost one was to be taken by Recce Squadron and 1st Battalion; Tiger, the middle one, was to be taken by 3rd Battalion; and Lion, the southernmost one closest to the river, by 2nd Battalion. In the event, only Lion proved viable, because the others were swiftly blocked by the Germans.

Page 127: Only an estimated 740 men from 1st Airborne Division actually made it to Arnhem bridge, the bulk of them from 2nd Parachute Battalion. None of the other units got much further than Arnhem's museum – about half a mile from the road bridge – before being either wiped out or driven back to what became the Oosterbeek perimeter.

Page 127: 'Cool, calm and collected . . . tall, a little aloof and full of confidence', **Maj. Digby Tatham-Warter DSO** was the thrusting officer who famously carried an umbrella at Arnhem bridge. On one occasion he used it to lead a bayonet charge, on another to disable a German armoured car by thrusting it through an observation slit so as to incapacitate the driver. His explanation later was that he could never remember the password and that it would be quite obvious that anyone foolish enough to carry a brolly could only be an Englishman.

His A Company, 2nd Battalion, was the first to reach Arnhem bridge – marching eight miles in seven hours, capturing or killing 150 Germans en route. Anticipating wireless problems, he revived Napoleonic War tradition by training his platoons beforehand in the use of bugle calls. These proved most effective, the calls proving audible even over the noise of bombardment.

After the bridge was overrun, the now-wounded Tatham-Warter was captured but escaped shortly afterwards from St Elizabeth's Hospital and spent weeks on the run, posing as a deaf-and-dumb

Dutchman. In this guise, he cycled freely round the region, his confidence enabling him to pass unnoticed by the Germans, coordinating the escape plans of nearly 140 fellow evaders in what became known as Operation Pegasus.

Page 129: The Battle of the Medway in June 1667 was the worst defeat in English Naval history. A Dutch fleet sailed up the River Thames, then up the River Medway to the Naval base at Chatham, burnt three capital ships and ten lesser vessels, and towed away the *Unity* and the English flagship *Royal Charles*.

Page 131: Mrs Kock was unlucky. One Dutch eyewitness account has another British machine-gunner in similar circumstances taking care to cover the table before he rests his Bren on it to kill a sniper. Generally, the British behaved towards Dutch civilians with a courtesy bordering on the excessive – asking permission before siting their positions in their gardens and always knocking at the front door rather than barging in (as might well have been safer, if the house was occupied by Germans) through the window.

Page 136: Maj. Gough's worst fears about the *coup de main* plan (see note *Page 91*) had been realised. The eight-mile journey from the Squadron RV point to the bridge, initially by minor tracks following the route of the railway line, should have taken no more than half an hour. But within ten minutes of the lead section's departure – less than half a mile from the start line – Gough's worst fears were realised. The able, very tactically minded SS commander Sepp Krafft had quickly worked out the probable line of the British advance and had formed his men in a defensive line directly across its path. First victims to the ambush by Krafft's well-concealed SS were two jeeps from C section. Seven Recce men were killed or mortally wounded, and four more were captured. The battle was over almost before it had begun. So was the Recce Squadron's role as the operation's spearhead unit.

Page 137: *Lady Chatterley's Lover* was written by D.H. Lawrence in 1927 and privately published in Florence in 1928. But apart from a rare underground edition, it was not published in Britain until 1960.

Page 144: Bud Flanagan and Chesney Allen were old-time music-hall stars – and members of the Crazy Gang – who became one of the war's most popular British singing double acts. Their hits included 'We're Gonna Hang Out The Washing On The Siegfried Line', 'Underneath The Arches' and 'Run Rabbit Run' (often changed to 'Run Adolf Run').

Page 148: Bernd Rosemeyer, one of Germany's greatest and most daring racing drivers, was killed trying to break the world land-speed record in 1938. Though it's true that Heinrich Himmler made him a member of the SS, it was an offer he could hardly have dared refuse. He never wore the uniform.

Page 159: '"That fucking German's gone and killed him."' Coward's having changed the names of some of those involved does not help us get to the bottom of this mystery. The unfortunate victim of friendly fire was named Maj. David Wallis, who, as Coward says, had a habit of speaking quietly and indistinctly. According to Martin Middlebrook in *Arnhem 1944*, he was shot with a burst of Bren fire, having failed to answer a sentry's challenge.

Page 173: '*Leck mich am Arsch*' – literally 'lick my arse' – is the title of a cheeky ditty tossed off by Mozart around 1782, based on a line from the Goethe play about the German knight Götz von Berlichingen.

Page 184: Disappointingly – I checked the last time it was repeated at Christmas – there is no mention in the end credits of *The Great Escape* of my grandfather's role as technical advisor.

Page 186: Johnny Weissmuller, American swimmer and actor, winner of five Olympic gold medals, was the sixth actor to play Tarzan and by far the best known. He invented the ululating Tarzan yell.

Page 193: 'Lt. Gen. Browning has commandeered as his Corps HQ . . .' Browning's insistence on flying into action with his Corps – when, for all the difference it made, he could have directed ops from England instead – used up 38 tug aircraft which might otherwise have carried extra men, munitions and supplies to Arnhem.

Browning was always immaculately turned out, in the distinctive uniform he had designed himself: zip-up barathea jacket with false uhlan-style front, grey kid gloves, highly polished Sam Browne belt and swagger stick, maroon beret.

Page 196: **Lt. Gen. Sir Brian Horrocks DSO, MC** commanded XXX Corps during Market Garden and later became a television presenter, military historian and Black Rod in the House of Lords.

His early career included two stints as a POW of the Germans in the First World War, and of the Red Army during the Russian Civil War (he had been acting as adviser to the White Army). Between the wars he represented Britain in the Pentathlon at the 1924 Paris Olympics.

During the Second World War, he distinguished himself at Dunkirk, El Alamein and at the Mareth Line in Tunisia, but nearly came to a sticky end during rehearsals for the Salerno landings when machine-gunned by a German fighter aircraft. When he had recovered from his wounds in August 1944 he was appointed commander of XXX Corps, whose perceived lack of urgency in the push for the final bridges has been held partly responsible for Market Garden's failure. Montgomery's order had been that the ground attack should be 'rapid and violent without regard to what is happening on the flanks'. As Middlebrook says, this was not complied with: while British and Polish airborne forces at Arnhem sustained 8,000 casualties, XXX Corps casualties were fewer than 1,500.

However, Horrocks himself was not personally blamed, and was held by Eisenhower to be 'the outstanding British general under Montgomery' and by Jim Gavin to be 'the finest general officer I met during the war'.

Page 199: The crossing of the Waal by 504 PIR – sometimes known as 'Little Omaha' – is widely revered as one of *the* great Allied feats of heroism of the Second World War. But these brave men's self-sacrifice would hardly have been necessary if a little more forethought had gone into the initial planning.

According to SS Commander Heinz Harmel, Operation Market Garden was lost not at Arnhem but at Nijmegen. 'If the Allies had taken the Nijmegen bridge on the first day, it would have been all over for us. Even if we had lost it on the second day, we would have had difficulty in stopping them.'

So why didn't they capture Nijmegen bridge on Day 1? This would have been the job of 82nd Airborne and it was indeed their commander Maj. Gen. Gavin's original plan to capture it by *coup de main*. But he was overruled by his senior officers, notably by Gen. Brereton of the USAAF but also by Lt. Gen. Browning who believed it was of greater priority for Gavin to secure an area of high ground to the south-west of Nijmegen called the Groesbeek Heights. The result of this was that the Germans had time to bolster their defences at the bridge and hold off the Allied advance for three vital days.

Page 225: Of all the incidents during Market Garden this is the most contentious. Coward's version of events tallies more or less with the one in *Strike and Hold* (Moffatt Burriss, see below), the autobiography of 82nd Airborne's T. Moffatt Burriss – the Captain in charge of I Coy 504 PIR who led the Waal crossing. He describes the British tank crews getting out their teapots. And berating the senior British officer as a 'yellow-bellied son of a bitch'.

But perhaps – as Coward appears to admit later – Coward's account has been coloured by his hatred of his brother James. Certainly, as far as most historians are concerned, the lead tanks of the Guards Armoured Division behaved impeccably.

First across Nijmegen bridge, under heavy fire, was Sgt. Peter Robinson of the Grenadier Guards. He reached the north side at around 18.30 hours on 20 September, about forty-five minutes before the Americans. He was lucky to make it. The German in charge of defending the bridge – SS Brigadeführer Heinz Harmel, commander of 10th SS Panzer Division – gave the signal to blow the bridge but the charges mysteriously failed to detonate. These charges were cleared shortly afterwards by a brave young Royal Engineers officer, Lt. Tony Jones.

Of the six Grenadier tanks that crossed the bridge, two were immediately knocked out by the Germans. Should the remaining four have pressed on for another eleven miles? Harmel seemed to hint as much in a 1967 interview when he said, 'The amazing thing was that instead of speeding full steam ahead the British seemed to hesitate.'

But to have done so with no infantry support would surely have been suicide. As historian and Arnhem veteran John Waddy has written: 'The road was narrow, with deep water-filled dikes on either side, and at night it would only need a few soldiers with hand-held weapons to stop them.' Not only did the Germans have armoured cars patrolling the roads, but also several tanks and SP guns.

Perhaps Horrocks could have exploited the bridge's capture by bringing forward a reserve force of infantry and armour to press the advance. But given the battles still raging south of the Waal he had none available.

Page 230: Lancashire comedienne and songstress Gracie Fields was one of the most popular Allied entertainers, performing to troops as far afield as New Guinea. Because her Italian film-director husband would have been interned had she remained in Britain, she had to stay away from her homeland throughout the war.

Page 230: 'Lili Marlene'. Originally written by a German schoolteacher during the First World War and a big hit with Axis forces during the Second, the love song 'Lili Marleen' was equally popular with Allied soldiers.

Page 238: The rapid advance of 5th Duke of Cornwall's Light Infantry (5th DCLI) from Oosterhout (nr Nijmegen) to Driel was one of Market Garden's rare successes. Not only did they cover the ten miles (through enemy-held territory) in forty-five minutes – one of the speediest advances of the whole operation – but en route they bumped into a column of German tanks (three Tigers and two Panthers) which a company of their infantrymen managed to ambush and destroy in the dark by laying mines across the road, then wiping them out with PIATs. This salutory example suggests that the tanks of the Grenadier Guards – see note *Page 225* – almost certainly took the right decision not to continue their advance on Arnhem.

Page 238: Quite typically of the Polish experience throughout the war, **Maj. Gen. Stanislaw F. Sosabowski** was horribly ill-used by his Allied 'comrades'. Originally he had been promised that his brigade of Poles would spearhead the eventual airborne invasion of occupied Poland. As the war drew on, it became clear that this was never going to happen, and that the Americans and the British had no intention of jeopardising their relationship with Stalin for the sake of rescuing Poland from his tyrannical rule. This did not prevent the Poles being given – and usually succeeding in – some of the most difficult tasks of the war, such as the capture of the monastery at Monte Cassino.

Though blamed – and subsequently sacked by Browning – for being 'difficult' during Market Garden, Sosabowski's only major crime was to be too free with the truth. It was his vociferous objections to Market Garden's predecessor – Operation Comet – which helped get the operation cancelled. And he saw all too clearly the problems with the Arnhem landings – not least the unhelpful decision to land his own paratroops south of the river and their vehicles and heavy equipment north of it.

Page 238: **Capt. the Hon. Richard Wrottesley** (later Lord Wrottesley) effected the first link-up between the GARDEN forces and the MARKET forces. Under cover of thick fog and taking a long, circuitous back route, Capt. Wrottesley slipped through the German lines with his Household Cavalry recce troop of armoured cars and scout cars and made it safely from Nijmegen to the Polish DZ at Driel without having to fire a shot. His wireless provided the first opportunity for Sosabowski to speak to Urquhart.

Page 243: **Brig. John 'Shan' Hackett** (later DSO and bar, MC), a brilliant linguist and classicist, was just thirty-three when he commanded 4th Parachute Brigade at Arnhem. His three parachute battalions – 156, 10th and 11th – would drop on the second day and be chewed to bits by an enemy which had had plenty of time to prepare for their arrival. Hackett was never under any illusions about the operation's prospects. 'Really, I think Market Garden was doomed before it started.'

But he still felt it should have gone ahead, despite the plan's obvious weaknesses, because there had already been far too many cancellations. 'You can't go on doing that to troops of quality. They were so good, so fit, so keyed up, so keen to get on that you had to get into the battle at almost any price.'

By the time of his arrival with the second lift on Monday 18 September, Hackett's role had more to do with damage limitation than tactical planning. The heathland surrounding his landing zone was on fire and swarming with Germans. On arriving at his HQ, he was informed that Maj. Gen. Urquhart was missing, that Brig. Hicks, the commander of 1st Airlanding Brigade, was now acting Divisional Commander, and that one third of his (Hackett's) command had been stolen away from him. Hicks had decided that 11th Battalion was urgently needed to support 1st Parachute Brigade in Arnhem.

This prompted a famously sharp exchange of words between Hackett and Hicks. Though they were old friends, Hackett was miffed at not having been given the chance to decide which of his battalions was detached. He felt in any case that the command of the division should, by rights, have been his because, though he was much younger than Hicks, his commission was senior, and so should have given him precedence.

On Tuesday 19 September, an attempt by 4th Parachute Brigade to seize areas of high ground around the Dreijenseweg in support of the assault on Arnhem was beaten back with heavy losses. As SS Sturmbannführer Krafft had done to 1st Parachute Brigade, so another SS Sturmbannführer Ludwig Spindler would do to 4th Parachute Brigade by forming a second blocking line as impenetrable as Krafft's. 156 Battalion was cut to pieces in the last major offensive action of Market. From now on it would be about retreat, defence and the struggle to stay alive.

Hackett remained throughout in the thick of the action. A friend of his, Lt. Col. Derick Heathcoat-Amory – subsequently Chancellor of the Exchequer in Harold Macmillan's government – was wounded and lying on a stretcher on the trailer of a jeep. Next to it was another jeep with a trailer full of mortar bombs which had caught fire and might explode at any moment. Heedless of his own safety, Hackett dashed over to the jeep and drove his friend out of danger.

Not long afterwards, Hackett found himself holed up with the 150 survivors of 156 Battalion in an area of hollow ground in the woods, where they held out for eight hours, their ammo dwindling. Most unusually for an officer of his rank, Hackett manned a rifle, threw grenades and led bayonet charges – the last of which led all his men to relative safety within the Oosterbeek perimeter. There is a brilliant account of this in Geoffrey Powell's *Men at Arnhem* (see below), Powell being one of the few officers from 156 Battalion to survive the battle.

During the Oosterbeek defence, Hackett's determination to lead by example – rarely seeking shelter even in the thickest bombardments, preferring to wander his positions nonchalantly – greatly encouraged the men but rather unnerved those of his officers who were expected to stand alongside him pretending to be unfazed by the shots and shells whizzing all about them.

His luck could not last. By the time Coward met him, Hackett had already been wounded once in the face and hands by the mortar bomb that killed the man next to him and wounded his driver. Then on the morning of Sunday 24 September he was seriously wounded by mortar splinters in his stomach and left thigh. With typical generosity of spirit he insisted, before allowing himself to be treated, on organising a stretcher party for his runner – a Recce man – who had been wounded in the same blast.

Hackett was among the many wounded who were captured when the Oosterbeek perimeter was finally overrun. With a 2-inch square piece of shrapnel in his intestine he should have died, but his life was saved by a brilliant South African surgeon, Capt. Lipmann Kessel. Hackett kept his rank secret, masquerading as a corporal, and as soon as he was fit enough, he escaped from hospital with the help of the Dutch Resistance. Nursed back to health by four kindly Dutch ladies, he eventually reached his own lines in February 1945 having cycled and canoed around half of Holland.

After the war Hackett rose to the rank of General and on retirement became a popular lecturer, TV pundit and unlikely bestselling author with his imaginary account of the next great global conflict (starting, of course, with the Soviet tanks rolling across Luneberg Heath), *The Third World War* (1979).

Page 244: 'Red bloody berets'. Geoffrey Powell describes a similar experience in *Men at Arnhem* (see below).

Page 245: Though Coward has changed most of his comrades' names, his description of 1st Airborne Recce Squadron's last days at the Oosterbeek perimeter – among them, the 'Brazil special' cigarettes made with coffee grounds, the SS boy getting his bottom spanked, the Toreador song and the duels with the StuG – tally with many of those in John Fairley's *Remember Arnhem* (see below).

Page 246: 'Angel of Mons'. According to popular wartime legend, a group of angels hovered protectively over the British Expeditionary Force at the Battle of Mons in 1914.

Page 262: The destruction of the mobile propaganda unit was recalled, in the December 2001 issue of *The Eagle*, the magazine of the Glider Pilot Regimental Association, by Staff Sgt. E.B.

'Bunny' Baker of 'F' Squadron. 'Several of us crept out with the last hand grenades and silenced the German unit.'

Page 267: **Maj. Robert Cain** won one of the most spectacular VCs not just of Arnhem, but the whole Second World War, with his outrageously heroic exploits while commanding 'B' Company, 2nd Battalion, South Staffordshire Regiment.

Most of his company having been wiped out by SPs and tanks in vicious fighting around St Elizabeth's Hospital, this generally mild and modest man determined to take revenge on as much German armour as possible. Sometimes with anti-tank guns, sometimes with PIATs – one of which blew up in his face and temporarily blinded him with fragments, and in desperation, when the PIAT bombs ran out, with 2-inch mortars, Maj. Cain managed to destroy or disable six tanks (four of them Tigers), plus a number of self-propelled guns. Despite being wounded in the face and having burst eardrums, he also rallied and inspired his men, saw that they held the perimeter and gave not an inch of ground, and was responsible for countless acts of courage, decency and generosity, such as giving his last cigarette to one of his men. His son-in-law is the *Top Gear* presenter Jeremy Clarkson, who made a TV documentary about him.

Page 270: '*Dulce et decorum est pro patria mori.*' Line from Horace's *Odes* later taken up ironically by the war poet Wilfred Owen. 'To die for one's mother country is a sweet and fitting thing.'

Page 283: Lt. Verney bears many similarities to the delightful and supremely modest glider pilot hero **Mike Dauncey DSO** – a lieutenant at the time of Market Garden – who narrowly missed a VC at Arnhem for feats of extraordinary heroism.

At Oosterbeek he oversaw the defence of the guns of Airlanding Light Regiment RA and on three occasions prevented his position from being overrun by superior forces of tanks and infantry by leading determined counter-attacks. Once, he led an impromptu patrol with two paratroopers and captured eight prisoners, a machine gun and several Luger pistols. Later he was grazed across his scalp by a sniper bullet, then wounded in the eye by a splinter – which a comrade painfully, but unavailingly tried to extract using a couple of matches. But despite his wounds Lt. Dauncey single-handedly disabled an SP gun with a Gammon grenade.

Afterwards, he was hit in the leg by a bullet and had his jaw broken by a German stick grenade. He was left among the wounded in the home of Kate Ter Horst and captured. He escaped from hospital with another officer and after months on the run made it back to the Allied lines.

Page 310: 'Arthur Bryant'. Popular English historian of the old school. Accused by historian Andrew Roberts of being a closet Nazi.

Page 312: 'Birkenhead Drill'. *HMS Birkenhead* was the troopship that sank in shark-infested waters near Capetown in 1852. There being not enough lifeboats, the soldiers aboard stood firm while their womenfolk and children rowed to safety.

Page 315: Of the 11,920 men who took part in the airborne operation at Arnhem, 1,485 were killed or died of wounds, 3,910 were evacuated across the river, leaving the remainder of 6,525 as prisoners of war or trying to evade capture (see Middlebrook, below)

Page 320: The assault on the Merville Gun Battery in Normandy by 9th Battalion, Parachute Regiment on 6 June 1944 was one of the great Allied feats of the war. Due to navigational errors only

150 men of the 650 men supposed to capture it arrived on target, and none of their transport, heavy weapons or sappers. Their commander, **Lt. Col. Terence Otway**, decided to press on regardless, and charged the heavily fortified position in a frontal assault through several minefields.

Page 324: 'Dumb crambo' – old-fashioned party game not unlike charades.

Further Reading

John Fairley, *Remember Arnhem* (Pegasus Journal, 1978) (out of print). The definitive history of 1st Airborne Recce Squadron. Well-written and extremely thorough, it abounds with detail found nowhere else. Much sought after by collectors – and justifiably so.

John Frost, *A Drop Too Many* (Pen & Sword, 1994). Lively, first-hand account of the battle from the man who held Arnhem bridge.

Louis Hagen, *Arnhem Lift* (Pen & Sword, 1993) (out of print). Fascinating autobiographical account of Arnhem from the perspective of a German Jew turned fighting glider pilot.

Robert J. Kershaw, *It Never Snows in September* (The Crowood Press, 1990). A definitive account of Market Garden from the German point of view, which leaves you full of admiration for the Germans' fighting spirit and tactical brilliance, and in no doubt as to why it was the Allied plans failed.

Karel Margry, *Operation Market Garden Then and Now, Vols 1 & 2 (After the Battle*, 2002). War-buff heaven: every picture ever taken during Market Garden, plus photos showing how the sites look now, plus detailed commentary.

James Megellas, *All the Way to Berlin* (Presidio Press, US, 2003), T. Moffatt Burriss, *Strike and Hold* (Brasseys, US, 2000). The US perspective from two of the boys who were there at the crossing of the Waal.

Martin Middlebrook, *Arnhem 1944: The Airborne Battle* (Westview Press, 1994). 'Without question the best book so far published on the Market Garden operation,' said Gen. Sir John Hackett. Actually it only deals with Market, and only the Allied experience, not the German one, but he's quite right: Middlebrook's book is the business. It's clear, it's thorough, it's full of first-hand accounts of the battle, and if you read one book only on the subject, then make it this one.

M.L. Peters, *Glider Pilots at Arnhem* (Pen & Sword Aviation, 2009). The GPs' story, as expertly told by a serving British Army officer and regular Arnhem tour guide.

Geoffrey Powell, *Men at Arnhem* (Pen & Sword, 1998). A (barely) fictionalised account of the horrendous experiences of 156 Battalion, the proud parachute unit which landed on Day 2 and was virtually wiped out. Powell, a major who commanded C Company, was one of very few officers to survive. Moving, compelling, immediate. Brilliant. Powell also wrote a good non-fiction account of Arnhem called *The Devil's Birthday* (Ashford, Buchan & Enright, 1984).

Cornelius Ryan, *A Bridge Too Far* (Simon & Schuster, 1974). The classic narrative history of Market Garden, colourfully recounted by the great Irish war correspondent who also wrote *The Longest Day*. In the early seventies most of the senior-ranking survivors were still alive and available for interview.

'Zeno', *The Cauldron* (Pan Books, 1968) (out of print). This spare, incredibly bleak and haunting fictionalised account of the experiences of 21st Independent Parachute Company (the Pathfinders) was a bestseller when reissued in 1977. Its author Gerald T. Lamarque served as an NCO with the unit, and was jailed after the war for stabbing to death a Swansea hotelier in a crime of passion. Why it's not still in print, I can't imagine, for it is a Second World War classic. Interestingly, Lamarque decides to kill off many more members of his unit than in fact died at Arnhem.

And, on the internet: www.pegasusarchive.org – a comprehensive, fantastically useful Arnhem resource with biographies of all the main players, unit histories etc. Highly recommended.

Glossary

Bar Thin metal bar attached to the ribbon of a medal, either to indicate the campaign in which it was won, or that the medal has been won more than once. E.g. **DSO** and bar means you have won the DSO twice.

BAR (US) Browning Automatic Rifle. A light machine gun – the US army equivalent of a **Bren**.

Battalion Army unit of between 700 and 900 men, commanded by a lieutenant colonel (armoured and artillery battalions in the British Army are called regiments).

Benzedrine Form of amphetamine ('speed') used as a pep pill during the war especially by tank crews and airmen, and a great deal by infantrymen at Arnhem.

Betuwe The 'island' between the Lower Rhine and the Waal, which separates Arnhem from Nijmegen.

Bn Battalion.

Bren British light machine gun (name comes from Brno, Czechoslovakia, where it was designed). It used the same .303 ammunition as the standard British Lee-Enfield rifle, and though its rate of fire was no match for the **Spandau** (q.v.) it was more easily portable and exceptionally accurate. It was issued on a scale of one per infantry section.

Bren Gun Carrier Lightly armoured tracked vehicle with two-man crew, used as a mobile gun platform and for carrying supplies.

Brewing up What a tank does when it catches fire and explodes.

Brigade Formation comprising roughly three battalions (and supporting arms) commanded by a brigadier.

Co-axial Turret-mounted machine gun that works side by side with the tank's main gun.

Comet Cancelled operation – the precursor to Market Garden.

Corps Formation of (usually) two or more **Divisions**, made up of 30,000-plus men, commanded by a **lieutenant general**.

Coup de main Dashing, rapid, small-scale assault which achieves operational effects out of all proportion to its size. The dramatic seizure of Pegasus Bridge by glider-borne troops of the Oxfordshire and Buckinghamshire Light Infantry on the eve of D-Day is the classic example.

CSM Company sergeant major.

Denison Loose-fitting, camouflaged paratrooper's jumping smock with a 'beaver tail' which fastened beneath the crotch from the back to the front, to stop it riding up during a parachute descent.

Division A division is made up of three brigades, each made up of three battalions. It is commanded by a **major general**.

Div HQ Divisional Headquarters.

DSO Distinguished Service Order (two narrow blue bands with broad red band in the middle). Gallantry medal, second to the Victoria Cross (**VC**), usually awarded only to officers of captain or above for exceptional leadership under fire. Sometimes awarded to junior officers to indicate they had only narrowly missed out on a VC.

DUKW (pronounced 'duck'). Six-wheeled, boat-shaped amphibious vehicle used by Allied forces for beach landings and river crossings.

DZ Dropping zone (where paratroops land; as opposed to **LZ** where gliders land).

88 German 88-mm gun, originally designed for anti-aircraft use, subsequently the war's deadliest anti-tank weapon capable of penetrating even the thickest allied armour.

Fairbairn-Sykes Legendary fighting knife with 7-inch blade, manufactured by Wilkinson Sword, issued to all British commandos. Developed in pre-war Shanghai by policemen and hand-to-hand combat experts William Ewart Fairbairn and Eric Anthony Sykes.

Fallschirmjäger German paratrooper (the elite of the Wehrmacht).

Flammpanzer German tank with flame-thrower attachment.

FOO Forward observation officer. An observer, usually attached to frontline infantry, who serves as the eyes of an artillery battery, by radioing back with target locations.

Gammon grenade Sticky bomb, popular with airborne troops, used for destroying tanks.

GP Glider pilot.

Half-track Armoured personnel carrier used by both Americans and Germans, with wheels for steering at the front and tracks for crossing rough terrain at the back.

Halifax Sturdy four-engine British heavy bomber, built by Handley Page.

Hamilcar Heavy-duty glider, much larger than the **Horsa**, capable of carrying light tanks or 17-pounder anti-tank guns.

Hauptmann Captain in the German Army.

Haupsturmführer SS rank equivalent to Hauptmann.

HE High explosive.

HMG Heavy machine gun.

HO Hostilities Only. Royal Navy and Royal Marines designation referring to civilians called up to serve only for the duration of the war – as opposed to career regulars.

Horsa Glider carrying up to twenty-five troops or supplies (e.g. two jeeps).

HQ Headquarters.

Kempitai Japanese secret police.

KOSB King's Own Scottish Borderers.

Lieutenant General Commander of a **corps**.

LMG Light machine gun (e.g. British **Bren** gun, German **Spandau**). Usually issued at squad level.

LZ Landing zone (where gliders land).

Major General Commander of a **division**.

MC Military Cross (white, purple-and-white ribbon). Third highest gallantry award (after VC and DSO), awarded to officers for 'gallantry during active operations against the enemy'.

Mc-109 Messerschmitt Bf 109 – German fighter aircraft, the most successful of the Second World War, destroying more aircraft than any other.

MG Machine gun.

MG34; MG42 German light machine guns much feared by Allied troops. Their exceptionally rapid rate of fire enabled small German infantry units to punch far above their weight. Nicknamed the **Spandau** by British troops.

MM Military Medal (dark blue with three white and two red stripes in the middle). Equivalent of Military Cross awarded to Other Ranks. Discontinued since 1993 on egalitarian grounds. Now all ranks are entitled to the **MC**.

MMG Medium machine gun (e.g. Vickers). Concentrated at battalion level and allocated by the OC to provide fire support at the *Schwerpunkt*.

MO Medical officer *or* method of operations (i.e. plan).

Moaning Minnie See *Nebelwerfer*.

Moffen Dutch nickname for the Germans.

Morning Hate Market Garden nickname for the Germans' morning wake-up call of mortars, *Nebelwerfers* and artillery at the Oosterbeek perimeter. Usually it started on the dot of 7 a.m.

Mortar Weapon carried by infantrymen comprising a base plate and tube which fires bombs at short distances, serving as highly effective portable artillery. (There were various types: 2-inch mortars were carried at platoon level; 3-inch mortars were a battalion support weapon; there were heavier mortars at Brigade.)

NCO Non-commissioned officer (e.g. sergeant major, sergeant, corporal, lance corporal).

Nebelwerfer (German for 'Fog launcher'.) Terrifying six-barrelled German mortar capable of carpeting a large area in seconds with high explosives. Known as the Moaning Minnie because of the distinctive screeching noise made by its rounds.

Neder Rhine Lower Rhine (the river that runs past Arnhem).

'O' Group Orders group. The briefing meeting at which officers and NCOs are given their tasks for the next engagement.

OC Commanding officer of a unit (e.g. lieutenant colonel in charge of a battalion).

Oflag German POW camp for officers.

Oosterbeek Leafy, genteel suburb, eight miles from Arnhem, where most of the fighting took place.

OP Observation post.

OR Other ranks. All soldiers/marines who are not officers.

Panther (PzKpw V) German tank, good all-rounder, rated by some as the best of the war (though strangely not by the Germans themselves).

Panzerfaust (literally tank fist). Portable anti-tank weapon used extensively by German infantry and much feared by Allied tank crews because it was so effective.

Panzerkampfwagen (literally 'armoured battle wagon'). Any German tank, usually abbreviated to 'Panzer'.

PFC (US rank). Private first class.

PIAT The projector, infantry anti-tank was the main British infantry anti-tank weapon of the war. Unlike its US and German equivalents – the bazooka and the **Panzerfaust** – it was fairly quiet and smokeless and had no backblast, meaning it could be fired from an enclosed space and would not give away its position after the weapon had been fired. But it was cumbersome to load and dangerous to use because it was only effective at short distances.

PIR (US). Parachute Infantry Regiment.

Platoon Army unit, comprising around thirty men, commanded by a lieutenant or second lieutenant, assisted by a platoon sergeant.

Polsten gun British 20-mm cannon which can be towed by a jeep.

POW Prisoner of war.

PW Prisoner of war.

RAF Royal Air Force.

RAMC Royal Army Medical Corps.

RAP Regimental aid post. Front-line treatment centre for wounded personnel.

RASC Royal Army Service Corps. The Army's logistical wing, responsible for keeping troops in supplies.

RE Royal Engineers.

Recce Reconnaissance.

RN Royal Navy.

RSM Regimental Sergeant Major.

2ic. Second in command .

77 Grenade White phosphorous grenade used both to lay down smoke cover during an assault and also as a particularly grisly anti-personnel weapon.

Sapper Royal Engineer.

Scharführer SS rank equivalent to platoon sergeant major.

Schmeisser Allied nickname for the German MP40 machine pistol.

Schuhmine German anti-personnel mine, 'shoe mine', contained a small explosive charge which was sufficient to blow off a foot or lower leg, without necessarily killing the victim.

Schwerpunkt The point where a commander concentrates his main effort.

Scrim Camouflage material.

Second Army At Arnhem, this was often used by the beleaguered British to refer to the land forces they imagined were coming to rescue them. Really, though, they meant XXX Corps, which was part of the Second Army.

Section In the British Army the smallest operational unit, usually comprising eight to ten men led by a corporal. Three sections make a **platoon**.

Sherman Mass-produced American tank, widely used by the Allies. Nicknamed the Tommycooker (and the Ronson by the Allies because it 'lights first time, every time') by the Germans because of its propensity for **brewing up** when struck in its relatively light armour.

S-Mine *(Schrapnellmine).* Much-feared German mine designed to leap into the air and explode at waist height with predictably hideous consequences. Also known as the Bouncing Betty and the Debollocker.

Sniper A specialist infantryman, the unit's best marksman, skilled in the arts of concealment and killing the enemy with a rifle at long distances. They were issued specially selected, 'hand-made' No. 4 (T) rifles.

SP Self-propelled (gun). Resembles a turretless tank, usually with an artillery gun mounted in the back.

Spandau British nickname for the German MG34 and MG42 machine guns, derived from the manufacturer's plates noting the part of Berlin in which some of the weapons were produced.

Sparks Wireless operators.

SS *Schutzstaffel* (German for 'protective squadron') – the security and military organisation of the Nazi Party. Its military wing, the Waffen-SS, operated in tandem with the regular German Army, the *Wehrmacht*. Often better trained and better equipped than their *Wehrmacht* counterparts, the SS were notoriously brutal and dedicated and were responsible for a disproportionately high number of war crimes. However, they were widely respected by their Allied opponents as superb fighting troops.

Stonk Mortar attack (derived, onomatopoeically, from the distinctive 'tonk' sound a mortar makes as it is fired).

StuG (*Sturmgeschütz* – assault gun). German self-propelled gun.

Sturmbannführer SS military rank equivalent to Wehrmacht and Allied major.

Sturmscharführer Most senior NCO rank in the SS, equivalent to British regimental sergeant major

Tellermine Plate-shaped German mine (*Teller* is German for plate) used primarily for anti-tank warfare.

Tiger German heavy tank, partly designed by Ferdinand Porsche, much feared for its near-impenetrable armour and its deadly 88-mm gun.

Tug Aircraft that pulls a glider (or a wank in British soldier parlance).

Typhoon Single-seat, rocket-firing, British fighter bomber; one of the Second World War's most successful ground-attack aircraft, very effective during the Normandy invasion.

USAAF United States Army Air Force.

VC Victoria Cross (crimson ribbon). The highest award for valour in the face of the enemy. Only 182 were awarded during the whole of the Second World War (compared to 626 in the First World War). Five were awarded at Arnhem.

'Waho Mohammed' Battle cry of British wartime paratroops, picked up during their North African campaign.

Wehrmacht German regular armed forces (as opposed to the SS) comprising *Heer* (army), *Luftwaffe* (air force) and *Kriegsmarine* (navy).

Vickers K Rapid-firing, drum-fed light machine gun, used by SAS and 1st Airborne Recce Squadron.

Acknowledgements

Huge thanks and maximum respect to those of my friends who were there at Market Garden: Brigadier Mike Dauncey, DSO; Leonard 'Nobby' Clarke; Major General Tony Deane-Drummond, DSO and Bar, MC; Col John Waddy.

Thanks to those of my other dear Second World War-era chums who weren't at Arnhem but whose fortitude, commonsense, kindness, generosity, encouragement and friendship are one of the things that make my life most worthwhile. They include: David 'COB' Hearsey DFC; Mickie O'Brien MC; Mike and Kathleen Peyton; John Clanwilliam; Jock Watt MM; George and Eileen Amos; Chuck Harris; Ian Bennett; John Lorimer DSO; Ken Perkins DFC; Pat and Christine Hagen; John Baker; Betty Field; Gordon 'Tim' Tye; Marjorie Dauncey; and all at 47 RM Commando Association.

Thanks to my expert advisers Adrian Weale (military arcana); Mike Peters (GPs); Guy Walters (Nazis); Ian Agg (technical); Mike Daunt (fish); the brilliant and indefatigable PG Urben (everything); Dr Marcel Waldinger, professor in sexual psychopharmacology (nymphomania); Stephen Daneff (language, tone, nuance); Malcolm Delingpole (moral support, gratifying enthusiasm); Richard Delingpole (jokes, maps); Dickie and Britta Bielenberg (German stuff); Wilton Barnhardt (US translation).

Thanks to Peter Straus for representing me, Mike Jones for continuing to have faith in me, Mary Tomlinson for copy-editing me so sympathetically, Ian Chapman for welcoming me, Rory Scarfe for marshalling me, and all at Simon & Schuster for doing such a splendid job packaging, marketing, advertising and promoting me.

Thanks to my wife and long suffering family for being bored rigid by my war obsessions, my hypochondria and my neuroses.

Finally, thanks to the late Field Marshal BL Montgomery, without whose crazy idea none of this could ever have been possible.